infinities

eric brown

ken macleod

alastair reynolds

adam roberts

infinities

edited and introduced by peter crowther

GOLLANCZ

London

Introduction by Peter Crowther © 2002
Copyright © Eric Brown 2001
Copyright © Ken MacLeod 2001
Copyright © Alastair Reynolds 2001
Copyright © Adam Roberts 2001

First published in this omnibus volume in 2002 by
Gollancz
An imprint of the Orion Publishing Group
Orion House, 5 Upper St Martin's Lane,
London WC2H 9EA

A CIP catalogue record for this book
is available from the British Library

ISBN 0 575 073551

Typeset at The Spartan Press Ltd,
Lymington, Hants
Printed in Great Britain by
Butler & Tanner Ltd, Frome and London

contents

a rose by any other name

An Introduction by Peter Crowther

I've always been interested – fascinated, even – by categorisation. The case in point, Science Fiction – where does it begin (at which point, presumably, so-called 'mainstream' ends) and where does it blur into other sub-genres of fantastical literature (horror, fantasy, suspense and so on). To answer that question of course, one first needs to define Science Fiction itself.

In the Introduction to the first volume (Ballantine Books, 1953) of his immensely enjoyable *Star Science Fiction* anthology series, editor Frederik Pohl took time to comment on the almost universal appeal of science fiction and, in so doing, effortlessly rendered as redundant the entire debate.

Citing the appearance of glowing reviews of one of his books in two magazines (*Advertising Age* and *The Industrial Worker*) whose readerships were as chalk is to cheese, Pohl had this to say about SF (and, in passing, about westerns and detective stories): 'One can get tired of cowboys or corpses; it's hard to tire of a field that can take you anywhere in space, time or the dimensions.'

Well, although I'd argue that statement – particularly with regard to detective stories (and I'm sure there are a whole passle of western fans who'd call Fred out into the street for a showdown for uttering such blasphemy) – the basic sentiment is true. It was true in 1953 and it's true still, half a century later.

With the shock – or perhaps 'surprise' would be more generous – of the 2001 Hugo Award for Best Novel going to J. K. Rowling for *Harry Potter And The Goblet of Fire* (50 years earlier, the same award went to Robert Heinlein's *Farmer In The Sky*), it's clear that SF in the 21st Century has become a very broad church indeed. But lest anyone infer that I'm being disparaging about that much-loved diminutive and bespectacled trainee wizard, let me add that such a seemingly radical development is no bad thing. Quite the contrary. For perhaps it's the long-overdue first step towards bestowing a greater acceptability – coupled with a refreshing erasing of the genrification parameters – on what is truly the literature of ideas.

Just as horror has morphed into the more respectable nomenclature of 'Dark Fantasy' and, occasionally, its sibling 'Dark Suspense', Science Fiction now embraces a multitude of styles and themes. But, of course, it was doing pretty much the same way back in 1953, as evidenced by *Star Science Fiction Stories*, wherein Arthur C. Clarke's cautionary parable about what will happen when all of the Divine Being's names have been revealed ('The Nine Billion Names of God') rubs shoulders with Ray Bradbury's achingly poignant tale of a man haunted by the past and his discovery of an attic that leads, somehow, to the stars ('A Scent of Sarsaparilla'), Clifford Simak's warm fable of an alien visitor's gift to a mistreated child ('Contraption') and Fritz Leiber's risqué and comical caper of subterfuge and milk glands ('The Night He Cried').

And that's what you'll discover in the pages of *Infinities* . . . though without the milk glands.

In this third book in the continuing *Foursight* series, we're following on pretty much with the scene we set in last year's *Futures* – namely, we're going into space. Kind of. Or, in some cases, space is coming into us.

But these are stories about possibilities, not about ray guns and star fleets and tentacled monsters. There *are* spaceships here. And there are aliens. And there's plenty of examples of science gone mad . . . or, at least, a little frayed around the edges. But there is also fear and mystery, plus a liberal helping of exceedingly dark fantasy.

The first story here – Eric Brown's 'A Writer's Life' – is also the first story of the four to be published under my PS imprint last year. It was both a shock and a wonderful surprise when it arrived. For Eric had, somewhat audaciously, taken a well-worn science-fictional staple and tinkered with it, blending in another theme . . . though this latter one, the mystical long-ago author whose books are feverishly sought by a modern-day writer, is one more usually found in works of Gothic melodrama and dark suspense. The result is a glorious amalgam of moods.

And that's the beauty of Eric's story and, indeed, the beauty of ALL the stories in this series: writers 'playing' with the genre's – perhaps even ALL genres' – conventions and giving them fresh air and new life.

In Ken MacLeod's 'The Human Front', a third world war has ravaged Earth since 1949. While communist partisans and Western conscript armies slug it out, the revolutionary core of the Human Front has raised the stakes. They're not looking for peace marchers any more. They're looking for returning soldiers to bring the war back home. But new recruit John Matheson carries more than a rifle to the streets and hills of Scotland. He carries a weight of knowledge which he's never dared to share, and which he knows exactly how to use.

Meanwhile, courtesy of Alastair Reynolds's 'Diamond Dogs', a small group of adventurers – led by a brilliant theorist and thinker on alien intelligence – pit their wits against gaining entry into a sinister alien structure on a nameless world light years from Earth. But they're not the first. Others have come before them – their bones littering the ground as a silent testament to the appalling punishments that the structure can inflict.

And, finally, in Adam Roberts's 'Park Polar', overpopulation has crammed the world full-to-bursting, with the only remaining natural wildernesses for wild animals to roam free being found at the two poles – Park Polar and Park Antarctica. But the animal inhabitants of these parks are genetically-engineered creatures, created and patented by the fiercely competitive giant companies that run the world, and when terrorists descend onto Park Polar's frozen wastes, the fragile equilibrium is disrupted . . . with violent consequences.

And there you have it. Four stories which truly do take you to new places in space, time and the dimensions.

In the closing part of his Introduction for *Star Science Fiction Stories* – the prototype volume, incidentally, for what was to become Ballantine Books' impressive line of SF anthologies, collections and novels – Fred Pohl referred back to the reviews in *Advertising Age* and *The Industrial Worker*: 'Of course,' he said, 'you need to be neither huckster nor Wobbly to enjoy science fiction – as I trust you will prove to yourself in the stories that follow. Some of the brightest stars in the science fiction firmament have done their best for you in these tales. To all of them, my thanks and – I hope – yours.'

Thanks, Fred – couldn't have said it better myself.

Peter Crowther
November 2001

a writer's life

Eric Brown

one

Edwards, Vaughan, (1930–1996?). English novelist, author of twelve novels and two collections of stories. His first novel, *Winter at the Castle*, (1951), received considerable critical acclaim but, like much of his subsequent output, little widespread popularity. Edwards was very much a writer's writer, eschewing the trappings of sensationalism in his fiction and concentrating instead on his own peculiar and unique vision. In book after book, this singular novelist wrote of a rural England haunted by ghosts of the past – both the spirits of humans and the more metaphorical apparitions of times long gone. The novel considered his finest, *The Miracle at Hazelmere*, (1968), tells, in his customary highly wrought prose, the story of William Grantham, an estranged and embittered artist, and his (perhaps imaginary – it is never revealed) affair with the phantom of a sixteen-year-old girl from the Elizabethan period. This novel, in common with the rest of his oeuvre, contains much striking imagery, pathos and a yearning for a long gone era of bucolic certainty. Artists and loners burdened with tragic pasts appear again and again in his writing, and there is speculation that the novels and stories drew much from the author's own life, though, as Edwards was an intensely private person, this has never been confirmed. Critics generally agree that his final novels, the *Secrets of Reality* series, marked the artistic low-point of his career. Though beautifully written, and containing much of ideative interest, the novels, beginning with *Those Amongst Us*, (1990), continuing with *A Several*

Fear, (1993), and *The Secret of Rising Dene*, (1996), show an obsessive preoccupation with the arcane, and found only a narrow readership. The series, a projected quartet, was unfinished at the time of the author's mysterious disappearance in the winter of 1996.

From *Encyclopaedia of Twentieth Century British Novelists*,

Macmillan, Third edition, 1998.

The above entry was the first mention I had ever heard of the writer Vaughan Edwards. I was surprised that I had never happened upon his work, as I have a pretty comprehensive knowledge of British writers of the last century and especially those publishing after the Second World War. The discovery filled me with a wonderful sense of serendipitous anticipation: there was something about the entry that told me I would take to the novels of Vaughan Edwards. The fact that he was relatively unknown now, and little regarded during his lifetime, gave me the sense that I would be performing a service to the memory of the man who had devoted his life, as the entry stated, to 'his own peculiar and unique vision'. Perhaps what gave me a certain empathy with the novelist was that I too was an unsuccessful writer, the author of half a dozen forgotten novels, as well as over fifty short stories buried away in long-defunct small-press magazines and obscure anthologies.

I showed the entry to Mina. For some reason – perhaps subsequent events have branded the very start of the episode on my consciousness – I recall the night well. It had been a grey, misty day in early November; a gale had blown up after dinner, and now a rainstorm lashed the windows of the cottage, instilling in me the romantic notion that we were aboard a storm-tossed galleon upon the high seas.

Mina was reading in her armchair before the blazing fire. Her favourites were the classic Victorians, the Brontës, Eliot and the rest. Now she laid the well-read paperback edition of *Wuthering Heights* upon her lap and blinked up at me, perhaps surprised at the summons back to the present day.

I set the thick tome on the arm of the chair and tapped the page with my forefinger. 'Why on earth haven't I come across him before?'

She pushed her reading glasses up her nose, pulled a frown, and read the entry. A minute later she looked up, a characteristic, sarcastic humour lighting her eyes. 'Perhaps because he's probably even more obscure and terrible than all those others you go on about.'

I leaned over and kissed her forehead. She laughed. The masochist in me found delight in setting myself up as the butt of her disdain.

I relieved her of the volume, sat before the fire and reread the entry.

Why was it that even then I knew, with a stubborn, innate certainty, that I would take to the works of this forgotten writer? There was enough in the entry to convince me that I had stumbled across a fellow romantic, someone obscurely haunted by an inexplicable sense of the tragedy that lies just beneath the veneer of the everyday – or perhaps I was flattering myself with knowledge gained of hindsight.

Mina stretched and yawned. 'I'm going to bed. I'm on an early tomorrow. Come up if you want.'

Even then, a year into our relationship, I was insecure enough to ascribe to her most innocent statements an ulterior intent. I remained before the fire, staring at the page, the words a blur, and tried to decide if she meant that she wished to sleep alone tonight.

At last, chastising myself for being so paranoid, I joined her in bed. Rain doused the skylight and wind rattled the eaves. I eased myself against her back, my right arm encircling her warm body, and closed my eyes.

* * *

Though the novels of Daniel Ellis are founded on a solid bedrock of integrity and honesty, yet they display the flaws of an excessive emotionalism which some might find overpowering.

From Simon Levi's review of the novel *Fair Winds* by Daniel Ellis.

But for Mina, I would never have come upon Vaughan Edwards' novel *A Bitter Recollection*. During the month following my discovery of his entry in the encyclopaedia, I wrote to a dozen second-hand bookshops enquiring if they possessed copies of any of his works.

Of the three replies I received, two had never heard of him, and a third informed me that in thirty years of bookdealing he had come across only a handful of Edwards' titles. I made enquiries on the Internet, but to no avail.

I forgot about Vaughan Edwards and busied myself with work. I was writing the novelisation of a children's TV serial at the time, working three hours in the mornings and taking the afternoons off to potter about the garden, read, or, if Mina was not working, drive into the Dales.

It was an uncharacteristically bright but bitterly cold day in mid-December when I suggested a trip to York for lunch and a scout around the bookshops.

As I drove, encountering little traffic on the mid-week roads, Mina gave me a running commentary on her week at work.

I listened with feigned attention. The sound of her voice hypnotised me. She had a marked Yorkshire accent that I have always found attractive, and an inability to pronounce the letter *r*. The word 'horrible', which she used a lot, came out sounding like 'howwible'. Perhaps it was the contradiction of the conjunction between the childishness of some of her phrases, and her stern and unrelenting practicality and pragmatism, which I found endearing.

She was a State Registered Nurse and worked on the maternity ward of the general hospital in the nearby town of Skipton. In the early days of our relationship I was conscious, perhaps to the point of feeling guilty, of how little I worked in relation to her. I could get away with three or four hours a day at the computer, five days a week, and live in reasonable comfort from my output of one novel and a few stories and articles every year. By contrast Mina worked long, gruelling shifts, looked after her two girls for three and a half days a week, and kept up with the daily household chores. When I met her she was renting a two-bedroom terrace house, which ate up most of her wage, and yet I never heard her complain. She had just walked out on a disastrous marriage that had lasted a little over eight years, and she was too thankful for her new-found freedom to worry about things like poverty and overwork.

Her practical attitude to life amazed me – me, who found it hard to manage my bank balance, who found the mundane chores of daily life too much of a distraction . . .

She once accused me of having it too easy, of never having to face real hardship, and I had to agree that she was right.

There were times, though, when her pragmatism did her a disservice. She often failed to appreciate the truly wondrous in life: she fought shy of my romanticism as if it were a disease. She could be cutting about my flights of fancy, my wild speculations about life on other worlds, the possibilities of the future. On these occasions she would stare at me, a frown twisting her features, and then give her head that quick irritable, bird-like shake. 'But what does all that matter!' she would say – as if all that did matter was a strict and limiting adherence to the banality of the everyday. She had gone through a lot: she was content with her present, when compared to her past. She feared, I thought, the uncertainty of the future.

We never argued about our differences, though. I loved her too much to risk creating a rift.

'Daniel,' she said, her sudden sharp tone causing me to flinch. 'You're miles away. You haven't been listening to a word . . . I might as well be talking to myself!'

'I was thinking about a dream I had last night.'

Why did I say this? I knew that she hated hearing about my dreams. She didn't dream herself, or if she did then she failed to recall them. It was as if the evidence of my over-active sleeping imagination was something that she could not understand, or therefore control.

I had dreamed of meeting a fellow writer in an ancient library filled with mouldering tomes. I had gestured around us, implying without words the insignificance of our efforts to add our slight fictions to the vast collection.

The writer had smiled, his face thin, hair gun-metal grey – a weathered and experienced face. He replied that the very act of imagining, of creating worlds that had never existed, was the true measure of our humanity.

The dream had ended there, faded from my memory even though I retained the subtle, nagging impression that our conversation had continued. Even stranger was the fact that, when I awoke, I was filled with the notion that my partner in the library had been Vaughan Edwards.

More than anything I wanted to recount my dream to Mina, but I was too wary of her scepticism. I wanted to tell her that to create worlds that had never existed was the true measure of our humanity.

* * *

I frequently feel the need to lie about my profession. When people ask what I do, I want to answer anything but that I am a freelance writer. I am sick and tired of repeating the same old clichés in response to the same old questions. When I told Mina this, she was horrified, appalled that I should lie about what I do. Perhaps it's because Mina is so sparing with the details of her personal life that she feels the few she does divulge must be truthful, and cannot imagine anyone else thinking otherwise.

From the personal journals of Daniel Ellis.

We parked on the outskirts and walked across the Museum Street bridge and into the city centre. Even on a freezing winter Thursday the narrow streets were packed with tourists, those latter-day disciples of commerce: mainly diminutive, flat-footed Japanese with their incorrigible smiles and impeccable manners. A few large Americans provided a stark contrast. We took in one bookshop before lunch, an expensive antiquarian dealer situated along Petergate. Mina lost herself in the classics section, while I scanned the packed shelves for those forgotten fabulists of the forties, fifties and sixties, De Polnay and Wellard, Standish and Robin Maugham, minor writers who, despite infelicities, spoke to something in my soul. They were absent from the shelves of this exclusive establishment – their third-rate novels neither sufficiently ancient, nor collectable enough, to warrant stocking.

Mina bought a volume of Jane Austen's letters, I an early edition of Poe. We emerged into the ice-cold air and hurried to our favourite tea-room.

Was it a failing in me that I preferred to have Mina to myself – the jealous lover, hoarding his treasure? I could never truly appreciate her when in the company of others. I was always conscious of wanting her attention, of wanting to give her my full attention, without being observed.

One to one we would chat about nothing in particular, the people we knew in town, friends, incidents that had made the news. That day she asked me how the book was going, and I tried to keep the weariness from my tone as I recounted the novelisation's hackneyed storyline.

Early in our relationship I had told her that my writing was just another job, something I did to keep the wolf from the door. I had been writing for almost twenty-five years, and though the act of creating still struck me as edifying and worthwhile, it no longer possessed the thrill I recalled from the first five years. She had said that I must be proud of what I did, and I replied that pride was the last thing I felt.

She had looked at me with that cool, assessing gaze of hers, and said, 'Well, I'm proud of you.'

Now I ate my salad sandwich and fielded her questions about my next serious novel.

How could I tell her that, for the time being, I had shelved plans for the next book, the yearly novel that would appear under my own name? The last one had sold poorly; my editor had refused to offer an advance for another. My agent had found some hackwork to tide me over, and I had put off thinking about the next Daniel Ellis novel.

I changed the subject, asked her about her sister, Liz, and for the next fifteen minutes lost myself in contemplation of her face: square, large-eyed, attractive in that worn, mid-thirties way that signals experience with fine lines about the eyes. The face of the woman I loved.

We left the tea-room and ambled through the cobbled streets towards the Minster. She took my arm, smiling at the Christmas window displays on either hand.

Then she stopped and tugged at me. 'Daniel, look. I don't recall . . .'

It was a second-hand bookshop crammed into the interstice between a gift shop and an establishment selling a thousand types of tea. The lighted window displayed a promising selection of old first editions. Mina was already dragging me inside.

The interior of the premises opened up like an optical illusion, belying the parsimonious dimensions of its frontage. It diminished in perspective like a tunnel, and narrow wooden stairs gave access to further floors.

Mina was soon chatting to the proprietor, an owl-faced, bespectacled man in his seventies. 'We moved in just last week,' he was saying. 'Had a place beyond the Minster – too quiet. You're looking for the Victorians? You'll find them in the first room on the second floor.'

I followed her up the precipitous staircase, itself made even narrower by shelves of books on everything from angling to bee-keeping, gardening to rambling.

Mina laughed to herself on entering the well-stocked room, turned to me with the conspiratorial grin of the fellow bibliophile. While she lost herself in awed contemplation of the treasures in stock, I saw a sign above a door leading to a second room: Twentieth Century Fiction.

I stepped through, as excited as a boy given the run of a toyshop on Christmas Eve.

The room was packed from floor to ceiling with several thousand volumes. At a glance I knew that many dated from the thirties and forties: the tell-tale blanched pink spines of Hutchinson editions, the pen and ink illustrated dust-jackets so popular at the time. The room had about it an air of neglect, the junk room where musty volumes were put out to pasture before the ultimate indignity of the council skip.

I found a Robert Nathan for one pound, a Wellard I did not possess for £1.50. I remembered Vaughan Edwards, and moved with anticipation to the E section. There were plenty of Es, but no Edwards.

I moved on, disappointed, but still excited by the possibility of more treasures to be found. I was scanning the shelves for Rupert Croft-Cooke when Mina called out from the next room, 'Daniel. Here.'

She had a stack of thick volumes piled beside her on the bare floorboards, and was holding out a book to me. 'Look.'

I expected some title she had been looking out for, but the book was certainly not Victorian. It had the modern, maroon boards of something published in the fifties.

'Isn't he the writer you mentioned the other week?'

I read the spine. *A Bitter Recollection* – Vaughan Edwards.

I opened the book, taking in the publishing details, the full-masted galleon symbol of the publisher, Longmans, Green and Company. It was his fourth novel, published in 1958.

I read the opening paragraph, and something clicked. I knew I had stumbled across a like soul.

An overnight frost had sealed the ploughed fields like so much stiffened corduroy, and in the distance, mist shrouded and remote, stood the village of Low Dearing. William Barnes, stepping from the second-class carriage onto the empty platform, knew at once that this was the place.

'Where did you find it?' I asked, hoping that there might be others by the author.

She laughed. 'Where do you think? Where it belongs, on the 50p shelf.'

She indicated a free-standing bookcase crammed with a miscellaneous selection of oddments, warped hardbacks, torn paperbacks, pamphlets and knitting patterns. There were no other books by Vaughan Edwards.

I laid my books upon her pile on the floor and took Mina in my arms. She stiffened, looking around to ensure we were quite alone: for whatever reasons, she found it difficult to show affection when we might be observed.

We made our way carefully down the stairs and paid for our purchases. I indicated the Edwards and asked the proprietor if he had any others by the same author.

He took the book and squinted at the spine. 'Sorry, but if you'd like to leave your name and address . . .'

I did so, knowing that it would come to nothing.

We left the shop and walked back to the car, hand in hand. We drove back through the rapidly falling winter twilight, the traffic sparse on the already frost-scintillating B-roads. The gritters would be out tonight, and the thought of the cold spell gripping the land filled me with gratitude that soon I would be home, before the fire, with my purchases.

For no apparent reason, Mina laid a hand on my leg as I drove, and closed her eyes.

I appreciated her spontaneous displays of affection all the more because they were so rare and arbitrary. Sometimes the touch of her hand in mine, when she had taken it without being prompted, was like a jolt of electricity.

The moon was full, shedding a magnesium light across the fields around the cottage. As I was about to turn into the drive, the thrilling, bush-tailed shape of a fox slid across the metalled road before the car, stopped briefly to stare into the headlights, then flowed off again and disappeared into the hedge.

* * *

Through focusing minutely on the inner lives of his characters, Vaughan Edwards manages to create stories of profound honesty and humanity . . .

From D. L. Shackleton's review of *The Tall Ghost and other stories*
by Vaughan Edwards.

I began *A Bitter Recollection* that night after dinner, and finished it in the early hours, emerging from the novel with surprise that so many hours had passed. It was the first time in years that I had finished a novel in one sitting, and I closed the book with a kind of breathless exultation. It was not the finest book I had ever read – the prose was too fastidious in places, and the plotting left much to be desired – but it was one of the most emotionally honest pieces of fiction I had ever come across. It swept me up and carried me along with its tortured portrayal of the central character, William Barnes, and his quest to find his missing lover. There was a magical quality to the book, an elegiac yearning for halcyon days, a time when things were better – and at the same time the novel was informed with the tragic awareness that all such desire is illusory. Barnes never found his lover – I suspected that he was an unreliable narrator, and that Isabella never really existed, was merely an extended metaphor for that harrowing sense of loss we all carry with us without really knowing why.

I was moved to tears by the novel, and wanted more.

I wrote to a dozen second-hand bookshops up and down the country, and logged onto the Websites of book-finders on the Internet, requesting the eleven novels I had yet to read, and his two collections.

Mina read the book, at my request. I was eager for her opinion, would even watch her while she read the novel, trying to gauge how she was enjoying it. She finished the book in three days, shrugged when I asked her what she thought of it, and said, 'It lacked something.'

I stared at her. 'Is that all? What do you mean? What did it lack?'

She frowned, pulled me onto the sofa and stroked my hair, her eyes a million miles away. 'I don't know . . . I mean, it had no story. Nothing happened. It lacked drama.'

'The drama was internalised in Barnes,' I began.

'Perhaps that was the problem. I couldn't identify with him. I couldn't even feel sympathy for him and his search for Isabella.'

'I don't think Isabella existed,' I said.

She blinked at me. 'She didn't?'

'She might have been a metaphor for loss.'

Mina shook her head, exasperated. 'No wonder I couldn't engage with the thing,' she said. 'If Isabella didn't exist, then it was even emptier than I first thought. It was about nothing . . .'

'Nothing but loss,' I said.

She smiled at me. 'You liked it, didn't you?'

'I loved it.'

She shook her head, as if in wonder. 'Sometimes, Daniel, I want to see inside your head, try to understand what you're thinking, but sometimes that frightens me.'

* * *

Today I met a wonderful woman, Mina Pratt. 'I wasn't born a Pratt,' she told me, 'I just married one.' She is 36, divorced, has two children. We met in the Fleece and talked for an hour about nothing but the novels we were reading. I was instantly attracted to her. She's practical, down-to-earth, level-headed – all the things I'm not. I told her I was a writer, and cursed myself in case she thought I was trying to impress her.

From the personal journals of Daniel Ellis.

Christmas came and went.

It was Mina's turn to have the girls for that year's festivities. Her parents came over from Leeds and the house was full, for the first time in ages, with goodwill and glad tidings. I disliked Christmas – the occasion struck me as tawdry and cheap, an excuse to party when no excuse was really needed, a time of sanctimonious bonhomie towards our fellow man, and the rest of the year be damned. I withheld my humbug from Mina. She loved Christmas day, the glitz and the cosiness, the present giving . . . It was a paradox, I know. She, the hard-hearted pragmatist, and me the romantic. I could take the romantic ideal of Yule, but not the actuality, while Mina enjoyed the occasion quite simply for what it was, a chance for the family to get together, enjoy good food and a classic film on TV.

The period following Christmas, and the even sadder occasion of New Year, strikes me as the nadir of the year. Spring is a distant promise, winter a grey, bitter cold reality: if the calendar were to be rendered as an abstract visualisation, then January and February would be coloured black.

The new year was brightened, on the second Saturday of January, by the unexpected arrival of a brown cardboard package. Mina was on an early shift, and the girls – Sam and Tessa, eight and six respectively – were filling in a colouring book at the kitchen table. I tended to keep in the background on the days when Mina had the girls; even after a year, and even though it was my house, I felt as though I were trespassing on emotional territory not rightfully mine. On the rare occasions when I was alone with the girls, I would give them pens and paper, or put a video on TV, and leave them to their own devices.

I carried the package to my study at the top of the house, attempting to divine from the postmark some idea of its content. The package came from York.

Intrigued, still not guessing, I ripped it open.

Books, and books, moreover, by Vaughan Edwards: his first and third novels, *Winter at the Castle* and *A Brighter Light*. They were in good condition, complete with pristine dust jackets. They looked as though they had never been read, though the passage of years had discoloured the pages to a sepia hue, and foxed the end-papers. A bargain at five pounds each, including postage and packing.

The back flap of the jackets each gave the same brief, potted biography: Vaughan Edwards was born in Dorset in 1930. After National Service in the RAF, he taught for five years at a public school in Gloucestershire. He is now a full-time writer and lives in the North Yorkshire village of Highdale.

These terse contractions of an individual's life filled me with sadness, especially those from years ago. I always read them in the knowledge that the life described was now no more, or was at least much altered in circumstance. I thought of Vaughan Edwards in the RAF, then teaching, and then living the writer's life in Highdale . . . before the tragedy of his disappearance.

Highdale was a small village situated thirty miles from Skipton on the North Yorkshire moors. It occurred to me that Edwards might still have been living there at the time of his disappearance, six years ago.

I rationed myself, over the course of the following bitter cold days, to just three hours a night with the novels of Vaughan Edwards. While Mina curled in her chair and reread the Brontës, I lay on the sofa and slowly immersed myself in the singular world of the vanished novelist. I began with his first novel, *Winter at the Castle*, a strange story of a group of lonely and embittered individuals who find themselves invited for a month to the remote North-umbrian castle of a reclusive landowner. That the recluse never appears to the guests, nor in the novel, came as no surprise. There was no explanation as to why they might have been invited to the castle. There was little action, but much introspection, as the characters met, interacted, and discussed their respective lives – and then left to resume their places in a century that hardly suited them . . . I refrained from asking Mina what she might make of this one.

His third novel, *A Brighter Light*, was a monologue from the viewpoint of a young girl imprisoned in an oak tree, her recollections of her early life, and how her essence had become one with the oak. She befriended, through a form of telepathy, a young novelist who moved into the cottage where the tree grew. The book ends ambiguously; there is a hint that the man joins the girl's spirit in the tree, and also that the monologue might have been a fictional work by the young writer.

Unpromising subject matter, I had to admit that. In the hands of a lesser writer, the novels would just not work. But something in Vaughan Edward's mature handling of his characters' emotions, their honestly wrought inner lives, lifted the books from the level of turgid emotionalism and invested them with art.

I finished *A Brighter Light* and laid it aside, my heart hammering.

Mina smiled across at me. 'Good?'

'Amazing.'

'I'll believe you,' she laughed.

Like all great art, which I believed these books to be, they had the effect of making me look anew at my life and the world around me; it was as if I saw Mina for the first time, was able now, with perceptions honed by Edwards' insight, to discern her essence, the bright light that burned at the core of her being. I felt then an overwhelming surge of love for this woman, and at the same time I was cut through with sadness like a physical pain.

Early in our relationship, she had told me that she did not love me, and that, 'I can't bring myself to feel love for anyone, other than the girls.'

I accepted this, rationalised that perhaps in time she might come to appreciate me, might even one day bring herself to love me.

I had asked her if she was unable to feel love because she had invested so much in her husband, only for that investment to turn sour. Perhaps she was afraid, I suggested, to risk giving love again, for fear of being hurt a second time. She denied this, said that she could not explain her inability to love me. I told myself that she was either deluding herself, or lying. Perhaps she was lying to save my feelings; perhaps she was capable of love, but I was not the right person. In the early days I was torn by the pain of what I saw as rejection . . . and yet she remained with me, gave a passable impression of, if not love, then a deep affection, and I refrained from quizzing her as to the state of her heart, and learned to live from day to day.

'Mina,' I said now. 'I love you.'

She sighed and closed her eyes, and then snapped them open and stared at me. 'Daniel, I wish you wouldn't . . .' Her plea was heartfelt.

'Sorry. Had to tell you. Sorry if that disturbs you. You know, most women like to be told that they're loved.'

'Well, I'm not most women—'

'I'm not going to leave you, Mina. You can tell me that you love me, and I won't walk out, hurt you again—'

'Oh, Christ!' She sat up and stared across at me. 'Why do you have to analyse? Why now? Everything's been fine, hasn't it? I'm here, with you. What more do you want?'

What more did I want?

Perhaps it was possessive of me to demand her love when I had everything else she could give me? Perhaps she was simply being honest when she admitted that she could not extend to me something that she claimed she no longer believed in. Perhaps I was an insecure, thoughtless bastard for demanding that she should open her heart.

'I'm sorry. I just wanted you to know.'

She sat and stared at me, as if at a wounded animal. In a small voice she said, 'I know, Daniel. I know.'

* * *

Mina's professed inability to feel love for me can only be a reaction to what she went through with her husband. She denies this – but is this denial her way of not admitting me past her defences, of not allowing me a glimpse of her true feelings and emotions?

From the personal journals of Daniel Ellis.

The following week I received an e-mail from a second-hand bookshop in Oxford, informing me that they had located three novels by Vaughan Edwards. I sent a cheque and the books arrived a few days later.

One of the novels was his very last, *The Secret of Rising Dene*, published shortly after his disappearance. The biographical details made no reference to the fact that he had vanished, but did give the interesting information that, in '96, he was still living in the North Yorkshire village of Highdale.

That weekend I suggested a drive up into the Dales. I told Mina that I wanted to visit Highdale, where Edwards had lived. After the spat the previous week, things had been fine between us. She made no mention of my interrogative *faux pas*, and I did my best not to rile her with further questions.

'Highdale? Don't we go through Settle to get there? There's that wonderful Thai place on the way.'

'Okay, we'll call in on the way back. How's that?'

She laughed at me. 'I hope you don't expect Highdale to be a shrine to your literary hero,' she said. 'He wasn't quite in the same league as the Brontës—'

'Then let's hope that Highdale isn't as trashily commercialised as Haworth, okay?'

Deuce.

She elbowed me in the ribs.

two

We set off after lunch on an unusually bright February afternoon, dazzling sunlight giving the false promise of the spring to come – which would soon no doubt be dashed by the next bout of bitter cold and rain.

The approach road to the village of Highdale wound through ancient woodland on the side of a steep hill. When we reached the crest I pulled off the road and braked the car.

I laughed in delight. The sunlight picked out the village with great golden searchlights falling through low banks of cumulus. Highdale was a collection of tiny stone-built cottages and farmhouses set amid hunched pastures; I made out a church, a public house, and what might have been a village hall, all laid out below us like some sanguine architect's scale model of a rural idyll.

We drove down the incline and into the village and parked on the cobbled market square before the White Lion.

The pub was empty, save for a barman chatting to someone who might have been a local farmer. They both looked up when we pushed through the door, as if unaccustomed to customers at this time of day.

I ordered a dry cider for Mina and a fresh orange juice for myself. While the barman poured the drinks and chatted to Mina, I looked around the snug. It was fitted out much like any typical village pub: a variety of moorland scenes by local artists, a selection of horse brasses, a battalion of Toby jugs hanging in ranks from the low, blackened beams.

Then I noticed the bookshelf, or rather the books that were upon it. One volume in particular stood out – I recognised the Val Biro pen and ink sketch on the spine of the dust jacket. It showed the attenuated figure of a man doffing his Trilby. It was the cover of Vaughan Edwards' third novel, *A Brighter Light*.

The barman said something.

'Excuse me?' I said, my attention on the books.

'I think he wants paying,' Mina said. 'Don't worry, I'll get these.'

She paid the barman and carried the drinks over to the table beneath the bookshelf. I was peering at the racked spines, head tilted.

'Good God,' I said. 'They're all Edwards.'

'Not all of them.' Mina tapped the spines of four books, older volumes than the Edwards. They were by a writer I had never come across before, E.V. Cunningham-Price. They looked Victorian, and caught her interest. She pulled them from the shelf, sat down and began reading.

I sorted through the Edwards. There were ten novels, eight of which I had never read, and a volume of short stories. I pulled them down and stacked them on the table, reading through the description of each book on the front inside flap.

I looked back at the shelf. I thought it odd that there should be no other books beside the Edwards and the four Cunningham-Price volumes.

The barman was watching me. I hefted one of the books. 'They're not for sale, by any chance . . . ?'

He was a big man in his sixties, with the type of stolid, typically northern face upon which scowls seem natural, like fissures in sedimentary rock.

'Well, by rights they're not for sale, like. They're for the enjoyment of the customers, if you know what I mean. Tell you what, though – take a couple with you, if you promise to bring them back.'

'I'll do that. That's kind—'

'You're not locals, then?'

Mina looked up. 'Almost. Skipton.'

'Local enough,' the barman said. 'Hope you enjoy 'em.'

'I'm sure I will.' I paused, regarding the books and wondering which two volumes to take with me. Mina looked up from her book. 'I wouldn't mind taking this one, Daniel.'

I selected the volume of stories, *The Tall Ghost and other stories*, and returned the others to the shelf.

I finished my drink and moved to the bar for a refill. I indicated the books. 'He was a local, wasn't he? Did he ever drop by?'

'Mr Vaughan?' the barman asked. 'Every Monday evening, regular as clockwork. Sat on the stool over there.' He indicated a high stool placed by the corner of the bar and the wall. 'Drank three Irish whiskeys from nine until ten, then left on the dot of the hour. Very rarely missed a Monday for over twenty years.'

'You knew him well?'

'Mr Vaughan?' He grunted a humourless laugh. 'No one knew Mr Vaughan. Kept himself to himself, if you know what I mean. Spoke to no one, and no one spoke to him. Reckon that's how he preferred it. Lived here nigh on forty years, and never said boo to a goose.'

'Strange,' I said, sipping my juice.

'Well,' the publican said, 'he was a writer chappie, you know?' He tapped his head. 'Lived up here most of the time.'

Over at her table, Mina was smiling to herself.

'He had a place in the village?' I asked.

'Not far off. He owned the big house up the hill on your left as you come in, set back in the woods. Edgecoombe Hall.'

The very title fired my imagination. It seemed somehow fitting, the very place where Vaughan Edwards would have lived his sequestered, writer's life.

I decided I'd like to take a look at the place. 'Who owns it now?'

'Edgecoombe Hall?' He shook his head. 'No one. It's been standing empty ever since Mr Vaughan went and disappeared.'

I nodded, digesting this. If it were a big house, with a fair bit of land, and perhaps dilapidated, then I imagined that no local would care to touch the place, and Highdale was just too far off the beaten track to make commuting to Leeds or Bradford an option for a prospective city buyer.

'Why's that?' I asked.

The publican shrugged. 'Well, it's not exactly brand spanking new,' he said. 'A bit tumbledown, if you know what I mean. And the ghost doesn't help.'

At this, Mina looked up from her book. 'The ghost?' She had scepticism daubed across her face in primary colours. She gave me a look that said, *if you believe that, Daniel . . .*

'Only reporting what I was told, love. Don't believe in 'em meself. Old wives' tales.'

Despite myself, I was intrigued. 'The ghost of Vaughan Edwards, right?'

He shook his head. Behind me, I heard Mina sigh with mock despair. 'That's where you're wrong, sir. The Hall was haunted – if you believe in that kind of thing – long before Mr Vaughan bought the place. Stories go way back, right to the turn of the century – and I mean the century before last. 1900s. Ghost of a young girl haunts the place every full moon, so they say. Many a local claims to have clapped eyes on it.'

I drank my orange juice and considered Vaughan Edwards. The scant biographical information I had come across had never mentioned whether or not he had ever married.

I asked the publican.

'Married? Mr Vaughan?' He chuckled. 'Never saw him with a woman – nor anyone else, for that matter. Bit of a recluse.'

'So he lived alone in the Hall?'

The publican laughed. 'Alone, if you don't count the ghost.'

I noticed that Mina had finished her drink and was gesturing to go. I signalled one minute and turned to my informant. 'You don't happen to know anything about how he disappeared?'

Mina sighed.

The publican said, 'Strange do, all things considered. His car was found in the woods, not a hundred yards up from the Hall, on the track leading to the escarpment above the river. A local youth found it and notified the police. They investigated, found he wasn't at the Hall, then traced his footprints on the path leading to the drop.' He shrugged. 'Strange thing was, his footprints stopped before they reached the edge.' He paused, considering. ''Course, he could always have stepped off the path and walked to the edge through the bracken.'

'You think that's what he did? Threw himself off the escarpment into the river?'

'Me?' He gave my question due consideration. 'I don't rightly know, sir. He didn't seem the kind to do a thing like that, but then who can tell? You see, his body was never found, which struck me as strange. The river's fast flowing, but there's a mill dam about two miles south of here. The body would've fetched up there, all things considered.'

'So if he didn't kill himself,' I asked, 'then what happened?'

'Aha,' the publican said, 'now that's the sixty-four thousand dollar question, isn't it?'

He paused, watching me. 'Funny thing, though,' he went on.

'Yes?'

'About a week before he disappeared, he brought in this carrier bag full of books. A dozen or so of his own and four or five others by the Cunningham chappie. He just dropped the bag on the counter and said that the far shelf needed filling, and that was it. Not another word.'

I nodded. 'Strange.'

We were interrupted by the arrival of another customer. 'Usual, Bill?' the publican called, and moved down the bar to pull a pint of Tetley's.

Mina took the opportunity to hurry me from the place. I picked up the Edwards collection, thanked the landlord and followed Mina outside.

As we drove up the hill and out of the village, she said, 'You really believed all that rubbish, didn't you?'

I glanced at her. 'What rubbish?'

'All that about the ghost.'

'I don't believe it – but then again I don't necessarily disbelieve.'

She said, 'I don't know . . .' under her breath.

'What's wrong with keeping your options open, Mina? "There are more things in heaven and Earth, Horatio . . ." Look at it this way, how many things were dismissed as impossible a hundred years ago, which have come to be accepted now?'

'Ghosts aren't one of them,' she said.

I sighed. I often found her world view severely limiting, and it irritated me when she took to mocking my open-mindedness.

I wondered if she had always been a sceptic, or if having to concentrate wholly on the practicalities of day to day survival during the traumatic separation from her husband had fostered in her such a narrow perspective. She would give credence to nothing that she could not see before her, that she could not grasp.

I drove slowly up the hillside, looking through the trees for sign of Edgecoombe Hall.

'Couldn't you see that he was leading you on, Daniel?' she continued.

'The publican?'

'He was spinning a yarn. I wonder how many times he's told the same story to visitors?'

I shook my head. 'I don't think so. He said himself that he didn't believe in ghosts.'

'And that story of Edwards' disappearance—'

I turned to her, wide-eyed. 'Don't tell me, Mina – you refuse to believe in that, too?'

She struck my arm with playful truculence. 'He was going on as if he might have survived – I don't know, staged his own disappearance. The chances are he left his car and went for a walk, went too near the edge and fell into the river.'

'So why was his body never discovered?'

She shrugged. 'Search me. Maybe it got snagged on the river-bottom.'

'Surely it would've been discovered by now.'

'So what do you think happened then?'

I smiled to myself. She loved certainty. I shook my head. 'I just don't know,' I said, knowing it would exasperate her. 'Ah . . . Look.'

I braked and pulled into the side of the road. Through the winter-denuded sycamore and elm, set perhaps half a mile from the road, I made out the gaunt towers of a Victorian building.

'Edgecoombe Hall, I presume. Mind if we take a look?'

She surprised me. She was staring at the severe outline of the Hall, something speculative in her gaze. 'Why not?' she said at last.

I drove on a little further, looking for the opening to the driveway in the overgrown hedge of ivy and bramble.

'There,' she called, pointing to a gap in the hedge. Once, many years ago, two tall stone pillars, topped with orbs, had marked the entrance to the grounds; now the pillars were cloaked with ivy. Wrought iron gates hung open and awry, their hinges having rusted long ago.

I turned the car into the pot-holed driveway and proceeded at walking pace through the gloomy tunnel between overgrown rhododendron and elderberry bushes.

Edgecoombe Hall hove into sight, more stark and intimidating at close quarters than when seen from the road. It was a foursquare pile with mock-Gothic towers at each corner, its façade having long ago given up the ghost against the creeping tide of ivy. Only the double doorway and a couple of upstairs windows were free of the verdant mass.

It struck me as the appropriate domicile of a lonely and reclusive writer. I almost expected to see a massive, haunted oak tree in the middle of the lawn, or the ghostly face of a young girl peering timidly out through an upper window.

I stopped the car before the plinth of steps rising to the entrance. Mina laid a hand on my arm and pointed.

A small truck, laden with timber, was parked around the far corner of the Hall. 'Perhaps someone has bought it after all,' she said. She peered at the façade and pulled a face. 'Certainly needs work.'

We climbed out. The sun was setting through the trees, slanting an intense orange light across the lawn and illuminating the ivied frontage of the building. I moved away from the car, stood and took in the atmosphere of the place.

Far from intimidating, the Hall seemed to me a place of melancholy. Perhaps it was merely that it was in a state of such disrepair, had seen far, far better days. But I imagined the Hall as it might have been, shorn of ivy and pristine, and it came to me still that it would have been a dour and eldritch place.

A steady tattoo of hammer blows sounded from within the Hall, and it cheered me that someone was at least making a start at renovation.

'Daniel,' Mina said. 'Look.'

She was pointing at the ground, the gravelled drive that swept around the front of the building. I joined her.

A series of fissures radiated from the Hall, wide where they issued from the wall and narrowing as they crossed the drive. I noticed great cracks in the grey brickwork beneath the ivy.

'Looks like it's been hit by an earthquake,' she said.

I approached the façade, where I guessed a window might be positioned behind the ivy, and pulled away the clinging growth. I came to a mullioned pane and peered within. A bright spear of sunlight fell over my shoulder and illuminated the room. To my surprise it was furnished: bookshelves lined the walls, and elephantine armchairs and sofas were positioned before the hearth.

'See anything?'

I held a swatch of vine aside as she peered in. She shivered theatrically. 'Creepy.'

I was about to suggest that we enter the Hall and find the wielder of the hammer, but Mina had other ideas. She took my arm. 'You've seen enough, Daniel. I'm hungry. A Thai banquet awaits us.'

The thought of food appealed to me, too. I wanted to stay a little longer, but I also wanted to investigate the track which Vaughan Edwards had taken prior to his disappearance.

'Okay, but there's something I must check, first.'

Mina rolled her eyes. I took her arm and we returned to the car. 'What?' she asked.

I reversed, then drove down the drive and onto the road. I turned right, continuing up the hill, and kept a lookout for a track leading into the woods.

I found it, and turned. Twilight enclosed us. 'Daniel,' Mina warned me.

'This, if I'm not mistaken, is where Vaughan Edwards left his car on the day he disappeared.'

Ahead of us the track terminated in a clearing made magical by the dying light of the sun. When I cut the engine and opened the door, a deathly hush pervaded the clearing and I received the distinct impression that the place regarded our arrival as an intrusion.

I climbed out and stood beside the car. In the gathering dusk I made out a worn path leading through the trees. I gestured for Mina to join me. She sat in the passenger seat, frowning her displeasure, waited a beat and then flounced out with ill grace.

'All I can think about is green Thai curry and you want to drag me through the mud on a wild goose chase.' As is often the case with Mina, the tone of her voice was betrayed by the humorous light of tolerance in her eyes.

She took my hand and we hurried side by side along the footpath.

Perhaps it was the writer in me, the pathological creator of tales, but I was storing away this setting, and the feelings I was experiencing, for use in some future work of fiction. I was filled with the sense that time had dissolved, that all events maintained simultaneously, and that any second I might behold the figure of Vaughan Edwards striding towards his destiny through the undergrowth before us.

The path took a sharp turn to the left, and the trees thinned out: an aqueous, twilight lacuna glimmered before us.

'Stop!' Mina screamed, clutching my arm.

I halted, stock still. At my feet the earth crumbled away, and only then did I make out the sudden drop.

Mina hauled me back and we stood, our arms about each other like frightened children, and stared in wonder and fright at the suddenly revealed precipice.

Emboldened by survival, I took a step forward and made out, a hundred feet below, the muscled torrent of a river in full spate.

I rejoined Mina. She was staring at me.

'Perhaps that's what happened to your writer,' she whispered, staring down. 'And his body?'

She shrugged, then gave a little shiver. 'I don't know.' She paused, as if considering. 'Let's go, Daniel. I don't like it here.'

'I thought you didn't believe in ghosts,' I said.

She snorted. 'I believe in the power of auto-suggestion,' she replied.

We retraced our way back along the path to the clearing. I was heartened to see the car – as if some primitive part of me had feared that it might have vanished in our absence, stranding us in the haunted wood. I kept my musings to myself as I backed from the clearing and once again resumed the road, heading for Settle.

Over piled plates of green curry and five mushroom satay, we chatted. Mina was animated and affectionate, as if she wished to put from her mind all thought of Vaughan Edwards and Edgecoombe Hall, and concentrate instead on the simple commerce of intimacy. She laughed a lot, reached across the table to touch my hand – an uncommon gesture – and got a little tipsy on Singha beer.

I'd often lose myself in the miracle of her physicality, staring into her wide eyes, or at her exquisite hands. Mina had the finest hands I had ever seen; small, ineffably graceful, with a lithe, articulated elegance and long, oval nails. And these were hands that made a dozen beds a day, that mopped up after incontinent patients, washed and cooked and cared for two children and myself . . .

Ten months ago her hours at the hospital had been cut and the rent of her terrace house increased, and for two weeks she had fretted without telling me of her concern. When at last I asked her what was wrong, and she told me, I rashly escalated the terms of our relationship by suggesting that she move in with me. Until then she had always stipulated that I stay over at her place only twice a week, that she was not committed to me – and I had feared that my offer might frighten her away.

To my joy she had agreed, and moved in, and I had adapted myself to part-time family life, careful not to impose myself on Mina in any way, to maintain a distance with the girls, not wanting to be seen to be usurping her maternal authority. For months I had walked on egg-shells.

I had never asked her if, even without the financial necessity, she would have eventually moved in with me. She hated my analysis of our relationship, the stripping to basics of her motivations. From time to time it came to me that she was with me not through bonds of strong affection, but merely because I was, to put it crudely, a meal ticket.

On these occasions I told myself that I should be thankful that I had found someone whom I could love, and left it at that.

We finished the meal and drove home through a frosty, star-filled night. It was as if we had agreed tacitly not to mention Edwards and the Hall. Mina laid a hand on my leg and talked of work, but I was conscious of the weight of the book in my jacket pocket, waiting to be read, at once inviting and, for some reason I could not quite fathom, not a little threatening.

* * *

'Vaughan Edwards manages to capture the tragic truth of the human condition in his timeless works of fiction . . .'

Graham Greene, cover quote for *A Summer's Promise*.

One month passed.

For some reason, I could not bring myself to read the Vaughan Edwards collection of stories I had borrowed from the White Lion. The book remained on my desk, unopened. From time to time I would pick it up, admire the Val Biro cover of a village scene with a Maypole as the centre-piece, and read the description of the stories on the inside flap, and the scant biographical paragraph on the back. But I felt a strange reluctance to begin the book.

I wondered if, subconsciously, I identified Vaughan Edwards and his books with Mina's uneasiness at Edgecoombe Hall that day. That weak core of my being, insecure in our relationship, was eager to appease Mina in whichever way possible – even if that meant not reading *The Tall Ghost and other stories*.

How Mina would have laughed at my tortured self-analysis!

However, as the weeks since Edgecoombe Hall elapsed, our relationship seemed to take on a new dimension, become deeper and more fulfilling. Mina did not go so far as to profess her undying love for me, but she did become more affectionate. Our love-making – never breathlessly passionate – increased in regularity and scope: it seemed that suddenly we each learned more of the other's desires, and adapted accordingly. As ever, these things went unspoken between us. Mina was a great believer that things should happen of their own accord, intuitively, an attitude which I – forever needing to question and analyse – found maddening. I bit my tongue, however. The last thing I wanted was to anger her by asking how she thought our relationship might be progressing.

A month after Edgecoombe Hall, it came to me that my reluctance to read the collection was nothing more than groundless insecurity. I looked back at my self-censorship and something in me, forever critical of my behaviour, mocked such feeble-mindedness.

I began the book when Mina was working a night-shift. While a wind keened around the cottage, rattling the windows in their frames, I lay on the sofa and immersed myself in Vaughan Edwards' singular visions.

The stories, written in the late forties and fifties and first published in magazines as diverse as *Lilliput* and the American *Magazine of Fantasy and Science Fiction*, were, if anything, even stranger than his novels. They comprised routine ghost stories, eerie fantasy tales set in the far future and the distant past, and two tales quite unclassifiable. These stories I found the most compelling. They told of visitors to Earth – though from where they came was never disclosed – their relations with lonely human beings, their perceptions of each other, and their attempts at conveying a sense of their separate realities. The impossibility of ever wholly comprehending an alien's viewpoint made for frustrating, if occasionally intriguing, reading. I finished the book in the early hours of the morning, convinced that I had been granted a privileged glimpse into the brilliant, if tortured, psyche of a fellow human being.

That morning we remained in bed until eleven, made love, and then lay in each other's arms. The harsh summons of the telephone propelled Mina to her feet. I watched her stalk around the bed and retrieve her dressing-gown from the back of the door. Short and heavy-breasted, she reminded me of the Earth-goddess figurines of the Palaeolithic period, full-bodied idols of fertility.

While she spoke on the phone – it was her sister, arranging a drink for that night – I stared at the ceiling and wondered whether to tell her that I was planning another trip to Highdale. I would return the two books we had borrowed, and ask if I could take the remaining Edwards if I left a monetary deposit.

Mina came back, shed her dressing-gown and slipped into bed beside me, gloriously naked. She slung a leg over my hip and told me that she was seeing Liz that night at the Fleece.

She met her sister perhaps once a week for a customary four halves of cider, and each time she left the house I could not help but experience an involuntary and wholly unwarranted pang of jealousy. Mina lived up to the archetype of a nurse in her extrovert ability to engage socially with all and everybody; men found her not only physically attractive, but open and approachable. She was popular, and outgoing, and the immature child in me, like a boy who demands his mother's total attention, bridled at the fact of her sociability.

Of course, I hated myself for this . . . And, of course, I had never mentioned it to Mina.

She had once, months ago, told me that she could never feel jealous. When I expressed disbelief, she quoted an instance. When she was leaving her husband he, in a bid to make her jealous and win her back, made it obvious that he was seeing another woman. She said she had felt nothing, other than relief that it made her decision to leave him all the more clear cut.

I refrained from pointing out to her that of course she would not feel jealous of someone who, by that point, she had come to hate.

Now I held her to me and let slip, quite casually, that the following day I intended to drive up to Highdale.

She pulled away to get a better look at me. 'You're not going to look around that house again, are you?'

I shook my head. 'I want to collect the remaining Edwards books I haven't read.'

'You can only take two at a time, remember?'

I laughed. 'It isn't a lending library. I'll leave him a deposit and take the lot.'

She regarded me. 'You really like his stuff, don't you?'

'It's magical.'

'I don't like it, Daniel. There's something . . . I don't know, not exactly creepy . . .' She stopped and stared at the ceiling. 'There's some quality about his books that frightens me. Perhaps it's just that I like certainty. I like to know that everything has its place. With his stories, his reality is off-centre, skewed.' She shivered. 'Enough of Vaughan Edwards. Aren't you getting up today?'

'Not working.' I yawned.

'No?' She looked at me, concerned. 'You haven't worked for weeks.'

Getting on for two months, to be precise. The creative urge had left me, and I had no pressing financial need to commit another novelisation. A week earlier my agent had phoned, asking how the latest novel was shaping up. He said that, despite the fact that my publisher might be wary of looking at the next one, he was sure he could interest a senior editor at HarperCollins.

I had lied – the fantasy springing easily to my lips – that it was going okay, was still in the early stages; that, as he knew, I didn't like to talk about work in progress. I had replaced the receiver with a nagging sense of shame at the lie.

'When there's no bread on the table, Mina, then we'll worry, okay?'

She looked at me. 'I'll make breakfast, Daniel.'

As I lay in bed and listened to the blissful sound of domesticity going on in the kitchen, the sizzling of eggs, the perking of the coffee, I wondered about the next book, and my lack of desire to start it. Never before had I been pole-axed by such apathy, even in my twenties when I had written novel after bad novel with no hope of finding a publisher.

I told myself that the muse would return, one day, and went downstairs to join Mina for breakfast.

* * *

'I don't give a damn about things like facts in my novels. My books aren't about the factual, physical world. They're about what's in here. Critics may call my work old-fashioned and over-emotional, but I contend that our emotions are the only true barometer of our humanity.'

Vaughan Edwards, in a rare radio interview,
BBC Third Programme, April 1959.

That afternoon, when I emerged from my study after doodling for a futile hour over the rewrite of a short story, Mina was kneeling on the rug before the fire, rump in the air. She had three books open on the floor, and was looking from one to the other, lost in concentration.

The girls were home from school, watching a noisy video on the TV in the kitchen.

Mina saw me and blinked, her face quite blank.

'What's wrong?' I asked.

I saw that the books she was studying were the E.V. Cunningham-Price and two of Vaughan Edwards' novels.

I moved to the kitchen and closed the door, diminishing the cartoon din.

'Daniel . . . This is strange.'

'What's strange?' Oddly enough, and for no apparent reason, I was aware of my increased pulse.

She stabbed at a book with a graceful forefinger. I sat on the sofa, watching her.

'This. I was reading the Cunningham-Price. There's a chapter set in North Yorkshire, about an artist who lives alone in a big house. It's haunted, and the artist has an affair with the ghost of a young girl . . .'

My stomach turned.

Mina went on, 'I remember you telling me about Edwards' book, *The Miracle at Hazelmere*. It sounded pretty much the same, so I checked. And look.'

She passed me the Cunningham-Price and *Miracle*. Disbelieving, and feeling a little strange, I read passages from both books that she had marked with yellow Post-it notes. For the next hour I went through the books, while Mina prepared the girls for ballet lessons. She looked in on me before setting off. 'What do you think?'

I looked up, nodded. 'Remarkable. He must have used the Cunningham book as a template . . .'

'You mean he plagiarised,' she said. 'I'll be back in an hour.'

I nodded again, absently. 'I'll have dinner ready.'

'That'd be great.' She hurried from the room. The video noise ceased, and suddenly the cottage was deathly quiet.

I read through the Cunningham-Price book, discovering many thematic similarities between it and other of Edwards' novels. My first fear, that Edwards had merely lifted great chunks of Cunningham-Price and claimed them as his own, was not borne out. Although, as Mina had rightly pointed out, Edwards had used an episode in the Cunningham-Price and expanded it, delving into the themes and ideas that Cunningham-Price had left unexplored, I was loath to accuse the modern novelist of plagiarising the Victorian. Rather, it was as if he had read the Cunningham-Price, found himself fascinated with the Victorian's ideas and concepts, and fleshed them out in his own fiction: Edwards' work, far from plagiarism, struck me as a tribute – acknowledged when he used certain of the older writer's characters and situations. A simple plagiarist without talent would simply have copied, not used Cunningham-Price as a starting point from which to explore his own ideas.

I recalled my promise to prepare dinner, and moved to the kitchen.

Later that night, with the girls in bed, I served dinner and opened a bottle of wine, and we discussed Mina's literary discovery.

'Think it'll earn me a footnote in some encyclopaedia?' she asked.

'More like a whole damn entry.'

She sipped her wine. 'But why would he do it, Daniel? Why would a writer simply steal another writer's work?'

I pointed my fork at her. 'I don't think he did,' I said. I explained my theory that Edwards had used Cunningham-Price as a starting point, and as a matter of course had acknowledged the Victorian writer by echoing some of his events and characters.

Mina stared at me. 'Echoing?' she laughed. 'That's the strangest euphemism for plagiarism I've ever heard.'

'Mina, Edwards is no plagiarist. He's too talented for that.'

'You just don't want to admit that your literary hero is a word-burglar, Daniel!'

I smiled at her turn of phrase. 'There's one way to find out for sure. Tomorrow I'll go up to Highdale and fetch the rest of the books, the Edwards and the Cunningham-Prices, okay? If Edwards used any more of Cunningham-Price's books on which to base his own . . . then okay, I might admit you have something.'

'It's a deal.'

'But I'll bet you a pound that my man will be vindicated.'

Her eyes flashed. 'I don't gamble, Daniel. Remember?'

I nodded, chastised. Her ex-husband had been an inveterate gambler. 'Okay, sorry. But if Edwards used any more of Cunningham's ideas and characters, I'll buy you a Thai meal, okay?'

She nodded and shook my hand with pantomime seriousness. 'Deal,' she said.

* * *

My dear Vaughan, I exhort you, as a friend as well as your agent, to consider again your preoccupation with the occult. We're living in an increasingly rationalistic age. Readers don't go for this kind of thing any more. Charlesworth at Hutchinson is having second thoughts about commissioning the next book . . .

A letter from Desmond Maitland to Vaughan Edwards,
July 1980.

The following afternoon I dropped Mina at the hospital and took the road due north to Highdale.

It had rained continuously all day, a monsoon downpour that reduced visibility to less than twenty metres. In consequence I drove slowly, and the journey seemed to take an age. I usually listen to Radio 4 when driving, but that afternoon my thoughts were too full of Vaughan Edwards to concentrate on the play.

It was almost four o'clock when I pulled onto the cobbled square outside the White Lion. Evidently it had been market day; a few sodden traders were dismantling their stalls with a distinct lack of enthusiasm. I jumped from the car and ran across the cobbles to the public house, avoiding puddles but not the torrent that lashed down from a leaden sky.

A few more drinkers than last time were propped against the bar, and the publican greeted me with, 'Not fit for a dog out there. Orange juice?'

Surprised that he remembered me, I nodded. I pulled the books from the inside pocket of my jacket. 'And I've returned these.'

He smiled as he fixed my drink. 'Hope you enjoyed them.'

I paid for the juice and carried it to the table beneath the bookshelf. Three volumes by E.V. Cunningham-Price, and nine by Edwards, still occupied the shelf. I pulled down the Cunningham-Prices and settled myself at the table. As with most Victorian novels, the date of publication was not given, though they had the look of books published in the last decade of the nineteenth century. I began speed-reading my way through, first, *Green Pastures*, and then *The Halfway House*.

Again and again I recognised turns of phrase, and sometimes entire descriptions, from those works of Edwards that I'd read. The plot of *Green Pastures* was pretty much recapitulated in Edwards' 1956 novel *Towards Sunset*. *The Halfway House* featured a character I recognised from one of his short stories.

And yet . . . I found it difficult to agree with Mina that Vaughan Edwards was a plagiarist. Certainly he had lifted from Cunningham-Price's work characters, descriptions, and certain lines – but from these he had fashioned his own unique novels, using, as it were, the original novels as a spring-board for his own imagination. If anything, he could be said to have been collaborating with the earlier writer – even though it was a collaboration that had gone uncredited.

Then again, perhaps my love of his work would not allow me to accede to the charge that he was a plagiarist: in a court of law, the similarities between the two novelists' works would be sufficient evidence to have him declared guilty as charged.

I suppose the question now was, why had Vaughan Edwards used the works of E.V. Cunningham-Price as the starting point for so many of his own fictions? As a writer, and a voracious reader, I well understood that there were certain authors whose work was so overwhelmingly powerful, and which spoke to one's heart – irrespective of literary merit – that it was often difficult not to be influenced. But in my experience these influences were strongest when the writer was young and had yet to develop his or her own voice: with time one's vision matured, one's voice became wholly one's own . . . And yet Vaughan Edwards had clearly been influenced by Cunningham's work when working on his very last novel, *The Secret of Rising Dene*, published in 1996.

The affair had about it, in common with the man's life and disappearance, an air of insoluble mystery.

I turned my attention to the novels by Edwards, leafing through the volumes with that comfortable sense of anticipation that one inevitably acquires when handling unread books by favourite writers – and what if others might accuse him of plagiarism? I would argue with Mina that in Edwards' case the borrowings had been wholly justifiable, as they had helped to produce lasting works of literature.

The publican left the bar and made a tour of the snug, collecting empties. I took the opportunity to broach the subject of borrowing the books wholesale.

I held up a fifty-pound note. 'And I'll leave this until I return them,' I offered.

He frowned at the note, and laughed. 'You look like a gentleman and a scholar,' he said, not without humour. 'And you brought the others back. Take 'em. I'll trust you.'

He moved away, balancing half a dozen pint glasses along the length of his right arm.

I waited until the rain had let up slightly, then thanked the publican and hurried out to the car. I stowed the books on the passenger seat and started the engine, wondering what Mina might have to say when I arrived home with enough reading material for the next few weeks.

I drove from the square and up the hill, my progress impeded by a small truck which laboured up the incline. It was not until it approached the crest of the rise, and turned right through the ivied gateposts of Edgecoombe Hall, that I recognised the vehicle as the one parked by the Hall on my first visit.

On impulse I braked, then sat and watched as the truck disappeared into the gloom of the driveway.

It came to me that I could always pose as someone interested in purchasing the tumbledown Hall, perhaps even ask the workman's permission to look around inside . . .

I turned down the drive and approached the Hall. The truck, parked around the corner as before, was emblazoned with the legend: Roy Giles, Builder. I saw a man, perhaps in his fifties, in baggy jeans and a red checked shirt, climb from the cab carrying a toolbox, and enter the building through a side door.

I braked and walked from the car, nervous now that the time had come to act the part of a prospective house buyer.

I rounded the corner and was approaching the side entrance when the man, presumably Giles, emerged.

'Can I help you?' Though his look was suspicious, his tone was friendly enough.

I gestured at the house. 'I was talking to the landlord of the White Lion,' I said. 'I hope to buy a place in the area. I don't suppose you know if it's for sale?'

'Matter of fact, I do.' He smiled. 'Chances are that it might be – but I won't know for sure for a year or so.'

He laughed at my puzzlement.

'Do you own the place?' I asked.

He scratched his head. 'Look, it's not as straightforward as all that.' He hesitated, considering. 'Why don't you come in and I'll explain.'

Bemused, I followed him through what I assumed was the tradesman's entrance into an old scullery. It had been stripped bare and repainted; plumbing fixtures and fittings lay around the floor, evidence of recent work.

He gestured to the only seat in the room, a wooden sawing horse, and I sat down.

He brewed a pot of scalding black tea on a Calor gas stove and handed me a chipped mug. I sipped experimentally: it tasted far better than it appeared.

He leaned against the wall beside a window darkened by ivy, gripping his mug in both hands. 'It's a long story, but I'll make it short,' Giles said. 'I worked for the owner of the Hall for almost twelve years, you see. Odd job man, gardener, things like that. Then six years ago my employer vanished—' He clicked his thumb and forefinger. 'Snap. Just like that.' He shrugged. 'A few months later I was contacted by his solicitor. Imagine my surprise when I found out that the owner had made a will, leaving the Hall and all its contents to me. Thing was, no one was sure that Mr Edwards – the owner – was dead. Until his remains were discovered, or seven years had elapsed, then the Hall was technically still his property. Well, his remains have never been found, and he's been missing six years now. So . . . until next year, I don't rightly know if I'm the owner or not. I come in from time to time, do the odd bit of work here and there to keep the place from falling down.'

He looked at me. 'Not that I hope they find his remains, understand? I'd be delighted if he walked back in here tomorrow.'

'Did you know him well?'

He frowned into his mug. 'Can't say that, but I respected him. He was a gentleman. He gave me work when I needed it and paid good money. He was a writer . . .' He shook his head and gave a wry smile. 'I tried one of his books once, but it wasn't my cup of tea.'

I nodded. 'It must have been quite a shock when he went missing?'

'To tell the truth, it wasn't. It wasn't so cut and dried. He'd been away from the Hall for a day or two when someone discovered his car in the woods, and footprints leading towards the river. The days passed, and I expected him to turn up at any time. I never really thought that he'd thrown himself over the scarp, and anyway no body was ever found, like I said. There was even a sighting of someone fitting Mr Edwards' description getting off a train at York.' He shrugged. 'It's a mystery what happened to him. I still sometimes think he'll walk in out of the blue.'

He laughed. 'So that's your answer. Come back in a year and I might be able to tell you one way or the other.'

I nodded, sipping my tea. 'It's not in the best of repair,' I began.

'I'll give you that,' he said. He hesitated, then went on: 'I'll show you around the place, if you like.'

He led the way from the scullery and down a long corridor, tripping light switches as he went. He flung open consecutive doors and stood aside to let me peer within, maintaining a running commentary as we went. 'Lumber room, still full of trunks and travelling cases.' And, 'Morning room, or that's what Mr Edwards called it, anyway.'

We came to a spacious hallway, illuminated by the light from a dusty chandelier, and crossed the chessboard tiles to a room he announced as, 'The study. This is where Mr Edwards wrote all his books.'

He flung open the door and switched on the light. I stepped inside, aware of my heartbeat. I was on the threshold of the room where Vaughan Edwards had created – with a little help from E.V. Cunningham-Price – his remarkable novels.

But for the film of dust that coated every horizontal surface, the room gave the appearance of still being in use. A typewriter sat on a desk by the ivy-choked window, and shelves of books lined the walls. A row of files – manuscripts, I guessed – occupied a bookshelf beside the desk. It was a pretty typical writer's study – the only thing missing being the writer himself.

My guide noticed me staring at the far wall, where a great crack in the brickwork, running from floor to ceiling, had been inexpertly plastered. I recalled the damage to the façade which I had noticed with Mina on our first visit, and the fissures in the grounds of the Hall.

'That's not the only one,' he said. 'I'll show you.'

He led me from the study and into the east wing of the house. There, in an empty room, he indicated yet another fissure that had been rendered over with discoloured plaster.

He opened a back door, which gave onto a spacious kitchen garden. He stepped out into the twilight and pointed to the rear wall of the building.

Along the length of the Hall, a series of great timber buttresses supported the bulging wall. The building seemed to bow outwards with the marked curvature of a galleon's hull; but for the sturdy props, the impression was that the Hall would have split open like an over-ripe fruit.

An ancient conservatory, with several panes of glass cracked or missing entirely, occupied the far end of the east wing.

'No doubt you'll have second thoughts about the place, now,' he said.

'Well, it does seem a bit tumbledown,' I ventured.

'Oh, it's surprisingly sturdy. These repairs were made a hundred years ago, and the place hasn't fallen down yet.'

The rain had abated, and in the light of the moon that appeared suddenly through the cloudrace I made out a series of crazed cracks in the garden – fissures that had been filled in over the years, but which still showed as slightly lower impressions radiating from the Hall itself.

'Mineshafts?' I asked at last. 'An underground stream?'

He looked at me and shook his head. 'An explosion.'

I stared at him. 'Explosion?'

'Well, that's what the locals said, those who were around at the time, and the story's passed into village folk lore.'

I turned and stared at the bulk of the house. Edgecoombe Hall was a dark shape against the moon-silvered clouds.

'What happened?' I asked.

'It's all a bit of a mystery. One night in December – this was in 1899 – a massive explosion was heard in the village. It came from up the hill – from

Edgecoombe Hall. When a posse of locals arrived here, they saw a faint blue light hovering over the roof. The walls of the Hall were split open, and the ground all about was cracked.' He shrugged. 'The local bobby was called out and took a statement from the owner. That was the last of the affair, and there was no satisfactory explanation about what had happened.'

'Was the owner some kind of scientist? An experiment backfired?'

He laughed. 'He wasn't no scientist. He was a gentleman landowner who wrote the odd novel.'

Quite involuntarily, the hair on the nape of my neck prickled, and a shiver ran down my spine. 'A writer?' I said.

'Gentleman by the name of Cunningham-Price,' my informant went on. 'Seems the Hall is popular with men of letters.'

'Cunningham-Price . . . ?'

I was not aware that I had uttered the name, and he stared at me. 'You've heard of him?'

'As a matter of fact I've read one of his books,' I managed. 'Quite a coincidence.'

My mind was racing. The coincidence that was uppermost in my thoughts, of course, was that Vaughan Edwards should have lived in the very same Hall, albeit many years later, as his literary hero. Then again, if he was so taken by Cunningham-Price's novels, what would be more natural than that he should seek out and purchase Edgecoombe Hall?

'Cunningham-Price was a bit of a recluse,' he was saying. 'Lived here alone, never married. Of course, after the explosion there was all manner of wild speculation and rumour. Locals swore he was deep into witchcraft, that the explosion was his attempt to summon the devil!'

'Has no one ever tried to work out scientifically what happened?' I asked.

'Not to my knowledge. That is, there's never been scientists in to investigate. Cunningham-Price hired some workmen to shore up the building – apparently he had them brick up the cellars.' He paused, looking at me. 'For what it's worth, I have a theory.'

I smiled. 'You do?'

'The area's riddled with underground streams and natural springs. It's a known fact that running water can accumulate static electricity. Perhaps a charge of electricity filled the cellar, reacted with something stored down there, and blew up.'

'And the blue glow that hung over the Hall?'

He shrugged. 'A result of the discharge – if a blue glow was present at all. We've only the word of the locals for that.'

He gestured inside, and we entered the Hall and made our way back to the scullery.

'What happened to Cunningham-Price?' I asked.

'He left the area around 1910. There was talk that he died in the First World War. The Hall was unoccupied for years, until Vaughan Edwards bought it in the mid-fifties. Two writers, one after the other –' he laughed '– don't suppose you're another pen-pusher?'

'Computers,' I lied, my thoughts miles away.

He was writing his name and telephone number on a scrap of old wallpaper. He handed it to me. 'Like I said, I'll know how things stand in a year or so, if you'd like to get in touch.'

I hesitated before taking my leave. 'The landlord said the place is haunted,' I began.

He pulled his chin, nodding to himself. 'He's not wrong, either. Ghost of a young girl haunts the place – or should I say *haunted*?'

'But not any more?'

He shook his head. 'It left six years ago, around the time Mr Vaughan disappeared.'

I stared at Giles, wondering what Mina might have said to this. 'You believe in such things?'

He nodded, his expression stern, as if put out at my scepticism. 'You see, I saw the ghost – just the once. It was following Mr Vaughan up the main staircase, a blonde-haired girl as plain as daylight. And I'd often hear her laughter around the place. But, like I said, never since Mr Vaughan vanished . . .'

* * *

I know there is more to this reality than we perceive with our strictly limited senses; we are like new-born babies who have yet to acquire polychromatic vision, and see the world only in black and white. Beyond our conditioned purview of the world are wonders of which we cannot even dream . . .

From the novel *Seasons of Wonder* by Vaughan Edwards.

The return journey seemed to pass in no time at all, my thoughts full of the Hall's strange history, the two reclusive writers separated by years and yet so obviously connected by a similarity of the soul.

It was almost eight by the time I arrived home. Mina was not due back until ten, so I fixed myself a quick meal and settled beside the fire with the books I had brought from the White Lion.

I scanned the first of the Cunningham-Prices, *The White Lodge*, a story of a country house and its inhabitants over the course of thirty years. It had the unmistakable feel of something that Vaughan Edwards might have written, a haunting, elegiac quality, a sympathy for the characters, that was familiar from the modern writer's work . . . I had another seven of Edwards' books yet to read – it was quite possible that among the books I had taken from Highdale there would be one that borrowed, as I thought of it, from *The White Lodge*.

I was still reading when Mina arrived home. She made herself a cup of tea and collapsed with a sigh on the sofa next to me. She frowned at the pile of novels on the coffee table. 'So the day was a success?'

'And that's not all,' I said. I told her about my visit to the Hall and the conversation with Giles.

'Strange, or what?' I said.

She cupped her mug in both hands and sipped, eyeing me over the horizon of the rim. I could almost hear her mind working, practical as ever. 'What's so strange about it?' she asked.

I enumerated the strange points on my fingers. 'Cunningham-Price, a reclusive writer. The mysterious explosion. Cunningham-Price's unconfirmed death in the Great War. The ghost—'

Mina snorted at this. 'You've only the word of some cowboy builder about that!'

I shrugged. 'Nevertheless.' I held up my fingers. 'Vaughan Edwards, reclusive writer. He buys the place where his literary mentor lived and wrote. He uses the Victorian writer's novels as a starting point of his own—'

'So you admit he was a plagiarist?'

'Not in so many words.'

'But you're still going to buy me that Thai meal?'

'Very well. Will you stop interrupting?' I pulled back my thumb. 'Then Vaughan Edwards goes and disappears in mysterious circumstances.'

Mina sighed. 'Sometimes I wonder about you, Daniel. What's so strange? So Cunningham was a reclusive writer – so were you before you met me!'

'That's not fair.'

'The explosion – your builder chap explained that. And then Cunningham died in the war, along with millions of others. Vaughan Edwards comes along, buys the house of his hero, copies his novels, goes out for a walk one day and falls down the hillside, his body buried in undergrowth or snagged at the bottom of the river.' She smiled at me. 'And the ghost – show me an old English building that isn't rumoured to be haunted. Why look for bizarre explanations, Daniel, when the obvious answer is so straightforward?'

I shrugged. 'Sometimes the bizarre is more appealing than the everyday.'

'But wholly impossible,' she said. She ruffled my hair. 'Come on, let's go to bed.'

I followed her upstairs, trying to refute her cold water douche of rationalism – convinced, of course, that there was much more to the affair than met the eye.

* * *

It is all very well to drag the occult into his novels, but what this writer signally fails to realise is that the modern reader demands that the novelist provides also an interesting story . . .

From Gerald Percival's review of *The White Lodge* by E.V. Cunningham-Price.

I read the Cunningham-Price books and the remaining Edwards novels over the course of the next fortnight. It came as no surprise to find that the Edwards borrowed heavily from the Cunningham-Prices. Minor characters in the Victorian novels cropped up in the modern novels as fully-fleshed protagonists. Themes hinted at in the early books were developed by Edwards and given full flight. Settings recurred, scenes, and even lines of dialogue.

I thought long and hard about what Edwards had done – a gifted novelist in his own right, he had no literary need to go about plundering someone else's work to use as the grist for his own books and stories. Except, of course, he obviously felt some kind of debt to the earlier writer – a duty to complete in his modern novels what the Victorian had left unsaid.

Weeks passed. I considered making my discovery public in the form of an article, but if I approached a newspaper with my findings they would only request a sensationalist story of literary plagiarism spanning the years. I mulled over the idea of writing an essay for a small-press literary magazine, citing the examples of Edwards' borrowings and attempting to make a positive case for what he had done. At length I set the idea aside; it seemed to me that I had insufficient facts, that something was missing, information that might allow me to understand fully Edwards' objectives and motivations.

Life resumed its normal course, and I received the subtle impression that Mina was gratified that I had stepped down my search for the facts behind the story.

Not a day passed when I did not give thanks for having met her; I was beset less and less by the gnawing fear of her leaving me, a fear that in the early days of our relationship had often soured my peace of mind. We entered a period of mutual affection which I had never before known with anyone else, and I wanted to do nothing to undermine our happiness. I did not so much as mention Edwards, or Edgecoombe Hall. When I suggested that we dine at the Thai restaurant in Settle, I did so without reference to her having won our wager over Edwards' so-called plagiarism.

I received a commission to novelise a computer game, which I did over the next week or so and submitted under a pseudonym. Still I felt disinclined to embark upon an original novel, despite a phone call from my agent asking how it was coming along. I knew from experience that the creative drought would end in time, of its own mysterious accord, and in the meantime I would get by on hackwork. At the back of my mind, however, was the thought that apathy and laziness might win out, that I might never again want to write seriously enough to begin a project that meant something to me, a project I would have to invest with integrity and effort. The spectre of filling the years with hackwork in order to scrape a living hung over my waking days.

I forgot about Vaughan Edwards and the mystery of Edgecoombe Hall for long periods. On occasion, seeing the books that I would some day have to return to the White Lion, I did dwell on the events at Highdale and the strange case of his plagiarism – but I knew that the passage of years had all but quashed any chance of ever discovering the truth.

That might have been the case, but for the arrival through the post, a week later, of two novels which the editor of a small literary magazine wanted me to review.

* * *

I have never demanded from Mina the affection she obviously finds so hard to give to me. More than anything I want to ask her to show some sign that she . . . not that she loves me . . . but that she *cares.* But I'm terrified of asking that for fear of frightening her away.

From the personal journals of Daniel Ellis.

I was still in bed at nine-fifteen the following morning when Mina returned from taking the girls to school. She shouted up that she was preparing breakfast – and that the postman had just delivered a parcel of what looked suspiciously like books. The promise of breakfast might not have propelled me downstairs, but the arrival of post was assured to get me up.

Over fried eggs on Marmite toast, I opened the package and read the enclosed letter.

'Anything interesting?' Mina asked.

I indicated the two hardback books on the table, and lifted the note. 'The editor of *The Coastal Quarterly* wants me to review these. He read my piece on the last Boyd in the *Yorkshire Post*. Says he was impressed.'

'Great,' Mina said, 'but does he pay?'

'Trust your grubby little mind to think of nothing but filthy lucre. As a matter of fact,' I went on, 'he does.'

That stirred her interest. 'More Thai banquets?' she said.

'Hardly. He's offering me a fiver per book.'

'That's not much.'

'About what a small literary magazine can stretch to. I get thirty from the *Post*. The London periodicals usually pay fifty or so, but not some small-press imprint based in Whitby.'

I picked up the books. They were handsome first editions by a writer I'd never heard of, Ed Cunningham.

In retrospect, I was surprised the alarm bells didn't start ringing – but at the time I was oblivious to the tenuous connection.

Mina glanced across at me. 'You will review them, won't you?'

'Of course. I've got to keep you in Thai food, haven't I?'

Mina began work at ten, and after driving her to the hospital I brewed myself a coffee, lay on the sofa before the fire, and began reading *Sundered Worlds* by Ed Cunningham.

How to describe the shock of recognition, and the subsequent turmoil of emotions, that passed through my head as I read?

My pulse throbbed at my temple. My mouth ran suddenly dry and I felt light-headed.

Ed Cunningham . . .

I read on, my hands trembling.

Sundered Worlds was about a soldier invalided out of the army at the end of the First World War, and his fight to regain his physical and mental well-being at a sanatorium high in the Yorkshire Dales. There he met and fell in love with a young girl who, by the end of the novel, is revealed as the spirit of a girl murdered by Roundhead soldiers in the Civil War nearly three hundred years before . . .

Lines and turns of phrase echoed those in the works of E.V. Cunningham-Price and Vaughan Edwards.

A minor character in *Sundered Worlds* was none other than the central character in Cunningham-Price's *The White Lodge*.

Descriptions of the Yorkshire landscape eerily mirrored those of the earlier writers.

I finished the first book in three hours, and began the second, *Winter Harvest*.

Again and again: repeated lines, familiar characters, themes in common with the earlier books . . .

I read about the author on the back flap. There was no photograph, and the merest biographical information. Ed Cunningham was in his thirties and lived in the North Yorkshire town of Whitby. *Winter Harvest* was his second book. His first, *Sundered Worlds*, was now out in paperback.

I laid the books aside and stared into space, my mind dizzy with the impossible.

* * *

God knows, there are times when my existence, what is happening to me, is more than I can humanly bear . . . and I desire nothing more than the balm of oblivion!

From the personal journals of E.V. Cunningham-Price.

'Daniel, are you okay?' She stood in the doorway of the front room, staring at me.

It was eight o'clock. The house was silent, and in darkness. The girls were with Mina's ex-husband across town. I had no idea how long had passed since I had stopped reading.

She switched on the light and approached cautiously, as if at any second I might jump from the sofa and attack her.

'Daniel?'

I stared at her, shaking my head. I pointed to the books. 'They're the same,' I said. 'I should have known. Ed Cunningham.'

Mina sat beside me on the sofa and picked up the books.

'They contain lines and characters and descriptions from the other books,' I said.

She looked at me. I could see the practical cogs of her mind spinning a reply. 'So some hack discovered the plagiarism before you and he's doing his own take on it. It's all a big con.'

'How did they know?'

She sighed. 'How did *who* know?'

'Whoever sent the books. How did they know that I knew about Edwards and Cunningham?'

She reached out and ruffled my hair. 'Haven't you ever heard of coincidence, Daniel?'

'Massive bloody coincidence,' I said.

She pulled the editor's letter from one of the books, read it and then regarded me. 'Daniel, this was written two days ago.'

The course of her logic defeated me. I blinked. 'So?'

'So . . . two days ago was April fool's day.'

I shook my head, impressed, despite myself, by her dogged pragmatism. 'Fact remains, how the bloody hell did they know?' I paused. 'And it can't be a coincidence if it's an April fool's joke, can it?'

Touché. I saw her flinch.

A long silence came between us. Mina perched on the edge of the cushion, legs together, the letter open on her lap, her eyes downcast.

At last she said, 'I'm sure there's some perfectly logical explanation, Daniel.'

I wanted to hug her, to cherish her unfailing existential belief that was so much a part of her; at the same time I wanted to lash out at her in blind fury, angered by her inability to look beyond the mundane for fear of seeing something that might fill her with terror.

For a while, back in the darkness of the afternoon, my mind had glimpsed something that it had had no right to glimpse, and I was filled with a trembling fear of a myriad terrible possibilities.

'Daniel, I'm going to ring him.'

'Who?'

'Who do you think?' she said, lifting the letter. 'The editor of the magazine.'

'Is there a number?'

She scanned the letter-heading. 'Damn. No, but there's an address. I'll ring directory enquiries.'

She hurried into the hall. I heard the low, reassuring sound of her voice as she spoke into the receiver.

She returned a minute later. 'Strange. The magazine doesn't have a number.'

She sat down beside me. I took the letter, read the address. 'What's happening, Mina?'

She shook her head, brow drawn in furious thought. 'It's a practical joke, Daniel. Or it's a coincidence. It's one or the other. It can't be anything else.'

'Can't it?'

She snorted. 'What else can it be?'

I was silent for a long time. At last I said, 'Perhaps, just perhaps, E.V. Cunningham, Vaughan Edwards and Ed Cunningham are one and the same person.'

She *tsk'd* in scornful disbelief.

'Think about it! There's no record of Cunningham-Price's death, Vaughan Edwards vanished, and now these turn up – books that bear a remarkable resemblance to the earlier novels—'

'Daniel,' Mina pointed out with the sweet patience of a saint, 'if he were still alive he'd be . . . good God, I don't know . . . *ancient.*'

'At least a hundred and thirty, give or take,' I said.

'Somehow, I don't think so.'

I reread the address on the letter-heading.

'What?' Mina said, watching me.

'I'm going over there,' I said. 'I'll drop you off at the hospital tomorrow. Then I'll go over to Whitby, try to find out what's going on. According to the blurb, Ed Cunningham lives in Whitby—' I stopped.

'Daniel?'

'Perhaps this is his way of contacting me,' I said.

Mina stared at me for a long time, and I relented.

'Or then again,' I said, 'perhaps it is one big practical joke.'

I slept badly that night, and again and again reached out to touch Mina's reassuring warmth.

* * *

All we have, when all is said and done, for good or bad, is the constancy of our humanity.

From the novel *Summer in Ithaca* by Daniel Ellis.

The following day at ten I dropped Mina off at the hospital.

She had been quiet for the duration of the drive, but before she climbed from the car she gave me an unaccustomed peck on the cheek and said, 'I hope you find the joker, Daniel. Take care, okay?'

I nodded and drove away.

Bright sunlight alternated with silvery showers as I took the long, high road over the North Yorkshire moors towards Whitby. I considered the events of the past few months, the strange occurrences at the Hall, the odd plagiarism that now connected three writers spanning as many centuries. I told myself that I had always kept an open mind as regards phenomena considered . . . let's say . . . *bizarre*, but now I felt that I was fast approaching someone who might be able to answer some of my many questions, and quite frankly I was more than a little apprehensive.

The sky over the North Sea was as leaden as the ocean itself as I came to the crest of the road and looked down on the bay and the tumbling town of Whitby. The sun was concealed behind a bank of cloud the colour of old bruises; the scene was drear and inhospitable, and I could well imagine why Bram Stoker had chosen as Dracula's point of arrival in England this grey and unprepossessing fishing port.

The address given on the note-paper was in the village of Throxton, a few miles north of Whitby on the coast road. I drove slowly, anxious now that the time had come to approach the man who had sent me the Cunningham books for review. He had signed himself as Gerald Melthem, the literary editor of *The Coastal Quarterly.*

What if Mina was right, and the whole affair was no more than a massive and unlikely coincidence? How might I explain myself to the editor then?

I decided to broach that eventuality if and when it occurred.

But if it were not a coincidence, then what might it be?

Throxton was a hamlet consisting of a dozen large houses strung out along the clifftop beside the coast road. I came upon Hapsley House quite by accident. I slowed and braked before the first big house in the village, intending to ask directions, and was surprised to read on a cross-section of tree-trunk, affixed to the gate, the title: Hapsley House.

The rain had abated, and the sun was out again. A mist hung over the road, and when I stepped from the car, my heart beating like a trip-hammer, I found that the afternoon was unseasonably mild.

I opened the gate and approached the front porch, only to be informed by a hand-written sign that visitors should ring at the side entrance.

I walked around the tall, grey-stone building, past rhododendron bushes spangled with rain, and found the side door.

Before I knocked, I heard the sound of a child's laughter emanating from the rear garden, and when I looked I saw, obscured by a stand of apple trees, the distant sight of a tall man in a white shirt, pushing a radiantly blonde girl in a swing. She was perhaps fifteen or sixteen, and her uninhibited laughter, as it carried over the garden on the sea wind, brought suddenly to mind the long gone summers of my youth.

I remembered myself, and rang the bell.

Almost immediately the door was opened by a grey-haired woman dressed in the old-fashioned garb of a housekeeper or maid. She looked at me severely, as if unaccustomed to receiving callers.

'Can I help you?'

'I've come to see Mr Melthem.'

She appeared unmoved, so I continued, 'If you could tell him that Daniel Ellis wishes to see him.'

She said, 'Are you a writer?' as if admission to this might prove the open sesame.

I nodded. 'Mr Melthem sent me some books to review.'

'In that case do come in, Mr Ellis. Please, follow me.'

She closed the door behind me and led the way up a narrow flight of stairs to a long room overlooking the sea. The lounge was stuffed with too much old-fashioned furniture, cabinets full of china, and an abundance of chintz.

'One moment while I inform Mr Melthem . . .' She left the room, and I moved to the window and stared out.

The tall man – I would guess that he was in his sixties – was leaning against the iron frame of the swing and talking to the girl. Even at this distance I was overcome with her Alice-like beauty; something in her laughing manner filled me with delight.

The housekeeper came into view in the garden beneath me and called to the man. He turned and looked up at the window where I stood, and involuntarily I took a backwards step so as to be out of sight.

When next I looked, the man was striding up the garden path towards the house, but of the young girl there was no sign.

A minute later I heard footsteps on the stairs, and the door opened suddenly.

He stood at the far end of the room for a second, lost in the shadows, as if assessing me. Then he strode forwards, his hand outstretched.

Closer to, I could see that he was much older than I had first assumed. Though he held himself stiffly upright with an almost military correctitude, the skin of his face and hands had the tissue-thin, translucent quality of great age.

I reached out to take his hand, my own trembling. I recalled the dream I had had, several months ago, of meeting a writer in an ancient library – and how I had been convinced, upon awakening, that the writer had been Vaughan Edwards.

The man before me bore an uncanny resemblance to the hazy figure in my dream . . .

'Mr Ellis,' he said warmly. 'Please, take a seat.' He indicated a wicker chair beside the window and took one positioned opposite, a wicker table between us.

The housekeeper appeared at the door, and Melthem asked me, 'A drink? Tea, coffee?'

'Tea, black,' I said.

The old man said, 'I have enjoyed your novels, Mr Ellis. They embody a spirit, let's say an attitude of mind, not often found in these modern times.'

I shrugged, at a loss. I always find flattery, on the infrequent occasions it is directed my way, more difficult to handle than criticism.

'That's kind of you. I try to write what I find most important to me.'

He sighed. 'Don't we all, Mr Ellis?' he said.

'You write yourself?' I asked, idiotically.

His reply was interrupted by the arrival of the housekeeper with our tea. Melthem poured the Earl Grey into two improbably delicate china cups.

I took mine on a saucer, the china chattering a quick signal of my nervousness.

Only then did I notice, on the table between us, a slim book. It was the collection of Vaughan Edwards' short stories – *Improbable Visions* – that I had yet to read.

I wondered if Mina would call this a coincidence, too?

My vision misted and my head reeled. I thought, for a second, that I was about to collapse. The feeling passed. I sipped my tea.

'I take it you received the Cunninghams?' he enquired.

I nodded. 'Yesterday. I've read them already. I was . . . impressed. They show a mature handling of character and situation—' I was aware that I was gabbling, running off at the mouth. 'A maturity surprising for a novelist's first books . . .'

'Quite. Exactly my feelings, too. I thought you might appreciate them. Isn't it wonderful to happen upon like souls in the appreciation of the noble art?'

I smiled and gulped my tea.

He noticed my glance towards the Vaughan Edwards collection. 'A gift,' he said, and an icy hand played a rapid arpeggio down my spine. 'I thought you might appreciate the volume.'

I thanked him with a whispered, '. . . most kind.' And took refuge behind my cup.

How had he known I would come here, I wanted to shout: for that matter, how did he know that this of all Vaughan Edwards' books was the one I had yet to read?

I felt as though I were participating in a dream over which I had no control, and from which I might at any second awake in fright.

'I was at Edgecoombe Hall just the other day,' Melthem was saying.

I nodded, at a loss quite how to respond. I sat rooted to my seat, my posture rigid, staring at him as he said, 'Would you care to meet me tomorrow at the Hall, between eleven and noon?'

I found myself assenting with a gesture.

'Splendid. There is so much to explain, and it would help if we were in the Hall where it all originally happened, don't you think?'

'Cunningham-Price, Edwards . . . ?' It was barely a whisper, a feeble attempt to articulate the many questions crowding my mind.

'Tomorrow, Mr Ellis.'

He reached out a papery hand, and when I looked into his sapphire-blue eyes it came to me that I was in the presence of someone who had experienced more than it was humanly possible to experience, and still survive.

The feeling was gone almost as soon as it arrived. I found myself shaking his hand. I rose from the chair and gestured farewell.

'Oh, Mr Ellis . . .' He called out as I made for the door. He held the volume of short stories towards me. I murmured an apology and took the book.

As I reached the door, he said, 'Tomorrow, between eleven and noon, Mr Ellis. I'll see you at Edgecoombe Hall.'

In a daze I hurried down the stairs and let myself out through the side door. The fresh air seemed to waken me, as if from the dream I had been so convinced I had fallen into. I made my way to the car, regretting now that I had not remained to question him – but at the same time not wishing in the slightest to return.

I made a three-point turn and accelerated up the road towards Whitby. As I came to the rise above the hamlet, I glanced back at the imposing grey pile of Hapsley House. I slowed the car and stopped, turning in my seat and staring.

Melthem had returned to the garden overlooking the sea, and once again he was pushing the laughing, golden-haired girl on the swing.

Sweating, I turned my back on Hapsley house and drove away.

* * *

Do I love him? What is love? Do I trust him? If trust is giving your fate to another, and knowing that you will not be harmed, then I trust him. But do I love him? After The Bastard, how can I bring myself to love anyone? So why, then, do I trust him?

From the diary of Mina Pratt.

I arrived home at six. Mina was still at work. I was relieved to have the house to myself. I would have found it hard to find rational answers to her questions; indeed, I found it hard myself to answer the many questions posed by the events of that afternoon.

I built the fire, taking my time with wadded newspapers, sticks of wood, coal and fire-lighters. I have always found the act of making a fire comforting, therapeutic. With the fire blazing, I sat on the sofa and considered eating – but I had no appetite.

I fetched *Improbable Visions* from my jacket where it hung in the hall, and returned to the front room. I resumed the sofa and began reading: the act seemed appropriate.

Mina returned at eight. The sound of the front door opening brought me back to reality. I was aware of my heartbeat, and the fact that I was not looking forward to facing her.

She appeared in the doorway and paused, gripping a bulky carrier bag of groceries. She stared at me. 'What happened, Daniel?'

I could not bring myself to reply. She disappeared into the kitchen, and I heard the sound of her unpacking the shopping and storing it away in cupboards. It struck me as the typical, practical thing that Mina would do at a time like this.

She emerged five minutes later, again halting in the doorway as if wary of approaching me. 'Are you going to tell me what happened?'

I found my voice at last. 'I met him,' I said.

She nodded. 'The editor?'

I could not bring myself to look at her. Instead I regarded the leaping flames. I licked my lips.

'Edwards,' I said. 'Or Cunningham-Price, or whatever he calls himself.'

The flames danced. Mina said nothing. The silence stretched painfully. I tore my eyes away from the fire and looked at her.

She was staring at me, and slowly shaking her head. She said, 'He told you he was Edwards?'

'No, not in so many words—'

'Then just what did he say?' I could hear the exasperation in her tone.

'It was strange, Mina. The meeting seemed unreal, like a dream. I wanted to ask so much, but I found myself unable to form the questions. He told me very little.'

'Then how on earth did you know he was Edwards?' she almost cried.

I shook my head. 'A feeling, an intuition. He was so old. At first I thought he was about sixty, seventy. Then . . . I don't know. When he spoke, when I looked into his eyes, I realised he was ancient.'

Mina moved to the armchair before the fire. She pulled her feet onto the cushion and hugged her shins, staring at the flames.

She glanced at me. 'Did you ask him why he sent the books?'

I shook my head. 'I think he wanted to communicate with me . . . tell someone about himself, after all those years.'

'But you said he told you next to nothing!'

My mouth ran dry. I considered my words. 'I think he wants to explain, tell someone who might be sympathetic. He said he liked my books, sympathised with their sentiments—'

'Wants to explain?' she asked, a note of what might have been apprehension in her voice. 'You're meeting him again?'

I nodded. 'He wants to meet me at Edgecoombe Hall tomorrow. He said that there's much to explain.'

'And you're going?'

I let the silence stretch, become almost unbearably tense, before it snapped and she asked, 'Well?'

I looked up at her, held her gaze. 'I've got to go, Mina. I want to find out.'

She gave a quick, bitter shake of her head and stared at the flames.

'Mina, something strange and wonderful happened at the Hall all those years ago . . . All my life I've been hoping that there was more to . . . to *this* . . . than what is apparent. We're so programmed by our limited perceptions and this reality's conditioning. There's more to existence than what is apparent to the senses. There has to be. If this is all there is, then I'd despair . . .'

She turned her head and stared at me, and I was shocked to see something almost like hatred in her eyes. 'You're a fool, Daniel. You're a bloody fool! Can't you be satisfied with what there is? Why all this searching?'

'I don't know.'

'Isn't what you've got enough?' She said this with her eyes downcast, unable to look at me.

I almost replied, then, cheaply, that if she would give me all her love, then that might be enough – but I held my tongue. 'It isn't about what I've got,' I said. 'It's about what's possible.'

'Listen to me, the editor is a con man – he's planning something.'

'He knew I was coming,' I interrupted, indicating the collection. 'He had this for me, the only Vaughan Edwards I haven't read. He knew that.'

'Impossible!'

'Another coincidence?' I sneered.

A silence developed, and the fire hissed and cracked. At last Mina said, 'Are you going?' in a small voice.

'What do you think? I've got to go. I must find out what's happening.'

Suddenly, surprising me, Mina stood and moved to the door. 'I'm meeting Liz at nine,' she said. 'We're going for a drink. You can fix your own dinner, can't you?'

The mention of such banalities angered me, but she hurried from the doorway and was climbing the stairs before I could reply.

I sat in silence, staring at the glowing coals.

She came down thirty minutes later, dressed in her short black coat, the collar turned up around her windswept-effect hair. She looked wonderful, and a part of me wanted to take her in my arms and apologise and tell her that I would not be going to Highdale in the morning.

I remained seated.

'Daniel,' she said, and I could tell that she had been giving the words great thought, 'I won't be back tonight. I'm staying over at Liz's.'

I nodded. 'Have a good time.'

She did not move from the door. 'So you're going up there, then?'

'That's what I said, isn't it?'

'I wish you wouldn't, Daniel,' she said, and made to leave.

I stopped her with, 'What do you fear, Mina?'

'What's that supposed to mean?'

'Do you care about what might happen to me, or fear I might discover something that might shatter your safe, limited little world view?'

She stared at me, slowly shaking her head. 'I don't have the slightest idea what you're talking about—'

'It's the latter, isn't it? You don't want your safe, cosy existence shattered by the knowledge that there's more to life than merely this . . .' I gestured about me . . . 'this physical existence. I've never met anyone as closed-minded as you.'

She could only stare at me, tears filming her eyes. 'That's not fair. I do care . . .'

I could not help myself. 'You've got a damned strange way of showing it, then. I know you've told me, again and again, that you don't love me . . . but what about affection?'

'Daniel . . .'

'Is it simply that you don't trust me, after all the love and affection I've shown you? Is that it? You know, never once in the year we've been together have you shown any spontaneous sign of intimacy. It's always me who has to make the first move. Do you know how galling that is? Do you ever stop to wonder what it's like to love someone, and not to have the slightest clue as to what the hell they feel about you in return?'

She was crying now, leaning against the door-frame and sobbing.

I twisted the knife. 'I sometimes wonder why the hell you bother staying with me!'

Shocked and angered, she looked up and stared at me, and I knew I had gone too far then, and would regret it. 'If that's how you feel . . .' she wept.

She hurried into the hall.

'What?' I called after her.

I heard the front door open. Then, suddenly, she was back, framed in the doorway, staring at me. 'You bastard,' she said. 'Don't expect me to be here when you get back.'

And, before I could reply, she was gone.

three

As a child I read a lot, lost myself in adventures and quests along with characters more real than anyone I had ever met in real life. Books were my refuge, a bolt-hole to other, better worlds than this one, an escape.

Perhaps they served much the same function now, though on a more sophisticated level: now I might lose myself in a book to escape the exigencies of this life, but at the same time fiction was a way of understanding others, of realising that one's own psychological viewpoint was not the only one. By engaging with the diversity and variation of thought and character to be found in literature, I was making my own life richer and more rewarding.

Vaughan Edwards' books had fulfilled both the above criteria; they had offered me a brief escape from this reality, and a means of understanding another person's unique world view. For me, the bizarre, other-worldly tales they told functioned as a grand metaphor for something very strange.

And I wanted to experience that strange reality for myself.

I awoke late the following morning in a bed cold without Mina. I forced myself to drink a cup of coffee, and at ten set off for Highdale.

As I drove, I considered Mina's declaration that she would not be at home when I returned. I decided that later, when I had met Vaughan Edwards – or whoever he might be – I would seek out Mina, and apologise. I could always tell her that I had acceded to her wishes, and not gone to the Hall.

But lies breed a subsequent duplicity, the need to follow up the original untruth with a series of others. I had never lied to Mina, and I did not want to begin now: what I was doing meant something to me – even though I was filled with apprehension at the same time – and I knew that it would devolve to me, upon my return, to attempt to explain this to Mina, somehow make her understand. If she were to share my life, then she must also share my mind. Relationships are founded on mutual understanding, and how could our partnership work if she failed to comprehend what the mystery of Vaughan Edwards and Edgecoombe Hall meant to me?

I arrived at Highdale just as cloud cover occluded the sun and a squall of heavy rain began. I drove past the Hall and into the village, glad of the excuse to delay the inevitable encounter: I had brought back the books I had borrowed from the White Lion on my last visit.

It was just after eleven when I pushed into the snug and returned the novels to their shelf. I was tempted to delay the rendezvous still further by ordering a drink, but resisted the urge. The sooner I learned the truth of Edgecoombe Hall, I reasoned, the sooner I could return to Mina.

I left the pub and drove slowly up the hill. The rain was torrential now, making ineffectual the laboured swipes of the windscreen-wipers. I slowed to a walking pace, hunching over the wheel so as to make out the road ahead.

I came to the ivied gateposts and turned, feeling as I did so the oppressive weight of something very much like fear settle over me. It was not, I told myself, too late to turn back. I could retreat now and be back home inside the hour, and I would be able to tell Mina that I had not set eyes on Edgecoombe Hall that day.

Even as I considered this option, I knew that I would not take it. I had set out with the express intention of meeting with Vaughan Edwards, if such was who he was, and I could not at this late stage deny myself the opportunity of discovering the truth.

By the time I emerged from the tunnel of shrubbery, the rain had abated, and the sun appeared from behind the clouds. Edgecoombe Hall stood before me, presenting an even more inimical façade for being so theatrically bathed in sudden sunlight.

I braked the car and remained inside for long minutes, aware that I was gripping the steering wheel as the survivor of a shipwreck might cling to flotsam. My pulse hammered at my temple, and sweat soaked my shirt.

I climbed from the car and approached the Hall, unsure now the time had come whether to knock on the main door or try the side entrance.

There was no sign of another vehicle: perhaps, I told myself, he had not yet arrived.

As I stood, momentarily paralysed by indecision, I heard a familiar sound from within the building.

The high joyous trill of a young girl's uninhibited laughter issued from the dour precincts of the Hall, a sound as golden as the sunlight without.

I attempted to peer through those windows not obscured by ivy, but what little I could make out of the interior was lost in shadow.

Then the great timber front door opened, and instantly the girl's laughter ceased.

He stood upon the top step, smiling down at me – and again I received the impression of great age and amiability.

'Mr Ellis, Daniel – splendid that you could make it.'

His face was thin, his hair gun-metal grey, and though there was about him a suggestion of infirmity – in the slight stoop of his frame, as opposed to his ramrod posture of yesterday – yet he seemed to glow with a lustrous vitality.

I found myself saying, quite unrehearsed, 'Who are you?'

He smiled, not at all put out by the question. 'Daniel, I think you know that by now, don't you?' It was almost a laugh.

I cleared my throat, began, 'You . . . are you—?' I halted, unable, for some reason, to bring myself to say the name.

He came to my assistance. 'I am Edward Vaughan Cunningham-Price, to give me my somewhat long-winded title.'

I opened my mouth to speak, but remained inarticulate.

He smiled. 'Would you care to come inside?'

I stood rooted to the spot, quite unable to move.

At last I said, 'What happened in '96, and before that, in the Great War?'

He considered my question. 'In '96 it was necessary for me to move on, and likewise before that in 1916—'

'How,' I said, hearing my words as if from a great distance, '. . . how old are you?'

He nodded, as if this were a perfectly reasonable question. 'I am one hundred and seventy-eight, Daniel.'

He peered into the sky; a cloud scudded across the sun, suddenly darkening the Hall. 'I think rain is on the way. You'll catch your death if you remain out there. Do come in.'

He stood back and gestured with an outstretched hand for me to enter. He was the epitome of genial hospitality, and for some reason it came to me that, despite everything, I could trust him.

I mounted the steps one by one. At the top I paused, facing him. 'How is that possible?' I murmured.

He laid a hand on my arm. 'Daniel, that is what I came here to explain. Please, this way . . .'

He turned and walked into the Hall. I followed him across the chessboard tiles, down a long corridor towards the back of the house. From time to time he made comments over his shoulder about the weather, and asked me if the drive up had been pleasant, as if such mundane smalltalk might put me at ease.

A part of me expected to see the laughing girl dancing in delight somewhere in the Hall. And yet, at the very same time, some intuitive part of my consciousness knew that she would not appear.

We passed though a double glass door, and for a second I thought that we were stepping outside: then I found myself in a vast conservatory, quite denuded of vegetation.

I looked around, bemused. I had expected to be shown something – I have no idea what – but the great glassed-in area was empty.

Cunningham-Price moved to the centre of the floor and stooped, lifting the ring of a trap-door to reveal a flight of steps descending into darkness. He took three steps down, then turned and smiled at me to follow.

'Where . . . where are we going?'

'The cellar, Daniel.'

I recalled what the builder, Giles, had told me weeks ago. 'The cellar? He – you . . . you had the cellar bricked up after the explosion.'

'All but this entrance,' he explained.

'What happened?' I asked. 'The explosion – what was it?'

He paused, regarding me. 'I was writing in my study at the time. It was late, midnight if I recall. The explosion shook the very foundations of the Hall. I made my way into the cellar, through the entrance in the scullery. I . . .' He paused, his vision misting over as he recalled the events of over one century ago. 'I beheld a remarkable sight, Daniel.'

I heard myself whisper, 'What?'

'It was the arrival here of something unique in the history of humankind,' he said, and continued down the steps.

My heart hammering, God help me, I followed.

We came to the foot of the steps. A naked bulb gave a feeble light, illuminating a short corridor, at the end of which was a door. Cunningham-Price paused before it, took a key from his pocket and turned it in the lock.

He looked at me over his shoulder. 'I would advise you to shield your eyes,' he counselled.

Puzzled, and not a little apprehensive, I did so, peering out beneath my hand as he turned the handle and eased open the door.

An effulgent glow, like the most concentrated lapis lazuli, sprang through the widening gap and dazzled me. I think I cried out in sudden shock and made to cover my eyes more securely. When I peered again, Cunningham-Price was a pitch black silhouette against the pulsing illumination as he stepped into the chamber.

Trembling with fright, I followed. As I crossed the threshold I heard, for the first time, a constant dull hum, as of some kind of dynamo, so low as to be almost subliminal.

I stepped inside and, as my vision grew accustomed to the glare, removed my hand from my eyes and peered across the chamber.

How to describe what I saw, then?

It seemed to me that, embedded in the far wall, was a great orb of dazzling blue-white light – like a swollen will-o'-the-wisp. It was as bright as the sun seen with the naked eye, and seemed to be spinning, constantly throwing off crazed filaments of crackling electricity; these filaments enwebbed the chamber, flowing around the walls and totally encapsulating us as we stood there in mute awe. Only then, belatedly, did I realise that the chamber was not a cellar room as such, but more like a cave, a great cavern excavated perhaps by the force of the explosion all those years ago.

'What . . .' I managed at last, 'what is it?'

In lieu of a reply, he said, 'When I heard the explosion I came down here forthwith – don't ask me how I knew its location. It was as if I were drawn here. I made my way cautiously down the stairs, afraid but at the same time unable to resist the impulse to investigate. Then suddenly I came upon this light occupying the space where my wine cellar had once been . . .'

He stopped there, a sad light in his eyes, as if the thought of what had happened then was too much. 'I . . . I have no idea how long I was down here. It seemed like hours, but later it came to me that only a matter of minutes had elapsed.'

He paused again, and I waited. I stared into the pulsating will-'o-the-wisp like someone hypnotised, then tore my gaze away and looked at him.

'And then?' I prompted.

'And then,' he went on, 'they communicated with me.'

I stared at him, at once wanting to disbelieve his bizarre story and yet, because of the very evidence of my eyes, unable to do so.

'They?' I echoed.

'Or perhaps I should say 'she',' he said. 'At least, that was the form they took to approach me. You see,' he went on, 'I was writing a novel at the time, about a soldier's love for a young girl . . . And they reached into my mind, and took this image of the child, and used it.' He paused there, on the verge of tears, his face drawn as he recalled the events of more than a century ago.

Seconds elapsed. A dizzy nausea gripped me. My conscious mind was exhorting me to run, to get out and never return, and yet at the same time another part of me, that part forever fascinated with the lure of the arcane, wanted nothing more than to hear the conclusion to his story.

He faced the light, tears now streaming down his cheeks. 'She came to me from the light, a fair innocent child emanating such an aura of purity that I was overcome. She explained that she was from elsewhere, that her kind had opened a channel from her realm to this world, and that they wished to study us . . .'

I said, 'Aliens? Beings from another dimension?'

He shook his head. 'Neither description quite fits the reality,' he said. 'She tried to make clear to me the nature of their realm, but my human mind, conditioned only to accept this world, could not begin to comprehend the place from whence she came. It was not from outer space, or from another dimension, or an alternate world – it was from a place that existed beyond matter as we understand it. Her universe was one of energy without physical form, and she herself consisted of pure energy. She, or it, or whatever, was bemused by the discovery of this world, and wanted to understand.'

He wept. 'The girl . . . It was as if she had the power to demand from me all the love, all the compassionate desire, I had ever felt for anyone. I stood before this ethereal creature and I was besotted. I could but accede to her desire . . .'

Something surged within me, a sudden, terrifying panic.

'What?' I began. 'What did she want?'

He forced his gaze away from the effulgence as if with great effort, and faced me, sobbing uncontrollably now and shaking his head.

As I stared at him, something in his lean, aquiline face altered. The lineaments of age seemed to dissolve, become suffused with a golden glow. I stepped backwards in alarm as the form of a young girl – the very girl I had beheld in the garden at Throxton – took shape within the old man and then stepped out, smiling at me.

Something hit me then, the full force of this creature's irresistible allure, and I cried out in rapture.

Behind her, Cunningham-Price, divested of energy, slumped suddenly, and in that second he seemed to age a hundred years.

I backed away, came up against the cavern wall.

The girl regarded me, smiling with angelic sweetness. It was hard to believe that she was a mere manifestation of pure energy, a being from another dimension; she seemed to possess, in her radiant form, the essence of all womanly pulchritude and sensuality.

'I wanted to dwell within the being of Cunningham-Price,' she said. 'He was a writer, and I was intrigued by his visions; more, by his heightened emotions. I had never before experienced such feelings, such emotion. I wanted to inhabit him.'

'You wanted to take him over!' the rational side of my mind protested.

'I would grant him powers of which he had never dreamed,' the girl continued. 'I would bestow upon him increased longevity, allow him to live beyond the paltry duration you poor beings are allotted. I would give him perfect health, and new abilities. He would have intuition as none of you might know, and foresight, and the ability to shape circumstances to his will . . .'

A sudden, dreadful realisation came to me. 'The books,' I began. 'He knew I was coming!'

She smiled, and the quick knowing look that crossed her face filled me with sudden panic. 'All along . . .' I cried. 'If he could shape circumstances . . .' My mind reeled, and I felt utterly powerless before this lambent being.

'Why?' I managed. 'What do you want?'

'Cunningham-Price is old,' she said. 'There is only so much that even I might do to sustain and prolong the life of the flesh. He is unable to host me any longer. I require someone with his sensibilities, with his innate under-standing of what it is to be human, someone in contact with their emotions. We read your books, Daniel. We knew you were the one.'

She stepped forward. Behind her, Cunningham-Price fell to the floor like a dead weight.

I cried out in an anguish of dilemma. I was overcome with a tidal wave of desire, the need to lavish upon this creature all the love I had within me, even though I knew that she was manipulating this desire. I wanted to love the girl as I loved Mina – but, even as I realised this, I knew too that the girl would be unable to reciprocate: what did this creature of energy know of the very attribute unique to the human race? She would inhabit me and use me, and I would live an extended life in thrall to this supernal creature, forever in love, while she would study me like some laboratory specimen, without the need or desire to love me in return.

I cried out. I wanted to take the easy option and step towards her, allow her to inhabit my being. I would be free then of the tangled web of emotions that make human relationships so terribly difficult. I would be her slave, and a part of me desired the ease of worshipping at the altar of her beauty.

And yet . . . and yet, what made human relations so joyous, so fulfilling, was that the effort of loving was often rewarded, that effort expelled was sometimes repaid, or at least we live in hope that our need to be needed might find in someone, somewhere, a like need . . .

I dived away from her outstretched hands. I fell to the floor and scrambled in the direction of the door. I heard her coaxing, mocking laughter trilling behind me, but I dared not bring myself to look back in case I weakened and allowed her entry.

On all fours I lunged at the door, hauling myself upright, flinging it open and running. I stumbled again and again, crying out as I imagined, at any second, to feel the warmth of her energy flow into me. Again and again I picked myself up, flung myself up the flight of stairs, my arms and legs bruised and painful, my heart labouring fit to burst. I came to the conservatory, the full moon silvering the panes of glass all around me, and without a backward glance ran through the darkened Hall in the direction of the entrance.

I hauled open the front door and bolted into the night. My car, a welcome symbol of banal modernity, stood where I had left it before the house. I dived into the driver's seat and started the engine – miraculously it fired first time – then steered in a crazy, careering u-turn and accelerated away from the Hall.

I did not look back – a fear like I had never known before would not allow me to turn my head to check if I was being pursued, even though every fibre of my being wanted to do so.

I sped from the Hall, down the hill away from the woodland. I wondered at the creature's range, its ability to chase me until I was caught. I told myself that, the greater distance I was able to put between myself and Edgecoombe Hall, the safer I would be. It had not, after all, possessed me when it had had the chance back in the cavern. Perhaps my headlong flight had saved my soul . . .

Still I accelerated, taking corners at breakneck sped, with no care at all for my safety, pursued as I imagined myself to be by a far, far greater danger.

I failed to see the oncoming vehicle until it was too late. Its glaring headlights appeared around the corner as if from nowhere, and instinctively I hauled on the wheel. My car careered from the road, bucked over a banking and rolled down what seemed like a never-ending incline. By the time it reached the bottom and halted, on its side, broken glass tinkling around me in a strangely beautiful glissando, my consciousness was rapidly ebbing away.

Seconds later I passed into oblivion.

* * *

There are times when I give thanks for what has happened to me, knowing that I am unique among all men; there are other times, however, when I feel the curse of this possession. To give love that cannot be returned, and to be denied the opportunity to exhibit love for any other . . .

From the personal journals of Vaughan Edwards.

I came awake to find myself slung on my side, cradled by the seat-belt. My body was frozen, and an intense pain gripped my head and legs. I waited, trapped, for the girl to find me, to take me over. I cried aloud in anguish at my inability to flee. I thought of Mina, and wanted nothing more than to apologise.

I passed out.

And awoke . . . to find myself in bed, and warm, the pain no more than a distant memory. I recall crying out in fear, and a soothing hand upon my forehead, before falling unconscious yet again.

The next time I came awake, I had a raging thirst. I tried to find the words to communicate my desire for water, but the effort was beyond me. I tried again, what seemed like hours later, and was rewarded. A disembodied hand – I could not move my head to see who it belonged to – lifted a beaker of water to my lips, and I drank.

Between moments of fleeting consciousness, I dreamed. I was in the cellar, and the girl-creature was reaching out, and I felt again the desire to give this being all the love that I possessed, and then it came to me with even more intense terror that that love could never be returned.

I awoke once in darkness, the hospital quiet around me, and the more I thought about the events at the Hall, the more I came to doubt the truth of what had happened . . .

Then I recalled, crying quietly to myself, what Mina had told me the last time I had seen her: that she would not be there for me when I returned from Edgecoombe Hall.

When I awoke again, it was morning. Intense sunlight cascaded through a window. A vase of brilliant daffodils seemed the most miraculous sight I had ever witnessed.

I felt a hand take mine, and squeeze.

With incredible effort, I moved my head, and the reward was worth the pain.

Mina sat beside the bed, smiling at me through her tears.

'You fractured your skull,' she reported in a small voice, 'broke both your legs. You were in a coma for a week. They thought—' She stopped herself, dried her eyes with a Kleenex. 'They thought you might not survive.'

I gripped her fingers. 'I'm sorry,' I said.

'Daniel,' she whispered, after a long silence, 'what happened?'

I shook my head. 'I don't know,' I said. 'I really don't know . . .'

A nightmare, I thought . . .

She smiled at me, and I slipped into unconsciousness.

She was by my side when I awoke again, maybe hours later. She was staring at a newspaper, her expression shocked.

'What is it?' I asked.

'Daniel, look . . .'

She held up the *Yorkshire Post*. The front-page headline declared: MISSING NOVELIST DISCOVERED DEAD.

'Vaughan Edwards,' she reported. 'He was found yesterday in the cellar of the Hall. He'd died of a heart attack. They give his age here as seventy-two.' She lowered the paper and smiled at me, shaking her head. 'All those crazy ideas of yours . . .'

I smiled at her. 'I was a fool,' I said.

I watched her, and wondered what had really happened at the Hall; had it all, actually, been nothing more than a figment of my overwrought desperation – a cathartic episode created by my desire to find love in this loveless world?

Quite suddenly, as I stared at Mina, an idea occurred to me. I smiled at the thought.

She looked up. 'What is it?'

I said, 'I want to write a new novel, Mina.'

Her face clouded. 'About what happened?'

I stared at her beautiful left hand, resting upon her knee. 'No,' I said. 'It will be about you . . . If you'll let me, that is.'

She had always been reluctant to have me write about her, as if by doing so I might claim possession of the part of her that she had been so careful to withhold.

Now she smiled. 'I think perhaps I might,' she said.

This novel is dedicated with love to Mina, for showing me that the true measure of love is one's actions, not words.

              Dedication in Daniel Ellis's novel *A Woman of Quality*.

the human front

Ken MacLeod

To Nick

Like most people of my generation, I remember exactly where I was on March 17, 1963, the day Stalin died. I was in the waiting-room of my father's surgery, taking advantage of the absence of waiting patients to explore the nicotine-yellowed stacks of *Reader's Digest*s and *National Geographic*s, and to play in a desultory fashion with the gnawed plastic soldiers, broken tin tanks, legless dolls and so forth that formed a disconsolate heap, like an atrocity diorama, in one corner. My father must have been likewise taking advantage of a slack hour towards the end of the day to listen to the wireless. He opened the door so forcefully that I looked up, guiltily, though on this particular occasion I had nothing to be guilty about. His expression alarmed me further, until I realised that the mixed feelings that struggled for control of his features were not directed at me.

Except one. It was with, I now think, a full awareness of the historic significance of the moment, as well as a certain sense of loss, that he told me the news. His voice cracked slightly, in a way I had not heard before.

'The Americans,' he said, 'have just announced that Stalin has been shot.'

'Up against a wall?' I asked, eagerly.

My father frowned at my levity and lit a cigarette.

'No,' he said. 'Some American soldiers surrounded his headquarters in the Caucasus mountains. After the partisans were almost wiped out they surrendered, but then Stalin made a run for it and the American soldiers shot him in the back.'

I almost giggled. Things like this happened in history books and adventure stories, not in real life.

'Does that mean the war is over?' I asked.

'That's a good question, John.' He looked at me with a sort of speculative respect. 'The Communists will be disheartened by Stalin's death, but they'll go on fighting, I'm afraid.'

At that moment there was a knock on the waiting-room door, and my father shooed me out while welcoming his patient in. The afternoon was clear and cold. I mucked about at the back of the house and then climbed up the hill behind it, sat on a boulder and watched the sky. A pair of eagles circled their eyrie on the higher hill opposite, but I didn't let that distract me. After a while my patience was rewarded by the thrilling sight of a V-formation of American bombers high above, flying east. Their circular shapes glinted silver when the sunlight caught them, and shadowed black against the blue.

* * *

The newspapers always arrived on Lewis the day after they were printed, so two days passed before the big black headline of the Daily Express blared **STALIN SHOT**, and I could read, without fully comprehending, the rejoicing of Beaverbrook, the grave commentary of Cameron, the reminiscent remarks of Churchill, and frown over Burchett's curiously disheartening reports from the front, and smile over the savage raillery of Cummings' cartoon of Stalin in hell, shaking hands with Satan while hiding a knife behind his back.

Obituaries traced his life: from the Tiflis seminary, through the railway yards and oilfields of Baku, the bandit years as Koba, the October Revolution and the Five-Year Plans, the Purges and the Second World War; his chance absence from the Kremlin during the atomic bombing of Moscow in Operation Dropshot, and his return in old age to the ways and vigour of his youth as a guerrilla leader, rallying Russia's remaining Reds to the protracted war against the Petrograd government; to the contested, gruesome details of his death and the final, bloody touch, the fingerprint identification of his hacked-off hands.

By then I had already had a small aftershock of the revolutionary's death myself, at school on the 18th. Hugh Macdonald, a pugnacious boy of nine or so but still in my class, came up to me in the playground and said: 'I bet you're pleased, *mac a dochter.*'

'Pleased about what?'

'About the Yanks killing Stalin, you *cac.*'

'And why should I not be? He was just a murderer.'

'He killed Germans.'

Hugh looked at me to see if this produced the expected change of mind, and when it didn't he thumped me. I kicked his shin and he ran off bawling, and I got the belt for fighting.

That evening I played about with the dial of my father's wireless, and heard through a howl of atmospherics a man with a posh Sassenach accent reading out eulogies on what the Reds still called Radio Moscow.

The genius and will of Stalin, great architect of the rising world of free humanity, will live forever.

I had no idea what it meant, or how anyone even remotely sane could possibly say it, but it remained in my mind, part of the same puzzle as that unexpected punch.

* * *

My father, Dr Malcolm Donald Matheson, was a native of the bleak long island. His parents were crofters who had worked hard and scraped by to support him in his medical studies at Glasgow in the 1930s. He had only just graduated when the Second World War broke out. He volunteered for combat duty and was immediately assigned to the Royal Army Medical Corps. Of his war service, mainly in the Far East, he said very little in my hearing. It may have been some wish to pay back something to the community that had supported him which led him to take up his far from lucrative practice in the western parish of Uig, but of sentiment towards that community he had none. He insisted on being addressed by the English form of his name, instead of as

'Calum' and I and my siblings were likewise identified: John, James, Margaret, Mary, Alexander – any careless references to Iain, Hamish, Mairead, Mairi or Alasdair met a frown or a mild rebuke. Though a fluent native speaker of Gaelic, he spoke the language only when no other communication were possible – there were, in those days, a number of elderly monoglots, and a much larger number of people who never used the English language for any purpose other than the telling of deliberate lies. There are two explanations, one fanciful and the other realistic, for the latter phenomenon. The fanciful one is that they believed that the Gaelic was the language of heaven (was the Bible not written in it?) and that the Almighty did not hear, or did not understand, the English; or, at the very least, that a lie not told in Gaelic didn't count. The realistic one is that English was the language of the state, and lying in its hearing was indeed legitimate, since the Gaels had heard so many lies from it, all in English.

My mother, Morag, was a Glaswegian of Highland extraction, who had met and married my father after the end of the Second World War and before the beginning of the Third. She, somewhat contrarily, taught herself the Gaelic and used it in all her dealings with the locals, though they always thought her dialect and her accent stuck-up and affected. The thought of her speaking a pure and correct Gaelic in a Glasgow accent is amusing; her neighbours' attitude towards her well-meant efforts less so, being an example of the characteristic Highland inferiority complex so often mistaken for class or national consciousness. The Lewis accent itself is one of the ugliest under heaven, a perpetual weary resentful whine – the Scottish equivalent of Cockney – and the dialect thickly corrupted with English words Gaelicised by the simple expedient of mispronouncing them in the aforementioned accent.

Before marriage she had been a laboratory assistant. After marriage she worked as my father's secretary, possibly for tax reasons, while raising me and my equally demanding brothers and sisters. Like my father, she was a smoker, a whisky-drinker, and an atheist. All of these were, at that time and place, considered quite inappropriate for a woman, but only the first was publicly known. Our non-attendance at any of the three doctrinally indistinguishable but mutually irreconcilable churches the parish supported was explained by the rumour – perhaps arising from my father's humanitarian contribution to the war effort – that the *dochter* was a Quaker. It was a notion he did nothing to encourage or to dispel. The locals wouldn't have recognised a Quaker if they'd found one in their porridge.

Because of my father's military service and medical connections, he had stroll-in access at the nearby NATO base. This sprawling complex of low, flat-roofed buildings, Nissen huts, and radar arrays disfigured the otherwise sublime headland after which the neighbouring village, Aird, was named. My father occasionally dropped in for cheap goods – big round tins of cigarettes, packs of American nylons for my mother, stacks of chewing-gum for the children, and endless tins of corned beef – at the NAAFI store.

It was thus that I experienced the event which became the second politically significant memory of my childhood, and the only time when my father expressed a doubt about the Western cause. He was, I should explain, a dyed-in-the-wool conservative and unionist, hostile even to the watery socialism of the Labour Party, but he would have died sooner than vote for the Conservative and Unionist Party. 'The Tories took our land,' he once spat, by way of explanation, before slamming the door in the face of a rare, hopeless canvasser. He showed less emotion at Churchill's death than he did at Stalin's. So, like most of our neighbours, he was a Liberal. The Liberals had, in their wishy-washy Liberal way, decried the Clearances, and the Highlanders have loyally returned them to Parliament ever since.

Why the Highlanders nurse a grievance over the Clearances was a mystery to me at the time, and still is. In no land in the world is the disproportion between natural attraction and sentimental attachment more extreme, except possibly Poland and Palestine. Expelled from their sodden Sinai to Canada and New Zealand the dispossessed crofters flourished, and those who remained behind had at last enough land to feed themselves, but their descendants still talk as if they'd been put on cattle trucks to Irkutsk.

It was my habit, when I had nothing better to do on a Saturday, to accompany my father on his rounds. I did not, of course, attend his consultations, but I would either wait in the car or brave the collies who'd press their forepaws on my shoulders and bark in my face, to the inevitable accompaniment of cries of 'Och, he's just being friendly,' and make my way through mud and cow-dung to the hospitality of black tea in the black houses, and the fussing of immense mothers girt in aprons and shod in wellingtons.

We'd visited an old man in Aird that morning in the summer of '63, and my father turned the Hillman off the main road and up to the NATO base. Gannets dropped like dive-bombs in the choppy sea of the bay below the headland's cliffs, and black on the Atlantic horizon the radar turned. Though militarily significant – Lewis commands a wide sweep of the North Atlantic, and Tupolev's deep-shelter factories in the Urals were turning out long-range jet bombers at a rate of about one a month, well above attrition – security was light. A nod to the squaddie on the gate, and we were through.

My father casually pulled up in the officers' car-park outside the NAAFI and we hopped out. He was just locking the door when an alarm shrieked. Men in blue uniforms were suddenly rushing about and pointing out to sea. Other men, in white helmets and webbing, were running to greater purpose. Somewhere a fire-engine and an ambulance joined in the clamour.

I spotted the incoming bomber before my father did, maybe two miles out.

'There – there it is!'

'It's *low*—'

Barely above the sea, flashing reflected sunlight as it yawed and wobbled, trailing smoke, the bomber limped in. On the wide concrete apron in front of us a team frantically pushed and dragged a big Wessex helicopter to the perimeter, while one man stood waving what looked like outsize ping-pong bats. The bomber just cleared the top of the cliff, skimmed the grass – I could see the plants bend beneath it, though no blast of air came from it – and with a screaming scrape and a shower of sparks it hit the concrete and slithered to a halt about a hundred yards from where we stood.

It was perhaps fifty feet in diameter, ten feet thick at the hub. Smoke poured from a ragged nick in its edge. The ambulance and fire-engine rushed up and stopped in a squeal of brakes, their crews leaping out just as a hatch opened on the bomber's upper side. More smoke puffed forth, but nothing else emerged. A couple of firemen, lugging fire-extinguishers, leapt on the sloping surface and dropped inside. Others hosed the rent in the hull.

My father ran forward, shouting 'I'm a doctor!' and I ran after him. The outstretched arm of one of the men in white helmets brought my father up short. After a moment of altercation, he was allowed to go on, while I struggled against a firm but not unfriendly grip on my shoulder. The man's armband read 'Military Police'. At that moment I was about ten yards from the bomber, close enough to see the rivets in its steel hull.

Close enough to see the body which the firemen lifted out, and which the ambulancemen laid on a stretcher and ran with, my father close behind, into the nearest building. It was wearing a close-fitting silvery flying-suit, and a visored helmet. One leg was crooked at a bad angle. That was not what shot me through with a thrill of horror. It was the body of a child, no taller than my five-year-old sister Margaret. The large helmet made its proportions even more child-like.

A moment later I was turned around and hustled away. The military policeman almost pushed me back into the car, told me to wait there, and shut me up with a stick of chewing-gum before he hurried off. Everybody else who'd come at all close to the craft was being rounded up into a huddle guarded by the military policemen and being lectured by a couple of men who I guessed were civilians, if their snap-brimmed hats, dark glasses and black suits were anything to go by. They reminded me of American detectives in comics. I wondered excitedly if they carried guns in shoulder holsters.

After about fifteen minutes my father came out of the building and walked over to the car. One of the civilians intercepted him. They talked for a few minutes, leaning towards each other, their faces close together, one or other of them shaking their fingers, pointing and jabbing. Each of them glanced over at me several times. Although I had the side window wound down, I couldn't hear what they were saying. Eventually my father turned on his heel and stalked over to the car, while the other man stood looking after him. As my father opened the car door the black-suited civilian shook his head a little, then rejoined his colleague as the small crowd dispersed.

A knot of military policemen formed up at the building's doorway, and surrounded two stretcher-bearers as they hurried to the Wessex. There was only the briefest glimpse of the stretcher as it was passed inside, moments before it took off and headed out to sea on a southerly course.

My father's face was pale and his hand shook as he took his hip-flask from the glove compartment. The top squeaked as he unscrewed it, the flask gurgled as he drank it dry.

'Leave the window down, John,' he said as he turned the key and pushed the starter. 'I need a cigarette.'

He lit up, fumbling, then engaged the gears and the car moved off with a lurch. As we passed the soldier on the gate my father gave him a wave that was almost a salute.

'What sort of people will that poor laddie be fighting for?' he asked me, or himself. His knuckles were white on the wheel. The swerve on to the main road threw me against the door. He didn't notice.

'Monsters,' he said. 'Monsters.'

I sat up straight again, rubbing my shoulder.

'It's awful to use wee children to fly bombers,' I said.

He looked across at me sharply, then turned his attention back to the single-track road.

'Is that what you saw?' he murmured. 'Well, John, we were told very firmly that the pilot was a midget, you know, a dwarf, and that this is a secret. If the enemy knew that, they would know something they shouldn't know about our bombers. About how much weight they can carry, or something like that.'

I squirmed on the plastic leather, swinging my legs as though I needed to pee. I had read about dwarfs and midgets in *Look and Learn*. They were not like in fairy stories.

'But that's not true,' I said. 'That wasn't a dwarf, the pro— the portions—'

' "Proportions".'

'The proportions were wrong. I mean, they were right – they were ordinary. The pilot was a child, wasn't he?'

The car swerved slightly, then steadied.

'Listen, John,' my father said. 'Whatever the pilot is, neither of us is supposed to talk about it, and we'll get into big trouble if we do. So if you're sure it was a child you saw, I'm not going to argue with you. And if the Air Force say the pilot is a midget, I'm not going to argue with them, either. I set and splinted the leg of that, that' – he hesitated, waving a hand dangerously off the wheel – '*craitur beag 'us bochd* – of the poor wee thing, I should say, and that's all I know of it.'

I was as startled by his lapse into the Gaelic as by the uncertainty and ambiguity of his reference to the pilot, and I thought it wise to keep quiet about the whole subject. But he didn't, not quite yet.

'Not a word about it, to anyone,' he said. 'Not to your mother, your brothers and sisters, your friends, anyone. Not a word. Promise me?'

'All right,' I said. I was young enough to feel that it was more exciting to keep a secret than to tell one.

The following day was a Sunday, and although it meant nothing to us but a day off school we had to conform to local custom by not playing outside. It was a sweltering hell of boredom, relieved only by the breath of air from the open back door and the arrival at the front door of two men in black suits, who weren't ministers. My father escorted them politely into his surgery. The waiting-room door (I found, on a cautious test) was locked. They did not stay long; but the following morning on the way out to catch the van to school I overheard my mother telephoning around to postpone the day's appointments, and noticed a freshly emptied whisky bottle on the trash.

* * *

A couple of years later, when I was ten, my father sold his practice to a younger, less financially straitened and more idealistic doctor (a Nationalist, to my father's private disgust) and took up a practice in Greenock, an industrial town on the Firth of Clyde. Our flitting was exciting, our arrival more so. It was another world. In the mid-sixties the Clyde was booming, its shipyards producing naval and civilian vessels in almost equal proportion, its harbours crowded with British and American warships, the Royal Ordnance Factory at Bishopton working around the clock. Greenock, as always, flourished from the employment opportunities upriver – beginning with the yards and docks of the adjacent town of Port Glasgow – and from its own industries, mainly the processing of colonial sugar, jute and tobacco. The pollution from the factories and refineries was light, but fumes from the heavy vehicular traffic that serviced them may well explain the high incidence of lung cancer in the area. (My father's death, though outside the purview of the present narrative, may also be so accounted.) Besides these traditional industries, a huge IBM factory had recently opened (the ceremonial ribbon cut by Sir Alan Turing himself) in the Kip Valley behind the town.

The town's division between middle class and working class was sharp. On the eastern side of Nelson Street lay the tenements and factories; to the west a classical grid of broad streets blocked out sturdy sandstone villas and semi-detached houses. Though our parents' disdain for private education saved us from the worst snobberies of fee-paying schools, the state system was just as blatantly segregated. The grammar schools filled the offices of management, and the secondary moderns manufactured workers. Class division shocked me: after growing up among the well-fed, if ill-clad, population of Lewis, I saw the poorer eight-tenths of the town as inhabited by misshapen dwarfs.

It was while exploring what to my imagination were dangerous, Dickensian slums, but which were in reality perfectly respectable working-class districts, that I first encountered evidence that this division was regarded, by some, as part of the greater division of the world. On walls, railway bridges and pavements I noticed a peculiar graffito, in the shape of an inverted 'Y' with a cross-bar – a childishly simple, and therefore instantly recognisable, representation of the human form. Sometimes it was enclosed by the outline of a five-pointed star, and frequently it was accompanied by a scrawled hammer and sickle. These last two symbols were, of course, already familiar to me from the red flags of the enemy.

It was at first as shocking a sight as if some Chinese or Russian guerrilla had popped out of a manhole in the street, and it gave me a strange thrill – a *frisson*, as the French say – to find that the remote and gigantic foe had his partisans in the streets of Greenock as much as in the jungles of Malaya or the rubble of Budapest. One day in 1966 I actually met one, on a street corner in the East End, down near the town centre where the big shops began.

This soldier of the Red horde was a bandy-legged old man in a cloth cap, selling copies of a broadsheet newspaper called the *Daily Worker*. He met with neither hostility nor interest from the passers-by. With boyish bravado, and some curiosity, I bought it. Its masthead displayed the two symbols I already knew, and an article inside was illustrated by, and explained, the third.

'Against the warmongers and arms profiteers, against the reckless drive to destruction, against the forces of death, it is necessary to rally all who yearn for peace. The situation cries out for the broadest possible united front, one broader even than the great People's Fronts against fascism, one in which every decent human being, every worker, every woman, every honest businessman, every farmer, every patriot can take their place with pride and determination. It is not for any political party, or class, or ideology that such a front shall stand, but for the very survival of the human race.

'This greatest of all united and people's fronts exists, and is growing.

'It is the Human Front.'

I understood barely a word of it, and the only reason why I clipped out the article and kept it, long after I had secretly disposed of the newspaper, long enough for me to re-read and finally understand it, years later, was because of coincidental resonances of its author's name – Dr John Lewis.

* * *

After that initial naive exploration I settled down to a sort of acceptance of the world as it was, and to learning more about it, at school and out. Science was more interesting than politics, and it soothed rather than disturbed the mind. The war was a permanent backdrop of news, and a distant prospect of National Service. The BBC brought it home on the wireless and, increasingly, on black-and-white television, with feigned neutrality and unacknowledged censorship. News items that raised questions about the war's conduct and its domestic repercussions were few: the Pauling trial, the Kinshasa atomic bombing, the occasional allusion to a speech by Foot in the Commons or Wedgwood Benn in the Lords.

The biggest jolt to the consensus came in 1968, with the May Offensive. Out of nowhere, it seemed, the supposedly defeated *maquis* stormed and seized Paris, Lyons, Nantes, and scores of other French cities. Only carpet-bombing of the suburbs dislodged them and saved the Versailles government. This could not be hidden, nor the first anti-war demonstrations in the United States: clean-cut students chanting 'Hey! Hey! JFK! How many kids did you kill today?' until the dogs and fire-hoses and tear-gas cleared the streets. At the time, I was more frightened by the unexpected closeness of the Communist threat than shocked by the measures taken against it.

My first act of dissidence wasn't until three years later, at the age of seventeen. I slipped out one April evening to attend a meeting in the Co-operative Hall held under the auspices of Medical Aid for Russia. The speaker was touring the country, and it may have been the controversy that followed him that drew the crowd of a hundred or so. It's certainly what drew me. He was flanked on the platform by a local trade union official, a pacifist lady, and Greenock's perennially unsuccessful Liberal candidate. (The local Labour MP had, naturally, denounced the meeting in the *Greenock Telegraph*.) The hall was bare, decorated with a few union banners and a portrait of Keir Hardie. I sat near the back, recognising no one except the little old man who'd once sold me the *Daily Worker*.

After some dull maundering from the union official, the pacifist lady stood up and introduced the speaker, the Argentine physician Dr Ernesto Lynch. A black-haired, bearded man, about forty, asthmatic, charismatic, apologetic about his cigar-smoking and his English, he brought the audience to their feet and sent me home in a fury.

'You're too gullible,' my father said. 'It's all just Communist propaganda.'

'Hiroshima, Nagasaki, Moscow, Magnitogorsk, Dien Bien Phu, Belgrade, Kinshasa!' I pounded the names with my fist on my palm. 'They happened! Nobody *denies* they happened!'

He lidded his eyes and looked at me through a veil of cigarette smoke. Bare elbows on the kitchen table, mother in the next room, the hiss of water on the iron, the Third Programme concerto in the background.

'If you had seen what I saw in Burma,' he said mildly, 'you wouldn't be so sorry about Hiroshima and Nagasaki. And the men who went into the Vorkuta camps weren't sorry about Moscow, and—'

'And what troops "liberated" Siberia?' I raged. 'The dirty Japs! With their hands still bloody from Vladivostok! Their hands *and* their—'

I stopped myself just in time.

'Look, John,' he said. 'We could go on shouting at each other all night about which side's atrocities are worse. The very fact that we can, that this Argentine johnny can tour the country and half the bloody Empire with his tales of heroic partisans in the Ukraine and sob stories about butchered villagers in Byelorussia, while nobody from our side could possibly do anything remotely similar in the Red territories, shows which side has the least to fear from the truth.'

'Britain didn't let the Nazis speak here during the war – William Joyce was hanged—'

He poured another whisky, and offered me one. I accepted it, ungraciously.

'We listened to Lord Haw-Haw and Tokyo Rose for a *laugh*,' he was saying. 'Then they were decently hanged, or decently jailed.'

'Pity we're on the same side now,' I said. 'Maybe the Yanks should let Tokyo Rose *out*. "Ruthki soldjah, you know what ith happening to you girrfliend? Big niggah boyth ith giving her big niggah—'

Again, I shut up just in time.

'Your racial prejudices are showing, young man,' Malcolm said. 'I thought Reds were supposed to be against the colour bar.'

'Huh!' I snorted. 'I thought Liberals were!'

'The colour bar will come down in good time,' he said. 'When both whites and coloureds are ready for it. Meanwhile, the Reds will be happy to agitate against it, while out of the other side of their mouths they'll spout the most blatant racialism and national prejudice, just as it suits them – anything to divide the free world.'

'Some free world that includes the American South, South Africa, Spain, Japan, and the Fourth Reich! That holds on to Africa with atom bombs! That relies on the dirty work of Nazi scientists!'

He tapped a cigarette and looked at it meditatively.

'What do you mean by that?'

'The bombers. They're what's made the whole war possible, from Dropshot onwards, and it was the Germans who invented them – to finish what Hitler started!'

He lit up, and shook his head.

'Werner von Braun died a very disappointed man,' he said. 'Unlike the rocket scientists the Russians got. They got to see their infernal researches put to use all right, with dire consequences for our side – mostly civilian targets, I might add, since you seem so upset about bombing civilians. At least our bomber pilots risk their own lives, unlike the Russian missilemen who deal out death from hundreds of miles away.'

I could see what he was doing, deflecting our moral dispute into a purely intellectual, historical debate, and I was having none of it.

'Yeah, I wonder if the Yanks are still sending *children* up to fly the bombers.'

He almost choked on his sip of whisky. Through the open door of the living-room came the sound of the iron crashing to the floor and my mother's shout of annoyance. A moment later she said, sharply: 'James! Margaret! Off to bed!' A faint protest, a scurry, a slam. She bustled through, hot in her pinny, and closed the door and sat down. Her flush paled in seconds. My father glanced at her and said nothing.

They both looked so frightened that I felt scared myself.

'What's— What did— ?'

My mother leaned forward and spoke quietly.

'Listen, Johnny,' she said. I bristled; she hadn't called me that for years. She sighed. 'John. You're old enough to do daft things. You could go off and join the Army tomorrow, or you could get married, and there's not a thing we could do about either. And it's the same with listening to Communists and repeating their rubbish. It's a free country. Ruin your prospects if you like. But there's one thing I ask you. Just one thing. Don't ever, *ever*, ever say anything about what you and your father saw in Aird. Don't even drop a hint. Because if you do, you'll ruin us all.'

'You never said this to me before!'

'Never thought we had to,' Malcolm said gruffly. 'You kept your mouth shut when you were a wee boy, as you promised, and good for you, and I thought that maybe over the years you had forgotten all about it.'

'How could I forget that?' I said.

He shrugged one shoulder.

'All right, all right,' I said. 'But I don't understand why it's such a big secret. I mean, surely the age or is it the *size* of the—'

My father leaned across the table and put his hand across my mouth – not as a gesture, as a physical shutting up.

'Not one word,' he said.

I leaned back and made wiping movements.

'OK, OK,' I said. 'Leave that aside. What were we talking about before? Oh yes, you were saying it wasn't the Nazis who invented the flying disc. So who do you think did?'

'Who knows? The Allies had Einstein and Oppenheimer and Turing and a lot of other very clever chaps, and it's all classified anyway, so, as I said – who knows?'

'How do you know it *wasn't* the Germans, then?'

'They weren't working along those lines.'

'Oh, come on!' I said. 'I've seen pictures of the things from during the war.'

'These were experimental circular airframes with entirely conventional propulsion,' he said. 'That doesn't describe the bombers, now does it? Have you ever heard of Nazi research into anti-gravity?'

'Have you ever heard of American?'

He shook his head.

'It's all classified, of course. But it was obviously a bigger breakthrough than the atomic bomb. Consider the Manhattan Project, and all the theory that led up to it.' He paused, to let this sink in. 'What I'd like you to do, John, is to use your head as well as keep your mouth shut. By all means rattle off the standard lefty rant about Nazi scientists, but do bear in mind that you're talking nonsense.'

I was baffled. My mother was looking worried.

'But,' I said, 'the *Americans* say it was German scientists who developed it.'

'They do indeed, John, they do indeed.'

He looked quite jovial; I think he was a little bit drunk.

'I think you've said enough,' my mother told him.

'That I have,' he said. 'Or too much. And you too, John. You have homework to do tonight and school to go to tomorrow. Goodnight.'

* * *

The following day I felt rather flat, whether as a result of the unaccustomed glass of whisky or my father's successful deflection of my moral outrage. After school I walked straight to the public library. My parents never worried if I didn't come home from school directly, so long as I phoned if I wasn't going to be home for my tea.

The library was a big Georgian-style pile in the town centre. I stepped in and breathed the exhilarating smell of dark polished wood and of old and new paper. It took me only a minute to Dewey-decimal my way around the high stacks to the aviation section. Sheer nostalgia made me reach for the first in the row of tiny, well-worn editions of the *Observer's Book of Aircraft*. I still had that 1960 edition, somewhere at home. Flicking past the familiar silhouettes of Lancaster and Lincoln and MiG, I looked again at the simplest outline of the lot: the circular plan and lenticular profile of the Advanced High Altitude Bomber, Mark 1. The description and specifications were understandably sparse ('outperforms all other aircraft, Allied and enemy') the history routine: first successful test flight, from White Sands to Roswell Army Air Field, New Mexico, July 1947; first combat use, Operation Dropshot, September 1949; extensive use in all theatres since.

I replaced the volume and pulled out the fresh 1970 edition, its cover colour photo of a Brabant still glossy. The AHAB's description, specs, and history were identical, and identically uninformative, but the designation had changed. Checking back a couple of volumes, I found that the AHAB-2 had come into service in 1964.

It didn't take me much longer to find that the biggest military innovation of the previous year had been the Russian MiG-24, capable of reaching a much higher altitude than its predecessors. I sought traces of the AHAB in more detailed works, one of which stated that none had ever been shot down over enemy territory. All of that got me thinking, but what struck me even more was that after more than twenty years there wasn't a dicky-bird about the machine's development, beyond the obviously (now that it was pointed out) misleading references to wartime German experimental aircraft. Nor were there any civilian or wider military applications of the revolutionary physical principles behind its anti-gravity engine.

I tried looking up anti-gravity in other stacks: physics, military history, biography. Beyond the obvious fact that it was used in the AHAB, there was nothing. No speculation. No theory. No big names. No obscure names. Nothing. Fuck all.

I walked home with a heavy load of books and a head full of anti-gravity.

* * *

'Outer space,' said Ian Boyd, confidently. Four or five of us were sitting out a free period on our blazers on damp grass on the slope of the hill above the playing-field. Below us the fourth-year girls were playing hockey. Now and again a run or swerve would lift the skirt of one of them above her knees. We were here for these moments, and for the more reliable sight of their breasts pushing out their crisp white shirts.

'What d'ye mean, outer space?' asked Daniel Orr.

'Where they came frae. The flying discs.'

'Oh aye. Dan Dare stuff.'

'Don't you Dan Dare me, Dan Orr.'

This variant on a then-popular catch-phrase had us all laughing.

'We know there's life out there,' Ian persisted. 'Astronomers say there's at least lichens on Mars, they can see the vegetation spreading up frae the equator every year. An it's no that far-fetched there's life on Venus an a', underneath the cloud cover.'

'No evidence of intelligent life, though,' Daniel said.

'No up there,' said Colin NcNicol. 'There is down there.'

'Aye, there's life, but is it intelligent?'

We all laughed and concentrated for a while on the hockey-playing aliens, with their strange bodies and high-pitched cries.

'It's intelligent,' said Ian. 'The problem is, how dae we communicate?'

'No, the *first* problem is, how do we let them know we're friendly?'

'Tell them we come in peace.'

'And we want to come inside.'

'*If,*' I said, mercilessly mimicking our Classics teacher, 'you gentlemen are quite ready to return the conversation to serious matters—'

'This is serious a' right!'

'Future ae the entire human race!'

'Patience, gentlemen, patience. Withhold your ejaculations. Your curiosity on these questions will be soon be fully satisfied. The annual lecture on "Human Reproduction In One Minute" will be prematurely presented to the boys later this year by Mr Hughes, in his class on Anatomy, Physiology, and Stealth. The girls will simultaneously and separately receive a lecture on "Human Reproduction In Nine Months" as part of their Domestic Science course. Boys and girls are not allowed to compare notes until after marriage, or pregnancy, whichever comes sooner. Meanwhile, I understand that Professor Boyd here has a point to make.'

'Oh aye, well, if it wisni the Yanks an' it wisni the Jerries, it must hae come frae somewhere else—'

'The annual prize for Logic—'

'—so it must hae been the Martians.'

'—has just been spectacularly lost at the last moment by Professor Boyd, after a serious objection from Brother William of Ockham—'

'Hey, nae papes in our school!'

'—who presents him, instead, with the conical paper cap inscribed in memory of Duns Scotus, for the *non sequitur* of the year.'

* * *

Near the High School was a park with a couple of reservoirs. Around the lower of them ran a rough path, and its circumambulation was a customary means of working off the stodge of school dinner. A day or two after our frivolous conversation, I was doing this unaccompanied when I heard a hurrying step behind me, and turned to see Dan Orr catch me up. He was a slim, dark, intense youth who, though a month or two younger than me, had always seemed more mature. The growth of his limbs, unlike mine, had remained proportionate, and their movements under the control of the motor centres of his brain. His father was, I believe, an engineer at the Thompson yard.

'Hi, Matheson.'

'Greetings, Orr.'

'Whit ye were saying the other day.'

'About the bombers?'

'Naw.' He waved a hand. 'That's no an issue. We'll never find out, anyway, and between you an me I couldni give a flying fuck if they were invented by Hitler himsel, or the Mekon of Mekonta fir that matter.'

'That's a point of view, I suppose.' We laughed. 'So what is the issue?'

'Come on, Matheson, ye know fine well whit the issue is. It isnae where they *came* frae. It's where they *go*, and whit they *dae* to folk.'

'Aye,' I said cautiously.

'Ye were at that meeting, right?'

'How would you know if I was?'

'Yir face is as red as yir hair, ya big teuchter. But not as red as Willie Scott of the AEU, who was on the platform and gave a very full account o the whole thing tae his Party branch.'

'Good God!' I looked sideways at him, genuinely astonished. 'You're in the CP?'

'No,' he said. 'The Human Front.'

'Well kept secret,' I said.

He laughed. 'It's no a secret. I just keep my mouth shut at school for the sake o the old man.'

'Does he know about it?'

'Oh, aye, sure. He's Labour, but kindae a left winger. Anyway, Matheson, what did you think about what Dr Lynch had tae say?'

I told him.

'Well, fine,' he said. 'The question is, d'ye want tae dae something about it?'

'I've already put my name down to raise money for Medical Aid.'

'That's good,' he said. 'But it's no enough.'

We negotiated an awkward corner of the path, leaping a crumbled culvert. Orr ended up ahead of me.

'Dr Lynch,' he said over his shoulder, 'had some other things tae say, about what people can do. And we're discussing them tonight.' He named a café. 'Back room, eight sharp. Drop by if ye like. Up tae you.'

He ran on, leaving me to think.

* * *

Heaven knows what Orr was thinking of, inviting me to that meeting. The only hypothesis which makes sense is that he had shrewdly observed me over the years of our acquaintance, and knew me to be reliable. I need not describe the discussion here. Suffice it to say that it was in response to a document written by Lin Piao which Dr Lynch had clandestinely distributed during his tour, and which was later published in full as an appendix to various trial records. I was not aware of that at the time, and the actual matters discussed were of a quite elementary, and almost entirely legal, character, quite in keeping with the broad nature of the Front. It was only later that I was introduced to the harsher regimens in Dr Lynch's prescription.

We started small. Over the next few weeks, what time I could spare from studying for my Highers, in evenings, early mornings, and weekends, was taken up with covering the town's East End and most of Port Glasgow with the slogans and symbols of the Front, as well as some creative interpretations of our own.

FREE DUBCEK, we wrote on the walls of the Port Glasgow Municipal

Cleansing works, in solidarity with a then-famous Czechoslovak guerrilla leader being held incommunicado by NATO. To the best of my knowledge it is still there, though time has worn the 'B' to a 'P'.

And, our greatest coup, on the enormous wall of the Thompson yard, in blazing white letters and tenacious paint that no amount of scrubbing could entirely erase:

FORGET KING BILLY AND THE POPE
UNCLE JOE'S OUR ONLY HOPE

The Saturday after the last of my Higher exams, I happened to be in the car with my father, returning from a predictably disastrous Morton match at Cappielow, when we passed that slogan. He laughed.

'I must say I agree with the first line,' he said. 'The second line, well, it takes me back. Good old Uncle Joe, eh? I must admit I left "Joe for King" on a few shit-house walls myself. Amazing that people still have faith in the old butcher.'

'But is it really?' I said. I told him of my long-ago (it seemed – seven years, my God!) playground scrap over the memory of Stalin.

'It's fair enough that he killed Germans,' Malcolm said. 'Or even that he killed Americans. The problem some people, you know, have with Stalin is that he killed *Russians*, in large numbers.'

'It was a necessary measure to prevent a counter-revolution,' I said stiffly.

Malcolm guffawed. 'Is that what they're teaching you these days? Well, well. What would have happened in the SU in the 30s if there had been a counter-revolution?'

'It would have been an absolute bloody massacre,' I said hotly. 'Especially of the Communists, and let's face it, they were the most energetic and educated people at the time. They'd have been slaughtered.'

'Damn right,' said Malcolm. 'So we'd expect – oh, let me see, most of the Red Army's generals shot? Entire cohorts of the Central Committee and the Politburo wiped out? Countless thousands of Communists killed, hundreds of thousands sent to concentration camps, along with millions of ordinary citizens? Honest and competent socialist managers and engineers and planners driven from their posts? The economy thrown into chaos by the turncoats and time-servers who replaced them? A brutal labour code imposed on the factory workers? Peasants rack-rented mercilessly? A warm handshake for Hitler? Vast tracts of the country abandoned to the fascist hordes? That the sort of thing you have in mind? That's what a counter-revolution would have been like, yes?'

'Something like that,' I said.

'That's exactly what happened, you dunderheid! Every last bit of it! Under Stalin!'

'How do we know that's not just propaganda from our side?'

'Here we go again,' he sighed. 'It's like arguing with a Free Presbyterian minister.'

'Come on,' I said. 'We know that a lot of what we're told in the press is lies. Look at the rubbish they were writing about how France was pacified, right up until the May Offensive! Look at—'

'Yes, yes,' he said. He pulled the car to a halt in the comfortable avenue where we lived, up by the golf course. He leaned back in his seat, took off his driving gloves and lit a cigarette.

'Look, John, let's not take this argument inside. It upsets your mother.'

'All right,' I said.

'You were saying about the press. Yes, it's quite true that a lot of lies are told about the war. I'll readily admit that, however much I still think the war is just. It was the same in the war with Hitler. Only to be expected. Censorship, misguided patriotism, wishful thinking – truth is the first casualty, and all that. So tell me this – who, in this country, has done the most to expose these lies?'

'Russell, I guess,' I said. After that I could only think of exiles and refugees from the ravaged Continent. 'And there's Sartre, and Camus, and Deutscher—'

'That's the man,' he said. 'Deutscher. Staunch Marxist. Former Communist. Respected alike by the *Daily Worker* and the *Daily Telegraph*. Man of the Left, man of integrity, right?'

'Yes,' I said, suspecting that he was setting me up for another fall. He was. When we went inside he handed me a worn volume from his study's bowed bookshelves.

Deutscher's *Stalin*, published in 1948, was a complete eye-opener to me. I had never before encountered criticism of Stalin or his regime from the Left, nor so measured a judgement and matchless a style. It seemed to come from a vanished world, the world before Dropshot, before the Fall.

* * *

'Fuck that,' said Dan Orr. 'Deutscher's a Trotskyite, for all that he's all right on the war. And Trotskyites are *scum*. I don't give a fuck how many o them Stalin killed. He didnae kill *enough*. There were still some alive tae be ministers in the Petrograd puppet government, alang wi all the Nazis and Ukrainian nationalists and NTS trash that the Yanks scraped out o the camps where they belonged.'

I didn't have an answer to that, at the time, so I shelved the matter. In any case we had more urgent decisions to make. Although we had not had our results yet, we both knew we had done well in our Highers, and could have gone straight to University the following September. This would have deferred our National Service until after graduation. Graduates could sign up for officer training. Most of our similarly successful classmates rejoiced at the opportunity to avoid the worst of the hardships and risks. Orr was adamant that we should not take it. It was a principle with him (and with the Front, and with the Young Communist League of which, unknown to me at the time, he was a clandestine member).

'It's a blatant class privilege,' he said. 'Every working-class laddie has tae go as soon as he turns eighteen. Why should we be allowed tae dodge the column for four mair years? What gies us the right tae a cushy number? And think about it – when we've done our stint that'll be it over, we can get on wi university wi none o that growing worry about what's at the end o it, and in the meantime we'll hae learned to use a rifle and we can look every young worker in the eye, because we'll hae been through the same shit as he has.'

'But,' I said, 'suppose we find ourselves shooting at the freedom fighters?'

Or shot by them, was what was really worrying me.

'Cannae be helped,' said Orr. He laughed. 'I'm told it seldom comes tae that anyway. It's no like in the comics.'

My mother objected, my father took a more fatalistic approach. There was a scene, but I got my way.

We spent the summer working to earn some spending money and hopefully put some by in our National Savings Accounts. In the permanent war economy it was easy enough to walk into a job. Orr, ironically enough, became a hospital porter for a couple of months, while I became a general labourer in the Thompson yard. We joked that we were working for each other's fathers.

The shipyard astounded me, in its gargantuan scale, its danger and din, and its peculiar combination of urgent pace and trivial delay. The unions were strong, management was complacent, work practices were restrictive and work processes were primitive. Parts of it looked like an Arab *souk*, with scores of men tapping copper pipes and sheets with little hammers over braziers. My accent had me marked instantly as a teuchter, a Highlander, which though humiliating was at least better than being written off as middle class. The older men had difficulty understanding me – I thought at first that this was an accent or language problem, and tried to conform to the Clydeside usage to ridiculous effect, until I realised that they were in fact partially deaf and I took to shouting in Standard English, like an ignorant tourist.

The Party branch at the yard must have known I was in the Front, but made no effort to approach me: I think there was a policy, at the time, of keeping students and workers out of each other's way. This backfired rather because it enabled me to encounter my first real live Trotskyist, who rather disappointingly was a second-year student working there for the summer. We had a lot of arguments. I have nothing more to say about that.

Most days after work I'd catch the bus to Nelson Street, slog up through the West End to our house, have a bath and sleep for half an hour before a late tea. If I had any energy left I would go out, ostensibly for a pint or two but more usually for activity for the Front. The next stage in its escalating campaign, after having begun to make its presence both felt and over-estimated, was to discourage collaboration. This included all forms of fraternisation with American service personnel.

Port Glasgow is to the east of Greenock, Gourock to the west. The latter town combines a douce middle-class residential area and a louche seafront playground. Its biggest dance-hall, the Cragburn, a landmark piece of 30s architecture with a famously spring-loaded dance floor, draws people from miles around.

Orr and I met in the Ashton Café one Friday night in July. Best suits, Brylcreemed hair; scarves in our pockets. Hip-flask swig and gasper puff on the way along the front. The Firth was in one of its Mediterranean moments, gay-spotted with yachts and dinghies, grey-speckled with warships. Pound notes at the door. A popular beat combo, then a swing band.

We chose our target carefully, and followed her at distance after the dance. Long black hair down her back. She kissed her American sailor goodbye at the pier, waved to him as the liberty-boat pulled away. We caught up with her at a dark stretch of Shore Street, in the vinegar smell of chip-shops. Scarves over our noses and mouths, my hand over her mouth. Bundled her into an alley, up against the wall. We didn't need the masks, not really. She couldn't look away from Orr's open razor.

'Listen, slag,' he said. 'Youse are no tae go out wi anybody but yir ain folk frae now on. Get it? Otherwise we'll cut ye.'

Tears glittered on her thick mascara. She attempted a nod.

'Something tae remind ye,' Orr said. 'And tae explain tae yir friends.'

He clutched her hair and cut it off with the razor, as close to the scalp as he could get. He threw the glistening hank at her feet and we ran before she could get out her first sob.

I threw up on the way home.

Three days later I overheard two lassies at the bus-stop. They were discussing the incident, or one like it. There had been several such, over the weekend, all the work of the Front.

'Looks like you're in deid trouble fae now on,' one of them concluded, 'if ye go out wi coons.'

* * *

Call-up papers arrived in August, an unwelcome 18th-birthday present. After nine weeks' basic training I was sent to Northern Ireland, where I spent the rest of my two-year stint guarding barracks, munitions dumps and coastal installations. Belfast, Londonderry, south Armagh: the most peaceful and friendly parts of the British Empire.

Orr was sent to Rhodesia. His grave is in the Imperial War Cemetery in Salisbury.

I was demobilised in September 1974, and went to Glasgow University. My fellow first-year students were all two years younger than me, including those in the Front. The Party line had changed. Young men were being urged to resist the war, to refuse conscription, to take any deferral available, to burn their call-up papers if necessary, to fill the jails. This was not because the Party had become pacifist. It was because the Party, and the Front, now had enough men with military experience for the next step up Lin Piao's ladder.

People's War.

* * *

It is necessary to understand the situation at the time. By 1974 the United States, Britain and the white Dominions, Germany, Spain, Portugal and Belgium were almost the only countries in the world without a raging guerrilla war. Although nominally on the Allied side, the governments of France and Italy were paralysed, large tracts of both countries ungovernable or already governed by the Resistance movements. Every colony had its armed independence movement, and every former socialist country had its re-liberated territory and provisional government, even if driven literally underground by round-the-clock bombing.

'The peoples of the anti-imperialist camp long for peace every day,' wrote Lin Piao. 'Why do the peoples of the imperialist camp not long for peace? Unfortunately it is because they have no idea of what horrors are being suffered by the majority of the peoples of the world. It is necessary to bring the real state of affairs sharply to their attention. In order for the masses to irresistibly demand that the troops be brought home, it is necessary for the people's vanguard to bring home the war.'

* * *

That later came to be called the Lin Piao 'Left' Deviation. At the time it was called the line. I swallowed it whole.

I lodged in a bed-sitting-room in Glasgow, near the University, and took my laundry home at weekends. During my National Service I had only been able to visit occasionally, and had followed the Front's advice to keep my head down and my mouth shut about politics, on duty or off. It was a habit that I found agreeable, and I kept it. My parents assumed that my National Service had knocked all that nonsense out of me.

Greenock had changed. The younger and tougher and more numerous successors of the likes of Orr and me had shifted their attacks from the sailors' girlfriends to the sailors, and the soldiers. They never attacked British servicemen, or even the police. At least a dozen Americans had been fatally stabbed, and two shot. Relations between the Americans and the town's population, hitherto friendly, had become characterised by suspicion on one side and resentment on the other. The cycle was self-reinforcing. Before long Americans were being attacked in quite non-political brawls, and off-duty Marines were picking fights with surly teenagers. The teenagers' angry parents would seek revenge. Other relatives would be drawn in. Before long an American serviceman couldn't be sure that any sweet-looking lass or little old lady wasn't an enemy.

Armed shore patrols in jeeps became a much more common sight. In the tougher areas, kids would throw stones at them. None of this was covered in the national press, and the *Greenock Telegraph* buried such accounts in brief reports of the proceedings of the Sheriff Court, but the *Daily Worker* reported similar events around US bases right across Britain.

I did not get involved in them. The first petrol-bombing, in January 1975, happened when I was in Glasgow. The first return fire from a group of US naval officers trapped in a stalled and surrounded staff car on the coast road –

they'd started going further afield, to the quieter, smaller resort of Largs – took place in February, also mid-week, when I was definitely not in Greenock. I read a brief report of it in the *Glasgow Herald*.

What was going on in Glasgow was political stuff, anti-war agitation, leafleting and picketing, that sort of thing. We took a hundred people from Glasgow to the big autumn demo in London. A hundred thousand or so converged on Grosvenor Square, with a militant contingent of ten thousand people chanting 'We shall fight! We shall win!' (we all agreed on that) and the Front's hotheads following it up with 'Joe! Joe! Joe Sta-lin!' or 'Long live Chairman Lin!' and the Trots trying to drown us out with a roar of 'London! Paris! Rome! Berlin!'

It was fun. I was serious. I knuckled down to the study of chemistry and physics (at Glasgow they still called the latter 'Natural Philosophy') which had always fascinated me. The Officer Training Corps would have been a risky proposition for me – even my very limited public political activity would have exposed me to endless hassles and security checks – but I joined the University's rifle club, which shared a shooting range and an armoury with the OTC. And I was still, of course, in the Reserves. Following the Front's advice, I kept out of trouble and bided my time.

* * *

I had seen the diagram a hundred times, and its physical manifestation, the iron filings forming furry field-lines on a sheet of paper with a magnet under it, in my first-year physics class at High School. I had balanced magnets on top of each other, my fingers preventing them from flicking around and clicking together, and had felt the uncanny invisible spring pushing them apart. It was late one night in February 1975 when I was alone in my room, propping my head over an open physics textbook, that I first connected that sensation with my childhood chance observation of the curiously unstable motion of an anti-gravity bomber close to the ground, and with the magnetic field lines.

Was it possible, I wondered, that anti-gravity was a polar opposite of gravity, that keeping it stable was like balancing two magnets one upon the other, and that the field generated by the ship had the same shape as that of a magnet? If so, any missile approaching an AHAB bomber from above or below would be deflected, whereas one directed precisely at its edge, where the two poles of the field balanced, might well get through. The crippled bomber I'd seen had taken a hit edge-on, if that distant memory was reliable. The chance of that happening accidentally, even in a long war, might be slim enough for it to have happened only once. Yet the consequences of doing it deliberately were so awesome that this very possibility might well be the secret which the dark-suited security men had been so anxious to maintain. It seemed much more significant than the minor, if grim, detail that the pilots were children or dwarfs.

It was an interesting thought, and I considered whether it might be possible to pass it upward through the Front and thence across to the revolutionary air forces. Come to think of it, to pass on all I knew, and all I'd seen at Aird. The thought made me shiver. I could not get away from the idea, so firmly instilled by my parents, that anything I might say along those lines would be traced back to me, and to them.

The Allied states, and Britain in particular, had at the time a sharp discontinuity in tolerance – their liberal and democratic self-definition almost forced them to put up with radical opposition, and to treat violent opposition as civil disorder rather than treason; while at the same time the necessities of the long war inclined them to totalitarian methods of maintaining military and state secrecy. A Front supporter could preach defeatism openly, and would receive at the worst police harassment and mob violence. A spy, or anyone under suspicion of materially aiding the enemy, would disappear and never be heard of again, or be summarily tried and executed. Rumours of torture cells and concentration camps proliferated. To what extent these were true was hard to judge, but irrelevant to their effect.

So I kept my theory to myself, and sought confirmation or refutation of it in war memoirs. Most from the Red side were stilted and turgid. Those from former Allied soldiers were usually better written, even if sensationalised. If these accounts were reliable at all, the AHAB bombers were occasionally used for close air support and even medevac, in situations where (as my careful cross-checking made clear) there was little actual fighting in the vicinity and the weather was too violent for helicopters or other conventional aircraft.

I put my ideas about that on the back burner and got on with my work, until the Front had work for me. I left my studies without regret. It was like another call-up, and another calling.

* * *

Davey stopped screaming when the morphine jab kicked in. Blood was still soaking from his trouser-leg all over the back seat of the stolen getaway car. He'd taken a high-velocity bullet just below the knee. Whatever was holding his shin on, it wasn't bone. In the yellow back-street sodium light all our faces looked sick and strange, but his was white. He sprawled, head and trunk in the rear footwell, legs on the back seat. I crouched beside him, holding the tourniquet, only slowing down the blood loss.

Andy, in the driver's seat, looked back over his shoulder.

'Take him tae the hospital?'

It was just up the road – we were parked, engine idling, in a back lane by the sugarhouse. The molasses smell was heavy, the fog damp and smoky.

'We could dump him and run,' Gordon added pointedly, looking out and not looking back.

Save his leg and maybe his life for prison or an internment camp. No chance. But the Front's clandestine field hospitals were already overloaded tonight – we knew that from the news on the car radio alone.

'West End,' I said. 'Top of South Street.'

Andy slid the car into gear and we slewed the corner, drove up past the hospital and the West Station and around the roundabout at a legal speed that had me seething, even though I knew it was necessary. No Army patrols in this part of town, but there was no point in getting pulled by the cops for a traffic offence.

We stopped in a dark spot around the corner from my parents' house. Andy drove off to dump the car and Gordon and I lugged Davey through a door in a wall, past the backs of a couple of gardens, over a fence and into the back porch. I still had the keys. It had been two years since I'd last used them.

Balaclava off, rifle left behind the doorway, into the kitchen, light on. Somebody was already moving upstairs. I heard the sound of a shotgun breech closing.

'Malcolm!' I shouted, past the living-room door. 'It's just me!'

He made some soothing sounds, then said something firmer, and padded downstairs and appeared in the living-room doorway, still knotting his dressing-gown. His face looked drawn in pencil, all grey lines. Charcoal shadows under the eyes. He started towards me.

'You're hurt!'

'It's not my blood,' I said.

His mouth thinned. 'I see,' he said. 'Bring him in. Kitchen floor.'

Gordon and I laid Davey out on the tiles, under the single fluorescent tube. The venetian blind in the window was already closed. My father reappeared, with his black bag. He washed his hands at the sink, stepped aside.

'Kettle,' he said.

I filled it and switched it on. He was scissoring the trouser-leg.

'Jesus Christ,' he said. 'Get this man to a hospital. I'm not a surgeon.'

'No can do,' I said. 'Do what you can.'

'I can stop him going into shock, and I can clean up and bandage.' He looked up at me. 'Top left cupboard. Saline bag, tube, needle.'

I held the saline drip while he inserted the needle. The kettle boiled. He sterilised a scalpel and forceps, tore open a bag of sterile swabs, and got to work quickly. After about five minutes he had Davey's wound cleaned and bandaged, the damaged leg splinted and both legs up on cushions on the floor. A dose of straight heroin topped up the morphine.

'Right,' Malcolm said. 'He'll live. If you want to save the leg, he must get to surgery right away.' He glared at us. 'Don't you bastards have field hospitals?'

'Overloaded,' I said.

His nose wrinkled. 'Busy night, huh?'

Davey was coming to.

'Take me in,' he said. 'I'll no talk.'

My father looked down at him.

'You'll talk,' he said; then, after a deep breath that pained him somehow: 'But I won't. I'll take him to the Royal, swear I saw him caught in crossfire.' He looked out at the rifles in the back porch, and frowned at me. 'Any powder on him?'

I shook my head, miserably.

'We didn't even get a shot in ourselves.'

'Too bad,' he said dryly. 'Right, you come with me, and you, mister,' he told Gordon, 'get yourself and your guns out of here before I see you, or them.'

Gordon glanced at me. I nodded.

'Through the cemetery,' I said.

I only just remembered to remove the revolver from Davey's jacket pocket. My mother suddenly appeared, gave me a tearful but silent hug, and started mopping the floor.

We straightened out a story on the way down, and I disappeared out of the car while my father went inside and got a couple of orderlies out with a stretcher. Ambulances came and went, sirens blaring, lights flashing. A lot of uniforms about. By this time we were fighting the Brits as well as the Yanks. After a few minutes Malcolm returned, and I stepped out of the shadows and slid into the car.

'They bought it,' he said. He lit a cigarette and coughed horribly. 'Back to the house for a minute? Talk to your mother?'

'Dangerous for us all,' I said. 'If you could drop me off up at Barr's Cottage, I'd appreciate it. Otherwise, I'll hop out now.'

'I'll take you.'

Past the station again, at a more sedate pace.

'Thank you,' I said, belatedly. 'For everything.'

He grinned, keeping his eye on the road. ' "First, do no harm",' he said. 'Sort of thing.'

He drove in silence for a minute, around the roundabout and out along Inverkip Road. The walls and high trees of the cemetery passed on the right. Gordon was probably picking his way through the middle of it by now.

'I'll give her your love,' he said. 'Yes?'

'Yes,' I said.

'Won't be seeing you again for another couple of years?'

'If that,' I answered, bleakly if honestly.

He turned off short of Barr's Cottage, into a council estate, and pulled in, under a broken streetlamp. The glow from another cigarette lit his face.

'All right,' he said. 'I have something to tell you.'

Another sigh, another bout of coughing.

'You may not see me again. Your mother doesn't know this yet, but I've got six months. If that.'

'Oh, God,' I said.

'Cancer of the lung,' he said. 'Lot of it about. Filthy air around here.' He crushed out the cigarette. 'Stick to rural guerrilla warfare in future, old chap. It's healthier than the urban variety.'

'I'll fight where I'm—'

His face blurred. I sobbed on his shoulder.

'Enough,' he said. He held me away, gently.

'There's no pain,' he assured me. 'Whisky, tobacco, and heroin, three great blessings. And as the Greek said, nothing is terrible when you know that being nothing is not terrible. I'll know when to ease myself out.'

'Oh, God,' I said again, very inaptly.

His yellow teeth glinted. 'I have no worries about meeting my maker. But, ah, I do have something on my conscience. A monkey on my back, which I want to offload on yours.'

'All right,' I said.

He leaned back and closed his eyes.

'Another time I treated a leg with a very similar injury . . .' he said. 'You were there then, too. You were much smaller, and so was the patient. You do remember?'

'Of course,' I said. My knees were shaking.

His eyes opened and he stared out through the windscreen.

'The last time we discussed this,' he said, 'I suggested that you look into the origin of the bomber. No doubt you have read some books, given the matter thought, and drawn your own conclusions.'

'Yes,' I said, 'I certainly have, it's a—'

He held up one hand. 'Keep it,' he said. 'I've had a lot longer to think about the origin of the pilot. My first thought was the same as yours, that it was a child. Then, when I got, ah, a closer look, I must confess that my second thought was that I was seeing the work of . . . another Mengele. The grey skin, the four digits on hands and feet, the huge eyes, the coppery colour of the blood . . . I thought for years that this was the result of some perverted Nazi science, you know. But, like you, I've read a great deal since. And as a medical man, I know what can and can't be done. No rare syndrome, no surgery, no mutation, no foul tinkering with the germ-plasm could have made that body. It was not a deformed human body. It was a perfectly healthy, normal body, but it was not human.'

He turned to me, shaking his head. 'The memory plays tricks, of course. But in retrospect, and even taking that into account, I believe that the pilot was not only not human, but not mammalian. I'm not even sure that he was a *vertebrate*. The bones in the leg were—'

His cheek twitched. 'Like broken plastic, and hollow. Thin-walled, and filled with rigid tubes and struts rather than spongy bone and marrow.'

I felt like giggling.

'You're saying the pilot was from *another planet*?'

'No,' he said, sharply. 'I'm not. I'm telling you what I *saw*.' He waved a hand, his cigarette tip tracing a jiggly red line. 'For all I know, the pilot may be a specimen of some race of intelligent beings that evolved on Earth and lurks unseen in the depths of the fucking Congo, or the Himalayas, like the Abominable Snowman!'

He laughed, setting off another wheezing cough.

'So there it is, John. A secret I won't be taking to the grave.'

We talked a bit more, and then I got out of the car and watched the tail-lights disappear around a corner.

* * *

Scotland is not a good country for rural guerrilla warfare, having been long since stripped of trees and peasants. Without physical or social shelter, any guerrilla band in the hills and glens would be easily spotted and picked off, if they hadn't starved first. The great spaces of the Highlands were militarily irrelevant anyway.

So everybody believed, until the guerrilla war. Night, clouds and rain, gullies, boulders, bracken, isolated clumps of trees, the few real forests, burns and bridges and bothies all provided cover. The relatively sparse population could do little to betray us and – voluntarily or otherwise – much to help, and supplied few targets for enemy reprisals against civilians. Deer, sheep and rabbits abounded, edible wild plants and berries grew everywhere, and vegetables were easily enough bought or stolen. The strategic importance of the coastline and the offshore oilfields, and the vulnerability and propaganda value of the larger towns – Fort William, Inverness, Aberdeen, Thurso – compelled the state's armed forces to hold the entire enormous area: to move troops and armour along the long, narrow moorland roads, through glens ideal for ambush, and to fly low over often-clouded hills; to guard hydro-electric power stations, railways, microwave relay masts, the military's own installations and training-grounds; to patrol hundreds of miles of pipelines and cables.

That was just the Highlands: the area where I was, for obvious reasons, sent. Those who fought in the Borders, the Pentlands, the Southwest, and even the rich farmland of Perthshire all discovered other options, other opportunities. And that is to say nothing of what the English and Welsh comrades were doing. By 1981 the Front was making the country burn. The line had changed – Deng Hsiao-Ping was making cautious advances in the Versailles negoti-ations – but the fighting continued and we felt proud that we had fulfilled the late Chairman's directive. We had brought home the war.

* * *

The Bren was heavy and the pack was heavier. I was almost grateful that I had to move slowly. Moving under cloud cover was frustrating and dangerous. Visibility that October morning was a couple of metres; the clouds were down to about a hundred, and there was a storm on the way. Behind me nine men followed in line, down from the ridge. I found the bed of a burn, just a trickle at that moment, its boulders and pebbles slick and slippery from the rain of a week earlier. We made our way down this treacherous stairway from the invisible skyline we'd crossed. The first *glomach* I slipped into soaked me to the thighs.

I waded out and moved on. My ankle would have hurt if it hadn't been so cold. The light brightened and quite suddenly I was below the cloud layer, looking down at the road and the railway line at the bottom of the glen, and off to my right and to the west, a patch of meadow on the edge of a small loch with a crannog in the middle. Three houses, all widely separated, were visible up and down the glen. We knew who lived there, and they knew we knew. There would be no trouble from them. Just ahead of us was a ruined barn, a rectangle of collapsed drystone walling within which rowans grew and rusty sheets of fallen corrugated iron roofing sheltered nettles and brambles.

We'd come down at the right place. A couple of hundred metres to the left, a railway bridge crossed the road at an awkward zigzag bend. The bridge had been mined the previous night; the detonation cable should be snaking back to the ruined barn. A train was due in an hour and ten minutes. Our job was to bring down the bridge, giving the train just enough time to stop – civilian casualties weren't necessary for this operation. We intended to levy a revolutionary tax on the passengers and any valuable goods in transit before turning them out on the road and sending the empty train over where the bridge had been, thus blocking the road and railway and creating an ambush chokepoint for any soldiers or cops who were sent to the scene. Booby-trapping the wreckage would be gravy, if we had the time.

I waved forward the next man behind me, and he did likewise, and one by one we all emerged from the fog and hunkered down behind the lip of a shallow gully. Andy and Gordon were there, they'd been with me since the street-fighting days in Greenock. Of the others, three – Sandy and Mike and Neil – were also from Clydeside and four were local (from our point of view –

in their own eyes Ian from Strome and Murdo from Torridon and Donald from Ullapool and Norman from Inverness were almost as distinct from each other in their backgounds as they were from ours).

'Tormod,' I said to Norman, 'you go and check out the bothy there, give us a wave if the electrician has done his job right. Two if he hasn't. Lie low and wait for the signal.'

'There's no signal.'

'The fucking whistle. My whistle.'

'Oh, right you are.'

Crouching, he ran to the ruin, and waved once after a minute. I sent Andy half a mile up the line to the nearest cutting, with a walkie-talkie, ready to confirm that the train had passed, and deployed the others on both sides of the bridge and both sides of the road. Apart from watching for any premature trouble, and being ready to raid the train when it had stopped, they were to stop any civilian vehicles that might chance to go under the bridge at the wrong moment. A light drizzle began to fall, and a front of heavier rain was marching up the glen from the west. It was still about five miles distant but with a good blow behind it, the opening breezes of which were already chilling my wet legs.

I had just settled myself and the Bren and the walkie-talkie behind a boulder on the hillside overlooking the bridge, with half an hour to spare before the train was due to pass at 12.11, when I heard the sound of a train far up the glen to the east. I couldn't see it, none of us could, except maybe Andy. I called him up.

'Passenger train,' he said. 'Wait a minute, it's got a couple of goods wagons at the back – shit, no! It's low-loaders! They're carrying two tanks!'

'Troop train,' I guessed. 'Maybe. Confirm when it passes.'

'I can check it frae here wi the glasses.'

He did, but still couldn't be certain.

Two minutes crawled by. The sound of the train filled the glen, or seemed to, until a sheep bleated nearby, startlingly loud. The radio crackled.

'Confirmed brown job,' said Andy, just as the train emerged from the cutting and into view. It wasn't travelling very fast, maybe just over twenty miles per hour.

I had a choice. I could let this one pass, and continue with the operation, or I could seize this immensely dangerous chance to wreak far more havoc than we'd planned.

I watched the train pass below me, waited until the engine had crossed the bridge, and blew the whistle. Norman didn't hesitate. The blast came when the third carriage of the train was on the bridge. It utterly failed to bring the bridge down, but it threw that carriage upwards and sideways, off the rails. It ploughed through the bridge parapet and its front end crashed on to the road. The remaining four carriages concertina'd into its rear end. One of them rolled on to the embankment, the one behind that was derailed, and the two tank-transporting flatbeds remained on the track.

The engine, and the two front carriages, had by this time travelled a quarter of a mile further down the track, and were accelerating rapidly away. There was nothing that could be done about that. I opened fire at once on the wreck, raking the bursts along the carriage windows. The rest of the squad followed up, then, like myself, they must have ducked down to await return fire.

In the silence that followed the crash and the firing, other noises gradually became audible. Among the screams and yells from the wreckage were the shouts of command. Within seconds a spatter of rifle and pistol fire started up. I raised my head cautiously, watched for the flashes, and directed single shots from the Bren in their direction.

Silence again. Neil and Murdo reported in on the walkie-talkie from the other side of the track, and up ahead a bit. They'd each hit one or two attempts at rescue work or flight. We seemed to have the soldiers on the train pinned down. At the same time it was difficult for us to break cover ourselves. In any sustained exchange of fire we were likely to be the first to run out of ammunition, and then to be picked off as we ran.

This impasse was brought to an end after half an hour by a torrential downpour and a further descent of the clouds. The scheduled train, either cancelled or forewarned, hadn't arrived. Any cars arriving at the scene had backed off and turned away, unmolested by us. We regrouped by the roadside, west of the bridge, well within earshot of the carriage that had crashed on the road.

'This is murder,' said Norman.

I was well aware of the many lives my decision had just ended or wrecked. I had no compunction about that, being even more aware of how many lives we had saved at the troops' destination.

'Seen any white flags, have you?' I snarled. 'Until you do, we're still fighting.'

'Only question is,' said Andy, 'do we pull back now while we're ahead?'

'There'll be rescue and reinforcement coming for sure,' said Murdo. 'The engine could come steaming back any minute, for one thing.'

'They're probably over-estimating us,' I said, thinking aloud in the approved democratic manner. 'I mean, who'd be mad enough to attack a troop train with ten men?'

We laughed, huddled in the pouring rain. The windspeed was increasing by the minute.

'There'll be no air support in this muck,' said Sandy.

'All the same,' I said, 'our best bet is to pull out now we have the chance and there's nothing more to— Wait a minute. What about the tanks?'

'Can't do much damage to them,' said Mike.

'Aye,' I said, 'but think of the damage we can do *with* them.'

* * *

It was easy. It was ridiculously, pathetically, trivially easy. Four of us had National Service experience with tanks, so we split into two groups and after firing a few shots to keep the enemy's heads down we knocked the shackles off the chains and commandeered both tanks. They were fuelled and armed, ready for action. We crashed them off the sides of the flatbeds and drove them perilously down the steep slope to the road, shelled the train, drove under the bridge, shelled the train again, then shelled the bridge. Then we drove over the tracks and around the back of the now-collapsed bridge and a couple of miles up the road, and off to one side, and when the relief column arrived – a dozen troop trucks and four armoured cars – we started shelling that.

By mid-afternoon we'd inflicted hundreds of casualties and had the remaining troops and vehicles completely pinned down. Reinforcements from our side began to arrive, pouring fire from the ridges into the glen, raiding more weapons and ammunition from the train and the relief column; and then attacking *its* relief column. The battle of Glen Carron was turning into the biggest engagement of the war in the British Isles. The increasingly appalling weather was entirely to our advantage, although my squad, at least, were on the point of pneumonia from the soaking we'd got earlier.

The first we knew of the bomber's arrival was when we lost contact with the men on the ridge. A minute later, I saw through the periscope the other tank – a few hundred metres away at the time – take a direct hit. That erupting flash of earth and metal told me without a doubt that Gordon was dead, along with Ian, Mike, Sandy and Norman.

'Reverse reverse reverse!' I shouted.

Murdo slammed us into reverse gear and hit the accelerator, throwing me painfully forward as we shot up a slope and into a birch-screened gully. The tank lurched upward as the bomb missed us by about twenty metres, then crashed back down on its tracks.

Blood poured from my brow and lip.

'Everybody all right?' I yelled.

No reply. Silence. I looked down and saw Andy tugging my leg, mouthing and nodding. He pointed to his ears. I grimaced acknowledgement and looked again through the periscope and saw the bomber descend towards the road just across the glen from us, by one of the trapped columns. Five hundred metres away, and exactly level with us.

There was a shell in the chamber. I swivelled the turret and racked the gun as hearing returned through a raging ringing in my ears, just in time to be deafened again as I fired. My aim was by intuition, with no use of the sights, pure Zen like a perfect throw of a stone. I knew it was going to hit, and it did.

The bomber shot upwards, skimmed towards us, then fluttered down to settle athwart the river at the bottom of the glen, just fifty metres away and ten metres below us, lying there like a fucking enormous landmine in our path.

I poked Murdo's shoulder with my foot and he engaged the forward gear. Andy set up a bit of suppressing fire with the machine-gun. We slewed to a halt beside the bomber. I grabbed a Bren, threw open the hatch and clambered through and jumped down. My ears were still ringing. The wind was fierce, the rain an instant skin-soaking, the wind-chill terrible. Water poured off the bomber like sea off a surfacing submarine. There was a smell of peat-bog and metal and crushed myrtle. Smoke drifted from a ragged notch in its edge, similar to the one on the crippled bomber I'd seen all those years ago.

I walked around the bomber, warily leaping past the snouts of machine-guns in its rim. With the Bren's butt I banged the hatch. The thing rang like a bell, even louder than my tinnitus.

The hatch opened. I stood back and levelled the Bren. A big visored helmet emerged, then long arms levered up a torso, and then the hips and legs swung up and out. The pilot slid down the side of the bomber and stood in front of me, arms raised high. Very slowly, the hands went to the helmet and lifted it off.

A cascade of blonde hair shook loose. The pilot was incredibly beautiful and she was about seven feet tall.

* * *

We left the tank sabotaged and blocking the road about five miles to the west, and took off into the hills. Through the storm and the gathering dusk we struggled to a lonely safe house, miles from anywhere. Our prisoner was tireless and silent. Her flying-suit was dark green and black, to all appearances standard for an American pilot, right down to the badges. She carried her helmet and knotted her hair deftly at her nape. Her Colt .45 and Bowie knife she surrendered without protest.

The safe house was a gamekeeper's lodge, with a kitchen and a couple of rooms, the larger of which had a fireplace. Dry wood was stacked on the hearth. We started the fire and stripped off our wet clothes – all of our clothes – and hung them about the place, then one by one we retrieved dry clothes from the stash in the back room. The prisoner observed us without a blink, and removed her own flying-suit. Under it she was wearing a closer-fitting garment of what looked like woven aluminium, with tubes running under its surface. It covered a well-proportioned female body. Too well-proportioned, indeed, for the giant she was. She sprawled on the worn armchair by the fire and looked at us, still silent, and carefully untied her wet hair and let it fall down her back.

Murdo, Andy, Neil and Donald huddled in front of the fire. I stood behind them, holding the prisoner's pistol.

'Donald,' I said, 'you take the first look-out. You'll find oilskins in the back. Neil, make some tea, and give it to Donald first.'

'Three sugars, if we have it,' said Donald, getting up and padding through to the other room. Neil disappeared into the kitchen. Sounds of him fiddling with and cursing the little gas stove followed. The prisoner smiled, for the first time. Her pale features were indeed beautiful, but somewhat angular, almost masculine; her eyes were a distinct violet, and very large.

'Talk,' I told her.

'Jodelle Smith,' she said. 'Flight-Lieutenant. Serial number . . .' She rattled it off.

The voice was deep, for a woman, but soft, the American accent perfect. Donald gave her a baleful glare as he headed for the door and the storm outside it.

'All right,' I said. 'We are not signatories to the Geneva Convention. We do not regard you as a prisoner of war, but as a war criminal, an air pirate. You have one chance of being treated as a prisoner of war, with all the rights that go with that, and that is to answer all our questions. Otherwise, we will turn you over to the nearest revolutionary court. They're pretty biblical around here. They'll probably stone you to death.'

I don't know how the lads kept a straight face through all that. Perhaps it was the anger and grief over the loss of our friends and comrades, the same feeling that came out in my own voice. I could indeed have wished her dead, but otherwise I was bluffing – there were no revolutionary courts in the region, and anyway our policy with prisoners was to disarm them, attempt to interrogate them, and turn them loose as soon as it was safe to do so.

The pilot sat silent for a moment, head cocked slightly to one side, then shrugged and smiled.

'Other bomber pilots have been captured,' she said. 'They've all been recovered unharmed.' She straightened up in the chair, and leaned forward. 'If you're not satisfied with the standard name, rank, and serial number, I'm happy to talk to you about anything other than military secrets. What would you like to know?'

I glanced at the others. I had never shared my father's story, or my own, with any of them, and I was glad of that now because the appearance of this pilot would have discredited it. Compared with what my father had described, she looked human. Compared with most people, she looked very strange.

'Where do you really come from?' I asked.

'Venus,' she said.

The others all laughed. I didn't.

'What happened to the other kind of pilots?' I asked. I held out one hand about a metre above the ground, as though patting a child's head.

'Oh, we took over from the Martians a long time ago,' she told us earnestly. 'They're still involved in the war, of course, but they're not on the front line any more. The Americans found their appearance disconcerting, and concealing them became too much of a hassle.'

I glared down the imminent interruptions from my men.

'You're saying there are two alien species fighting on the American side?'

'Yes,' she said. She laughed suddenly. 'Greys are from Mars, blondes are from Venus.'

'Total fucking *cac*,' said Neil. 'She's a Yank. They're always tall. Better food.'

'Maybe she is,' I said, 'but she is not the kind of pilot I was expecting. And I've seen one of the other kind. My father saw it up close.'

The woman's eyebrows went up.

'The Aird incident? 1964?'

I nodded.

'Ah,' she said. 'Your father must be . . . Dr Malcolm Donald Matheson, and you are his son, John.'

'How the hell do you know that?'

'I've read the reports.'

'This is insane,' said Andy. 'It's some kind of trick, it's a trap. We shouldnae say another word, or listen tae any.'

'There's eggs and bacon and tatties in the kitchen,' I said. 'See if you can make yourself useful.'

He glowered at me and stalked out.

'But he's right, you know,' I said, loud enough for Andy to overhear. 'We are going to have to send you up a level or two, for interrogation, as soon as the storm passes. Will you still talk then?'

She spread her hands. 'On the same basis as I've spoken to you, yes. No military secrets.'

'Aye, just disinformation,' said Murdo. 'You're not telling us that it wouldn't be a military secret if the Yanks really were getting help from *outer space*? But making people believe it, now, that would be worth something. Christ, it's enough of a job fighting the Americans. Who would fight the fucking Martians?'

He leaned back and laughed harshly.

The woman who called herself Jodelle gazed at him with narrowed, thoughtful eyes.

'There is that argument,' she said. 'There is the other argument, that if the Communists could claim the real enemy was not human they would unite even more people against the Allied side, and that the same knowledge would create all kinds of problems – political, religious, philosophical – for Allied morale. So far, the latter argument has prevailed.'

My grip tightened on the pistol.

'You are talking about psychological warfare,' I said. 'And you are doing it, right here, now. Shut the fuck up.'

She gave us a pert smile and shrugged.

'No more talking to her,' I said.

My own curiosity was burning me inside, but I knew that to pursue the conversation – with the mood here as it was – really would be demoralising and confusing. I got everybody busy guarding the prisoner, cleaning weapons, laying the table. Andy brought through plates laden with steaming, fragrant thick bacon and fried eggs and boiled potatoes. I relieved Donald on the outside watch before taking a bite myself, and prowled around in the howling wet dark with my M-16 under the oilskin cape and my belly grumbling. The window blinds were keeping the light in all right, and only the wind-whipped smoke from the chimney could betray our presence. I kept my closest attention to downwind, where someone might smell it. There was no chance of anyone seeing it.

I was looking that way, peering and listening intently through the dark to the east, when I felt a prickle in the back of my neck and smelled something electric.

I turned with a sort of reluctance, as though expecting to see a ghost. What I saw was a bomber, haloed in blue, descending between me and the house. There might have been a fizzing sound, or that may be just a memory of the hissing rain. For a moment I stood as still as the bomber, which floated preternaturally above the ground. Then I raised the rifle. Something flashed out from the bomber, and I was knocked backwards, and senseless.

* * *

I woke to voices, and pain. My skin smarted all over; my eyelids hurt to open. I was lying on my side on a slightly yielding smooth grey floor. The light was pearly and sourceless. Moving slightly, I found I had some bruises and what felt like scrapes on my back, but apart from that and the burning feeling everything seemed to be fine. My oilskins were gone, as were my weapons and, curiously enough, my watch. I raised my head, propped myself on one elbow and looked around. The room I lay in was circular, about fifteen metres across. My comrades were lying beside me, unconscious, looking sunburned, but breathing normally and apparently uninjured. There was a sort of bench or shelf around the room, which in one section looped away from the wall to form a seat, at which a tall person with long fair hair sat facing away from me, hands on a pair of knobbed levers. Other parts of the shelf were not padded seating but tables and odd panels. Above the bench was a black screen or window which likewise encircled the room.

Sitting on the bench, on either side of the person I guessed was the pilot, were three similar people – one of them, just then noticing that I was stirring, being the woman we'd captured – and a small creature with a large head, slit mouth, tiny nostrils and enormous black eyes. Its skin was grey, but somehow not an unhealthy grey – it had a glow to it, a visible warmth underneath; though hairless it reminded me of the skin of a seal. Its legs were short, its arms long, and its hands – I recalled my father's words, and felt a slight thrill at their confirmation – bore four long digits.

It too noticed me, and it looked directly at me and – it didn't blink, something flicked sideways across its eyes, like an eagle's. The woman stood up and stepped over and stood looking down at me.

'There's no need to be afraid of the Martian,' she said.

'I'm not afraid,' I said, then caught myself. 'John Matheson, unit commander, MB 246.'

She reached down, took my hand and hauled me to my feet, without effort. There was something wrong about my weight. I felt curiously light.

'Your friends will wake up shortly,' she said. 'OK, consider yourself a prisoner of war if you like, but there's no need to not be civil. We have nothing to hide from you any more, and there really isn't anything we want to find out from you.'

I said nothing. She pointed to the bench.

'Relax,' she said, 'sit down, have a coffee.' Then she giggled, in a very disarming way. ' "For you, Johnny, the vor iss over." '

Her fake, Ealing-studio German accent was as perfect as her genuine-sounding American one. I couldn't forbear to smile back, and walked over to the seat. On the way I stumbled a little. It was like the top step that isn't there.

'Martian gravity,' Jodelle said, steadying me. The Martian bowed his big head slightly, as though in apology. I sat down beside one of the other people, the 'Venusians' as I perforce mentally labelled them. All except Jodelle were evidently male, though their hair was as long and fair as hers. One of them passed me a mug of coffee; out of the corner of my eye, I noticed a coffee pot and electric kettle on one of the table sections, and some mugs and, banally enough, a kilogramme packet of Tate & Lyle sugar.

'My name is Soren,' the man said. He waved towards the others. 'The pilot is Olaf, and the man next to him is Harold.'

'And my name is Chuck,' said the Martian. His small shoulders shrugged. 'That's what I'm called around here, anyway.' His voice was like that of a tough wee boy, his accent American, but he sounded like he was speaking a learned second language.

I nodded at them all and said nothing, gratefully sipping the coffee. Outside, the view was completely black, though the movements of the pilot's eyes, head, and hands appeared to be responding to some visible exterior environment.

One by one, Neil, Donald, Murdo and Andy came round, and went through the same process of disorientation, astonishment, reassurance and suspicion as I had. We ended up sitting together, not speaking to each other or to our captors, perhaps silently mourning the loss of our comrades and friends in the other tank. The bomber's crew talked amongst themselves in a language I did not recognise, and attended to instruments. None of us was in anything but a hostile mood, and if the aliens had been less unknown in their intentions and capabilities we might have regarded their evident lack of concern as an opportunity to try to overwhelm them, rather than – as we tacitly acknowledged – evidence that they had no reason to fear us.

After about half an hour, they relaxed, and all sat down on the long seat.

'Almost there,' Jodelle Smith said.

Before any of us could respond, one side of the encircling window filled with the glare of the sun, instantly dimmed by some property of the display; the other with the light of that same sun reflected on white clouds, of which I glimpsed a dazzling, visibly curved expanse a second before we plunged into them. Moments later we were underneath them, and a green surface spread below us. Looking up, I could see the silvery underside of the clouds. Our rapid descent soon brought the green surface into focus as an apparently endless forest, broken by lakes and rivers, and by plateaus or gentler rises covered with grass. After a few seconds we were low enough for the shadow of the bomber to be visible, skimming across the treetops. The circle of shade enlarged, and then disappeared. I blinked, and saw that we were now stationary above a broad valley bounded by high sandstone cliffs and divided by a wide, meandering river.

Then, with a yawing motion which we could see but not feel – so it seemed that the landscape swayed, and not the ship – we descended, and settled on a grassy plain. Around us, in the middle distance, were rows of Nissen huts; in the farther distance, watchtowers and barbed wire.

'Welcome to Venus,' said the pilot.

* * *

The camp held about a thousand people, from all over the world. Most of them were Front soldiers or cadre. There were as many women as there were men, and there were some children. The Front basically ran the camp, through committees of the various national sections, and an international committee for which the main qualification seemed to be fluency in Russian. The only rule that the Venusians enforced was a curfew and blackout between sunset and sunrise. They didn't bother about which hut you spent the night in, so long as you were in a hut.

They gave us no work to do, and watched unconcerned as we practised drill and unarmed combat, sweltering in the heat and humidity. Food and drink were adequate, and in fact more varied and nutritious than the fare to which most of the inmates, including myself, had become accustomed. This is not to say that our confinement was pleasant. The continuous cloud cover felt like a great shining lid pressing down on us, day after day. Every day it seemed to, or perhaps actually did, descend a little lower. The nightly lock-downs were hellish, even though the huts did in fact cool down somewhat. The wire around the camp was almost equally suffocating, although we'd realised that it wasn't so much there to keep us in as to keep the dinosaurs out. The same was true of the guards' strange weapons, which could – if turned to a much higher setting than was ever used against prisoners – fire bolts of electricity or plasma sufficient to turn back even the biggest of the great blundering beasts which flocked to the river every couple of days, their feet making the plain shake. We called them dinosaurs, because they resembled the reconstructions of dinosaurs which most of us had seen in books, but I knew from my scientific education that they could not be dinosaurs – they were too vigorous, too obviously hot-blooded, to be the sluggish reptilian giants of the Triassic and Jurassic eras. Whatever they may have been, their presence certainly discouraged attempts to escape.

The British contingent was in two Nissen huts: twenty men in one, twenty women in the other. They had a committee of three men, three women, and a chairman, and they spent a lot of time trying to regulate sexual relations. It was all very British and messy, uncomfortably between the strict puritanism of the Chinese comrades and the easy-going, if occasionally violent, mores of the Latin Americans and Africans. My unit decided to ignore all that and do what we considered the proper British thing.

We set up an escape committee.

* * *

'What the hell are you doing, Matheson?'

I waved my free hand. 'Just a minute—'

It didn't interrupt my counting. When I'd finished, I put the one-metre line and the 250-gramme tin of peas on the table and glanced over my calculations before looking up at Purdie. The young Englishman was on our hut committee and the camp committee, but not the escape committee, which he regarded as a diversion in both senses of the word.

'We're not on Venus,' I said.

He glanced over his shoulder, as if to confirm that we were still alone in the hut, then sat on a corner of the table.

'How d'you figure that out?'

'Pendulum swing,' I said. 'Galileo's experiment. The gravity here is exactly the same as on Earth. Venus has about eighty per cent of the mass of Earth.'

'H'mm,' he said. 'Well done. Most people begin by wondering why nothing feels lighter, and then put it down to our muscles adapting to the supposed lower gravity. Still, can't say it's a surprise, old chap. Some of us reckon they keep us in at night because if we went outside we could see the moon through the cloud cover, and even the least educated of us is aware that Venus doesn't *have* a bloody moon.'

'So where are we?' I waved a hand. 'It seems a wee bit out of the way, if this is Earth.'

He crooked one leg over the other and lit a cigarette.

'Well, the camp committee has considered that. The usual explanation is that we're in some unexplored region of a South American jungle, something like what's-his-name's *The Lost World*.'

'Conan Doyle,' I said automatically. I screwed up my eyes against the smoke and the glaring light from the open door of the hut. 'Doesn't seem likely to me.'

'Me neither,' said Purdie cheerfully. 'For one thing, the midday sun isn't high enough in the sky for this to be a tropical latitude, but it's *bloody* hot. Any other ideas?'

'What if instead we're in somewhere out of *The Time Machine*? Well, you know . . . *dinosaurs*?'

Purdie frowned and probed in his ear with a finger.

'That has come up. Our Russian comrades shot it down in flames. Time travel is ruled out by dialectical materialism, I gather. But I must say, this place does strike me as frightfully Cretaceous, the anomaly of hot-blooded dinosaurs aside. My personal theory is that we're on a planet around another star, which resembles Earth in the Cretaceous period.'

He cracked a smile. 'That, however, implies a vastly more advanced civilization which either isn't Communist or *is* Communist and fights on the side of the imperialists. Neither of which are acceptable speculations to the, ah, leading comrades here, who thus stick with the line that the self-styled Venusians and Martians are the spawn of Nazi medical experiments, or some such.'

'Bollocks,' I said.

Purdie shrugged. 'You may well say that, but I wouldn't. I myself am troubled by the thought that my own theory at least strongly suggests – even if it doesn't, strictly speaking, require – faster-than-light travel, which is ruled out by Einstein – an authority who to me carries more weight on matters of physics than Engels or Lenin, I'm afraid.'

'Relativity doesn't rule out time travel,' I said. 'Even if dialectical materialism does.'

'And no science whatever rules out lost-world relict dinosaur populations,' said Purdie. He shrugged. 'Occam's razor and all that, keeps up morale, so lost-world is the official line.'

'First I've heard of it,' I said. 'Nobody's even suggested we're not on Venus in the two weeks I've been here.'

'Bit of a test, comrade,' he said dryly. He stubbed out his cigarette, hopped off the table and stuck out his right hand for me to shake. 'Congratulations on passing it. Now, how would you like to join the *real* escape committee?'

* * *

The official escape committee had long since worked through and discarded the laughable expedients – tunnels, gliders and so on – which I and my mates, perhaps over-influenced by such tales of derring-do as *The Colditz Story* and *The Wooden Horse*, had earnestly evaluated. The only possibility was for a mass break-out, exploiting the only factor of vulnerability we could see in the camp's defences, and one which itself was implicitly part of them: the dinosaur herds. It would also exploit the fact that, as far as we knew, the guards were reluctant to use lethal force on prisoners. So far, at least, they'd only ever turned on us the kind of electrical shock which had knocked out me and my team, and indeed most people here at the time of their capture or subsequent resistance.

The tedious details of how a prison-camp escape attempt is prepared have been often enough recounted in the genre of POW memoirs referred to above, and need not be repeated here. Suffice it to say that about fifty days after my arrival, the preparations were complete. From then on, all those involved in the scheme waited hourly for the approach of a suitably large herd, and on the second day of our readiness, conveniently soon after breakfast, one arrived.

About a score of the great beasts: bulls, cows, and calves, their tree-trunk-thick legs striding across the plain, their tree-top-high heads swaying to sniff and stooping to browse, were marching straight towards the eastern fence of the camp, which lay athwart their route to the river. The guards were just bestirring themselves to rack up the setting on their plasma rifles when the riot started.

At the western end of the camp a couple of Chinese women started screaming, and on this cue scores of other prisoners rushed to surround them and pile in to a highly realistic and noisy fight. Guards from the perimeter patrol raced towards them, and were immediately turned on and overwhelmed by a further crowd that just kept on coming, leaping or stepping over those who'd fallen to the low-level electric blasts. At that the guards from the watchtowers on that side began to descend, some of them firing.

My team was set for the actual escape, not the diversion. I was crouched behind the door of our hut with Murdo, Andy, Neil, Donald and a dozen others, including Purdie. We'd grabbed our stashed supplies and our improvised tools, and now awaited our chance. Another human wave assault, this time a crowd of Russians heading for the fence where the guards were belatedly turning to face the oncoming dinosaurs, thundered past. We dashed out behind them and ran for an empty food-delivery truck, temporarily unguarded. It even had a plasma-rifle, which I instantly commandeered, racked inside.

The Russians swarmed up the wire, standing on each other's shoulders like acrobats. The guards, trying to deal with them and the dinosaurs, failed to cope with both. A bull dinosaur brought down the fence and two watch-towers, and by the time he'd been himself laid low with concerted plasma fire, we'd driven over the remains of the fence and hordes of prisoners were fleeing in every direction.

Within minutes the first bombers arrived, skimming low, rounding up the escapees. They missed us, perhaps because they'd mistaken the truck – a very standard US Army Dodge – for one of their own. We abandoned it at the foot of the cliffs, scaled them in half an hour of frantic scrambling up corries and chimneys, and by the time the bombers came looking for us we'd disappeared into the trees.

* * *

Heat, damp, thorns, and very large dragonflies. Apart from that last and the small dinosaur-like animals – some, to our astonishment, with feathers – scuttling through the undergrowth, the place didn't look like another planet, or even the remote past. Since my knowledge of what the remote past was supposed to look like was derived entirely from dim memories of *Look and Learn* and slightly fresher memories of a stroll through the geological wing of the Hunterian Museum, Glasgow, this wasn't saying much. I vaguely expected giant ferns and cycads and so forth, and found perfectly recognisable conifers, oaks and maples. The flowers were less instantly recognisable, but didn't look particularly primitive, or exotic.

I shared these thoughts with Purdie, who laughed.

'You're thinking of the Carboniferous, old chap,' he said. 'This is all solidly Cretaceous, so far.'

'Could be modern,' I said.

'Apart from the animals,' he pointed out, as though this wasn't obvious. 'And as I said, it's not tropical, but it's too bloody hot to be a temperate latitude.'

I glanced back. Our little column was plodding along behind us. We were heading in an approximately upward direction, on a reasonably gentle slope.

'I've thought about this,' I said. 'What if this whole area is some kind of artificial reserve in *North* America? If it's possible to genetically . . . engineer, I suppose would be the word . . . different kinds of humans, why shouldn't it be possible to do the same with birds and lizards and so on, and make a sort of botched copy of dinosaurs?'

'And keep it all under some vast artificial cloud canopy?' He snorted. 'You over-estimate the imperialists, let alone the Nazi scientists, comrade.'

'Maybe we're under a huge dome,' I said, not entirely seriously. I looked up at the low sky, which seemed barely higher than the tree-tops. It really had become lower since we'd arrived. 'Buckminster Fuller had plans that were no less ambitious than that.'

Purdie wiped sweat from his forehead with the back of his hand. 'Now that,' he said, 'is quite a plausible suggestion. It sure *feels* like we're in a bloody greenhouse. Mind you, none of us saw anything like that from the bomber.'

'That was a screen, not a window.'

'Hmm. A remarkably realistic screen, in that case. Back to implausibly advanced technology.'

We wouldn't have to speculate for long, because our course was taking us directly up to the cloud level, which we reached within an hour or so. I assigned my lads the task of guiding the others, who were quite unfamiliar with the techniques of low-visibility walking, and we all headed on up. First wisps then dense damp billows of fog surrounded us. I led the way and moved forward cautiously, whistling signals back and forth. Behind me I could just see Purdie and two of the English women comrades. Underfoot the ground became grassier, and around us the trees became shorter and the bushes more sparse. The only way to follow a particular direction was to go upslope, and that – with a few inevitable wrong turnings that led us into declivities – we did.

The fog thinned. Clutching the plasma rifle, hoping I had correctly figured out how to use it, I walked forward and up and into clear air. A breeze blew refreshingly into my face, and as I glanced back I saw that it had pushed back the fog and revealed all of our straggling party. We were on one of the wide, rounded hilltops I'd seen from the bomber. In the far distance I could see other green islands above the clouds. The sky was blue, the sun was bright.

All around us, people rose out of the long grass, aiming plasma rifles. I dropped mine and raised my hands.

About a hundred metres in front of us was the wire fence of another camp.

* * *

We went into the camp without resistance, but without being searched or, in my case, disarmed: I was told to pick up my rifle and sling it over my shoulder. The people were human beings like us, but they were weird. They spoke English, in strange accents and with a lot of unfamiliar words. Several of them were coloured or half-caste, but their accents were as English as those of the rest. I found myself walking beside a young woman with part of her hair dyed violet. I knew it was a dye because it was growing out: the roots were black. She had several rings and studs in her ear, and not just in the earlobe. She was wearing baggy grey trousers with pockets at the thighs, and a silky scarlet sleeveless top with a silver patch shaped like a rabbit. Around her bicep was a tattoo of thorns. Under her tarty make-up her face was quite attractive. Her teeth looked amazingly white and even, like an American's.

'My name's Tracy,' she said. She had some kind of Northern English accent; I couldn't place it more than that. 'You?'

Name, rank, serial number . . .

'Where you from?'

Name, rank, serial number . . .

'Forget that,' she said. 'You're not a prisoner.'

A massive gate made from logs and barbed wire was being pushed shut behind us. Nissen huts inside a big square of fence, a bomber parked just outside it.

'Oh no?' I said.

'Keeps the fucking dinosaurs out, dunnit?'

Somebody handed me a tin mug of tea, black with a lot of sugar. I sipped it and looked around. If this was a camp it was one where prisoners had guns. Or one run by trusties . . . I was still suspicious.

'Where are the aliens?' I asked.

'The what?'

'The Venusians, the Martians . . .' I held my free hand above my head, then at chest height.

Tracy laughed, 'Is that what they told you?'

I nodded. 'Not sure if I believe them, though.'

She was still chuckling. 'You lot must be from Commie World. Never built the rockets, right?'

'The Russians have rockets,' I said with some indignation. 'The biggest in the world – they have a range of hundreds of kilometres!'

'Exactly. No ICBMs.' She smiled at my frown. 'Inter-Continental Ballistic Missiles. None of them, and no space-probes. Jeez. You could still half-believe this might be Venus, with jungles and tall Aryans. And that the Greys are Martians.'

'Well, what are they?' I asked, becoming irritated by her smug teasing.

'Time travellers,' she said. 'From the future.' She shivered slightly. 'From *another* world's future. The ones you call the Venusians are from about half a million years up ahead of the twentieth century, the Greys're from maybe five million. In your world's twentieth century they fly bombers and fight Commies. In mine they're just responsible for flying saucers, alien abductions, cattle mutilations and odd sock phenomena.'

I let this incomprehensibly pass.

'So where are we now?'

I meant the camp. I knew where we were in general, but that was what she answered.

'This Johnny-boy, is the past. They can never go back to the same future, but they can go back to the same place in the past, where they can make no difference. The common past, the past of us all – the Cretaceous.'

She looked at me with a bit more sympathy. My companions were finishing off their tea and gazing around, looking as baffled and edgy as I felt. The other prisoners, if that was what they were, gathered around us seemed more alien than the bomber pilots.

'Come on,' Tracy said, gesturing towards some rows of seats in front of which a table had been dragged. 'Debriefing time. You have a lot to learn.'

* * *

I have learned a lot.

I tug the reins and the big Clydesdale turns, and as I follow the plough around I see a porpoise leap in the choppy water of the Moray Firth. My hands and back are sore but I'm getting used to it, and the black soil here is rich, and arable after the trees have been cut down and their stumps dynamited. The erratic boulders have been cleared away long ago, by the long-dead first farmers of this land, and no glaciers have revisited it since its last farmers passed away. The rougher ground is pasture, grazed by half-wild long-horns, a rugged synthetic species. The village is stockaded on a hilltop nearby. We have no human enemies, but wolves, bears and lions prowl the forests and moors. We are not barbarians – the plough that turns the furrow I walk has an iron blade, and the revolver on my hip was made in Hartford, Connecticut, millennia ago and worlds away. The post-humans settled us – and other colonies – on this empty Earth with machinery and medicines, weapons and tools and libraries, and enough partly-used ball-point pens to keep us all scribbling until our descendants can make their own.

On countless other empty Earths they have done the same. Somewhere unreachable, but close to hand, another man, perhaps another John Matheson, may be tramping a slightly different furrow. I wish him well.

There are many possible worlds, and in almost all of them humanity didn't survive the time from which most of us have been taken. Either the United States and the Soviet Union destroyed each other and the rest of civilization in an atomic war in the fifties or sixties, or they didn't, and the collapse of the socialist states in the late twentieth century so discredited socialism and international co-operation that humanity failed utterly to unite in time to forestall the environmental disasters of the twenty-first.

In a few, a very few possible worlds, enough scattered remnants of humanity survived as savages to eventually – hundreds of thousands of years later – become the ancestors of the post-human species we called the Venusians. Who in turn – millions of years later – themselves gave rise to the post-human species we called the Martians. It was the latter who discovered time travel, and with it some deep knowledge about the future and past of the universe.

I don't pretend to understand it. As Feynmann said – in a world where he didn't die in jail – it all goes back to the experiment with the light and the two slits, and Feynmann himself didn't pretend to understand *that*. What we have been told is simply this – that the past of the universe, its very habitability for human beings, depends on its future being one – or rather, many – which contain as many human beings and their successors as possible, until the end of time.

It is not enough for the time-travellers to intervene in histories such as the one from which I come, and by defeating Communism while avoiding atomic war, save a swathe of futures for co-operation and survival. They also have to repopulate the time-lines in which humanity destroyed itself, and detonate new shock-waves of possibility that will spread humanity across time and forward through it, on an ever-expanding, widening front.

The big mare stops and looks at me, and whinnies. The sun is low above the hills to the west, the hills where I once – or many times – fought. Its light is red in the sky. The dust from the last atomic war is no longer dangerous, but it will linger in the high atmosphere for thousands of years to come.

I unharness the horse, heave the plough to the shed at the end of the field, and lead the beast up the hill towards the village. The atomic generator is humming, the lights are coming on, and dinner in the communal kitchen will soon be ready. Tracy will be putting away the day's books in the library, and yawning and stretching herself. Maybe this evening, after we've all eaten, she can be persuaded to tell us some stories. For me she has many fascinations – she's quite unlike any woman I've ever met – and the only one I'm happy for her to share with everybody else is her stories from the world where, I still feel, history turned out almost as it would have done without any meddling at all by the time-travellers: her world, the world where the prototype bomber didn't work; the world where, as she puts it, the Roswell saucer crashed.

diamond dogs

Alastair Reynolds

one

I met Childe in the Monument to the Eighty.

It was one of those days when I had the place largely to myself, able to walk from aisle to aisle without seeing another visitor; only my footsteps disturbing the air of funereal silence and stillness.

I was visiting my parents' shrine. It was a modest affair: a smooth wedge of obsidian shaped like a metronome, undecorated save for two cameo portraits set in elliptical borders. The sole moving part was a black blade which was attached near the base of the shrine, ticking back and forth with magisterial slowness. Mechanisms buried inside the shrine ensured that it was winding down; destined to count out days and then years with each tick. Eventually it would require careful measurement to detect its movement.

I was watching the blade when a voice disturbed me.

'Visiting the dead again, Richard?'

'Who's there?' I said, looking around, faintly recognising the speaker but not immediately able to place him.

'Just another ghost.'

Various possibilities flashed through my mind as I listened to the man's deep and taunting voice: a kidnapping, an assassination, before I stopped flattering myself that I was worthy of such attention.

Then the man emerged from between two shrines a little way down from the metronome.

'My God,' I said.

'Now do you recognise me?'

He smiled and stepped closer; as tall and imposing as I remembered. He had lost the devil's horns since our last meeting – they had only ever been a bio-engineered affectation – but there was still something satanic about his appearance, an effect not lessened by the small and slightly pointed goatee he had cultivated in the meantime.

Dust swirled around him as he walked towards me, suggesting that he was not a projection.

'I thought you were dead, Roland.'

'No, Richard,' he said, stepping close enough to shake my hand. 'But that was most certainly the effect I desired to achieve.'

'Why?' I said.

'Long story.'

'Start at the beginning, then.'

Roland Childe placed a hand on the smooth side of my parents' shrine. 'Not quite your style, I'd have thought?'

'It was all I could do to argue against something even more ostentatious and morbid. But don't change the subject. What happened to you?'

He removed his hand, leaving a faint damp imprint. 'I faked my own death. The Eighty was the perfect cover. The fact that it all went so horrendously wrong was even better. I couldn't have planned it like that if I'd tried.'

No arguing with that, I thought. It *had* gone horrendously wrong.

More than a century and a half ago, a clique of researchers led by Calvin Sylveste had resurrected the old idea of copying the essence of a living human being into a computer-generated simulation. The procedure – then in its infancy – had the slight drawback that it killed the subject. But there had still been volunteers, and my parents had been amongst the first to sign up and support Calvin's work. They had offered him political protection when the powerful Mixmaster lobby opposed the project, and they had been amongst the first to be scanned.

Less than fourteen months later, their simulations had also been among the first to crash.

None could ever be restarted. Most of the remaining Eighty had succumbed, and now only a handful remained unaffected.

'You must hate Calvin for what he did,' Childe said, still with that taunting quality in his voice.

'Would it surprise you if I said I didn't?'

'Then why did you set yourself so vocally against his family after the tragedy?'

'Because I felt justice still needed to be served.' I turned from the shrine and started walking away, curious as to whether Childe would follow me.

'Fair enough,' he said. 'But that opposition cost you dearly, didn't it?'

I bridled, halting next to what seemed a highly realistic sculpture but which was almost certainly an embalmed corpse.

'Meaning what?'

'The Resurgam expedition, of course, which just happened to be bankrolled by House Sylveste. By rights, you should have been on it. You were Richard Swift, for heaven's sake. You'd spent the better part of your life thinking about possible modes of alien sentience. There should have been a place for you on that ship, and you damned well knew it.'

'It wasn't that simple,' I said, resuming my walk. 'There were a limited number of slots available and they needed practical types first – biologists, geologists, that kind of thing. By the time they'd filled the most essential slots, there simply wasn't any room for abstract dreamers like myself.'

'And the fact that you'd pissed-off House Sylveste had nothing whatsoever to do with it? Come off it, Richard.'

We descended a series of steps down into the lower level of the Monument. The atrium's ceiling was a cloudy mass of jagged sculptures; interlocked metal birds. A party of visitors was arriving, attended by servitors and a swarm of bright, marble-sized float-cams. Childe breezed through the group, drawing annoyed frowns but no actual recognition, although one or two of the people in the party were vague acquaintances of mine.

'What is this about?' I asked, once we were outside.

'Concern for an old friend. I've had my tabs on you, and it was pretty obvious that not being selected for that expedition was a crushing disappointment. You'd thrown your life into contemplation of the alien. One marriage down the drain because of your self-absorption. What was her name again?'

I'd had her memory buried so deeply that it took an effort of will to recall any exact details about my marriage.

'Celestine. I think.'

'Since when you've had a few relationships, but nothing lasting more than a decade. A decade's a mere fling in this town, Richard.'

'My private life's my own business,' I responded sullenly. 'Hey. Where's my volantor? I parked it here.'

'I sent it away. We'll take mine instead.'

Where my volantor had been was a larger, blood-red model. It was as baroquely-ornamented as a funeral barge. At a gesture from Childe it clammed open, revealing a plush gold interior with four seats, one of which was occupied by a dark, slouched figure.

'What's going on, Roland?'

'I've found something. Something astonishing that I want you to be a part of; a challenge that makes every game you and I ever played in our youth pale in comparison.'

'A challenge?'

'The ultimate one, I think.'

He had pricked my curiosity, but I hoped it was not too obvious. 'The city's vigilant. It'll be a matter of public record that I came to the Monument, and we'll have been recorded together by those float-cams.'

'Exactly,' Childe said, nodding enthusiastically. 'So you risk nothing by getting in the volantor.'

'And should I at any point weary of your company?'

'You have my word that I'll let you leave.'

I decided to play along with him for the time being. Childe and I took the volantor's front pair of seats. Once ensconced, I turned around to acquaint myself with the other passenger, and then flinched as I saw him properly.

He wore a high-necked leather coat which concealed much of the lower half of his face. The upper part was shadowed under the generous rim of a homburg, tipped down to shade his brow. Yet what remained visible was sufficient to shock me. There was only a blandly handsome silver mask; sculpted into an expression of quiet serenity. The eyes were blank silver surfaces, what I could see of his mouth a thin, slightly-smiling slot.

'Doctor Trintignant,' I said.

He reached forward with a gloved hand, allowing me to shake it as one would the hand of a woman. Beneath the black velvet of the glove I felt armatures of hard metal. Metal that could crush diamond.

'The pleasure is entirely mine,' he said.

* * *

Airborne, the volantor's baroque ornamentation melted away to mirror-smoothness. Childe pushed ivory-handled control sticks forward, gaining altitude and speed. We seemed to be moving faster than the city ordinances allowed, avoiding the usual traffic corridors. I thought of the way he had followed me, researched my past and had my own volantor desert me. It would also have taken considerable resourcefulness to locate the reclusive Trintignant and persuade him to emerge from hiding.

Clearly Childe's influence in the city exceeded my own, even though he had been absent for so long.

'The old place hasn't changed much,' Childe said, swooping us through a dense conglomeration of golden buildings, as extravagantly-tiered as the dream pagodas of a fever-racked Emperor.

'Then you've really been away? When you told me you'd faked your death, I wondered if you'd just gone into hiding.'

He answered with a trace of hesitation. 'I've been away, but not as far as you'd think. A family matter came up that was best dealt with confidentially, and I really couldn't be bothered explaining to everyone why I needed some peace and quiet on my own.'

'And faking your death seemed the best way to go about it?'

'Like I said, I couldn't have planned the Eighty if I'd tried. I had to bribe a lot of minor players in the project, of course, and I'll spare you the details of how we provided a corpse . . . but it all worked swimmingly, didn't it?'

'I never had any doubts that you'd died along with the rest of them.'

'I didn't like deceiving my friends. But I couldn't go to all that trouble and then ruin my plan with a few indiscretions.'

'You were friends, then?' solicited Trintignant.

'Yes, Doctor,' Childe said, glancing back at him. 'Way back when. Richard and I were rich kids – relatively rich, anyway – with not enough to do. Neither of us were interested in the stock market or the social whirl. We were only interested in games.'

'Oh. How charming. What kinds of game, may I ask?'

'We'd build simulations to test each other – extraordinarily elaborate worlds filled with subtle dangers and temptations. Mazes and labyrinths; secret passages; trapdoors; dungeons and dragons. We'd spend months inside them, driving each other crazy. Then we'd go away and make them even harder.'

'But in due course you grew apart,' the Doctor said. His synthesized voice had a curious piping quality.

'Yeah,' Childe said. 'But we never stopped being friends. It was just that Richard had spent so much time devising increasingly alien scenarios that he'd become more interested in the implied psychologies behind the tests. And I'd become interested only in the playing of the games; not their construction. Unfortunately Richard was no longer there to provide challenges to me.'

'You were always much better than me at playing them,' I said. 'In the end it got too hard to come up with something you'd find difficult. You knew the way my mind worked too well.'

'He's convinced that he's a failure,' Childe said, turning round to smile at the Doctor.

'As are we all,' Trintignant answered. 'And with some justification, it must be said. I have never been allowed to pursue my admittedly controversial interests to their logical ends. You, Mister Swift, were shunned by those who you felt should have recognised your worth in the field of speculative alien psychology. And you, Mister Childe, have never discovered a challenge worthy of your undoubted talents.'

'I didn't think you'd paid me any attention, Doctor.'

'Nor had I. I have surmised this much since our meeting.'

The volantor dropped below ground level, descending into a brightly-lit commercial plaza lined with shops and boutiques. With insouciant ease, Childe skimmed us between aerial walkways, and then nosed the car into a dark side-tunnel. He gunned the machine faster, our speed indicated only by the passing of red lights set into the tunnel sides. Now and then another vehicle passed us, but once the tunnel had branched and re-branched a half a dozen times, no further traffic appeared. The tunnel lights were gone now, and when the volantor's headlights glanced against the walls they revealed ugly cracks and huge, scarred absences of cladding. These old sub-surface ducts dated back to the city's earliest days, before the domes were thrown across the crater.

Even if I had recognised the part of the city where we had entered the tunnel system, I would have been hopelessly lost by now.

'Do you think Childe has brought us together to taunt us about our lack of respective failures, Doctor?' I asked, beginning to feel uneasy again despite my earlier attempts at reassurance.

'I would consider that a distinct possibility, were Childe himself not conspicuously tainted by the same lack of success.'

'Then there must be another reason.'

'Which I'll reveal in due course,' Childe said. 'Just bear with me, will you? You two aren't the only ones I've gathered together.'

* * *

Presently we arrived somewhere.

It was a cave in the form of a near-perfect hemisphere; the great domed roof arching a clear three hundred metres from the floor. We were obviously well below Yellowstone's surface now. It was even possible that we had passed beyond the city's crater wall, so that above us lay only poisonous skies.

But the domed chamber was inhabited.

The roof was studded with an enormous number of lamps, flooding the interior with synthetic daylight. An island stood in the middle of the chamber, moated by a ring of uninviting water. A single bone-white bridge connected the mainland to the island, shaped like a great curved femur. The island was dominated by a thicket of slender, dark poplars partly concealing a pale structure situated near its middle.

Childe brought the volantor to a rest near the edge of the water and invited us to disembark.

'Where are we?' I asked, once I had stepped down.

'Query the city and find out for yourself,' Trintignant said.

The result was not what I was expecting. For a moment there was a shocking absence inside my head; the neural equivalent of a sudden, unexpected amputation.

The Doctor's chuckle was an arpeggio played on a pipe organ. 'We have been out of range of city services from the moment we entered his conveyance.'

'You needn't worry,' Childe said. 'You are beyond city services, but only because I value the secrecy of this place. If I imagined it'd have come as a shock to you, I'd have warned you already.'

'I'd have at least appreciated a warning, Roland,' I said.

'Would it have changed your mind about coming here?'

'Conceivably.'

The echo of his laughter betrayed the chamber's peculiar acoustics. 'Then are you at all surprised that I didn't tell you?'

I turned to Trintignant. 'What about you?'

'I confess my use of city services has been as limited as your own, but for rather different reasons.'

'The good Doctor needed to lie low,' Childe said. 'That meant he couldn't participate very actively in city affairs. Not if he didn't want to be tracked down and assassinated.'

I stamped my feet, beginning to feel cold. 'Good. What now?'

'It's only a short ride to the house,' Childe said, glancing towards the island.

* * *

Now a noise came steadily nearer. It was an antiquated, rumbling sound, accompanied by a odd, rhythmic sort of drumming, quite unlike any machine I had experienced. I looked towards the femoral bridge, suspecting as I did that it was exactly what it looked like: a giant, bio-engineered bone, carved with a flat roadbed. And something was approaching us over the span; a dark, complicated and unfamiliar contraption, which at first glance resembled an iron tarantula.

I felt the back of my neck prickle.

The thing reached the end of the bridge and swerved towards us. Two mechanical black horses provided the motive power. They were emaciated black machines with sinewy, piston-driven limbs, venting steam and snorting from intakes. Malignant red laser-eyes swept over us. The horses were harnessed to a four-wheeled carriage slightly larger than the volantor, above which was perched a headless humanoid robot. Skeletal hands gripped iron control cables which plunged into the backs of the horses' steel necks.

'Meant to inspire confidence, is it?' I asked.

'It's an old family heirloom,' Childe said, swinging open a black door in the side of the carriage. 'My uncle Giles made automata. Unfortunately – for reasons we'll come to – he was a bit of a miserable bastard. But don't let it put you off.'

He helped us aboard, then climbed inside, sealed the door and knocked on the roof. I heard the mechanical horses snort; alloy hooves hammering the ground impatiently. Then we were moving, curving around and ascending the gentle arc of the bridge of bone.

'Have you been here during the entire period of your absence, Mister Childe?' Trintignant asked.

He nodded. 'Ever since that family business came up, yeah. I've allowed myself the occasional visit back to the city – just like I did today – but I've tried to keep such excursions to a minimum.'

'Didn't you have horns the last time we met?' I said.

He rubbed the smooth skin of his scalp, where the horns had been. 'Had to have them removed. I couldn't very well disguise myself otherwise.'

We crossed the bridge and navigated a path between the tall trees which sheltered the island's structure. Childe's carriage pulled up to a smart stop in front of the building, and I was afforded my first unobstructed view of our destination. It was not one to induce great cheer. The house's architecture was haphazard: whatever basic symmetry it might once have had lost under a profusion of additions and modifications. The roof was a jumbled collision of angles and spires, jutting turrets and sinister oubliettes. Not all of the embellishments had been arranged at strict right-angles to their neighbours, and the style and apparent age of the house varied jarringly from place to place. Since our arrival in the cave the overhead lights had dimmed, simulating the onset of dusk, but only a few windows were illuminated; clustered together in the left-hand wing. The rest of the house had a foreboding aspect; the paleness of its stone, the irregularity of its construction and the darkness of its many windows suggesting a pile of skulls.

Almost before we had disembarked from the carriage, a reception party emerged from the house. It was a troupe of servitors – humanoid household robots, of the kind anyone would have felt comfortable with in the city proper – but they had been reworked to resemble skeletal ghouls or headless knights. Their mechanisms had been sabotaged so that they limped and creaked, and they had all had their voiceboxes disabled.

'Had a lot of time on his hands, your uncle,' I said.

'You'd have loved Giles, Richard. He was a scream.'

'I'll take your word for it, I think.'

The servitors escorted us into the central part of the house, then took us through a maze of chill, dark corridors.

Finally we reached a large room walled in plush red velvet. A holoclavier sat in one corner, with a book of sheet music spread open above the projected

keyboard. There was a malachite escritoire, a number of well-stocked book-
cases, a single chandelier, three smaller candelabra, and two fireplaces of
distinctly gothic appearance, one of which roared with an actual fire. But the
room's central feature was a mahogany table, around which three additional
guests were gathered.

'Sorry to keep everyone waiting,' Childe said, closing a pair of sturdy
wooden doors behind us. 'Now. Introductions.'

The others looked at us with what seemed no more than mild interest.

The only man among them wore an elaborately ornamented exoskeleton; a
baroque support structure of struts, hinged plates, cables and servo-mechan-
isms. His face was a skull papered with deathly white skin, shading to black
under his bladelike cheekbones. His eyes were concealed behind goggles, his
hair a spray of stiff black dreadlocks.

Periodically he inhaled from a glass pipe, connected to a miniature refinery
of bubbling apparatus placed before him on the table.

'Allow me to introduce Captain Forqueray,' Childe said. 'Captain – this is
Richard Swift and . . . um, Doctor Trintignant.'

'Pleased to meet you,' I said, leaning across the table to shake Forqueray's
hand. His grip felt like the cold clasp of a squid.

'The Captain is an Ultra; the master of the lighthugger *Apollyon*; currently
in orbit around Yellowstone,' Childe added.

Trintignant refrained from approaching him.

'Shy, Doctor?' Forqueray said, his voice simultaneously deep and flawed,
like a cracked bell.

'No, merely cautious. It is a matter of common knowledge that I have
enemies among the Ultras.'

Trintignant removed his homburg and patted his crown delicately, as if
smoothing down errant hairs. Silver waves had been sculpted into his head-
mask, so that he resembled a bewigged Regency fop dipped in mercury.

'You've enemies everywhere,' said Forqueray, between gurgling inhalations.
'But I bear you no personal animosity for your atrocities, and I guarantee that
my crew will extend you the same courtesy.'

'Very gracious of you,' Trintignant said, before shaking the Ultra's hand for the minimum time compatible with politeness. 'But why should your crew concern me?'

'Never mind that.' It was one of the two women speaking now. 'Who is this guy, and why does everyone hate him?'

'Allow me to introduce Hirz,' Childe said, meaning the woman who had spoken. She was small enough to have been a child, except that her face was clearly that of an adult woman. She was dressed in austere, tight-fitting black clothes which only emphasized her diminutive build. 'Hirz is – for want of a better word – a mercenary.'

'Except I prefer to think of myself as an information retrieval specialist. I specialise in clandestine infiltration for high-level corporate clients in the Glitter Band – physical espionage some of the time. Mostly, though, I'm what used to be called a hacker. I'm also pretty damned good at my job.' Hirz paused to swig down some wine. 'But enough about me. Who's the silver dude, and what did Forqueray mean about atrocities?'

'You're seriously telling me you're unaware of Trintignant's reputation?' I said.

'Hey, listen. I get myself frozen between assignments. That means I miss a lot of shit that goes down in Chasm City. Get over it.'

I shrugged and – with one eye on the Doctor himself – told Hirz what I knew about Trintignant. I sketched in his early career as an experimental cyberneticist, how his reputation for fearless innovation had eventually brought him to Calvin Sylveste's attention.

Calvin had recruited Trintignant to his own research team, but the collaboration had not been a happy one. Trintignant's desire to find the ultimate fusion of flesh and machine had become obsessive; even – some said – perverse. After a scandal involving experimentation on unconsenting subjects, Trintignant had been forced to pursue his work alone; his methods too extreme even for Calvin.

So Trintignant had gone to ground, and continued his gruesome experiments with his only remaining subject.

Himself.

'So let's see,' said the final guest. 'Who have we got? An obsessive and thwarted cyberneticist with a taste for extreme modification. An intrusion specialist with a talent for breaking into highly-protected – and dangerous – environments. A man with a starship at his disposal and the crew to operate it.'

Then she looked at Childe, and while her gaze was averted I admired the fine, faintly familiar profile of her face. Her long hair was the sheer black of interstellar space, pinned back from her face by a jewelled clasp which flickered with a constellation of embedded pastel lights. Who was she? I felt sure we had met once or twice before. Perhaps we had passed each other among the shrines in the Monument to the Eighty, visiting the dead.

'And Childe,' she continued. 'A man once known for his love of intricate challenges, but long assumed dead.' Then she turned her piercing eyes upon me. 'And, finally, you.'

'I know you, I think . . .' I said, her name on the tip of my tongue.

'Of course you do.' Her look, suddenly, was contemptuous. 'I'm Celestine. You used to be married to me.'

* * *

All along, Childe had known she was here.

'Do you mind if I ask what this is about?' I said, doing my best to sound as reasonable as possible, rather than someone on the verge of losing their temper in polite company.

Celestine withdrew her hand once I had shaken it. 'Roland invited me here, Richard. Just the same way he did you, with the same veiled hints about having found something.'

'But you're . . .'

'Your ex-wife?' She nodded. 'Exactly how much do you remember, Richard? I heard the strangest rumours, you know. Ones that said you'd had me deleted from your long-term memory.'

'I had you suppressed, not deleted. There's a subtle distinction.'

She nodded knowingly. 'So I gather.'

I glanced at the other guests, who were observing us. Even Forqueray was waiting, the pipe of his apparatus poised an inch from his mouth in expectation. They were waiting for me to say something; anything.

'Why exactly are you here, Celestine?'

'You don't remember, do you?'

'Remember what?'

'What it was I used to do, Richard, when we were married.'

'I confess I don't, no.'

Childe coughed. 'Your wife, Richard, was as fascinated by the alien as you were. She was one of the city's foremost specialists on the Pattern Jugglers, although she'd be entirely too modest to admit it herself.' He paused, apparently seeking Celestine's permission to continue. 'She visited them, long before you met; spending several years of her life at the study station on Spindrift. You swam with the Jugglers, didn't you, Celestine?'

'Once or twice.'

'And allowed them to reshape your mind; transforming its neural pathways into something deeply – albeit usually temporarily – alien.'

'It wasn't that big a deal,' Celestine said.

'Not if you'd been fortunate enough to have it happen to you, no. But for someone like Richard – who craved knowledge of the alien with every fibre of his existence – it would have been anything but mundane.' He turned to me. 'Isn't that true?'

'I admit I'd have done a great deal to experience communion with the Jugglers,' I said, knowing that it was pointless to deny it. 'But it just wasn't possible. My family lacked the resources to send me to one of the Juggler worlds, and the bodies that might ordinarily have funded that kind of trip – the Sylveste Institute, for instance – had turned their attentions else-where.'

'In which case Celestine was deeply fortunate, wouldn't you say?'

'I don't think anyone would deny that,' I said. 'To speculate about the shape of alien consciousness is one thing; but to drink it; to bathe in the full flood of it – to know it intimately, like a lover . . .' I trailed off for a moment. 'Wait a minute. Shouldn't you be on Resurgam, Celestine? There isn't time for the expedition to have gone there and come back.'

She eyed me with raptorial intent before answering.

'I never went.'

Childe leant over and refreshed my glass. 'She was turned down at the last minute, Richard. Sylveste had a grudge against anyone who'd visited the Jugglers; suddenly deciding they were all unstable and couldn't be trusted.'

I looked at Celestine wonderingly. 'Then all this time . . . ?'

'I've been here, in Chasm City. Oh, don't look so crushed, Richard. By the time I learned I'd been turned down, you'd already decided to flush me out of your past. It was better for both of us this way.'

'But the deception . . .'

Childe put one hand on my shoulder, calmingly. 'There wasn't any. She just didn't make contact again. No lies; no deception; nothing to hold a grudge about.'

I looked at him, angrily. 'Then why the hell is she here?'

'Because I happen to have use of someone with the skills that the Jugglers gave to Celestine.'

'Which included?' I said.

'Extreme mathematical prowess.'

'And why would that have been useful?'

Childe turned to the Ultra, indicating that the man should remove his bubbling apparatus.

'I'm about to show you.'

* * *

The table housed an antique holo-projection system. Childe handed out viewers which resembled lorgnette binoculars, and – like so many myopic opera buffs – we studied the apparitions which floated into existence above the polished mahogany surface.

Stars; incalculable numbers of them – hard white and blood-red gems, strewn in lacy patterns against deep velvet blue.

Childe narrated.

'The better part of two and a half centuries ago, my uncle Giles – whose somewhat pessimistic handiwork you have already seen – made a momentous decision. He embarked on what we in the family only ever referred to as the Program, and then only in terms of extreme secrecy.'

Childe told us that the Program was an attempt at covert deep space exploration.

Giles had conceived the work, funding it directly from the family's finances. He had done this with such ingenuity that the apparent wealth of House Childe had never faltered, even as the Program entered its most expensive phase. Only a few select members of the Childe dynasty had even known of the Program's existence, and that number had dwindled as time passed.

The bulk of the money had been paid to the Ultras, who had already emerged as a powerful faction by that time.

They had built the autonomous robot space probes according to this uncle's desires, and then launched them towards a variety of target systems. The Ultras could have delivered his probes to any system within range of their lighthugger ships, but the whole point of the exercise was to restrict the knowledge of any possible discoveries to the family alone. So the envoys crossed space by themselves, at only a fraction of the speed of light, and the targets they were sent to were all poorly-explored systems on the ragged edge of human space.

The probes decelerated by use of solar sails, picked the most interesting worlds to explore, and then fell into orbit around them.

Robots were sent down, equipped to survive on the surface for many decades.

Childe waved his hand across the table. Lines radiated out from one of the redder suns in the display, which I assumed was Yellowstone's star. The lines reached out towards other stars, forming a three-dimensional scarlet dandelion several dozen light-years wide.

'These machines must have been reasonably intelligent,' Celestine said. 'Especially by the standards of the time.'

Childe nodded keenly. 'Oh, they were. Cunning little blighters. Subtle and stealthy and diligent. They had to be, to operate so far from human supervision.'

'And I presume they found something?' I said.

'Yes,' Childe said testily, like a conjurer whose carefully scripted patter was being ruined by a persistent heckler. 'But not immediately. Giles didn't expect it to be immediate, of course – the envoys would take decades to reach the closest systems they'd been assigned to, and there'd still be the communicational timelag to take into consideration. So my uncle resigned himself to forty or fifty years of waiting, and that was erring on the optimistic side.' He paused and sipped from his wine. 'Too bloody optimistic, as it happened. Fifty years passed . . . then sixty . . . but nothing of any consequence was ever reported back to Yellowstone, at least not in his lifetime. The envoys did, on occasion, find something interesting – but by then other human explorers had usually stumbled on the same find. And as the decades wore on, and the envoys failed to justify their invention, my uncle grew steadily more maudlin and bitter.'

'I'd never have guessed,' Celestine said.

'He died, eventually – bitter and resentful; feeling that the universe had played some sick cosmic trick on him. He could have lived for another fifty or sixty years with the right treatments, but I think by then he knew it would be a waste of time.'

'You faked your death a century and a half ago,' I said. 'Didn't you tell me it had something to do with this family business?'

He nodded in my direction. 'That was when my uncle told me about the Program. I didn't know anything about it until then – not even the tiniest hint of a rumour. No one in the family did. By then, of course, the project was costing us almost nothing, so there wasn't even a financial drain to be concealed.'

'And since then?'

'I vowed not to make my uncle's mistake. I resolved to sleep until the machines sent back a report, and then sleep again if the report turned out to be a false alarm.'

'Sleep?' I said.

He clicked his fingers and one entire wall of the room whisked back to reveal a sterile, machine-filled chamber.

I studied its contents.

There was a reefersleep casket of the kind Forqueray and his ilk used aboard their ships, attended by numerous complicated hunks of gleaming green support machinery. By use of such a casket, one might prolong the four hundred-odd years of a normal human lifespan by many centuries, though reefersleep was not without its risks.

'I spent a century and a half in that contraption,' he said. 'Waking every fifteen or twenty years whenever a report trickled in from one of the envoys. Waking is the worst part. It feels like you're made of glass; as if the next movement you make – the next breath you take – will cause you to shatter into a billion pieces. It always passes, and you always forget it an hour later, but it's never easier the next time.' He shuddered visibly. 'In fact, sometimes I think it gets harder each time.'

'Then your equipment needs servicing,' Forqueray said dismissively. I suspected it was bluff. Ultras often wore a lock of braided hair for every crossing they had made across interstellar space and survived all the myriad misfortunes which might befall a ship. But that braid also symbolised every occasion on which they had been woken from the dead, at the end of the journey.

They felt the pain as fully as Childe did, even if they were not willing to admit it.

'How long did you spend awake each time?' I asked.

'No more than thirteen hours. That was usually more than sufficient to tell if the message was interesting or not. I'd allow myself one or two hours to catch up on the news; what was going on in the wider universe. But I had to be disciplined. If I'd stayed awake longer, the attraction of returning to city life would have become overwhelming. That room began to seem like a prison.'

'Why?' I asked. 'Surely the subjective time must have passed very quickly?'

'You've obviously never spent any time in reefersleep, Richard. There's no consciousness when you're frozen, granted – but the transitions to and from the cold state can seem like an eternity, crammed with strange dreams.'

'But you hoped the rewards would be worth it?'

Childe nodded. 'And, indeed, they may well have been. I was last woken six months ago, and I've not returned to the chamber since. Instead, I've spent that time gathering together the resources and the people for a highly unusual expedition.'

Now he made the table change its projection, zooming in on one particular star.

'I won't bore you with catalogue numbers. Suffice to say that this is a system which no one around this table – with the possible exception of Forqueray – is likely to have heard of. There've never been any human colonies there, and no crewed vessel has ever passed within three light-years of it. At least, not until recently.'

The view zoomed in again; enlarging with dizzying speed.

A planet swelled up to the size of a skull, suspended above the table.

It was hued entirely in shades of grey and pale rust, cratered and gouged here and there by impacts and what must have been very ancient weathering processes. Though there was a suggestion of a wisp of atmosphere – a smoky blue halo encircling the planet – and though there were icecaps at either pole, the world looked neither habitable nor inviting.

'Cheerful-looking place, isn't it?' Childe said. 'I call it Golgotha.'

'Nice name,' Celestine said.

'But not, unfortunately, a very nice planet.' Childe made the view enlarge again, so that we were skimming the world's bleak, seemingly lifeless surface. 'Pretty dismal, to be honest. It's about the same size as Yellowstone, receiving about the same amount of sunlight from its star. Doesn't have a moon. Surface gravity's close enough to one gee that you won't know the difference once you're suited up. A thin carbon dioxide atmosphere, and no sign that anything's ever evolved there. Plenty of radiation hitting the surface, but that's about your only hazard, and one we can easily deal with. Golgotha's tectonically dead, and there haven't been any large impacts on her surface for a few million years.'

'Sounds boring,' Hirz said.

'And it very probably is, but that isn't the point. You see, there's something on Golgotha.'

'What kind of something?' Celestine asked.

'That kind,' Childe said.

It came over the horizon.

It was tall and dark, its details indistinct. That first view of it was like the first glimpse of a cathedral's spire through morning fog. It tapered as it rose, constricting to a thin neck before flaring out again into a bulb-shaped finial, which in turn tapered to a needle-sharp point.

Though it was impossible to say how large the thing was, or what it was made of, it was very obviously a structure, as opposed to a peculiar biological or mineral formation. On Grand Teton, vast numbers of tiny single-celled organisms conspired to produce the slime towers which were that world's most famous natural feature, and while those towers reached impressive heights and were often strangely shaped, they were unmistakably the products of unthinking biological processes rather than conscious design. The structure on Golgotha was too symmetric for that, and entirely too solitary. If it had been a living thing, I would have expected to see others like it, with evidence of a supporting ecology of other organisms.

Even if it were a fossil, millions of years dead, I could not believe that there was just one on the whole planet.

No. The thing had most definitely been put there.

'A structure?' I asked Childe.

'Yes. Or a machine. It isn't easy to decide.' He smiled. 'I call it Blood Spire. Almost looks innocent, doesn't it? Until you look closer.'

We spun round the Spire, or whatever it was, viewing it from all directions. Now that we were closer, it was clear that the thing's surface was densely-detailed; patterned and textured with geometrically-complex forms, around which snaked intestinal tubes and branching, veinlike bulges. The effect was to make me undermine my earlier certainty that the thing was non-biological.

Now it looked like some sinewy fusion of animal and machine; something that might have appealed in its grotesquerie to Childe's demented uncle.

'How tall is it?' I asked.

'Two hundred and fifty metres,' Childe said.

I saw that now there were tiny glints on Golgotha's surface; almost like metallic flakes which had fallen from the side of the structure.

'What are those?' I said.

'Why don't I show you,' Childe said.

He enlarged the view still further, until the glints resolved into distinct shapes.

They were people.

Or – more accurately – the remains of what had once been people. It was impossible to say how many there had been. All had been mutilated in some fashion; crushed or pruned or bisected; the tattered ruins of their spacesuits still visible in one or two places. Severed parts accompanied the bodies, often several tens of metres from the rightful owner.

It was as if they had been flung away in a fit of temper.

'Who were they?' Forqueray asked.

'A crew who happened to slow down in this system to make shield repairs,' Childe said. 'Their captain was called Argyle. They chanced upon the Spire and started exploring it, believing it to contain something of immense technological value.'

'And what happened to them?'

'They went inside in small teams, sometimes alone. Inside the Spire they passed through a series of challenges, each of which was harder than the last. If they made a mistake, the Spire punished them. The punishments were initially mild, but they became steadily more brutal. The trick was to know when to admit defeat.'

I leaned forward. 'How do you know all this?'

'Because Argyle survived. Not long, admittedly, but long enough for my machine to get some sense out of him. It had been on Golgotha the whole time, you see – watching Argyle's arrival, hiding and recording them as they confronted the Spire. And it watched him crawl out of the Spire, shortly before the last of his colleagues was ejected.'

'I'm not sure I'm prepared to trust either the testimony of a machine or a dying man,' I said.

'You don't have to,' Childe answered. 'You need only consider the evidence of your eyes. Do you see those tracks in the dust? They all lead into the Spire, and there are almost none leading to the bodies.'

'Meaning what?' I said.

'Meaning that they got inside, the way Argyle claimed. Observe also the way the remains are distributed. They're not all at the same distance from the Spire. They must have been ejected from different heights, suggesting that some got closer to the summit than others. Again – it accords with Argyle's story.'

With a sinking feeling of inevitability I saw where this was heading. 'And you want us to go there and find out what it was they were so interested in. Is that it?'

He smiled. 'You know me entirely too well, Richard.'

'I thought I did. But you'd have to be quite mad to want to go anywhere near that thing.'

'Mad? Possibly. Or simply very, very curious. The question is . . .' He paused and leaned across the table to refill my glass, all the while maintaining eye contact. 'Which are you?'

'Neither,' I said.

* * *

But Childe could be persuasive. A month later I was frozen aboard Forqueray's ship.

two

We reached orbit around Golgotha.

Thawed from reefersleep we convened for breakfast, riding a travel pod upship to the lighthugger's meeting room.

Everyone was there, including Trintignant and Forqueray, the latter inhaling from the same impressive array of flasks, retorts and spiralling tubes he had brought with him to Yellowstone. Trintignant had not slept with the rest of us, but seemed none the worse for wear. He had, Childe said, his own rather specialised plumbing requirements, incompatible with standard reefersleep systems.

'Well, how was it?' Childe asked, throwing a comradely arm around my shoulders.

'Every bit as . . . dreadful as I'd been led to expect.' My voice was slurred; sentences taking an age to form in whatever part of my brain it was that handled language. 'Still a bit fuzzy.'

'Well, we'll soon fix that. Trintignant can synthesize a medichine infusion to pep up those neural functions, can't you, Doctor?'

Trintignant looked at me with his handsome, immobile mask of a face. 'It would be no trouble at all, my dear fellow . . .'

'Thanks.' I steadied myself; my mind crawling with half-remembered images of the botched cybernetic experiments which had earned Trintignant his notoriety. The thought of him pumping tiny machines into my skull made my skin crawl. 'But I'll pass on that for now. No offence intended.'

'And absolutely none taken.' Trintignant gestured towards a vacant chair. 'Come. Sit with us and join in the discussion. The topic, rather interestingly, is the dreams some of us experienced on the way here.'

'Dreams . . . ?' I said. 'I thought it was just me. Are you saying I wasn't the only one?'

'No,' Hirz said. 'You weren't the only one. I was on a moon in one of them. Earth's, I think. And I kept on trying to get inside this alien structure. Fucking thing kept killing me, but I'd always keep going back inside, like I was being brought back to life each time just for that.'

'I had the same dream,' I said, wonderingly. 'And there was another dream in which I was inside some kind of . . .' I halted, waiting for the words to assemble in my head. 'Some kind of underground tomb. I remember being chased down a corridor by an enormous stone ball which was going to roll over me.'

Hirz nodded. 'The dream with the hat, right?'

'My God, yes.' I grinned like a madman. 'I lost my hat, and I felt this ridiculous urge to rescue it!'

Celestine looked at me with something between icy detachment and outright hostility. 'I had that one too.'

'Me too,' Hirz said, chuckling. 'But I said fuck the hat. Sorry, but with the kind of money Childe's paying us, buying a new one ain't gonna be my biggest problem.'

An awkward moment followed, for only Hirz seemed at all comfortable about discussing the generous fees Childe had arranged as payment for the expedition. The initial sums had been large enough, but upon our return to Yellowstone we would all receive nine times as much; adjusted to match any inflation which might occur during the time – between sixty and eighty years – which Childe said the journey would span.

Generous, yes.

But I think Childe knew that some of us would have joined him even without that admittedly sweet bonus.

Celestine broke the silence, turning to Hirz. 'Did you have the one about the cubes, too?'

'Christ, yes,' the infiltration specialist said, as if suddenly remembering. 'The cubes. What about you, Richard?'

'Indeed,' I answered, flinching at the memory of that one. I had been one of a party of people trapped inside an endless series of cubic rooms, many of which contained lethal surprises. 'I was cut into pieces by a trap, actually. Diced, if I remember accurately.'

'Yeah. Not exactly on my top ten list of ways to die, either.'

Childe coughed. 'I feel I should apologise for the dreams. They were narratives I fed into your minds – Doctor Trintignant excepted – during the transition to and from reefersleep.'

'Narratives?' I said.

'I adapted them from a variety of sources, thinking they'd put us all in the right frame of mind for what lies ahead.'

'Dying nastily, you mean?' Hirz asked.

'Problem-solving, actually.' Childe served pitch-black coffee as he spoke, as if all that lay ahead of us was a moderately bracing stroll. 'Of course, nothing that the dreams contained is likely to reflect anything that we'll find inside the Spire . . . but don't you feel better for having had them?'

I gave the matter some thought before responding.

'Not exactly, no,' I said.

* * *

Thirteen hours later we were on the surface, inspecting the suits Forqueray had provided for the expedition.

They were sleek white contraptions, armoured, powered and equipped with enough intelligence to fool a roomful of cyberneticians. They enveloped themselves around you, forming a seamless white surface which lent the wearer the appearance of a figurine moulded from soap. The suits quickly learned how you moved, adjusting and anticipating all the time like perfect dance partners.

Forqueray told us that each suit was capable of keeping its occupant alive almost indefinitely; that the suit would recycle bodily wastes in a near-perfect closed cycle, and could even freeze its occupant if circumstances merited such action. They could fly and protect their user against just about any external environment, ranging from a vacuum to the crush of the deepest ocean.

'What about weapons?' Celestine asked, once we had been shown how to command the suits to do our bidding.

'Weapons?' Forqueray asked blankly.

'I've heard about these suits, Captain. They're supposed to contain enough firepower to take apart a small mountain.'

Childe coughed. 'There won't be any weapons, I'm afraid. I asked Forqueray to have them removed from the suits. No cutting tools, either. And you won't be able to achieve as much with brute force as you would with an unmodified suit. The servos won't allow it.'

'I'm not sure I understand. You're handicapping us before we go in?'

'No – far from it. I'm just abiding by the rules that the Spire sets. It doesn't allow weapons inside itself, you see – or anything else that might be used against it, like fusion torches. It senses such things and acts accordingly. It's very clever.'

I looked at him. 'Is this guesswork?'

'Of course not. Argyle already learned this much. No point making exactly the same mistakes again, is there?'

'I still don't get it,' Celestine said, when we had assembled outside the shuttle, standing like so many white soap statuettes. 'Why fight the thing on its own terms at all? There are bound to be weapons on Forqueray's ship we could use from orbit; open it like a carcass.'

'Yes,' Childe said, 'and in the process destroy everything we came this far to learn?'

'I'm not talking about blowing it off the face of Golgotha. I'm just talking about clean, surgical dissection.'

'It won't work. The Spire is a living thing, Celestine. Or at least a machine intelligence many orders of magnitude cleverer than anything we've encountered to date. It won't tolerate violence being used against it. Argyle learned that much.

'Even if it can't defend itself against such attacks – and we don't know that – it will certainly destroy what it contains. We'll still have lost everything.'

'But still . . . no weapons?'

'Not quite,' Childe said, tapping the forehead region of his suit. 'We still have our minds, after all. That's why I assembled this team. If brute force would have been sufficient, I'd have had no need to scour Yellowstone for such fierce intellects.'

Hirz spoke from inside her own, smaller version of the armoured suit. 'You'd better not be taking the piss.'

* * *

'Forqueray?' Childe said. 'We're nearly there now. Put us down on the surface two klicks from the base of the Spire. We'll cross the remaining distance on foot.'

Forqueray obliged; bringing the triangular formation down. Our suits had been slaved to his, but now we regained independent control.

Through the suit's numerous layers of armour and padding I felt the rough texture of the ground beneath my feet. I held up a thickly gauntleted hand and felt the breeze of Golgotha's thin atmosphere caress my palm. The tactile transmission was flawless, and when I moved the suit flowed with me so effortlessly that I had no sense of being encumbered by it. The view was equally impressive, with the suit projecting an image directly into my visual field rather than forcing me to peer through a visor.

A strip along the top of my visual field showed a three-hundred-and-sixty-degree view all around me, and I could zoom in on any part of it almost without thinking. Various overlays – sonar, radar, thermal, gravimetric – could be dropped over the existing visual field with the same ease. If I looked down I could even ask the suit to edit me out of the image, so that I viewed the scene from a disembodied perspective. As we walked along the suit threw traceries of light across the scenery; an etchwork of neon which would now and then coalesce around an odd-shaped rock or peculiar pattern of ground markings. After several minutes of this I had adjusted the suit's alertness threshold to what I felt was a useful level of protectivity; neither too watchful nor too complacent.

Childe and Forqueray had taken the lead on the ground. They would have been difficult to distinguish, but my suit had partially erased their suits, so that they seemed to walk unprotected save for a ghostly second skin. When they looked at me they would perceive the same consensual illusion.

Trintignant followed a little way behind, moving with the automaton-like stiffness I had now almost grown accustomed to.

Celestine followed, with me a little to her stern.

Hirz brought up the rear; small and lethal and – now that I knew her a little better – quite unlike any of the few children I had ever met.

And ahead – rising, ever rising – was the thing we had come all this way to best.

It had been visible, of course, long before we set down. The thing was a quarter of a kilometre high, after all. But I think we had all chosen to ignore it; to map it out of our perceptions, until we were much closer. It was only now that we were allowing those mental shields to collapse; forcing our imaginations to confront the fact of the tower's existence.

Huge and silent, it daggered into the sky.

It was much as Childe had shown us, except that it seemed infinitely more massive; infinitely more present. We were still a quarter of a kilometre from the thing's base, and yet the flared top – the bulb-shaped finial – seemed to be leaning back over us; constantly on the point of falling and crushing us. The effect was exacerbated by the occasional high-altitude cloud that passed overhead, writhing in Golgotha's fast, thin jetstreams. The whole tower seemed to be toppling. For a long moment, taking in the immensity of the thing that stood before us – its vast age; its vast, brooding capacity for harm – the idea of trying to reach the summit seemed uncomfortably close to insanity.

Then a small, rational voice reminded me that this was exactly the effect the Spire's builders would have sought.

Knowing that, it was fractionally easier to take a step closer to the base.

* * *

'Well,' Celestine said. 'It looks like we've found Argyle.'

Childe nodded.

'Yes. Or what's left of the poor bastard.'

We had found several body parts by then, but his was the only one that was anywhere near being complete. He had lost a leg inside the Spire, but had been able to crawl to the exit before the combination of bleeding and asphyxiation killed him. It was here – dying – that he had been interviewed by Childe's envoy, which would only then have emerged from its hiding place.

Perhaps he had imagined himself in the presence of a benevolent steel angel.

He was not well-preserved. There was no bacterial life on Golgotha, and nothing that could be charitably termed weather, but there were savage dust-storms, and these must have intermittently covered and revealed the body, scouring it in the process. Parts of his suit were missing, and his helmet had cracked open, exposing his skull. Papery sheets of skin adhered to the bone here and there, but not enough to suggest a face.

Childe and Forqueray regarded the corpse uneasily, while Trintignant knelt down and examined it in more detail. A float-cam belonging to the Ultra floated around, observing the scene with goggling arrays of tightly-packed lenses.

'Whatever took his leg off did it cleanly,' the Doctor reported, pulling back the tattered layers of the man's suit fabric to expose the stump. 'Witness how the bone and muscle have been neatly severed along the same plane, like a geometric slice through a platonic solid? I would speculate that a laser was responsible for this, except that I see no sign of cauterization. A high-pressure water-jet might have achieved the same precision of cut, or even an extremely sharp blade.'

'Fascinating, Doc,' Hirz said, kneeling down next to him. 'I'll bet it hurt like fuck, too, wouldn't you?'

'Not necessarily. The degree of pain would depend acutely on the manner in which the nerve ends were truncated. Shock does not seem to have been the primary agent in this man's demise.' Doctor Trintignant fingered the remains of a red fabric band a little distance above the end of the leg. 'Nor was the blood loss as rapid as might have been expected given the absence of cauterisation. This band was most likely a tourniquet; probably applied from his suit's medical kit. The same kit almost certainly included analgesics.'

'It wasn't enough to save him, though,' Childe said.

'No.' Trintignant stood up, the movement reminding me of an escalator. 'But you must concede that he did rather well, considering the impediments.'

*　*　*

For most of its height Blood Spire was no thicker than a few dozen metres, and considerably narrower just below the bulb-like upper part. But – like a slender chess piece – its lower parts swelled out considerably to form a wide base. That podium-like mass was perhaps fifty metres in diameter; a fifth of the structure's height. From a distance it appeared to rest solidly on the base; a mighty obelisk requiring the deepest of foundations to anchor it to the ground.

But it didn't.

The Spire's base failed to contact the surface of Golgotha at all, but floated above it; spaced by five or six clear metres of air. It was as if someone had constructed a building slightly above the ground, kicked away the stilts, and it had simply stayed there.

We all walked confidently towards the rim and then stopped; none of us immediately willing to step under that overhang.

'Forqueray?' Childe said.

'Yes?'

'Let's see what that drone of yours has to say.'

Forqueray had his float-cam fly under the rim, orbiting the underside of the Spire in a lazily-widening spiral. Now and then it fingered the base with a spray of laser-light, and once or twice even made contact; skittering against the flat surface. Forqueray remained impassive, glancing slightly down as he absorbed the data being sent back to his suit.

'Well?' Celestine said. 'What the hell's keeping it up?'

Forqueray took a step under the rim. 'No fields; not even a minor perturbation of Golgotha's own magnetosphere. No significant alterations in the local gravitational vector, either. And – before we assume more sophistication than is strictly necessary – there are no concealed supports.'

Celestine was silent for a few moments before answering. 'All right. What if the Spire doesn't weigh anything? There's air here; not much of it I'll grant you – but what if the Spire's mostly hollow? There might be enough buoyancy to make the thing float, like a balloon.'

'There isn't,' Forqueray said, opening a fist to catch the cam, which flew into his grasp like a trained kestrel. 'Whatever's above us is solid matter. I can't read its mass, but it's blocking an appreciable cosmic ray flux, and none of our scanning methods can see through it.'

'Forqueray's right,' Childe said. 'But I understand your reluctance to accept this, Celestine. It's perfectly normal to feel a sense of denial.'

'Denial?'

'That what we are confronting is truly alien. But I'm afraid you'll get over it, just the way I did.'

'I'll get over it when I feel like getting over it,' Celestine said, joining Forqueray under the dark ceiling.

She looked up and around, less in the manner of someone admiring a fresco than in the manner of a mouse cowering beneath a boot.

But I knew exactly what she was thinking.

In four centuries of deep space travel there had been no more than glimpses of alien sentience. We had long suspected they were out there somewhere. But that suspicion had grown less fervent as the years passed; world after world revealing only faint, time-eroded traces of cultures that might once have been glorious but which were now utterly destroyed. The Pattern Jugglers were clearly the products of intelligence, but not necessarily intelligent themselves. And – though they had been spread from star to star in the distant past – they did not now depend on any form of technology that we recognised. The Shrouders were little better; secretive minds cocooned inside shells of restructured spacetime.

They had never been glimpsed, and their nature and intentions remained worryingly unclear.

Yet Blood Spire was different.

For all its strangeness; for all that it mocked our petty assumptions about the way matter and gravity should conduct themselves, it was recognisably a manufactured thing. And – I told myself – if it had managed to hang above Golgotha's surface until now, it was extremely unlikely to choose this moment to come crashing down.

I stepped across the threshold, followed by the others.

'Makes you wonder what kind of beings built it,' I said. 'Whether they had the same hopes and fears as us, or whether they were so far beyond us as to seem like Gods.'

'I don't give a shit who built it,' Hirz said. 'I just want to know how to get into the fucking thing. Any bright ideas, Childe?'

'There's a way,' he said.

We followed him, until we stood in a small, nervous huddle under the centre of the ceiling. It had not been visible before, but directly above us was a circle of utter blackness against the mere gloom of the Spire's underside.

'That?' Hirz said.

'That's the only way in,' Childe said. 'And the only way you get out alive.'

I said: 'Roland – how exactly did Argyle and his team get inside?'

'They must have brought something to stand on. A ladder or something.'

I looked around. 'There's no sign of it now, is there?'

'No, and it doesn't matter. We don't need anything like that – not with these suits. Forqueray?'

The Ultra nodded and tossed the float-cam upwards.

It caught flight and vanished into the aperture. Nothing happened for several seconds, other than the occasional stutter of red light from the hole. Then the cam emerged, descending again into Forqueray's hand.

'There's a chamber up there,' Forqueray said. 'Flat-floored, surrounding the hole. It's twenty metres across, with a ceiling just high enough to let us stand.

It's empty. There's what looks like a sealed door leading out of the chamber, into the rest of the Spire.'

'Can we be sure there's nothing harmful in it?' I asked.

'No,' Childe said. 'But Argyle said the first room was safe. We'll just have to take his word on that one.'

'And there's room for all of us up there?'

Forqueray nodded. 'Easily.'

I suppose there should have been more ceremony to the act, but there was no sense of significance, or even foreboding, as we rose into the ceiling. It was like the first casual step onto the tame footslopes of a mountain; unweighted by any sense of the dangers that undoubtedly lay ahead.

Inside it was exactly as Forqueray had described it.

The chamber was dark but the float-cam provided some illumination, and our suits' sensors were able to map out the chamber's shape and overlay this information on our visual fields.

The floor had a metalled quality to it; dented here and there, and the edge where it met the hole was rounded and worn.

I reached down to touch it; feeling a hard, dull alloy which nonetheless seemed as if it would yield given sufficient pressure. Data scrolled onto my visual readout, informing me that the floor had a temperature only one hundred and fifteen degrees above absolute zero. My palm chemosensor reported that the floor was mainly iron, laced with carbon woven into allotropic forms it could not match against any in its experience. There were microscopic traces of almost every other stable isotope in the periodic table, with the odd exception of silver. All of this was inferred, for when the chemosensor attempted to shave off a microscopic layer of the flooring for more detailed analysis, it gave a series of increasingly heated error messages before falling silent.

I tried the chemosensor against part of my own suit.

It had stopped working.

'Fix that,' I instructed my suit, authorising it to divert whatever resources it required to the task.

'Problem, Richard?' asked Childe.

'My suit's damaged. Minor, but annoying. I don't think the Spire was too thrilled about my taking a sample of it.'

'Shit. I probably should have warned you of that. Argyle's lot had the same problem. It doesn't like being cut into, either. I suspect you got off with a polite warning.'

'Generous of it,' I said.

'Be careful, all right?' Childe then told everyone else to disable their chemosensors until told otherwise. Hirz grumbled, but everyone else seemed to accept what had to be done.

In the meantime I continued my survey of the room, counting myself lucky that my suit had not provoked a stronger reaction. The chamber's circular wall was fashioned from what looked like the same hard, dull alloy, devoid of detail except for the point where it framed what was obviously a door, raised a metre above the floor. Three blocky steps led up to the door.

The door itself was one metre wide and perhaps twice that in height.

'Hey,' Hirz said. 'Feel this.'

She was kneeling down, pressing a palm against the floor.

'Careful,' I said. 'I just did that and—'

'I've turned off my chemo-whatsit, don't worry.'

'Then what are you—'

'Why don't you reach down and see for yourself.'

Slowly, we all knelt down and touched the floor. When I had touched it before it had felt as cold and dead as the floor of a crypt, yet that was no longer the case. It was vibrating; as if somewhere not too far from here a mighty engine was shaking itself to pieces; a turbine on the point of breaking loose from its shackles. The vibration rose and fell in throbbing waves. Once every thirty seconds or so it reached a kind of crescendo, like a great slow inhalation.

'It's alive,' Hirz said.

'It wasn't like that just now.'

'I know.' Hirz turned and looked at me. 'The fucking thing just woke up, that's why. It knows we're here.'

three

I moved to the door and studied it properly for the first time.

Its proportions were reassuringly normal, requiring only that we stoop down slightly to step through. But for now the door was sealed by a smooth sheet of metal, which would presumably slide across once we had determined how to open it. The only guidance came from the door's thick metal frame, which was inscribed with faint geometric markings.

I had not noticed them before.

The markings were on either side of the door, on the vertical members of the frame. Beginning from the bottom on the left-hand side, there was a dot – it was too neatly circular to be accidental – a flat-topped equilateral triangle, a pentagon and then a heptagonal figure. On the right-hand side there were three more figures with eleven, thirteen and twenty sides respectively.

'Well?' Hirz was looking over my shoulder. 'Any bright ideas?'

'Prime numbers,' I said. 'At least, that's the simplest explanation I can think of. The number of vertices of the shapes on the left-hand frame are the first four primes: one, three, five and seven.'

'And on the other frame?'

Childe answered for me. 'The eleven-sided figure is the next one in the sequence. Thirteen's one prime too high, and twenty isn't a prime at all.'

'So you're saying if we choose eleven, we win?' Hirz reached out her hand, ready to push her hand against the lowest figure on the right, which she could reach without ascending the three steps. 'I hope the rest of the tests are this simp—'

'Steady, old girl.' Childe had caught her wrist. 'Mustn't be too hasty. We shouldn't do anything until we've arrived at a consensus. Agreed?'

Hirz pulled back her hand. 'Agreed . . .'

It only took a few minutes for everyone to agree that the eleven-sided figure was the obvious choice. The only one who did not immediately accede was Celestine, who looked long and hard at the right-hand frame before concurring with the original choice.

'I just want to be careful, that's all,' she said. 'We can't assume anything. They might think from right to left, so that the figures on the right form the sequence which those on the left are supposed to complete. Or they might think diagonally, or something even less obvious.'

Childe nodded. 'And the obvious choice might not always be the right one. There might be a deeper sequence – something more elegant – which we're just not seeing. That's why I wanted Celestine along. If anyone'll pick out those subtleties, it's her.'

She turned to him. 'Just don't put too much faith in whatever gifts the Jugglers might have given me, Childe.'

'I won't. Unless I have to.' Then he turned to the infiltration specialist, still standing by the frame. 'Hirz – you may go ahead.'

She reached out and touched the frame, covering the eleven-sided figure with her palm.

After a heart-stopping pause there was a clunk, and I felt the floor vibrate even more strongly than it had before. Ponderously, the door slid aside, revealing another dark chamber.

We all looked around, assessing each other.

Nothing had changed; none of us had suffered any sudden, violent injuries.

'Forqueray?' Childe said.

The Ultra knew what he meant. He tossed the float-cam through the open doorway and waited several seconds until it flew back into his grasp like an obedient tennis-ball.

'Another metallic chamber, considerably smaller than this one. The floor is level with the door, so we'll have gained a metre or so in height. There's another raised door on the opposite side, again with markings. Other than that, I don't see anything except bare metal.'

'What about the other side of *this* door?' Childe said. 'Are there markings on it as well?'

'Nothing that the drone could make out.'

'Then let me be the guinea pig. I'll step through and we'll see what happens. I'm assuming that even if the door seals behind me, I'll still be able to open it. Argyle said the Spire didn't prevent anyone from leaving provided they hadn't attempted to access a new room.'

'Try it and see,' Hirz said. 'We'll wait on this side. If the door shuts on you, we'll give you a minute and then we'll open it ourselves.'

Childe walked up the three steps and across the threshold. He paused, looked around and then turned back to face us, looking down on us now.

Nothing had happened.

'Looks like the door stays open for now. Who wants to join me?'

'Wait,' I said. 'Before we all cross over – shouldn't we take a look at the problem? We don't want to be trapped in there if it's something we can't solve.'

Childe walked over to the far door. 'Good thinking. Forqueray – pipe my visual field through to the rest of the team, will you?'

'Done.'

We saw what Childe was seeing, his gaze tracking along the doorframe. It looked much like the one we had just solved, except that the markings were different. Four unfamiliar shapes were inscribed on the left side of the door, spaced vertically. Each of the shapes was composed of four rectangular elements of differing sizes, butted together in varying configurations. Childe then looked at the other side of the door. There were four more shapes on the right; superficially similar to those we had already seen.

'Definitely not a geometric progression,' Childe said.

'No. Looks more like a test of conservation of symmetry through different translations,' Celestine said, her voice barely a murmur. 'The lowest three shapes on the left have just been rotated through an integer number of right angles, giving their corresponding forms on the right. But the top two shapes aren't rotationally symmetric. They're mirror images, plus a rotation.'

'So we press the top right shape, right?'

'Could be. But the left one's just as valid.'

Hirz said: 'Yeah. But only if we ignore what the last test taught us. Whoever the suckers were that made this thing, they think from left to right.'

Childe raised his hand above the right-side shape. 'I'm prepared to press it.'

'Wait.' I climbed the steps and walked over the threshold, into the same room as Childe. 'I don't think you should be in here alone.'

He looked at me with something resembling gratitude. None of the others had stepped over yet, and I wondered if I would have done so had Childe and I not been old friends.

'Go ahead and press it,' I said. 'Even if we get it wrong, the punishment's not likely to be too severe at this stage.'

He nodded and palmed the right-side symbol.

Nothing happened.

'Maybe the left-side . . . ?'

'Try it. It can't hurt. We've obviously done *something* wrong already.'

Childe moved over and palmed the other symbol on the top row.

Nothing.

I gritted my teeth. 'All right. Might as well try one of the ones we definitely know is wrong. Are you ready for that?'

He glanced at me and nodded. 'I didn't go to the hassle of bringing in Forqueray just for the free ride, you know. These suits are built to take a lot of crap.'

'Even alien crap?'

'About to find out, aren't we.'

He moved to palm one of the lower symmetry pairs.

I braced myself, unsure what to expect when we made a deliberate error, wondering even if the Spire's punishment code would apply in such a case. After all, what was clearly the correct choice had elicited no response, so what was the sense in being penalised for making the wrong one?

He palmed the shape; still nothing happened.

'Wait,' Celestine said, joining us. 'I've had an idea. Maybe it won't respond – positively or negatively – until we're all in the same room.'

'Only one way to find out,' Hirz said, joining her.

Forqueray and Trintignant followed.

When the last of them had crossed the threshold, the rear door – the one we had all come through – slid shut. There were no markings on it, but nothing that Forqueray did made it open.

Which, I supposed, made a kind of sense. We had committed to accepting the next challenge now; the time for dignified retreats had passed. The thought was not a pleasant one. This room was smaller than the last one, and the environment was suddenly a lot more claustrophobic.

We were almost standing shoulder to shoulder.

'You know, I think the first chamber was just a warm-up,' Celestine said. 'This is where it starts getting more serious.'

'Just press the fucking thing,' Hirz said.

Childe did as he was told. As before, there was an uncomfortable pause which probably only lasted half a second, but which seemed abysally longer; as if our fates were being weighed by distant judicial machinery. Then thumps and vibrations signalled the opening of the door.

Simultaneously, the door behind us had opened again. The route out of the Spire was now clear again.

'Forqueray . . .' Childe said.

The Ultra tossed the float-cam into the darkness.

'Well?'

'This is getting a tiny bit monotonous. Another chamber, another door, another set of markings.'

'No booby-traps?'

'Nothing the drone can resolve, which I'm afraid isn't saying much.'

'I'll go in this time,' Celestine said. 'No one follow me until I've checked out the problem, understood?'

'Fine by me,' Hirz said, glancing back at the escape route.

Celestine stepped into the darkness.

I decided that I was no longer enjoying the illusion of seeing everyone as if we were not wearing suits – we all looked far too vulnerable, suddenly – and ordered my own to stop editing my visual field to that extent. The transition was smooth; suits forming around us like thickening auras. Only the helmet parts remained semi-transparent, so that I could still identify who was who without cumbersome visual tags.

'It's another mathematical puzzle,' Celestine said. 'Still fairly simple. We're not really being stretched yet.'

'Yeah, well I'll settle for not being really stretched,' Hirz said.

Childe looked unimpressed. 'Are you certain of the answer?'

'Trust me,' Celestine said. 'It's perfectly safe to enter.'

* * *

This time the markings looked more complicated, and at first I feared that Celestine had been over-confident.

On the left-hand side of the door – extending the height of the frame – was a vertical strip marked by many equally-spaced horizontal grooves, in the manner of a ruler. But some of the cleanly-cut grooves were deeper than the others. On the other side of the door was a similar ruler, but with a different arrangement of deeper grooves, not lining up with any of those on the right.

I stared at the frame for several seconds, thinking the solution would click into my mind; willing myself back into the problem-solving mode that had once seemed so natural. But the pattern of grooves refused to snap into any neat mathematical order.

I glanced at Childe, seeing no greater comprehension in his face.

'Don't you see it?' Celestine said.

'Not quite,' I said.

'There are ninety-one grooves, Richard.' She spoke with the tone of a teacher who had begun to lose patience with a tardy pupil. 'Now, counting from the bottom, the following grooves are deeper than the rest: the third, the sixth, the tenth, the fifteenth . . . shall I continue?'

'I think you'd better,' Childe said.

'There are seven other deep grooves, concluding with the ninety-first. You must see it now, surely. Think geometrically.'

'I am,' I said testily.

'Tell us, Celestine,' Childe said, between what was obviously gritted teeth.

She sighed. 'They're triangular numbers.'

'Fine,' Childe said. 'But I'm not sure I know what a triangular number is.'

Celestine glanced at the ceiling for a moment, as if seeking inspiration. 'Look. Think of a dot, will you?'

'I'm thinking,' Childe said.

'Not surround that dot by six neighbours, all the same distance from each other. Got that?'

'Yes.'

'Now keep on adding dots, extending out in all directions, as far as you can imagine – each dot having six neighbours.'

'With you so far.'

'You should have something resembling a Chinese chequer board. Now concentrate on a single dot again, near the middle. Draw a line from it to one of its six neighbours, and then another line to one of the two dots either side of the neighbour you just chose. Then join the two neighboring dots. What have you a got?'

'An equilateral triangle.'

'Good. That's three taken care of. Now imagine that the triangle's sides are twice as long. How many dots are connected together now?'

Childe answered after only a slight hesitation. 'Six. I think.'

'Yes.' Celestine turned to me. 'Are you following, Richard?'

'More or less . . .' I said, trying to hold the shapes in my head.

'Then we'll continue. If we triple the size of the triangle, we link together nine dots along the sides, with an additional dot in the middle. That's ten.

Continue – with a quadruple-sized triangle – and we hit fifteen.' She paused, giving us time to catch up. 'There are eight more; up to ninety-one, which has thirteen dots along each side.'

'The final groove,' I said, accepting for myself that whatever this problem was, Celestine had probably understood it.

'But there are only seven deep grooves in that interval,' she continued. 'That means all we have to do is identify the groove on the right which corresponds to the missing triangular number.'

'All?' Hirz said.

'Look, it's simple. I *know* the answer, but you don't have to take my word for it. The triangles follow a simple sequence. If there are N dots in the lower row of the last triangle, the next one will have N plus one more. Add one to two and you've got three. Add one to two to three, and you've got six. One to two to three to four, and you've got ten. Then fifteen, then twenty-one . . .' Celestine paused. 'Look, it's senseless taking my word for it. Graph up a chequer board display on your suits – Forqueray, can you oblige? – and start arranging dots in triangular patterns.'

We did. It took a quarter of an hour, but after that time we had all – Hirz included – convinced ourselves by brute force that Celestine was right. The only missing pattern was for the fifty-five dot case, which happened to coincide with one of the deep grooves on the right side of the door.

It was obvious, then. That was the one to press.

'I don't like it,' Hirz said. 'I see it now . . . but I didn't see it until it was pointed out to me. What if there's another pattern none of us are seeing?'

Celestine looked at her coldly. 'There isn't.'

'Look, there's no point arguing,' Childe said. 'Celestine saw it first, but we always knew she would. Don't feel bad about it, Hirz. You're not here for your mathematical prowess. Nor's Trintignant, nor's Forqueray.'

'Yeah, well remind me when I can do something useful,' Hirz said.

Then she pushed forward and pressed the groove on the right side of the door.

* * *

Progress was smooth and steady for the next five chambers. The problems to be solved grew harder, but after consultation the solution was never so esoteric that we could not all agree on it. As the complexity of the tasks increased, so did the area taken up by the frames, but other than that there was no change in the basic nature of the challenges. We were never forced to proceed more quickly than we chose, and the Spire always provided a clear route back to the exit every time a doorway had been traversed. The door immediately behind us would only seal once we had all entered the room where the current problem lay, which meant that we were able to assess any given problem before committing ourselves to its solution. To convince ourselves that we were indeed able to leave, we had Hirz go back the way we had come in. She was able to return to the first room unimpeded – the rear-facing doors opened and closed in sequence to allow her to pass – and then make her way back to the rest of us by using the entry codes we had already discovered.

But something she said upon her return disturbed us.

'I'm not sure if it's my imagination or not . . .'

'What?' Childe snapped.

'I think the doorways are getting narrower. And lower. There was definitely more headroom at the start than there is now. I guess we didn't notice when we took so long to move from room to room.'

'That doesn't make much sense,' Celestine said.

'As I said, maybe I imagined it.'

But we all knew she had done no such thing. On the last two times when I had stepped across a door's threshold my suit had bumped against the frame. I had thought nothing of it at the time – putting it down to carelessness – but that had evidently been wishful thinking.

'I wondered about the doors already,' I said. 'Doesn't it seem a little convenient that the first one we met was just the right size for us? It could have come from a human building.'

'Then why are they getting smaller?' Childe asked.

'I don't know. But I think Hirz is right. And it does worry me.'

'Me too. But it'll be a long time before it becomes a problem.' Childe turned to the Ultra. 'Forqueray – do the honours, will you?'

I turned and looked at the chamber ahead of us. The door was open now, but none of us had yet stepped across the threshold. As always we waited for Forqueray to send his float-cam snooping ahead of us, establishing that the room contained no glaring pitfalls.

Forqueray tossed the float-cam though the open door.

We saw the usual red stutters as it swept the room in visible light. 'No surprises,' Forqueray said, in the usual slightly absent tone he adopted when reporting the cam's findings. 'Empty metallic chamber . . . only slightly smaller than one we're standing in now. A door at the far end with a frame that extends half a metre out on either side. Complex inscriptions this time, Celestine.'

'I'll cope, don't you worry.'

Forqueray stepped a little closer to the door, one arm raised with his palm open. His expression remained calm as he waited for the drone to return to its master. We all watched, and then – as the moment elongated towards seconds – began to suspect that something was wrong.

The room beyond was utterly dark; no stammering flashes now.

'The cam . . .' Forqueray said.

Childe's gaze snapped to the Ultra's face. 'Yes?'

'It isn't transmitting anymore. I can't detect it.'

'That isn't possible.'

'I'm telling you.' The Ultra looked at us, his fear not well concealed. 'It's gone.'

* * *

Childe moved into the darkness, through the frame.

Just as I was admiring his bravery I felt the floor shudder. Out of the corner of my eye I saw a flicker of rapid motion, like an eyelid closing.

The rear door – the one that led out of the chamber in which we were standing – had just slammed shut.

Celestine fell forward. She had been standing in the gap.

'No . . .' she said, hitting the ground with a detectable thump.

'Childe!' I shouted, unnecessarily. 'Stay where you are – something just happened.'

'What?'

'The door behind us closed on Celestine. She's been injured . . .'

I was fearing the worst; that the door might have snipped off an arm or a leg as it closed – but it was, mercifully, not that serious. The door had damaged the thigh of her suit – grazing an inch of its armour away as it closed – but Celestine herself had not been injured. The damaged part was still airtight, and the suit's mobility and critical systems remained unimpaired.

Already, in fact, the self-healing mechanisms were coming into play, repairing the wound.

She sat up on the ground. 'I'm OK. The impact was hard, but I don't think I've done any permanent damage.'

'You sure?' I said, offering her a hand.

'Perfectly sure,' she said, standing up without my assistance.

'You were lucky,' Trintignant said. 'You were only partly blocking the door. Had that not been the case, I suspect your injuries would have been more interesting.'

'What happened?' Hirz asked.

'Childe must have triggered it,' Forqueray said. 'As soon as he stepped into the other room, it closed the rear door.' The Ultra stepped closer to the aperture. 'What happened to my float-cam, Childe?'

'I don't know. It just isn't here. There isn't even a trace of debris, and there's no sign of anything that could have destroyed it.'

The silence that followed was broken by Trintignant's piping tones. 'I believe this makes a queer kind of sense.'

'You do, do you?' I said.

'Yes, my dear fellow. It is my suspicion that the Spire has been tolerating the drone until now – lulling us, if you will, into a false sense of security. Yet now the Spire has decreed that we must discard that particular mental crutch. It will no longer permit us to gain any knowledge of the contents of a room until one of us steps into it. And at that moment it will prevent any of us *leaving* until we have solved that problem.'

'You mean it's changing the rules as it goes along?' Hirz asked.

The Doctor turned his exquisite silver mask towards her. 'Which rules did you have in mind, Hirz?'

'Don't fuck with me, Doc. You know what I mean.'

Trintignant touched a finger to the chin of his helmet. 'I confess I do not. Unless it is your contention that the Spire has at some point agreed to bind by a set of strictures, which I would ardently suggest is far from the case.'

'No,' I said. 'Hirz is right, in one way. There have been rules. It's clear that it won't tolerate us inflicting physical harm against it. And it won't allow us to enter a room until we've all stepped into the preceding one. I think those are pretty fundamental rules.'

'Then what about the drone, and the door?' asked Childe.

'It's like Trintignant said. It tolerated us playing outside the rules until now, but we shouldn't have assumed that was always going to be the case.'

Hirz nodded. 'Great. What else is it tolerating now?'

'I don't know.' I managed a thin smile. 'I suppose the only way to find out is to keep going.'

* * *

We passed through another eight rooms, taking between one and two hours to solve each.

There had been one or two occasions when we had debated whether to continue, with Hirz usually the least keen of us, but so far the problems had not become insurmountably difficult. And we were making a kind of progress. Mostly the rooms were blank, but every now and then there was a narrow, trellised window, panelled in stained sheets of what was obviously a substance very much more resilient than glass or even diamond. Sometimes these windows opened only into gloomy interior spaces, but on one occasion were were able to look outside, able to sense some of the height we had attained. Forqueray, who had had been monitoring our journey with an inertial compass and gravitometer, confirmed that we had ascended at least fifteen vertical metres since the first chamber. That almost sounded impressive, until one considered the several hundred meters of Spire that undoubtedly lay above us. Another few hundred rooms, each posing a challenge more testing than the last?

And the doors were definitely getting smaller.

It was an effort to squeeze through now, and while the suits were able to reshape themselves to some extent, there was a limit to how compact they could become.

It had taken us sixteen hours to reach this point. At this rate it would take many days to get anywhere near the summit.

But none of us had imagined that this would be over quickly.

'Tricky,' Celestine said, after studying the latest puzzle for many minutes. 'I think I see what's going on here, but . . .'

Childe looked at her. 'You think, or you know?'

'I mean what I said. It's not easy, you know. Would you rather I let someone else take first crack at it?'

I put a hand on Celestine's arm and spoke to her privately. 'Easy. He's just anxious, that's all.'

She brushed my hand away. 'I didn't ask you to defend me, Richard.'

'I'm sorry. I didn't mean . . .'

'Never mind.' Celestine switched off private mode and addressed the group. 'I think these markings are shadows. Look.'

By now we had all become reasonably adept at drawing figures using our suits' visualisation systems. These sketchy hallucinations could be painted on any surface, apparently visible to all.

Celestine – who was the best at this – drew a short red hyphen on the wall.

'See this? A one-dimensional line. Now watch.'

She made the line become a square; splitting into two parallel lines joined at their ends. Then she made the square rotate until it was edge-on again, and all we could see was the line.

'We see it . . .' Childe said.

'You can think of a line as the one-dimensional shadow of a two-dimensional object, in this case a square. Understand?'

'I think we get the gist,' Trintigant said.

Celestine made the square freeze, and then slide diagonally, leaving a copy of itself to which it was joined at the corners. 'Now. We're looking at a two-dimensional figure this time; the shadow of a three-dimensional cube. See how it changes if I rotate the cube, how it elongates and contracts?'

'Yes. Got that,' Childe said, watching the two joined squares slide across each other with a hypnotically smooth motion; only one square visible as the imagined cube presented itself face-on to the wall.

'Well, I think these figures . . .' Celestine sketched a hand an inch over the intricate designs worked into the frame. 'I think what these figures represent are two-dimensional shadows of four-dimensional objects.'

'Fuck off,' Hirz said.

'Look, just concentrate, will you? This one's easy. It's a hypercube. That's the four-dimensional analogue of a cube. You just take a cube and extend it *outwards*; just the same way that you make a cube from a square.' Celestine paused, and for a moment I thought she was going to throw up her hands in despair. 'Look. Look at this.' And then she sketched something on the wall: a cube set inside a slightly larger one, to which it was joined by diagonal lines. 'That's what the three-dimensional shadow of a hypercube would look like. Now all you have to do is collapse that shadow by one more dimension, down to two, to get *this* . . .' And she jabbed at the beguiling design marked on the door.

'I think I see it,' Childe said, without anything resembling confidence.

Maybe I did, too – though I felt the same lack of certainty. Childe and I had certainly taunted each other with higher-dimensional puzzles in our youth, but never had so much depended on an intuitive grasp of those mind-shattering mathematical realms. 'All right,' I said. 'Supposing that *is* the shadow of a tesseract . . . what's the puzzle?'

'This,' Celestine said, pointing to the other side of the door, to what seemed like an utterly different – though no less complex – design. 'It's the same object, after a rotation.'

'The shadow changes that drastically?'

'Start getting used to it, Richard.'

'All right.' I realised she was still annoyed with me for touching her. 'What about the others?'

'They're all four-dimensional objects; relatively simple geometric forms. This one's a 4-simplex; a hypertetrahedon. It's a hyper-pyramid with five tetrahedral faces . . .' Celestine trailed off, looking at us with an odd expression on her face. 'Never mind. The point is, all the corresponding forms on the right should be the shadows of the same polytopes after a simple rotation through higher-dimensional space. But one isn't.'

'Which is?'

She pointed to one of the forms. 'This one.'

'And you're certain of that?' Hirz said. 'Because I'm sure as fuck not.'

Celestine nodded. 'Yes. I'm completely sure of it now.'

'But you can't make any of us see that this is the case?'

She shrugged. 'I guess you either see it or you don't.'

'Yeah? Well maybe we should have all taken a trip to the Pattern Jugglers. Then maybe I wouldn't be about to shit myself.'

Celestine said nothing, but merely reached out and touched the errant figure.

* * *

'There's good news and there's bad news,' Forqueray said, after we had traversed another dozen or so rooms without injury.

'Give us the bad news first,' Celestine said.

Forqueray obliged, with what sounded like the tiniest degree of pleasure. 'We won't be able to get through more than two or three more doors. Not with these suits on.'

There had been no real need to tell us that. It had become crushingly obvious during the last three or four rooms that we were near the limit; that the Spire's subtly-shifting internal architecture would not permit further movement within the bulky suits. It had been an effort to squeeze through the last door, only Hirz oblivious to these difficulties.

'Then we might as well give up,' I said.

'Not exactly.' Forqueray smiled his vampiric smile. 'I said there was good news as well, didn't I?'

'Which is?' Childe said.

'You remember when we sent Hirz back to the beginning, to see if the Spire was going to allow us to leave at any point?'

'Yes,' Childe said. Hirz had not repeated the exercise since, but she had gone back a dozen rooms, and found that the Spire was just as co-operative as it had been before. There had seemed no reason to think she would not have been able to make her way to the exit, had she wished.

'Something bothered me,' Forqueray said. 'When she went back, the Spire opened and closed doors in sequence to allow her to pass. I couldn't see the sense in that. Why not just open all the doors along her route?'

'I confess it troubled me as well,' Trintignant said.

'So I thought about it, and decided there must be a reason not to have all the doors open at once.'

Childe sighed. 'Which was?'

'Air,' Forqueray said.

'You're kidding, aren't you?'

The Ultra shook his head. 'When we began, we were moving in vacuum – or at least through air that was as thin as that on Golgotha's surface. That continued to be the case for the next few rooms. Then it began to change. Very slowly, I'll grant you – but my suit sensors picked up on it immediately.'

Childe pulled a face. 'And it didn't cross your mind to tell any of us about this?'

'I thought it best to wait until a pattern became apparent.' Forqueray glanced at Celestine, whose face was impassive.

'He's right,' Trintignant said. 'I have also become aware of the changing atmospheric conditions. Forqueray has also doubtless noticed that the temperature in each room has been a little warmer than the last. I have extrapolated these trends and arrived at a tentative conclusion. Within two – possibly three – rooms, we will be able to discard our suits and breathe normally.'

'Discard our suits?' Hirz looked at him as if he were insane. 'You have got to be fucking kidding.'

Childe raised a hand. 'Wait a minute. When you said air, Doctor Trintignant, you didn't say it was anything we'd be able to breathe.'

The Doctor's answer was a melodious piped refrain. 'Except it is. The ratios of the various gases are remarkably close to those we employ in our suits.'

'Which isn't possible. I don't remember providing a sample.'

Trintignant dipped his head in a nod. 'Nonetheless, it appears that one has been taken. The mix, incidentally, corresponds to precisely the atmospheric preferences of Ultras. Argyle's expedition would surely have employed a slightly different mix, so it is not simply the case that the Spire has a long memory.'

I shivered.

The thought that the Spire – this vast, breathing thing in which we scurried like rats – had somehow reached inside the hard armour of our suits to snatch a sample of air, without our knowing, made my guts turn cold. It not only knew of our presence, but it knew – intimately – what we were.

It understood our fragility.

As if wishing to reward Forqueray for his observation, the next room contained a substantially thicker atmosphere than any of its predecessors, and was also much warmer. It was not yet capable of supporting life, but one would not have died instantly without the protection of a suit.

The challenge that the room held was by far the hardest, even by Celestine's reckoning. Once again the essence of the task lay in the figures marked on either side of the door, but now these figures were linked by various symbols and connecting loops, like the subway map of a foreign city. We had encountered some of these hieroglyphics before – they were akin to mathematical operators, like the addition and subtraction symbol – but we had never seen so many. And the problem itself was not simply some numerical exercise, but – as far as Celestine could say with any certainty – a problem about topological transformations in four dimensions.

'Please tell me you see the answer immediately,' Childe said.

'I . . .' Celestine trailed off. 'I think I do. I'm just not absolutely certain. I need to think about this for a minute.'

'Fine. Take all the time you want.'

Celestine nodded, and then fell into a reverie which lasted minutes and then tens of minutes. Once or twice she would open her mouth and take a breath of air as if in readiness to speak, and on one or two other occasions she took a promising step closer to the door, but none of these things heralded the sudden, intuitive breakthrough we were all hoping for. She always returned to the same silent, standing posture, and the time dragged on; first an hour and then the better part of two hours.

All this, I thought, before even Celestine had seen the answer.

It might take days if we were all expected to follow her reasoning.

Finally, however, she spoke. 'Yes. I see it.'

Childe was the first to answer. 'Is it the one you thought it was originally?'

'No.'

'Great,' Hirz said.

'Celestine . . .' I said, trying to defuse the situation. 'Do you understand why you made the wrong choice originally?'

'Yes. I think so. It was a trick answer; an apparently correct solution which contained a subtle flaw. And what looked like the clearly wrong answer turned out to be the right one.'

'Right. And you're certain of that?'

'I'm not certain of anything, Richard. I'm just saying this is what I believe the answer to be.'

I nodded. 'I think that's all any of us can honestly expect. Do you think there's any chance of the rest of us following your line of argument?'

Her answer was not immediately forthcoming. 'I don't know. How much do you understand about Kaluza-Klein spaces?'

'Not a vast amount, I have to admit.'

'That's what I feared. I could probably explain my reasoning to some of you, but there'd always be someone who didn't get it . . .' Celestine looked pointedly at Hirz. 'We could be in this bloody room for weeks before any of us grasp the solution. And the Spire may not tolerate that kind of delay.'

'We don't know that,' I cautioned.

'No,' Childe said. 'On the other hand, we can't afford to spend weeks solving every room. There's going to have to come a point where we put our faith in Celestine's judgement. I think that time may have come.'

I looked at him, remembering that his mathematical fluency had always been superior to mine. The puzzles I had set him had seldom defeated him, even if it might takes weeks for his intensely methodical mind to arrive at the solution. Conversely, he had often managed to beat me by setting a mathematical challenge of similar intricacy to the one now facing Celestine. They were not quite equals, I knew, but neither were their abilities radically different. It was just that Celestine would always arrive at the answer with the superhuman speed of a savant.

'Are you saying I should just press it, with no consultation?' Celestine said.

Childe nodded. 'Provided everyone else agrees with me . . .'

It was not an easy decision to make, especially after having navigated so many rooms via such a ruthlessly democratic process. But we all saw the sense, even Hirz coming around to our line of thinking in the end.

'I'm telling you,' she said. 'We get through this door, I'm out of here, money or not.'

'You're giving up?' Childe asked.

'You saw what happened to those poor bastards outside. They must have thought they could keep on solving the next test.'

Childe looked sad but nodded. 'I understand perfectly. But I trust you'll reassess your decision as soon as we're through?'

'Sorry, but my mind's made up. I've had enough of this shit.' Hirz turned to Celestine. 'Put us all out of our misery, will you? Make the choice.'

Celestine looked at each of us in turn. 'Are you ready for this?'

'We are,' Childe said, answering for the group. 'Go ahead.'

Celestine pressed the symbol. There was the usual yawning moment of expectation; a moment that stretched tortuously. We all stared at the door, willing it to begin sliding open.

This time nothing happened.

'Oh God . . .' Hirz began.

Something happened then, almost before she had finished speaking, but it was over almost before we had sensed any change in the room. It was only afterwards – playing back the visual record captured by our suits – that we were able to make any sense of events.

The walls of the chamber – like every room we had passed through, in fact – had appeared totally seamless. But in a flash something emerged from the wall; a rigid, sharp-ended metal rod spearing out at waist-height. It flashed through the air from wall to wall, vanishing like a javelin thrown into water. None of us had time to notice it; let alone react bodily. Even the suits – programmed to move out of the way of obvious moving hazards – were too slow. By the time they began moving, the javelin had been and gone. And if there had been only that one javelin, we might almost have missed it happening at all.

But a second emerged; a fraction of a second after the first, spearing across the room at a slightly different angle.

Forqueray happened to be standing in the way.

The javelin passed through him as if he were made of smoke; its progress unimpeded by his presence. But it dragged behind it a comet-tail of gore, exploding out of his suit where he had been speared, just below the elbow. The pressure in the room was still considerably less than atmospheric.

Forqueray's suit reacted with impressive speed, but it still managed to seem sluggish compared to the javelin.

It assessed the damage that had been inflicted on the arm, aware of how quickly its self-repair systems could work to seal that inch-wide hole, and came to a rapid conclusion. The integrity could be restored, but not before unacceptable blood and pressure loss. Since its duty was always to keep its wearer alive, no matter what the costs, it opted to sever the arm above the wound; hyper-sharp irised blades snicking through flesh and bone in an instant.

All that took place long before any pain signals had a chance to reach his brain. The first thing Forqueray knew of his misfortune was when his arm clanged to his feet.

'I think . . .' he started saying. Hirz dashed over to the Ultra and did her best to support him.

Forqueray's truncated arm ended in a smooth silver iris.

'Don't talk,' Childe said.

Forqueray, who was still standing, looked at his injury with something close to fascination. 'I . . .'

'I said don't talk.' Childe knelt down and picked up the amputated arm, showing the evidence to Forqueray. The hole went right through it, as cleanly-bored as a rifle barrel.

'I'll live,' Forqueray managed.

'Yes, you will,' Trintignant said. 'And you may also count yourself fortunate. Had the projectile pierced your body, rather than one of its extremities, I do not believe we would be having this conversation.'

'You call this fortunate?'

'A wound such as yours can be made good with only trivial intervention. We have all the equipment we need aboard the shuttle.'

Hirz looked around uneasily. 'You think the punishment's over?'

'I think we'd know if it wasn't,' I said. 'That was our first mistake, after all. We can expect things to be a little worse in future, of course.'

'Then we'd better not make any more screw-ups, had we?' Hirz was directing her words at Celestine.

I had expected an angry rebuttal. Celestine would have been perfectly correct to remind Hirz that – had the rest of us been forced to make that choice – our chances of hitting the correct answer would have been a miserable one in six.

But instead Celestine just spoke with the flat, soporific tones of one who could not quite believe she had made such an error.

'I'm sorry . . . I must have . . .'

'Made the wrong decision. Yes.' I nodded. 'And there'll be undoubtedly be others. You did your best, Celestine – better than any of us could have managed.'

'It wasn't good enough.'

'No, but you narrowed the field down to two possibilities. That's a lot better than six.'

'He's right,' Childe said. 'Celestine, don't cut yourself up about this. Without you we wouldn't have got as far as we did. Now go ahead and press the other answer – the one you settled on originally – and we'll get Forqueray back to base camp.'

The Ultra glared at him. 'I'm fine, Childe. I can continue.'

'Maybe you can, but it's still time for a temporary retreat. We'll get that arm looked at properly, and then we'll come back with lightweight suits. We can't carry on much further with these, anyway – and I don't particularly fancy continuing with no armour at all.'

Celestine turned back to the frame. 'I can't promise that this is the right one, either.'

'We'll take that chance. Just hit them in sequence – best choice first – until the Spire opens a route back to the start.'

She pressed the symbol that had been her first choice, before she had analysed the problem more deeply and seen a phantom trap.

As always, Blood Spire did not oblige us with an instant judgement on the choice we had made. There was a moment when all of us tensed, expecting the javelins to come again . . . but this time we were spared further punishment.

The door opened, exposing the next chamber.

We did not step through, of course. Instead, we turned around and made our way back through the succession of rooms we had already traversed, descending all the while, laughing at the childish simplicity of the very earliest puzzles compared to those we had faced before the attack.

As the doors opened and closed in sequence, the air thinned out and the skin of Blood Spire became colder; less like a living thing, more like an ancient, brooding machine. But still that distant, throbbing respiratory vibration rattled the floors – lower now, and slower – the Spire letting us know it was aware of our presence and, perhaps, the tiniest bit disappointed at this turning back.

'All right, you bastard,' Childe said. 'We're retreating, but only for now. We're coming back, understand?'

'You don't have to take it personally,' I said.

'Oh, but I do,' Childe said. 'I take it very personally indeed.'

We reached the first chamber, and then dropped down through what had been the entrance hole. After that, it was just a short flight back to the waiting shuttle.

It was dark outside.

We had been in the Spire for more than nineteen hours.

four

'It'll do,' Forqueray said, tilting his new arm this way and that.

'Do?' Trintignant sounded mortally wounded. 'My dear fellow, it is a work of exquisite craftsmanship; a thing of beauty. It is unlikely that you will see its like again, unless I am called upon to perform a similar procedure.'

We were sitting inside the shuttle, still parked on Golgotha's surface. The ship was a squat, aerodynamically-blunt cylinder which had landed tail-down and then expanded a cluster of eight bubbletents around itself; six for our personal quarters during the expedition; one commons area, and a general medical bay equipped with all the equipment Trintignant needed to do his work. Surprisingly — to me, at least, who admitted some unfamiliarity with these things — the shuttle's fabricators had been more than able to come up with the various cybernetic components that the Doctor required, and the surgical tools at his disposal — glistening, semi-sentient things which moved to his will almost before they were summoned — were clearly more than adequate; state of the art by any reasonable measure.

'Yes, well I'd have rather you'd re-attached my old arm,' Forqueray said, opening and closing the sleek metal gauntlet of his replacement.

'It would have been trivial to do; almost insultingly so,' Trintignant said. 'A new hand could have been cultured and regrafted in a few hours. If that did not appeal to you, I could have programmed your stump to regenerate a hand of its own accord; a perfectly simple matter of stem-cell manipulation. But what would have been the point? You would be very likely to lose it as soon as we suffer our next punishment. Now you will only be losing machinery – a far less traumatic prospect.'

'You're enjoying this,' Hirz said. 'Aren't you?'

'It would be churlish to deny it,' Trintignant said. 'When you have been deprived of willing subjects as long as I have, it seems only natural to take pleasure in those little opportunities for practice that fate sees fit to present.'

Hirz nodded knowingly. She had not heard of Trintignant upon our first meeting, I recalled, but she had lost no time in forming her subsequent opinions of the man. 'Except you won't just stop with a hand, will you? I checked up on you, Doc – after that meeting in Childe's house. I hacked into some of the medical records that the Stoner authorities still haven't declassified, because they're just too damned disturbing. You really went the whole hog, didn't you? Some of the things I saw in those files – your victims – they stopped me from sleeping.'

And yet still she had chosen to come with us, I thought. Evidently the allure of Childe's promised reward outweighed any reservations she might have had about sharing a room with Trintignant. But I wondered about those medical records. Certainly, the publicly released data had contained more than enough atrocities for the average nightmare. It chilled the blood to think that Trintignant's most heinous crimes had never been fully revealed.

'Is it true?' I said. 'Were there really worse things?'

'That depends,' Trintignant said. 'There were subjects upon whom I pushed my experimental techniques further than is generally realised, if that is what you mean. But did I ever approach what I considered were the true limits? No. I was always hindered.'

'Until, perhaps, now,' I said.

The rigid silver mask swivelled to face us all in turn. 'That is as maybe. But please give the following matter some consideration. I can surgically remove all your limbs now, cleanly, with the minimum of complications. The detached members could be put into cryogenic storage, replaced by prosthetic systems until we have completed the task that lies ahead of us.'

'Thanks . . .' I said, looking around at the others. 'But I think we'll pass on that one, Doctor.'

Trintigant offered his palms magnanimously. 'I am at your disposal, should you wish to reconsider.'

* * *

We spent a full day in the shuttle before returning to the Spire. I had been mortally tired, but when I finally slept, it was only to submerge myself in yet more labyrinthine dreams, much like those Childe had pumped into our heads during the reefersleep transition. I woke feeling angry and cheated, and resolved to confront him about it.

But something else snagged my attention.

There was something wrong with my wrist. Buried just beneath the skin was a hard rectangle, showing darkly through my flesh. Turning my wrist this way and that, I admired the object, acutely – and strangely – conscious of its rectilinearity. I looked around me, and felt the same visceral awareness of the other shapes which formed my surroundings. I did not know whether to feel more disturbed at the presence of the alien object under my flesh, or my unnatural reaction to it.

I stumbled groggily into the common quarters of the shuttle, presenting my wrist to Childe, who was sitting there with Celestine.

She looked at me before Childe had a chance to answer. 'So you've got one too,' she said, showing me the similar shape lurking just below her own skin. The shape rhymed – there was no other word for it – with the surrounding panels and extrusions of the commons. 'Um, Richard?' she added.

'I'm feeling a little strange.'

'Blame Childe. He put them there. Didn't you, you lying rat?'

'It's easily removed,' he said, all innocence. 'It just seemed more prudent to implant the devices while you were all asleep anyway, so as not to waste any more time than necessary.'

'It's not just the thing in my wrist,' I said. 'Whatever it is.'

'It's something to keep us awake,' Celestine said, keeping her anger just barely under control. Feeling less myself than ever, I watched the way her face changed shape as she spoke, conscious of the armature of muscle and bone lying just beneath the skin.

'Awake?' I managed.

'A . . . shunt, of some kind,' she said. 'Ultras use them, I gather. It sucks fatigue poisons out of the blood, and puts other chemicals back into the blood to upset the brain's normal sleeping cycle. With one of these you can stay conscious for weeks, with almost no psychological problems.'

I forced a smile, ignoring the sense of wrongness I felt. 'It's the almost part that worries me.'

'Me too.' She glared at Childe. 'But much as I hate the little rat for doing this without my permission, I admit to seeing the sense in it.'

I felt the bump in my wrist again. 'Trintignant's work, I presume?'

'Count yourself lucky he didn't hack your arms and legs off while he was at it.'

Childe interrupted her. 'I told him to install the shunts. We can still catnap, if we have the chance. But these devices will let us stay alert when we need alertness. They're really no more sinister than that.'

'There's something else . . .' I said tentatively. I glanced at Celestine, trying to judge if she felt as oddly as I did. 'Since I've been awake, I've . . . experienced things differently. I keep seeing shapes in a new light. What exactly have you done to me, Childe?'

'Again, nothing irreversible. Just a small medichine infusion . . .'

I tried to keep my temper. 'What sort of medichines?'

'Neural modifiers.' He raised a hand defensively, and I saw the same rectangular bulge under his skin. 'Your brain is already swarming with Demarchist implants and cellular machines, Richard, so why pretend that what I've done is anything more than a continuation of what was already there?'

'What the fuck is he talking about?' said Hirz, who had been standing at the door to the commons for the last few seconds. 'Is it to do with the weird shit I've been dealing with since waking up?'

'Very probably,' I said, relieved that at least I was not going insane. 'Let me guess – heightened mathematical and spatial awareness?'

'If that's what you call it, yeah. Seeing shapes everywhere, and thinking of them fitting together . . .' Hirz turned to look at Childe. Small as she was, she looked easily capable of inflicting injury. 'Start talking, dickhead.'

Childe spoke with quiet calm. 'I put modifiers in your brain, via the wrist shunt. The modifiers haven't performed any radical neural restructuring, but they are suppressing and enhancing certain regions of brain function. The effect – crudely speaking – is to enhance your spatial abilities, at the expense of some less essential functions. What you are getting is a glimpse into the cognitive realms that Celestine inhabits as a matter of routine.' Celestine opened her mouth to speak, but he cut her off with a raised palm. 'No more than a glimpse, no, but I think you'll agree that – given the kinds of challenges the Spire likes to throw at us – the modifiers will give us an edge that we lacked previously.'

'You mean you've turned us all into maths geniuses, overnight?'

'Broadly speaking, yes.'

'Well, that'll come in handy,' Hirz said.

'It will?'

'Yeah. When you try and fit the pieces of your dick back together.'

She lunged for him.

'Hirz, I . . .'

'Stop,' I said, interceding. 'Childe was wrong to do this without our consent, but – given the situation we find ourselves in – the idea makes sense.'

'Whose side are you on?' Hirz said, backing away with a look of righteous fury in her eyes.

'Nobody's,' I said. 'I just want to do whatever it takes to beat the Spire.'

Hirz glared at Childe. 'All right. This time. But you try another stunt like that, and . . .'

But even then it was obvious that Hirz had already come to the conclusion that I had arrived at for myself. That, given what the Spire was likely to test us

with, it was better to accept these machines than ask for them to be flushed
out of our systems.

There was just one troubling thought which I could not quite dismiss.

Would I have welcomed the machines so willingly before they had invaded my head, or were they partly influencing my decision?

I had no idea.

But I decided to worry about that later.

five

'Three hours,' Childe said triumphantly. 'Took us nineteen to reach this point on our last trip through. That has to mean something, doesn't it?'

'Yeah,' Hirz said snidely. 'It means it's a piece of piss when you know the answers.'

We were standing by the door where Celestine had made her mistake the last time. She had just pressed the correct topological symbol and the door had opened to admit us to the chamber beyond, one we had not so far stepped into. From now on we would be facing fresh challenges again, rather than passing through those we had already faced. The Spire, it seemed, was interested in probing the limits of our understanding rather than forcing us to solve permutations of the same basic challenge.

It wanted to break us; not stress us.

More and more I was thinking of it as a sentient thing; inquisitive and patient and – when the mood took it – immensely capable of cruelty.

'What's in there?' Forqueray said.

Hirz had gone ahead into the unexplored room.

'Well fuck me if it isn't another puzzle.'

'Describe it, would you?'

'Weird shape shit, I think.' She was quiet for a few seconds. 'Yeah. Shapes in four dimensions again. Celestine – you wanna take a look at this? I think it's right up your street.'

'Any idea what the nature of the task is?' Celestine asked.

'Fuck, I don't know. Something to do with stretching, I think . . .'

'Topological deformations,' Celestine murmured, before joining Hirz in the chamber.

For a minute or so the two of them conferred, studying the marked doorframe like a pair of discerning art critics.

On the last run through, Hirz and Celestine had shared almost no common ground, but now it was unnerving to see how much Hirz grasped. The machines Childe had pumped into our skulls had improved the mathematical skills of all of us – with the possible exception of Trintignant, whom I suspected had not received the therapy – but the effects had differed in nuance, degree and stability. My mathematical brilliance came in feverish unpredictable waves, like inspiration to a laudanum-addicted poet. Forqueray had gained an astonishing fluency in arithmetic, able to count huge numbers of things simply by looking at them for a moment.

But Hirz's change had been the most dramatic of all, something even Childe seemed taken aback by. On the second pass through the Spire she had been intuiting the answers to many of the problems at a glance, and I was certain that she was not always remembering what the correct answer had been. Now – as we entered the realms of the tasks that had challenged even Celestine – Hirz was still able to perceive the essence of a problem, even if it was beyond her to articulate the details in the formal language of mathematics.

And if she could not yet see her way to selecting the correct answer, she could at least see the one or two answers that were clearly wrong.

'Hirz is right,' Celestine said eventually. 'It's about topological deformations; stretching operations on solid shapes.'

She explained that once again we were seeing the projected shadows of four-dimensional lattices. On the right side of the door, however, the shadows were of the same objects after they had been stretched and squeezed and generally distorted. The problem was to identify the shadow that could only be formed with a shearing, in addition to the other operations.

It took an hour, but eventually Celestine felt certain that she had selected the right answer. Hirz and I attempted to follow her arguments, but the best we could do was agree that two of the other answers would have been wrong. That, at least, was an improvement on anything we would have been capable of before the medichine infusions, but it was only moderately comforting.

Nonetheless, Celestine had selected the right answer. We moved into the next chamber.

'This is as far as we can go with these suits,' Childe said, indicating the door that lay ahead of us. 'It'll be a squeeze, even with the lighter suits – except for Hirz, of course.'

'What's the air like in here?' I asked.

'We could breathe it,' Forqueray said. 'And we'll have to, briefly. But I don't recommend that we do that for any length of time – at least not until we're forced into it.'

'Forced?' Celestine said. 'You think the doors are going to keep getting smaller?'

'I don't know. But doesn't it feel as if this place is forcing us to expose ourselves to it, to make ourselves maximally vulnerable? I don't think it's done with us just yet.' He paused, his suit beginning to remove itself. 'But that doesn't mean we have to humour it.'

I understood his reluctance. The Spire had hurt him, not us.

Beneath the Ultra suits which had brought us this far we had donned as much of the lightweight versions as was possible. They were skintight suits of reasonably modern design, but they were museum pieces compared to the Ultra equipment. The helmets and much of the breathing gear had been impossible to put on, so we had carried the extra parts strapped to our backs. Despite my fears, the Spire had not objected to this, but I remained acutely aware that we did not yet know all the rules under which we played.

It only took three or four minutes to get out of the bulky suits and into the new ones; most of which time was taken up running status checks. For a minute or so, with the exception of Hirz, we had all breathed Spire air.

It was astringent, blood-hot, humid, and smelt faintly of machine oil.

It was a relief when the helmets flooded with the cold, tasteless air of the suits' backpack recyclers.

'Hey.' Hirz, who was the only one still wearing her original suit, knelt down and touched the floor. 'Check this out.'

I followed her, pressing the flimsy fabric of my glove against the surface.

The structure's vibrations rose and fell with increased strength, as if we had excited it by removing our hard protective shells.

'It's like the fucking thing's getting a hard-on,' Hirz said.

'Let's push on,' Childe said. 'We're still armoured – just not as effectively as before – but if we keep being smart, it won't matter.'

'Yeah. But it's the being smart part that worries me. No one smart would come within pissing distance of this fucking place.'

'What does that make you, Hirz?' Celestine asked.

'Greedier than you'll ever know,' she said.

Nonetheless we made good progress for another eleven rooms. Now and then a stained-glass window allowed a view out of Golgotha's surface, which seemed very far below us. By Forqueray's estimate we had gained forty-five vertical metres since entering the Spire. Although two hundred further metres lay ahead – the bulk of the climb, in fact – for the first time it began to seem possible that we might succeed. That, of course, was contingent on several assumptions. One was that the problems, while growing steadily more difficult, would not become insoluble. The other was that the doorways would not continue to narrow now that we had discarded the bulky suits.

But they did.

As always, the narrowing was imperceptible from room to room, but after five or six it could not be ignored. After ten or fifteen more rooms we would again have to scrape our way between them.

And what if the narrowing continued beyond that point?

'We won't be able to go on,' I said. 'We won't fit – even if we're naked.'

'You are entirely too defeatist,' Trintignant said.

Childe sounded reasonable. 'What would you propose, Doctor?'

'Nothing more than a few minor readjustments of the basic human body-plan. Just enough to enable us to squeeze through apertures which would be impassable with our current . . . encumberances.'

Trintignant looked avariciously at my arms and legs.

'It wouldn't be worth it,' I said. 'I'll accept your help after I've been injured, but if you're thinking that I'd submit to anything more drastic . . . well, I'm afraid you're severely mistaken, Doctor.'

'Amen to that,' Hirz said. 'For a while back there, Swift, I really thought this place was getting to you.'

'It isn't,' I said. 'Not remotely. And in any case, we're thinking many rooms ahead here, when we may not be able to get through the next.'

'I agree,' Childe said. 'We'll take it one at a time. Doctor Trintignant – put your wilder fantasies aside, at least for now.'

'Consider them relegated to mere daydreams,' Trintignant said.

So we pushed on.

Now that we had passed through so many doors, it was possible to see that the Spire's tasks came in waves; that there might, for instance, be a series of problems which depended on prime number theory, followed by another series which hinged on the properties of higher-dimensional solids. For several rooms in sequence we were confronted by questions related to tiling patterns – tesselations – while another sequence tested our understanding of cellular automata; odd chequer-board armies of shapes which obeyed simple rules and yet interacted in stunningly complex ways. The final challenge in each set would always be the hardest; the one where we were most likely to make a mistake. We were quite prepared to take three or four hours to pass each door, if that was the time it took to reach certainty – in Celestine's mind at least – that the answer was clear.

And though the shunts were leaching fatigue poisons from our blood, and though the modifiers were enabling us to think with a clarity we had never known before, a kind of exhaustion always crept over us after solving one of the hard challenges. It normally passed in a few tens of minutes, but until then we generally waited before venturing through the now-open door, gathering our strength again.

In those quiet minutes we spoke amongst ourselves, discussing what had happened and what we could expect.

'It's happened again,' I said, addressing Celestine on the private channel.

Her answer came back, no more terse than I had expected. 'What?'

'For a while the rest of us could keep up with you. Even Hirz. Or if not keep up, then at least not lose sight of you completely. But you're pulling ahead again, aren't you? Those Juggler routines are kicking in again.'

She took her time replying. 'You have Childe's medichines.'

'Yes. But all they can do is work with the basic neural topology; suppressing and enhancing activity without altering the layout of the connections in any significant way. And the 'chines are broad-spectrum; not tuned specifically to any one of us.'

Celestine glanced at the only one of us still wearing one of the original suits. 'They worked on Hirz.'

'Must have been luck. But yes, you're right. She couldn't see as far as you, though, even with the modifiers.'

Celestine tapped the shunt in her wrist, still faintly visible beneath the tight-fitting fabric of her suit. 'I took a spike of the modifiers as well.'

'I doubt that it gave you much of an edge over what you already had.'

'Maybe not.' She paused. 'Is there a point to this conversation, Richard?'

'Not really,' I said, stung by her response. 'I just . . .'

'Wanted to talk, yes.'

'And you don't?'

'You can hardly blame me if I don't, can you? This isn't exactly the place for small-talk, let alone with someone who chose to have me erased from his memory.'

'Would it make any difference if I said I was sorry about that?'

I could tell from the tone of her response that my answer had not been quite the one she was expecting. 'It's easy to say you're sorry, now . . . now that it suits you to say as much. That's not how you felt at the time, is it?'

I fumbled for an answer which I felt was not too distant from the truth. 'Would you believe me if I said I'd had you suppressed because I still loved you, and not for any other reason?'

'That's just a little too convenient, isn't it?'

'But not necessarily a lie. And can you blame me for it? We were in love, Celestine. You can't deny that. Just because things happened between us . . .' A question I had been meaning to ask her forced itself to the front of my mind. 'Why didn't you contact me again, after you were told you couldn't go to Resurgam?'

'Our relationship was over, Richard.'

'But we'd parted on reasonably amicable terms. If the Resurgam expedition hadn't come up, we might not have parted at all.'

Celestine sighed; one of exasperation. 'Well, since you asked, I *did* try and contact you.'

'You did?'

'But by the time I'd made my mind up, I learned about the way you'd had my memory suppressed. How do you imagine that made me feel, Richard? Like a small, disposable part of your past – something to be wadded up and flicked away when it offended you?'

'It wasn't like that at all. I never thought I'd see you again.'

She snorted. 'And maybe you wouldn't have, if it wasn't for dear old Roland Childe.'

I kept my voice level. 'He asked me along because we both used to test each other with challenges like this. I presume he needed someone with your kind of Juggler transform. Childe wouldn't have cared about our past.'

Her eyes flashed behind the visor of her helmet. 'And you don't care either, do you?'

'About Childe's motives? No. They're neither my concern nor my interest. All that bothers me now is this.'

I patted the Spire's thrumming floor.

'There's more here than meets the eye, Richard.'

'What do you mean by that?'

'Haven't you noticed how . . .' She looked at me for several seconds, as if on the verge of revealing something, then shook her head. 'Never mind.'

'What, for pity's sake?'

'Doesn't it strike you that Childe has been just a little too well-prepared?'

'I wouldn't say there's any such thing as being too well-prepared for a thing like Blood Spire, Celestine.'

'That's not what I mean.' She fingered the fabric of her skintight. 'These suits, for instance. How did he know we wouldn't be able to go all the way with the larger ones?'

I shrugged, a gesture that was now perfectly visible. 'I don't know. Maybe he learned a few things from Argyle, before he died.'

'Then what about Doctor Trintignant? That ghoul isn't remotely interested in solving the Spire. He hasn't contributed to a single problem yet. And yet he's already proved his value, hasn't he?'

'I don't follow.'

Celestine rubbed her shunt. 'These things. And the neural modifiers – Trintignant supervised their installation. And I haven't even mentioned Forqueray's arm, or the medical equipment aboard the shuttle.'

'I still don't see what you're getting at.'

'I don't know what leverage Childe's used to get his co-operation – it's got to be more than bribery or avarice – but I have a very, very nasty idea. And all of it points to something even more disturbing.'

I was wearying of this. With the challenge of the next door ahead of us, the last thing I needed was paranoiac theory-mongering.

'Which is?'

'Childe knows too much about this place.'

* * *

Another room, another punishment.

It made the last seem like a minor reprimand. I remembered a swift metallic flicker of machines emerging from hatches which opened in the seamless walls; not javelins now but jointed, articulated pincers and viciously curved scissors. I remembered high-pressure jets of vivid arterial blood spraying the room like pink banners; the shards of shattered bone hammering against the walls like shrapnel. I remembered an unwanted and brutal lesson in the anatomy of the human body; the elegance with which muscle, bone and sinew were anchored to each other and the horrid ease with which they could be flensed apart – filleted – by surgically sharp metallic instruments.

I remembered screams.

I remembered indescribable pain, before the analgesics kicked in.

Afterwards, when we had time to think about what had happened, I do not think any of us thought of blaming Celestine for making another mistake. Childe's modifiers had given us a healthy respect for the difficulty of what she was doing, and – as before – her second choice had been the correct one; the one that opened a route back to the Spire's exit.

And besides.

Celestine had suffered as well.

It was Forqueray who had caught the worst of it, though. Perhaps the Spire, having tasted his blood once, had decided it wanted much more of it. Certainly more than could be provided by the sacrifice of a mere limb. It had quartered him; two quick opposed snips with the nightmarish scissors; a bisection followed an instant later by a hideous transection.

Four pieces of Forqueray had thudded to the Spire's floor; his interior organs laid open like a wax model in a medical school. Various machines nestled neatly among his innards, sliced along the same planes. What remained of him spasmed once or twice, then – with the exception of his replacement arm, which continued to twitch – he was mercifully still. A moment or two passed, and then – with whiplash speed – jointed arms seized his pieces and pulled him into the wall, leaving slick red skidmarks.

Forqueray's death would have been bad enough, but by then the Spire was already inflicting further punishment.

I saw Celestine drop to the ground, one arm pressed around the stump of another; blood spraying from the wound despite the pressure she was applying. Through her visor her face turned ghostly.

Childe's right hand was missing all the fingers. He pressed the ruined hand against his chest, grimacing, but managed to stay on his feet.

Trintignant had lost a leg. But there was no blood gushing from the wound; no evidence of severed muscle and bone. I saw only damaged mechanisms; twisted and snapped steel and plastic armatures; buzzing cables and stuttering optic fibres; interrupted feedlines oozing sickly green fluids.

Trintignant, nonetheless, fell to the floor.

I also felt myself falling, looking down to see that my right leg ended just below the knee; realising that my own blood was hosing out in a hard scarlet stream. I hit the floor – the pain of the injury having yet to reach my brain – and reached out in reflex for the stump. But instead only one hand presented itself; my left arm curtailed neatly above the wrist. In my peripheral vision I saw my detached hand, still gloved, perched on the floor like an absurd white crab.

Pain flowered in my skull.

I screamed.

six

'I've had enough of this shit,' Hirz said.

Childe looked up at her from his recovery couch. 'You're leaving us?'

'Damn right I am.'

'You disappoint me.'

'Fine, but I'm still shipping out.'

Childe stroked his forehead, tracing its shape with the new steel gauntlet Trintignant had attached to his arm. 'If anyone should be quitting, it isn't you, Hirz. You walked out of the Spire without a scratch. Look at the rest of us.'

'Thanks, but I've just had my dinner.'

Trintignant lifted his silver mask towards her. 'Now there is no call for that. I admit the replacements I have fashioned here possess a certain brutal *aesthetique*, but in functional terms they are without equal.' As if to demonstrate his point, he flexed his own replacement leg.

It was a replacement, rather than simply the old one salvaged, repaired and re-attached. Hirz – who had picked up as many pieces of us as she could manage – had never found the other part of Trintignant. Nor had an examination of the area around the Spire – where we had found the pieces of Forqueray – revealed any significant part of the Doctor. The Spire had allowed us to take back Forqueray's arm after it had been severed, but now it appeared to have decided to keep all metallic things for itself.

I stood up from my own couch, testing the way my new leg supported my weight. There was no denying the excellence of Trintignant's work. The prosthesis had interfaced with my existing nervous system so perfectly that I had already accepted the leg into my body image. When I walked on it I did so with only the tiniest trace of a limp, and that would surely vanish once I had grown accustomed to the replacement.

'I could take the other one off as well,' Trintignant piped, rubbing his hands together. 'Then you would have perfect neural equilibrium . . . shall I do it?'

'You want to, don't you?'

'I admit I have always been offended by asymmetry.'

I felt my other leg; the flesh and blood one that now felt so vulnerable; so unlikely to last the course.

'You'll just have to be patient,' I said.

'Well, all things come to he who waits. And how is the arm doing?'

Like Childe, I now boasted one steel gauntlet instead of a hand. I flexed it, hearing the tiny, shrill whine of actuators. When I touched something I felt prickles of sensation, and the hand was capable of registering subtle gradations of warmth or coldness. Celestine's replacement was very similar, although sleeker and somehow more feminine. At least our injuries had demanded as much, I thought: unlike Childe, who had lost only his fingers, but who had seemed to welcome more of the Doctor's gleaming handiwork than was strictly necessary.

'It'll do,' I said, remembering how much Forqueray had irritated the Doctor with the same remark.

'Don't you get it?' Hirz said. 'If Trintignant had his way, you'd be like him by now. Christ only knows where he'll stop.'

Trintignant shrugged. 'I merely repair what the Spire damages.'

'Yeah. The two of you make a great team, Doc.' She looked at him with an expression of pure loathing. 'Well, sorry, but you're not getting your hands on me.'

Trintignant appraised her. 'No great loss, when there is so little raw material with which to work.'

'Screw you, creep.'

Hirz left the room.

'Looks like she means it when says she's quitting,' I said, breaking the silence that ensued.

Celestine nodded. 'I can't say I entirely blame her, either.'

'You don't?' Childe asked.

'No. She's right. This whole thing is in serious danger of turning into some kind of sick exercise in self-mutilation.' Celestine looked at her own steel hand, not quite masking her own revulsion. 'What will it take, Childe? What will we turn into by the time we beat this thing?'

He shrugged. 'Nothing that can't be reversed.'

'But maybe by then we won't want it reversed, will we?'

'Listen, Celestine.' Childe propped himself against a bulkhead. 'What we're doing here is trying to beat an elemental thing. Reach its summit, if you will. In that respect Blood Spire isn't very different to a mountain. It punishes us when we make mistakes, but then so do mountains. Occasionally, it kills. More often than not it only leaves us with a reminder of what it can do. Blood Spire snips off a finger or two. A mountain achieves the same effect with frostbite. Where's the difference?'

'A mountain doesn't enjoy doing it, for a start. But the Spire *does*. It's alive, Childe; living and breathing.'

'It's a machine, that's all.'

'But maybe a cleverer one than anything we've ever known before. A machine with a taste for blood, too. That's not a great combination, Childe.'

He sighed. 'Then you're giving up as well?'

'I didn't say that.'

'Fine.'

He stepped through the door which Hirz had just used.

'Where are you going?' I said.

'To try and talk some sense into her, that's all.'

seven

Ten hours later – buzzing with unnatural alertness; the need for sleep a distant, fading memory – we returned to Blood Spire.

'What did he say to make you come back?' I said to Hirz, between one of the challenges.

'What do you think?'

'Just a wild stab in the dark, but did he by any chance up your cut?'

'Let's just say the terms were renegotiated. Call it a performance-related bonus.'

I smiled. 'Then calling you a mercenary wasn't so far off the mark, was it?'

'Sticks and stones may break my bones . . . sorry. Given the circumstances, that's not in the best possible good taste, is it?'

'Never mind.'

We were struggling out of our suits now. Several rooms earlier we had reached a point where it was impossible to squeeze through the door without first disconnecting our air-lines and removing our backpacks. We could have done without the packs, of course, but none of us wanted to breathe Spire air until it was necessary. And we would still need the packs to make our retreat, back through the unpressurised rooms. So we kept hold of them as we wriggled between rooms, fearful of letting go. We had seen the way the Spire harvested first Forqueray's drone and then Trintignant's leg, and it was likely it would do the same with our equipment if we left it unattended.

'Why are you doing it, then?' asked Hirz.

'It certainly isn't the money,' I said.

'No. I figured that part out. What, then?'

'*Because it's there.* Because Childe and I go back a long way, and I can't stand to give up on a challenge once I've accepted it.'

'Old-fashioned bullheadedness, in other words,' Celestine said.

Hirz was putting on a helmet and backpack assembly for the first time. She had just been forced to get out of her original suit and put on one of the skintights; even her small frame now too large to pass through the constricted doors. Childe had attached some additional armour to her skintight – scablike patches of flexible woven diamond – but she must still have felt more vulnerable than she had before.

I answered Celestine. 'What about you, if it isn't the same thing that keeps me coming back?'

'I want to solve the problems, that's all. For you they're just a means to an end, but for me they're the only thing of interest.'

I felt slighted, but she was right. The nature of the challenges seemed less important to me than discovering what was at the summit; what secret the Spire so jealously guarded.

'And you're hoping that through the problems they set us you'll eventually understand the Spire's makers?'

'Not just that. I mean, that's a significant part of it, but I also want to know what my own limitations are.'

'You mean you want to explore the gift that the Jugglers have given you?' Before she had time to answer I continued: 'I understand. And it's never been possible before, has it? You've only ever been able to test yourself against problems made by other humans. You could never map the limits of your ability; anymore than a lion could test its strength against paper.'

She looked around her. 'But now I've met something that tests me.'

'And?'

Celestine smiled thinly. 'I'm not sure I like it.'

* * *

We did not speak again until we had traversed half a dozen new rooms, and then rested while the shunts mopped up the excess of tiredness which came after such efforts.

The mathematical problems had now grown so arcane that I could barely describe them, let alone grope my way towards a solution. Celestine had to do most of the thinking, therefore – but the emotional strain which we all felt was just as wearying. For an hour during the rest period I teetered on the edge of sleep, but then alertness returned like a pale, cold dawn. There was something harsh and clinical about that state of mind – it did not feel completely normal – but it enabled us to get the job done, and that was all that mattered.

We continued, passing the seventieth room – fifteen further than we had reached before. We were now at least sixty metres higher than when we had entered, and for a while it seemed that we had found a tempo that suited us. It was a long time since Celestine had shown any hesitation in her answers, even though it might take a couple of hours for her to reach the solution. It was as if she had found the right way of thinking, and that now none of the challenges would seem truly alien to her. For a while, as we passed room after room, a dangerous optimism began to creep over us.

It was a mistake.

In the seventy-first room, the Spire began to enforce a new rule. Celestine, as usual, spent at least twenty minutes studying the problem, skating her fingers over the shallowly-etched markings on the frame, her lips moving silently as she mouthed possibilities.

Childe studied her with a peculiar watchfulness I had not observed before.

'Any ideas?' he said, looking over her shoulder.

'Don't crowd me, Childe. I'm thinking.'

'I know, I know. Just try and do it a little faster, that's all.'

Celestine turned away from the frame. 'Why? Are we on a schedule, suddenly?'

'I'm just a little concerned about the amount of time it's taking us, that's all.' He stroked the bulge on his forearm. 'These shunts aren't perfect, and . . .'

'There's something else, isn't there?'

'Don't worry. Just concentrate on the problem.'

But this time the punishment began before we had begun our solution.

It was lenient, I suppose, compared to the savage dismembering that had concluded our last attempt to reach the summit. It was more of a stern admonishment to make our selection; the crack of a whip rather than the swish of a guillotine.

Something popped out of the wall and dropped to the floor.

It looked like a metal ball, about the size of a marble. For several seconds it did nothing at all. We all just stared at it, knowing that something unpleasant was going to happen, but unsure what.

Then the ball trembled, and – without deforming in any way – bounced itself off the ground, to knee-height.

It hit the ground and bounced again; a little higher this time.

'Celestine . . .' Childe said. 'I strongly suggest that you come to a decision . . .'

Horrified, Celestine forced her attention back to the puzzle marked on the frame. The ball continued bouncing; reaching higher each time.

'I don't like this,' Hirz said.

'I'm not exactly thrilled by it myself,' Childe told her, watching as the ball hit the ceiling and slammed back to the floor, landing to one side of the place where it had begun its bouncing. This time its rebound was enough to make it hit the ceiling again, and on the recoil it streaked diagonally across the room, hitting one of the side walls before glancing off at a different angle. The ball slammed into Trintignant, ricocheting off his metal leg, and then connected with the walls twice – gaining speed with each collision – before hitting me in the chest. The force of it was like a hard punch, driving the air from my lungs.

I fell to the ground, emitting a groan of discomfort.

The little ball continued arcing around the room, its momentum not sapped in any appreciable way. It kept getting faster, in fact, so that its trajectory came to resemble a constantly shifting silver loom which occasionally intersected one of us. I heard groans, and then felt a sudden pain in my leg, and the ball kept on getting faster. The sound it made was like a fusillade of gunshots, the space between each detonation growing smaller.

Childe, who had been hit himself, shouted: 'Celestine! Make your choice!'

The ball chose that moment to slam into her, making her gasp in pain. She buckled down on one knee, but in the process reached out and palmed one of the markings on the right side of the frame.

The gunshot sounds – the silver loom – even the ball itself – vanished.

Nothing happened for several more seconds, and then the door ahead of us began to open.

We inspected our injuries. There was nothing life-threatening, but we had all been bruised badly, and it was likely that a bone or two had been fractured. I was sure I had broken a rib, and Childe grimaced when he tried to put weight on his right ankle. My leg felt tender where the ball had struck me, but I could still walk, and after a few minutes the pain abated; soothed by a combination of my own medichines and the shunt's analgesics.

'Thank God we'd put the helmets back on,' I said, fingering a deep bump in the crown. 'We'd have been pulped otherwise.'

'Would someone please tell me what just happened?' Celestine asked, inspecting her own wounds.

'I guess the Spire thought we were taking too long,' Childe said. 'It's given us as long as we like to solve the problems until now, but from now on it looks like we'll be up against the clock.'

Hirz said: 'And how long did we have?'

'After the last door opened? Forty minutes, or so.'

'Forty-three, to be precise,' Trintignant said.

'I strongly suggest we start work on the next door,' Childe said. 'How long do you think we have, Doctor?'

'As an upper limit? In the region of twenty-eight minutes.'

'That's nowhere near enough time,' I said. 'We'd better retreat and come back.'

'No,' Childe said. 'Not until we're injured.'

'You're insane,' Celestine said.

But Childe ignored her. He just stepped through the door, into the next room. Behind us the exit door slammed shut.

'Not insane,' he said, turning back to us. 'Just very eager to continue.'

* * *

It was never the same thing twice.

Celestine made her selection as quickly as she could, every muscle in her tense with concentration, and that gave us – by Trintignant's estimation – five or six clear minutes before the Spire would demand an answer.

'We'll wait it out,' Childe said, eyeing us all to see if anyone disagreed. 'Celestine can keep checking her results. There's no sense in giving the fucking thing an answer before we have to; not when so much is at stake.'

'I'm sure of the answer,' Celestine said, pointing to the part of the frame she would eventually palm.

'Then take five minutes to clear your head. Whatever. Just don't make the choice until we're forced into it.'

'If we get through this room, Childe . . .'

'Yes?'

'I'm going back. You can't stop me.'

'You won't do it, Celestine, and you know it.'

She glared at him, but said nothing. I think what followed was the longest five minutes in my life. None of us dared speak again; unwilling to begin anything – even a word – for fear that something like the ball would return. All I heard for five minutes was our own breathing; backgrounded by the awful slow thrumming of the Spire itself.

Then something slithered out of one wall.

It hit the floor, writhing. It was an inch-thick, three-metre-long length of flexible metal.

'Back off . . .' Childe told us.

Celestine looked over her shoulder. 'You want me to press this, or not?'

'On my word. Not a moment before.'

The cable continued writhing; flexing, coiling and uncoiling like a demented eel. Childe stared at it, fascinatedly. The writhing grew in strength, accompanied by the slithering, hissing sounds of metal on metal.

'Childe?' Celestine asked.

'I just want to see what this thing actually . . .'

The cable flexed and writhed, and then propelled itself rapidly across the floor in Childe's direction. He hopped nimbly out of the way, the cable passing under his feet. The writhing had become a continuous whipcracking now, and we all pressed ourselves against the walls. The cable – having missed Childe – retreated to the middle of the room and hissed furiously. It looked much longer and thinner than it had a moment ago, as if it had elongated itself.

'Childe . . .' Celestine said. 'I'm making the choice in five seconds, whether you like it or not.'

'Wait, will you?'

The cable moved with blinding speed now, rearing up so that its motion was no longer confined to a few inches above the floor. Its writhing was so fast that it took on a quasi-solidity; an irregularly-shaped pillar of flickering, whistling metal. I looked at Celestine, willing her to palm the frame, no matter what Childe said. I appreciated his fascination – the thing was entrancing to look at – but I suspected he was pushing curiosity slightly too far.

'Celestine . . .' I started saying.

But what happened next happened with lightning speed; a silver-grey tentacle of the blur – a thin loop of the cable – whipping out to form a double coil around Celestine's arm. It was the one Trintignant had already worked on. She looked at it in horror; the cable tightened itself and snipped the arm off. Celestine slumped to the floor, screaming.

The tentacle tugged her arm to the centre of the room, retreating back into the hissing, flickering pillar of whirling metal.

I dashed for the door, remembering the symbol she had pressed. The whirl reached a loop out to me, but I threw myself against the wall and the loop merely brushed the chest of my suit before flicking back into the mass. From the whirl, tiny pieces of flesh and bone dribbled to the ground. Then another loop flicked out and snared Hirz, wrapping around her midsection and pulling her towards the whirl.

She struggled – cartwheeling her arms, her feet skidding against the floor – but it was no good. She started shouting, and then screaming.

I reached the door.

My hand hesitated over the markings. Was I remembering accurately, or had Celestine intended to press a different solution? They all looked so similar now.

Then Celestine, who was still clutching her ruined arm, nodded emphatically.

I palmed the door.

I stared at it, willing it to move. After all this, what if her choice had been wrong? The Spire seemed to draw out the moment sadistically, while behind me I continued to hear the frantic hissing of the whirling cable. And something else, which I preferred not to think about.

Suddenly, the noise stopped.

In my peripheral vision I saw the cable retreating back into the wall, like a snake's tongue laden with scent.

Before me, the door began to open.

Celestine's choice had been correct. I examined my state of mind and decided that I ought to be feeling relief. And perhaps, distantly, I did. At least now we would have a clear route back out of the Spire. But we would not be going forward, and I knew not all of us would be leaving.

I turned around, steeling against what I was about to see.

Childe and Trintignant were undamaged.

Celestine was already attending to her injury, fixing a tourniquet from her medical kit above the point where her arm ended. She had lost very little blood, and did not appear to be in very much discomfort.

'Are you alright?' I said.

'I'll make it out, Richard.' She grimaced; tugging the tourniquet tighter. 'Which is more than can be said for Hirz.'

'Where is she?'

'It got her.'

With her good hand, Celestine pointed to the place where the whirl had been, only moments before. On the floor – just below the volume of air where the cable had hovered and thrashed – lay a small, neat pile of flailed human tissue.

'There's no sign of Celestine's hand,' I said. 'Or Hirz's suit.'

'It pulled her apart,' Childe said, his face drained of blood.

'Where is she?'

'It was very fast. There was just a . . . blur. It pulled her apart and then the parts disappeared into the walls. I don't think she could have felt much.'

'I hope to God she didn't.'

Doctor Trintignant stooped down and examined the pieces.

eight

Outside, in the long, steely-shadowed light of what was either dusk or dawn, we found the pieces of Hirz for which the Spire had had no use.

They were half-buried in dust, like the bluffs and arches of some ancient landscape rendered in miniature. My mind played gruesome tricks with the shapes; turning them from brutally detached pieces of human anatomy into abstract sculptures; jointed formations that caught the light in a certain way and cast their own pleasing shadows. Though some pieces of fabric remained, the Spire had retained all the metallic parts of her suit for itself. Even her skull had been cracked open and sucked dry, so that the Spire could winnow the few small precious pieces of metal she carried in her head.

And what it could not use, it had thrown away.

'We can't just leave her here,' I said. 'We've got to do something, bury her . . . at least put up some kind of marker.'

'She's already got one,' Childe said.

'What?'

'The Spire. And the sooner we get back to the shuttle, the sooner we can fix Celestine and get back to it.'

'A moment, please,' Trintignant said, fingering through another pile of human remains.

'Those aren't anything to do with Hirz,' Childe said.

Trintignant rose to his feet, slipping something into his suit's utility belt pocket in the process.

Whatever it had been was small; no larger than a marble or small stone.

* * *

'I'm going home,' Celestine said, when we were back in the safety of the shuttle. 'And before you try and talk me out of it, that's final.'

We were alone in her quarters. Childe had just given up trying to convince her to stay, but he had sent me in to see if I could be more persuasive. My heart, however, was not in it. I had seen what the Spire could do, and I was damned if I was going to be responsible for any blood other than my own.

'At least let Trintignant take care of your hand,' I said.

'I don't need steel now,' she said, stroking the glistening blue surgical sleeve which terminated her arm. 'I can manage without a hand until we're back in Chasm City. They can grow me a new one while I'm sleeping.'

The Doctor's musical voice interrupted us; Trintignant's impassive silver mask poking through into Celestine's bubbletent partition. 'If I may be so bold . . . it may be that my services are the best you can now reasonably hope to attain.'

Celestine looked at Childe, and then at the Doctor, and then at the glistening surgical sleeve.

'What are you talking about?'

'Nothing. Only some news from home which Childe has allowed me to see.' Uninvited, Trintignant stepped fully into the room and sealed the partition behind him.

'What, Doctor?'

'Rather disturbing news, as it happens. Not long after our departure, something upsetting happened to Chasm City. A blight which afflicted everything contingent upon any microscopic, self-replicating system. Nano-technology, in other words. I gather the fatalities were numbered in the millions . . .'

'You don't have to sound so bloody cheerful about it.'

Trintignant navigated to the side of the couch where Celestine was resting.

'I merely stress the point that what we consider state of the art medicine may be somewhat beyond the city's present capabilities. Of course, much may change before our return . . .'

'Then I'll just have to take that risk, won't I?' Celestine said.

'On your own head be it.' Trintignant paused, and placed something small and hard on Celestine's table. Then he turned as if to leave, but stopped and spoke again. 'I am accustomed to it, you know.'

'Used to what?' I said.

'Fear and revulsion. Because of what I have become, and what I have done. But I am not an evil man. Perverse, yes. Given to peculiar desires, most certainly. But emphatically not a monster.'

'What about your victims, Doctor?'

'I have always maintained that they gave consent for the procedures I inflicted . . .' He corrected himself. 'Performed . . . upon them.'

'That's not what the records say.'

'And who are we to argue with records?' The light played on his mask in such a fashion as to enhance the half-smile that was always there. 'Who are we, indeed.'

* * *

When Trintignant was gone, I turned to Celestine and said: 'I'm going back into the Spire. You realise that, don't you?'

'I'd guessed, but I still hope I can talk you out of it.' With her good hand, she fingered the small, hard thing Trintignant had placed on the table. It looked like a misshapen dark stone – whatever the Doctor had found among the dead – and for a moment I wondered why he had left it behind.

Then I said: 'I really don't think there's much point. It's between me and Childe now. He must have known that there'd come a point when I wouldn't be able to turn away.'

'No matter what the costs?' Celestine asked.

'Nothing's without a little risk.'

She shook her head, slowly and wonderingly. 'He really got to you, didn't he.'

'No,' I said, feeling a perverse need to defend my old friend, even when I knew that what Celestine said was perfectly true. 'It wasn't Childe, in the end. It was the Spire.'

'Please, Richard. Think carefully, won't you?'

I said I would. But we both knew it was a lie.

nine

Childe and I went back.

I gazed up at it, towering over us like some brutal cenotaph. I saw it with astonishing, diamond-hard clarity. It was as if a smoky veil had been lifted from my vision, permitting thousands of new details and nuances of hue and shade to blast through. Only the tiniest, faintest hint of pixelation – seen whenever I changed my angle of view too sharply – betrayed the fact that this was not quite normal vision, but a cybernetic augmentation.

Our eyes had been removed; the sockets scrubbed and packed with far more efficient sensory devices, wired back into our visual cortices. Our eyeballs waited back at the shuttle, floating in jars like grotesque delicacies. They could be popped back in when we had conquered the Spire.

'Why not goggles?' I said, when Trintignant had first explained his plans.

'Too bulky, and too liable to be snatched away. The Spire has a definite taste for metal. From now on, anything vital had better be carried as part of us – not just worn, but internalised.' The Doctor steepled his silver fingers. 'If that repulses you, I suggest you concede defeat now.'

'I'll decide what repulses me,' I said.

'What else?' Childe said. 'Without Celestine we'll need to crack those problems ourselves.'

'I will increase the density of medichines in your brains,' Trintignant said.

'They will weave a web of fullerene tubes; artificial neuronal connections supplanting your existing synaptic topology.'

'What good will that do?'

'The fullerene tubes will conduct nerve signals hundreds of times more rapidly than your existing synaptic pathways. Your neural computation rate will increase. Your subjective sense of elapsed time will slow.'

I stared at the Doctor, horrified and fascinated at the same time. 'You can do that?'

'It's actually rather trivial. The Conjoiners have being doing it since the Transenlightenment, and their methods are well documented. With them I can make time slow to a subjective crawl. The Spire may give you only twenty minutes to solve a room, but I can make it seem like several hours; even one or two days.'

I turned to Childe. 'You think that'll be enough?'

'I think it'll be a lot better than nothing, but we'll see.'

But it was better than that.

Trintignant's machines did more than just supplant our existing and clumsily slow neural pathways. They reshaped them; configuring the topology to enhance mathematical prowess. It took us onto a plateau beyond what the neural modifiers had been capable of doing. We lacked Celestine's intuitive brilliance, but we had the advantage of being able to spend longer – subjectively, at least – on a given problem.

And for a while, at least, it worked.

ten

'You're turning into a monster,' she said.

I answered: 'I'm turning into whatever it takes to beat the Spire.'

I stalked away from the shuttle, moving on slender articulated legs like piston-driven stilts. I no longer needed armour now. Trintignant had grafted it to my skin. Tough black plaques slid over each other like the carapacial segments of a lobster.

'You even sound like Trintignant now,' Celestine said, following me. I watched her asymmetric shadow loom next to mine; she lopsided; me a thin, elongated wraith.

'I can't help that,' I said, my voice piping from the speech synthesizer that replaced my sealed-up mouth.

'You can stop. It isn't too late.'

'Not until Childe stops.'

'And then? Will even that be enough to make you give up, Richard?'

I turned to face her. Behind her faceplate I watched her try and conceal the revulsion she obviously felt.

'He won't give up,' I said.

Celestine held out her hand. At first I thought she was beckoning me, but then I saw there was something in her palm. Small, dark and hard.

'Trintignant found this outside, by the Spire. It's what he left in my room. I think he was trying to tell us something. Trying to redeem himself. Do you recognise it, Richard?'

I zoomed in on the object. Numbers flickered around it. Enhancement phased in. Surface irregularity. Topological contours. Albedo. Likely composition. I drank in the data like a drunkard.

Data was what I lived for now.

'No.'

eleven

'I can hear something.'

'Of course you can. It's the Spire, the same as it's always been.'

'No.' I was silent for several moments, wondering whether my augmented auditory system was sending false signals into my brain.

But there it was again – an occasional rumble of distant machinery, but one that was coming closer.

'I hear it now,' Childe said. 'It's coming from behind us. Along the way we've come.'

'It sounds like the doors opening and closing in sequence.'

'Yes.'

'Why would they do that?'

'Something must be coming through the rooms, towards us.'

Childe thought about that for what seemed like minutes, but which was probably only a matter of actual seconds. Then he shook his head, dismissively. 'We have eleven minutes to get through this door, or we'll be punished. We don't have time to worry about anything extraneous.'

Reluctantly, I agreed.

I forced my attention back to the puzzle; feeling the machinery in my head pluck at the mathematical barbs of the problem. The ferocious clockwork that Trintignant had installed in my skull spun giddily. I had never understood mathematics with any great agility, but now I sensed it as a hard grid of truth underlying everything; bones shining through the thin flesh of the world.

It was almost the only thing I was now capable of thinking of at all. Everything else felt painfully abstract, whereas before the opposite had been the case. This, I knew, must be what it felt like to an idiot savant; gifted with astonishing skill in one highly specialised field of human expertise.

I had become a tool shaped so efficiently for one purpose that it could serve no other.

I had become a machine for solving the Spire.

Now that we were alone – and no longer reliant on Celestine – Childe had revealed himself as a more than adequately capable problem-solver. More than once I had found myself staring at a problem, with even my new mathematical skills momentarily unable to crack the solution, when Childe had seen the answer. Generally he was able to articulate the reasoning behind his choice, but sometimes there was nothing for it but for me to either accept his judgement or wait for my own sluggard thought processes to arrive at the same conclusion.

And I began to wonder.

Childe was brilliant now, but I sensed there was more to it than the extra layers of cognitive machinery Trintignant had installed. He was so confident now that I began to wonder if he had merely been holding back before, preferring to let the rest of us make the decisions. If that was the case, he was in some way responsible for the deaths that had already happened.

But, I reminded myself, we had all volunteered.

With three minutes to spare, the door eased open, revealing the room beyond. At the same moment the door we had come through opened as well, as it always did at this point. We could leave now, if we wished. At this time, as had been the case with every room we had passed through, Childe and I made a decision on whether to proceed further or not. There was always the danger that the next room would be the one that killed us – and every second that we spent before stepping through the doorway meant one second less available for cracking the next problem.

'Well?' I said.

His answer came back, clipped and automatic. 'Onwards.'

'We only had three minutes to spare on this one, Childe. They're getting harder now. A hell of a lot harder.'

'I'm fully aware of that.'

'Then maybe we should retreat. Gather our strength and return. We'll lose nothing by doing so.'

'You can't be sure of that. You don't know that the Spire will keep letting us make these attempts. Perhaps it's already tiring of us.'

'I still—'

But I stopped, my new, wasp-waisted body flexing easily at the approach of a footfall.

My visual system scanned the approaching object, resolving it into a figure, stepping over the threshold from the previous room. It was a human figure, but one that had, admittedly, undergone some alterations – although none that were as drastic as those that Trintignant had wrought on me. I studied the slow, painful way she made her progress. Our own movements seemed slow, but were lightning fast by comparison.

I groped for a memory; a name; a face.

My mind, clotted with routines designed to smash mathematics, could not at first retrieve such mundane data.

Finally, however, it obliged.

'Celestine,' I said.

I did not actually speak. Instead, laser light stuttered from the mass of sensors and scanners jammed into my eyesockets. Our minds now ran too rapidly to communicate verbally, but – though she moved slowly herself, she deigned to reply.

'Yes. It's me. Are you really Richard?'

'Why do you ask?'

'Because I can hardly tell the difference between you and Childe.'

I looked at Childe; paying proper attention to his shape for what seemed the first time.

At last, after so many frustrations, Trintignant had been given free rein to do with us as he wished. He had pumped our heads full of more processing machinery, until our skulls had to be reshaped to accommodate them, becoming sleekly elongated. He cracked our ribcages open and carefully removed our lungs and hearts, putting these organs into storage. The space vacated by one lung was replaced by a closed-cycle blood oxygenating system of the kind carried in spacesuit backpacks, so that we could endure vacuum and had no need to breathe ambient air. The other lung's volume was filled by a device which circulated refrigerated fluid along a loop of tube, draining the excess heat generated by the stew of neural machines filling our heads. Nutrient systems crammed the remaining thoracic spaces; our hearts tiny fusion-powered pumps. All other organs – stomach, intestines, genitalia – were removed, along with many bones and muscles. Our remaining limbs were detached and put into storage; replaced by skeletal prosthetics of immense strength, but which could fold and deform to enable us to squeeze through the tightest door. Our bodies were encased in exoskeletal frames to which these limbs were anchored. Finally, Trintignant gave us whiplike counterbalancing tails, and then caused our skins to envelope our metal parts, hardening here and there in lustrous grey patches of organic armour, woven from the same diamond mesh that had been used to reinforce Hirz's suit.

When he was done, we looked like diamond-hided greyhounds.

Diamond dogs.

* * *

I bowed my head. 'I am Richard.'

'Then for God's sake please come back.'

'Why have you followed us?'

'To ask you. One final time.'

'You changed yourself just to come after me?'

Slowly, with the stone grace of a statue, she extended a beckoning hand. Her limbs, like ours, were mechanical, but her basic form was far less canine.

'Please.'

'You know I can't go back now. Not when I've come so far.'

Her answer was an eternity arriving. 'You don't understand, Richard. This is not what it seems.'

Childe turned his sleek, snouted face to mine.

'Ignore her,' he said.

'No,' Celestine said, who must have also been attuned to Childe's laser signals. 'Don't listen to him, Richard. He's tricked and lied to you all along. To all of us. Even to Trintignant. That's why I came back.'

'She's lying,' Childe said.

'No. I'm not. Haven't you got it yet, Richard? Childe's been here before. This isn't his first visit to the Spire.'

I convulsed my canine body in a shrug. 'Nor mine.'

'I don't mean since we arrived on Golgotha. I mean before that. Childe's been to this planet already.'

'She's lying,' Childe repeated.

'Then how did you know what to expect, in so much detail?'

'I didn't. I was just prudent.' He turned to me, so that only I could read the stammer of his lasers. 'We are wasting valuable time here, Richard.'

'Prudent?' Celestine said. 'Oh yes; you were damned prudent. Bringing along those other suits, so that when the first ones became too bulky we could still go on. And Trintignant – how did you know he'd come in so handy?'

'I saw the bodies lying around the base of the Spire,' Childe answered. 'They'd been butchered by it.'

'And?'

'I decided it would be good to have someone along who had the medical aptitude to put right such injuries.'

'Yes.' Celestine nodded. 'I don't disagree with that. But that's no more than part of the truth, is it?'

I glanced at Childe and Celestine in turn. 'Then what is?'

'Those bodies aren't anything to do with Captain Argyle.'

'They're not?' I said.

'No.' Celestine's words arrived agonisingly slowly, and I began to wish that

Trintignant had turned her into a diamond-skinned dog as well. 'No. Because Argyle never existed. He was a necessary fiction – a reason for Childe knowing at least something about what the Spire entailed. But the truth . . . well, why don't you tell us, Childe?'

'I don't know what you want me to say.'

Celestine smiled. 'Only that the bodies are yours.'

His tail flexed impatiently, brushing the floor. 'I won't listen to this.'

'Then don't. But Trintignant will tell you the same thing. He guessed first, not me.'

She threw something towards me.

I willed time to move more slowly. What she had thrown curved lazily through the air, following a parabola. My mind processed its course and extrapolated its trajectory with deadening precision.

I moved and opened my foreclaw to catch the falling thing.

'I don't recognise it,' I said.

'Trintignant must have thought you would.'

I looked down at the thing, trying to see it anew. I remembered the Doctor fishing among the bones around the Spire's base; placing something in one of his pockets. This hard, black, irregular, dully pointed thing.

What was it?

I half remembered.

'There has to be more than this,' I said.

'Of course there is,' Celestine said. 'The human remains – with the exception of what's been added since we arrived – are all from the same genetic individual. I know. Trintignant told me.'

'That isn't possible.'

'Oh, it is. With cloning, it's almost child's play.'

'This is nonsense,' Childe said.

I turned to him now, feeling the faint ghost of an emotion Trintignant had not completely excised. 'Is it really?'

'Why would I clone myself?'

'I'll answer for him,' Celestine said. 'He found this thing, but long, long before he said he did. And he visited it, and set about exploring it, using clones of himself.'

I looked at Childe, expecting him to at least proffer some shred of explanation. Instead, padding on all fours, he crossed into the next room.

The door behind Celestine slammed shut like a steel eyelid.

Childe spoke to us from the next room. 'My estimate is that we have nine or ten minutes in which to solve the next problem. I am studying it now and it strikes me as . . . challenging, to say the least. Shall we adjourn any further discussion of trivialities until we're through?'

'Childe,' I said. 'You shouldn't have done that. Celestine wasn't consulted . . .'

'I assumed she was on the team.'

Celestine stepped into the new room. 'I wasn't. At least, I didn't think I was. But it looks like I am now.'

'That's the spirit,' Childe said. And I realised then where I had seen the small, dark thing that Trintignant had retrieved from the surface of Golgotha.

I might have been mistaken.

But it looked a lot like a devil's horn.

twelve

The problem was as elegant, Byzantine, multi-layered and potentially treacherous as any we had encountered.

Simply looking at it sent my mind careering down avenues of mathematical possibility, glimpsing deep connections between what I had always assumed were theoretically distant realms of logical space. I could have stared at it for hours, in a state of ecstatic transfixion. Unfortunately, we had to solve it, not admire it. And we now had less than nine minutes.

We crowded around the door and for two or three minutes – what felt like two or three hours – nothing was said.

I broke the silence, when I sensed that I needed to think about something else for a moment.

'Was Celestine right? Did you clone yourself?'

'Of course he did,' she said. 'He was exploring hazardous territory, so he'd have been certain to bring the kind of equipment necessary to regenerate organs.'

Childe turned away from the problem. 'That isn't the same as cloning equipment.'

'Only because of artificially-imposed safeguards,' Celestine answered. 'Strip those away and you can clone to your heart's content. Why regenerate a single hand or arm when you can culture a whole body?'

'What good would that do me? All I'd have done was make a mindless copy of myself.'

I said: 'Not necessarily. With memory trawls and medichines, you could go some way towards imprinting your personality and memory on any clone you chose.'

'He's right,' Celestine said. 'It's easy enough to rescript memories. Richard should know.'

Childe looked back at the problem, which still seemed as fiercely intractable as when we had entered.

'Six minutes left,' he said.

'Don't change the fucking subject,' Celestine said. 'I want Richard to know exactly what happened here.'

'Why?' Childe said. 'Do you honestly care what happens to him? I saw that look of revulsion when you saw what we'd done to ourselves.'

'Maybe you do revolt me,' she said, nodding. 'But I also care about someone being manipulated.'

'I haven't manipulated anyone.'

'Then tell him the truth about the clones. And the Spire, for that matter.'

Childe returned his attention to the door, evidently torn between solving the problem and silencing Celestine. Less than six minutes now remained, and though I had distracted myself, I had not come closer to grasping the solution, or even seeing a hint of how to begin.

I snapped my attention back to Childe. 'What happened with the clones? Did you send them in, one by one, hoping to find a way into the Spire for you?'

'No.' He almost laughed at my failure to grasp the truth. 'I didn't send them in ahead of me, Richard. Not at all. I sent them in *after* me.'

'Sorry, but I don't understand.'

'I went in first, and the Spire killed me. But before I did that, I trawled myself and installed those memories in a recently grown clone. The clone wasn't a perfect copy of me, by any means – it had some memories, and some of my grosser personality traits, but it was under no illusions that it was anything but a recently made construct.' Childe glanced back towards the problem. 'Look, this is all very interesting, but I really think . . .'

'The problem can wait,' Celestine said. 'I think I see a solution, in any case.'

Childe's slender body stiffened in anticipation. 'You do?'

'Just a hint of one, Childe. Keep your hackles down.'

'We don't have much time, Celestine. I'd very much like to hear your solution.'

She looked at the pattern, smiling faintly. 'I'm sure you would. I'd also like to hear what happened to the clone.'

I sensed him seethe with anger, then bring it under control. 'It – the new me – went back into the Spire, and attempted to make further progress than its predecessor. Which it did, advancing several rooms beyond the point where the old me died.'

'What made it go in?' Celestine said. 'It must have known it would die in there as well.'

'It thought it had a significantly better chance of survival than the last one. It studied what had happened to the first victim and took precautions – better armour; drugs to enhance mathematical skills; some crude stabs at the medichine therapies we have been using.'

'And?' I said. 'What happened after that one died?'

'It didn't die on its first attempt. Like us, it retreated once it sensed it had gone as far as it reasonably could. Each time, it trawled itself – making a copy of its memories. These were inherited by the next clone.'

'I still don't get it,' I said. 'Why would the clone care what happened to the one after it?'

'Because . . . it never expected to die. None of them did. Call that a character trait, if you will.'

'Overweening arrogance?' Celestine offered.

'I'd prefer to think of it as a profound lack of self-doubt. Each clone imagined itself better than its predecessor; incapable of making the same errors. But they still wanted to be trawled, so that – in the unlikely event that they were killed – something would go on. So that, even if that particular clone did not solve the Spire, it would still be something with my genetic heritage that did. Part of the same lineage. Family, if you will.' His tail flicked impatiently. 'Four minutes. Celestine . . . are you ready now?'

'Almost, but not quite. How many clones were there, Childe? Before you, I mean?'

'That's a pretty personal question.'

She shrugged. 'Fine. I'll just withhold my solution.'

'Seventeen,' Childe said. 'Plus my original; the first one to go in.'

I absorbed this number; stunned at what it implied. 'Then you're . . . the nineteenth to try and solve the Spire?'

I think he would have smiled at that point, had it been anatomically possible. 'Like I said, I try and keep it in the family.'

'You've become a monster,' Celestine said, almost beneath her breath.

It was hard not to see it that way, as well. He had inherited the memories from eighteen predecessors; all of whom had died within the Spire's pain-wracked chambers. It hardly mattered that he had probably never inherited the precise moment of death; the lineage was no less monstrous for that small mercy. And who was to say that some of his ancestor clones had not crawled out of the Spire, horribly mutilated, dying, but still sufficiently alive to succumb to one last trawl?

They said a trawl was all the sharper if it was performed at the moment of death, when damage to the scanned mind mattered less.

'Celestine's right,' I said. 'You've become something worse than the thing you set out to beat.'

Childe appraised me; those dense clusters of optics sweeping over me like gun barrels. 'Have you looked in a mirror lately, Richard? You're not exactly the way nature intended, you know.'

'This is just cosmetic,' I said. 'I still have my memories. I haven't allowed myself to become a . . .' I faltered; my brain struggling with vocabulary now that so much of it had been reassigned to the task of cracking the Spire. 'A perversion,' I finished.

'Fine.' Childe lowered his head; a posture of sadness and resignation. 'Then go back, if that's what you want. Let me stay to finish the challenge.'

'Yes,' I said. 'I think I will. Celestine? Get us through this door, and I'll come back with you. We'll leave Childe to his bloody Spire.'

* * *

Celestine's sigh was one of heartfelt relief. 'Thank God, Richard. I didn't think I'd be able to convince you quite that easily.'

I nodded towards the door, suggesting that she sketched out what she thought was the likely solution. It still looked devilishly hard to me, but now that I refocused my mind on it, I thought I began to see the faintest hint of an approach, if not a full-blooded solution.

But Childe was speaking again. 'Oh, you shouldn't sound so surprised,' he said. 'I always knew he'd turn back as soon as the going got tough. That's always been his way. I shouldn't have deceived myself that he'd have changed.'

I bristled. 'That isn't true.'

'Then why turn back, when we've come so far?'

'Because it isn't worth it.'

'Or is it simply that the problem's become too difficult; the challenge too great?'

'Ignore him,' Celestine said. 'He's just trying to goad you into following him. That's what this has always been about, hasn't it, Childe? You think you can solve the Spire, where eighteen previous versions of you have failed. Where eighteen previous versions of you were butchered and flayed by the thing.' She looked around, almost as if she expected the Spire to punish her for speaking so profanely. 'And perhaps you're right, too. Perhaps you really have come closer than any of the others.'

Childe said nothing, perhaps unwilling to contradict her.

'But simply beating the Spire wouldn't be good enough,' Celestine said. 'For you'd have no witnesses. No one to see how clever you'd been.'

'That isn't it at all.'

'Then why did we all have to come here? You found Trintignant useful, I'll grant you that. And I helped you as well. But you could have done without us, ultimately. It would have been bloodier, and you might have needed to run off a few more clones . . . but I don't doubt that you could have done it.'

'The solution, Celestine.'

By my estimate we had not much more than two minutes left in which to make our selection. And yet I sensed that it was time enough. Magically, the problem had opened up before me where a moment ago it had seemed insoluble; like one of those optical illusions which suddenly flip from one state to another. The moment was as close to a religious experience as I cared to come.

'It's all right,' I said. 'I see it now. Have you got it?'

'Not quite. Give me a moment . . .' Childe stared at it, and I watched as the lasers from his eyes washed over the labyrinthine engravings. The red glare skittered over the wrong solution, and lingered there. It flickered away and alighted on the correct answer, but only momentarily.

Childe flicked his tail. 'I think I've got it.'

'Good,' Celestine replied. 'I agree with you. Richard? Are you ready to make this unanimous?'

I thought I had misheard her, but I had not. She was saying that Childe's answer was the right one; that the one I had been sure of was the wrong one . . .

'I thought . . .' I began. Then, desperately, stared at the problem again. Had I missed something? Childe had seemed to have his doubts, but Celestine seemed so certain of herself. And yet what I had glimpsed had appeared beyond question. 'I don't know,' I said, weakly. 'I don't know.'

'We haven't time to debate it. We've got less than a minute.'

The feeling in my belly was one of ice. Somehow, despite the layers of humanity that had been stripped from me, I could still taste terror. It was reaching me anyway; refusing to be daunted.

I felt so certain of my choice. And yet I was outnumbered.

'Richard?' Childe said again, more insistent this time.

I looked at the two of them, helplessly. 'Press it,' I said.

Childe placed his forepaw over the solution that he and Celestine had agreed on, and pressed.

I think I knew, even before the Spire responded, that the choice had not been the correct one. And yet when I looked at Celestine I saw nothing resembling shock or surprise in her expression. Instead, she looked completely calm and resigned.

And then the punishment commenced.

It was brutal, and once it would have killed us. Even with the augmentations Trintignant had given us, the damage inflicted was considerable, as a scythe-tipped, triple-jointed pendulum descended from the ceiling and began swinging in viciously widening arcs. Our minds might have been able to compute the future position of a simpler pendulum, steering our bodies out of its harmful path. But the trajectory of a jointed pendulum was ferociously difficult to predict; a nightmarish demonstration of the mathematics of chaos.

But we survived, as we had survived the previous attacks. Even Celestine made it through; the flashing arc snipping off only one of her arms. I lost an arm and leg on one side, and watched – half in horror, half in fascination – as the room claimed these parts for itself; tendrils whipping out from the wall to salvage those useful conglomerations of metal and plastic. There was pain, of a sort, for Trintignant had wired those limbs into our nervous systems, so that we could feel heat and cold. But the pain abated quickly, replaced by digital numbness.

Childe got the worst of it, though.

The blade had sliced him through the middle, just below what had once been his ribcage, spilling steel and plastic guts, bone, viscera, blood and noxious lubricants onto the floor. The tendrils squirmed out and captured the twitching prize of his detached rear end; flicking tail and all.

With the hand that she still had, Celestine pressed the correct symbol. The punishment ceased and the door opened.

In the comparative calm that followed, Childe looked down at his severed trunk.

'I seem to be quite badly damaged,' he said.

But already various valves and gaskets were stemming the fluid loss; clicking shut with neat precision. Trintignant, I saw, had done very well. He had equipped Childe to survive the most extreme injuries.

'You'll live,' Celestine said, with what struck me as less than total sympathy.

'What happened?' I asked. 'Why didn't you press that one first?'

She looked at me. 'Because I knew what had to be done.'

* * *

Despite her injuries she helped us on the retreat.

I was able to stumble from room to room, balancing myself against the wall and hopping on my good leg. I had lost no great quantity of blood, for while I had suffered one or two gashes from close approaches of the pendulum, my limbs had been detached above the points where they were anchored to flesh and bone. But I still felt the shivering onset of shock, and all I wanted to do was make it out of the Spire, back to the sanctuary of the shuttle. There, I knew, Trintignant could make me whole again. Human again, for that matter. He had always promised it would be possible, and while there was much about him that I did not like, I did not think he would lie about that. It would be a matter of professional pride that his work was technically reversible.

Celestine carried Childe, tucked under her arm. What remained of him was very light, she said, and he was able to cling to her with his undamaged forepaws. I felt a spasm of horror every time I saw how little of him there was, while shuddering to think how much more intense that spasm would have been were I not already numbed by the medichines.

We had made it back through perhaps one third of the rooms when he slithered from her grip, thudding to the floor.

'What are you doing?' Celestine asked.

'What do you think?' He supported himself by his forelimbs; his severed trunk resting against the ground. The wound had begun to close, I saw: his diamond skin puckering tight to seal the damage.

Before very long he would look as if he had been made this way.

Celestine took her time before answering.

'Quite honestly, I don't know what to think.'

'I'm going back. I'm carrying on.'

Still propping myself against a wall, I said: 'You can't. You need treatment. For God's sake; you've been cut in half.'

'It doesn't matter,' Childe said. 'All I've done is lose a part of me I would have been forced to discard before very long. Eventually the doors would have been a tight squeeze even for something shaped like a dog.'

'It'll kill you,' I said.

'Or I'll beat it. It's still possible, you know.' He turned around, his rear part scraping against the floor, and then looked back over his shoulder. 'I'm going to retrace my steps back to the room where this happened. I don't think the Spire will obstruct your retreat until I step – or crawl, as it may be – into the last room we opened. But if I were you, I wouldn't take too long on the way back.' Then he looked at me, and again switched on the private frequency. 'It's not too late, Richard. You can still come back with me.'

'No,' I said. 'You're wrong. It's much too late.'

Celestine reached out to help me make my awkward way to the next door. 'Leave him, Richard. Leave him to the Spire. It's what he's always wanted, and he's had his witnesses now.'

Childe eased himself onto the lip of the door leading into the room we had just come through.

'Well?' he said.

'She's right. Whatever happens now, it's between you and the Spire. I suppose I should wish you the best of luck, except it would sound irredeemably trite.'

He shrugged; one of the few human gestures now available to him. 'I'll take whatever I can get. And I assure that we *will* meet again, whether you like it or not.'

'I hope so,' I said, while knowing it would never be the case. 'In the meantime, I'll give your regards to Chasm City.'

'Do that, please. Just don't be too specific about where I went.'

'I promise you that. Roland?'

'Yes?'

'I think I should say goodbye now.'

Childe turned around and slithered into the darkness, propelling himself with quick, piston-like movements of his forearms.

Then Celestine took my arm and helped me towards the exit.

thirteen

'You were right,' I told her as we made our way back to the shuttle. 'I think I would have followed him.'

Celestine nodded. 'But I'm glad you didn't.'

'Do you mind if I ask something?'

'As long as it isn't to do with mathematics.'

'Why did you care what happened to me, and not Childe?'

'I did care about Childe,' she said firmly. 'But I didn't think any of us were going to be able to persuade him to turn back.'

'And that was the only reason?'

'No. I also thought you deserved something better than to be killed by the Spire.'

'You risked your life to get me out,' I said. 'I'm not ungrateful.'

'Not ungrateful? Is that your idea of an expression of gratitude?' But she was smiling, and I felt a faint impulse to smile as well. 'Well, at least that sounds like the old Richard.'

'There's hope for me yet, then. Trintignant can put me back the way I should be, after he's done with you.'

But when we got back to the shuttle there was no sign of Doctor Trintignant. We searched for him, but found nothing; not even a set of tracks leading away. None of the remaining suits were missing, and when we contacted the orbiting ship they had knowledge of the Doctor's where-abouts.

Then we found him.

He had placed himself on his operating couch, beneath the loom of swift, beautiful surgical machinery. And the machines had dismantled him, separating him into his constituent components, placing some pieces of him in neatly-labelled fluid-filled flasks and others in vials. Chunks of eviscerated bio-machinery floated like stinger-laden jellyfish. Implants and mechanisms glittered like small, precisely jewelled ornaments.

There was surprisingly little in the way of organic matter.

'He killed himself,' Celestine said. Then she found his hat – the homburg – which he had placed at the head of the operating couch. Inside, tightly folded and marked in precise handwriting, was what amounted to Trintignant's suicide note.

My dear friends, he had written.

After giving the matter no little consideration, I have decided to dispose of myself. I find the prospect of my own dismantling a more palatable one than continuing to endure revulsion for a crime I do not believe I committed. Please do not attempt to put me back together; the endeavour would, I assure you, be quite futile. I trust however that the manner of my demise – and the annotated state to which I have reduced myself – will provide some small amusement to future scholars of cybernetics.

I must confess that there is another reason why I have chosen to bring about this somewhat terminal state of affairs. Why, after all, did I not end myself on Yellowstone?

The answer, I am afraid, lies as much in vanity as anything else.

Thanks to the Spire – and to the good offices of Mister Childe – I have been given the opportunity to continue the work that was so abruptly terminated by the unpleasantness in Chasm City. And thanks to yourselves – who were so keen to learn the Spire's secrets – I have been gifted with subjects willing to submit to some of my less orthodox procedures.

You in particular, Mister Swift, have been a Godsend. I consider the series of transformations I have wrought upon you to be my finest achievement to date. You have become my magnum opus. I fully accept that you saw the surgery merely as a means to an end, and that you would not otherwise have consented to my ministrations, but that in no way lessens the magnificence of what you have become.

And therein, I am afraid, lies the problem.

Whether you conquer the Spire, or retreat from it – assuming, of course, that it does not kill you – there will surely come a time when you will desire to return to your prior form. And that would mean that I would be compelled to undo my single greatest work.

Something I would rather die than do.

I offer my apologies, such as they are, while remaining –

Your obedient servant,

T

* * *

Childe never returned. After ten days we searched the area about the Spire's base, but there were no remains that had not been there before. I supposed that there was nothing for it but to assume that he was still inside; still working his way to whatever lay at the summit.

And I wondered.

What ultimate function did the Spire serve? Was it possible that it served none but its own self-preservation? Perhaps it simply lured the curious into it, and forced them to adapt – becoming more like machines themselves – until they reached the point when they were of use to it.

At which point it harvested them.

Was it possible that the Spire was no more purposeful than a flytrap?

I had no answers. And I did not want to remain on Golgotha pondering such things. I did not trust myself not to return to the Spire. I still felt its feral pull.

So we left.

'Promise me,' Celestine said.

'What?'

'That whatever happens when we get home – whatever's become of the city – you won't go back to the Spire.'

'I won't go back,' I said. 'And I promise you that. I can even have the memory of it suppressed, so it doesn't haunt my dreams.'

'Why not,' she said. 'You've done it before, after all.'

But when we returned to Chasm City we found that Childe had not been lying. Things had changed, but not for the better. The thing that they called the Melding Plague had plunged our city back into a festering, technologically-decadent dark age. The wealth we had accrued on Childe's expedition meant nothing now, and what small influence my family had possessed before the crisis had diminished even further.

In better days, Trintignant's work could probably have been undone. It would not have been simple, but there were those who relished such a challenge, and I would probably have had to fight off several competing offers; rival cyberneticists vying for the prestige of tackling such a difficult project. Things were different now. Even the crudest kinds of surgery were now difficult or impossibly expensive. Only a handful of specialists retained the means to even attempt such work, and they were free to charge whatever they liked.

Even Celestine, who had been wealthier than me, could only afford to have me repaired, not rectified. That – and the other matter – almost bankrupted us.

And yet she cared for me.

There were those who saw us and imagined that the creature with her – the thing that trotted by her like a stiff, diamond-skinned, grotesque mechanical dog – was merely a strange choice of pet. Sometimes they sensed something unusual in our relationship – the way she might whisper an aside to me, or the way I might seem to be leading her – and they would look at me, intently, before I stared into their eyes with the blinding red scrutiny of my vision.

Then they would always look away.

And for a long time – until the dreams became too much – that was how it was.

Yet now I pad into the night, Celestine unaware that I have left our apartment. Outside, dangerous gangs infiltrate the shadowed, half-flooded streets. They call this part of Chasm City the Mulch and it is the only place where we can afford to live now. Certainly, we could have afforded something better – something much better – if I had not been forced to put aside money in readiness for this day. But Celestine knows nothing of that.

The Mulch is not as bad as it used to be, but it would still have struck the earlier me as a vile place in which to exist. Even now I am instinctively wary, my enhanced eyes dwelling on the various crudely fashioned blades and cross-bows that the gangs flaunt. Not all of the creatures who haunt the night are technically human. There are things with gills that can barely breathe in open air. There are other things that resemble pigs, and they are the worst of all.

But I do not fear them.

I slink between shadows, my thin, doglike form confusing them. I squeeze through the gaps in collapsed buildings, effortlessly escaping the few who are foolish enough to chase me. Now and then I even stop and confront them, standing with my back arched.

My red gaze stabs through them.

I continue on my way.

Presently I reach the appointed area. At first it seems deserted – there are no gangs here – but then a figure emerges from the gloom, trudging through ankle-deep caramel-brown floodwater. The figure is thin and dark, and with each step it makes there is a small, precise whine. It comes into view and I observe that the woman – for it is a woman, I think – is wearing an exoskeleton. Her skin is the black of interstellar space, and her small, exquisitely-featured head is perched above a neck which has been extended by several vertebrae. She wears copper rings around her neck, and her fingernails – which I see clicking against the thighs of her exoskeleton – are as long as stilettos.

I think she is strange, but she sees me and flinches.

'Are you . . . ?' she starts to say.

'I am Richard Swift,' I answer.

She nods almost imperceptibly – it cannot be easy, bending that neck – and introduces herself. 'I am Triumvir Verika Abebi, of the lighthugger *Poseidon*. I sincerely hope you are not wasting my time.'

'I can pay you, don't you worry.'

She looks at me with something between pity and awe. 'You haven't even told me what it is you want.'

'That's easy,' I say. 'I want you to take me somewhere.'

park polar

Adam Roberts

The sky raced like a shaggy wolf with a rabbit pinned
in its jaws, its fur flying with the first snow,
then gnawed at the twilight with its incisors skinned;
the light bled, flour flew past the window.

Walcott, *Omeros* xlii

one

Park Polar moved beneath them, white as bleached sheets.

'I still don't see,' said McCullough, 'why we need the military protection.'

'Terrorists,' said Kodwo, offhandedly. 'These terrorists think we're desecrating the last great wilderness.' And the wind sliced through the chinks in the front-loader of the air-truck, and McCullough pulled the rims of her hood tighter around the front of her face. The air-truck passenger floor was constructed entirely of transparent panels, a see-through bubble slung underneath the main cargo body of the plane. McCullough hated it. No matter how hard she told herself not to look, she found her eyes drawn down between her feet. The polar landscape slid by beneath. A sort of optical illusion, and not one that made McCullough feel very comfortable. Her brain told her she was standing on nothing, and that felt very wrong. She was only momentarily suspended, and would soon start falling to the pack-ice below. Nasty sort of death; the inevitability of the anticipation. Knowing as you fell that you were about to die, no escape. McCullough went back over to the coffee nipple and filled another bowlbeaker. Then, half-heartedly, she tried to take her mind off it by staring at the surface of the coffee; but it jiggled and arranged itself into tiny standing ripples. Not letting her forget that she was on a plane. She shuffled back over to the group of genengineers, who now seemed to be sharing a joke. The three interDefence soldiers sat on the benches at the rim of the compartment, with their rifles between their knees. The sight of them didn't help calm McCullough's nerves either. Maybe another stab at conversation with the scientists would help take her mind off it, off everything. Except that every time she tried it, they somehow managed to bring the conversation back to death and dying. She wondered if they were doing it on purpose to wind her up, except that they did it with an ease that suggested it was their constant topic whether she was there or not.

She stood next to Bronovski. 'God, I hate flying,' she said. 'It's stupid, isn't it? The way I hate flying? It's a real old-time phobia.'

He looked at her. His long, smooth face, haloed completely by the red of his hood, looked weirdly detached from his body, incorporeal. 'Well, it is a pretty dangerous way of moving around,' he said. 'Specially up here. The weather is all to fuck up here. Had a friend,' he went on, prodding Hartmann's arm with his mitten to get his attention, 'called Wu. You remember Wu? His plane crashed on a Zembla island, one of them. It was the strangest thing.'

'I remember Wu,' said Hartmann, turning to them. 'God, that was a nasty way to go.'

'The plane he was on hit the ground, some malfunction or other. But the point is, it hit the ground, broke up. The front part, with the pilot, happened to go right into a fat drift. That guy broke an arm, but was otherwise alright. But Wu's half struck hard ice and broke into tiny little pieces. He was mashed up like mince.'

'Who you talking about?' said Kodwo, coming over.

'Wu,' said Hartmann.

'Oh God, I remember him,' said Kodwo, with a wide grin.

McCullough said, abruptly: 'Tell me more about these terrorists.' She certainly didn't want any more gung-ho stories of arctic aircraft accidents. Even the terrorists would be better a better topic of conversation than that.

'I think they've got a point,' said Kodwo, switching conversation topics smoothly. They all did that, McCullough had decided, all three of them seguing from one talking point to the next. It was like hanging out with kids. They moved from one thing to another indiscriminately as if bored too easily;

they never expressed surprise, never transgressed the code of Cool that defined them.

'You're on the side of the terrorists,' said Bronovski without surprise. 'Figures.'

'Meaning what?' retorted Kodwo. But even when they bickered, like this, or to be more precise (McCullough thought) even when they went through the *motions* of bickering, like this, there was never any heat in it. Pieces moved about a board, just a well-worn conversational game.

'Meaning,' said Bronovski, 'last week you were saying there should be death penalties for terrorists, but this week you're on their side. Is it your period, or something?'

Kodwo was a short Eurasian woman whose figure spread consistently from her neck to her hips. The padding of her jacket made her look even more bulky. She was a much more imposing figure than stalky Bronovski. Her coin-shaped face wrinkled in disdain, the eyes disappearing into creases.

'Interesting thing about arctic menstruation,' said Hartmann, about to move the conversation onto something else. 'Without the usual cycles of twenty-four hours day and night—'

But McCullough stopped him.

'No, wait a moment,' she said. 'Go on with what you were saying, please. What's the deal with these terrorists?'

Kodwo shrugged; or perhaps shuddered a little, it was difficult to tell underneath all that padding. The air coming in through the gaps in the front-loader was certainly chilly. 'They think we should keep the Parks as wildernesses. You ask me, there's a certain point to that argument.'

'A point?' said Bronovski in a bored tone. 'An anti-life point. What good are wildernesses? Gigahectares of nothing. There's plenty of nothing in the universe. The universe is mostly made up of nothing. If they like that, why don't they move on up?'

'Of course they're anti-life,' said Kodwo. 'That's why they're terrorists. That's why they blow things up.'

'What I don't understand,' said Hartmann, 'is how that squares with them.

They believe Park Polar should be left entirely unspoiled, but then they blow up whole stations. The debris from that kind of thing is going to do far more damage to the wilderness status of Arctica than any number of herds of snow-wildebeest.'

'Their latest thing,' said Bronovski, nodding, 'is to poison the ice in some way. To kill all the animals from the ground up. Now that's a pretty nihilistic philosophy, I do think.'

'Poison, huh,' said Hartmann. 'I'd not heard that one.'

'Sure,' said Bronovski. 'That's the latest. Some bacterial agent, introduced into the ice, kills off the whole ecosystem here.'

'Well would you look at that?' said Kodwo. Everybody looked down, following her gaze. McCullough couldn't help herself. They were flying over patches of green ice now, and the blotchy patterns of colour against the brightness of the white ice gave it a surreal effect, as if they were passing slowly over a large abstract painting held a few feet below the air-truck. Long sprawling fingers of green, stretches and blobs of white. McCullough crouched down, holding her bowlbeaker in both hands as if for comfort. She found the whole optical illusion of having nothing between her and the ground a little easier to cope with if she were squatting down. The three scientists were unfazed by the apparent drop. They all stood with their legs apart, and their heads down. 'What is it?' McCullough asked. 'What's wrong?'

It was Kodwo who answered. 'Look at the algae patterning,' she said.

'That patterning,' said Bronovski, 'is all to fuck.'

'When we lay it out we lay it out in geometric patterns. The wildebeest should graze it enough to keep it to those patterns. But these algae are spreading in great fingers – look there, for instance.'

McCullough forced herself to look again. Picked out against the smooth, table-top green of the algae-ice she could just make out the white backs of snow-wildebeest. They looked impossibly tiny, like white maggots. She tried to think of them as maggots. If she thought of them as the huge, shaggy, white monsters she knew from the lab, then she'd be forced to confront exactly how far up she was. The three scientists were bickering again.

'It's undergrazed,' said Hartmann, lazily. 'Any fool from Mars can see it's undergrazed.'

'Any fool from Mars can see they're down there grazing it *now*,' countered Kodwo. 'There they are. Its the algae; it's hyperfecund.'

'I can see, what, a dozen animals? That's not enough to graze it back. We need more wildebeest, then the green is kept in check.'

'We need a less fecund strain of algae,' said Kodwo. 'Or pretty soon the whole of Park Polar is going to be green.'

'More wildebeest,' said Bronovski, putting his hand on McCullough's shoulders, 'means more dung for you, Dr McCullough.'

'More dung,' said McCullough. 'That's lovely. Thank you, Dr Bronovski.'

When they landed an hour and a half later, Kodwo and Hartmann were still discussing what difference it would make if the whole of the arctic circle were colonised by the snow algae. Hartmann, just to be contrary (or so it seemed to McCullough) was arguing it would make no difference at all. 'We'd need to give the animals a different colouring, I guess, or their camouflage would be all messed up. But we could do that. Get their hides to grow chlorophyll.' He riffed on the topic of photosynthesising animal hide for a bit. Kodwo looked as though she could barely gather the energy to contradict such idiocy.

'It would utterly change the refractive index,' she said. 'Probably melt the whole pack. It would be Armageddon for Park Polar.'

The front-loaders opened, and tiny gusts of gritty ice blew in. 'That,' Bronovski told McCullough, putting his padded arm around her back and pointing with his free mitten to a lumbering figure coming in through the front-loader. 'That is Natty. That's the name you should use, Natty.'

'That's his name?' asked McCullough, weakly.

'Ah, no,' said Bronovski ponderously. 'Nobody knows the real name. But we all use 'Natty' and it seems to serve.'

two

Natty had a beard, and looked pretty bulky in a red padded jacket, so it took McCullough a while before she realised that Natty was a woman.

'I genengineered the beard,' she said, and then she grinned widely at her own rhyme. 'A little poem,' she said. 'I genengin*eered* the *beard*. Just as she *feared*.'

'And it looks *weird*,' chipped in Kodwo.

McCullough must have been staring a little, because Natty then said, 'it's OK to touch it, bright girl. It's real. It keeps my chin warm.' She grabbed McCullough's hand, tugging the mitten off, and pulling the fingers so that they connected with the surprisingly soft hairs.

'I'm sorry,' said McCullough, blushing, pulling her hand away. 'I didn't mean to be rude.' Natty's boisterous manner contrasted so sharply from the laid-back cynicism of the scientists that she was a little wrongfooted

Natty laughed, a weird peeping sort of noise. 'You aren't rude, my darling-lovely,' she said. 'You're a sweet. You really are.' She put her chin forward so that the hairs bristled. 'I get rid of it when I leave post here, and make my way back home,' she said. 'Haven't found a man yet who'll admit to finding facial hair attractive on a woman. Nor yet a woman. But it keeps me warm when I'm up here by myself.'

Hartmann came through. His own beard looked meagre beside Natty's splendid bush. 'Natty,' he said. 'The pilot wants to be off now. Is there any more junk you want taking back?'

'We *are* careful of our junk,' said Natty. 'In case there are any terrorists listening in, we are *most* careful to have all the bio-undegradable stuff flown back to Russian incinerators. Wouldn't want people to think we were *polluting* this pristine wilderness.' She went through a door at the back of the chamber.

'Don't worry about her,' said Hartmann. 'She's acting up a little because you're new. It's a sort of show-off thing.'

'She fancies you,' said Kodwo, coming up behind with a pack and dumping it on the floor.

'Actually, I doubt if she does,' said Hartmann. 'But you'll get used to her. She's a *mensch*.'

Natty came back through complaining. 'Three soldiers?' she was saying, in a high-pitched voice. 'Why three? Why not two? Or one?'

'Come along,' said Hartmann. 'You know as good as any of us. There have been attacks all along the Harris Ridge. Animals killed, stations exploded.'

'Like these soldiers are going to do any good about that,' said Natty. 'Where are they supposed to stay, answer me that?'

'They can bivouac here, in the store,' said Kodwo.

'Fucking right on the button they can,' said Natty.

* * *

The entrance to the body of the complex was through a door at the back of the hangar, over by the corner. McCullough went through and down the slope, passing through the kitchen, the corridor, and making her way to a cell-like room carved from the ice itself. Natty was right behind her.

'You cut all this out of the ice yourself?' McCullough asked, trying to find a topic of neutral conversation.

'I didn't,' was the reply. 'Construction did. Or construction drones did, whilst two construction workers stood around and tried to worm their way into my knickers. This is your place. You want to unload your samples? That pilot is itching to be off.'

So McCullough dumped her pack, and hurried through to the ice-hangar at the front. It took her twenty minutes to get her containers off the air-truck, and another ten to go from each to each checking the seals and the internal conditions. Whilst she was doing this she looked through the wide mouth of the hangar as the bulbous shape of the air-truck shuddered and lifted into the sky on a swarm of clouding ice particles.

'What are these, anyway?' asked Natty.

'Kangaroos,' said McCullough. For the first time since the beginning of the flight she was feeling more in control of the situation, a little calmer. Each of her containers seemed OK.

'Alright,' said Natty. 'Kangaroos. You Australian?'

McCullough looked at her. 'As it happens, yes,' she said. 'Although my parents moved around a lot when I was young.'

'I went to Australia once,' said Natty, leaning against the door-jamb. Her hands were ungloved, and she was twirling a forefinger in her beard. It distantly crossed McCullough's mind that this might have been meant as a flirtatious gesture.

'Really?' said McCullough, keen to keep the conversation on non-contentious topics. 'Whereabouts?'

'Oh I can't remember the names. Somewhere west, I think. Or was it right in the middle? Anyway, all I can remember was soya. Soya plants stretching in every direction, far as the eye could see. It was like this place, in a way. Like this place to fly over. Just soya plants for hours and hours, and every now and again some huge automated harvester, like a bug.'

'The West and Centre is pretty much all soya now,' said McCullough. 'Although there are some wheat-fields in the South East.'

'It's the monotony of it, is my point.' Natty stood up, picked her gloves from where they dangled from her sleeves, and slid her hands back inside. 'I wonder if it makes that much difference in the end: a wilderness of life, or a wilderness of death. Amounts to the same, wouldn't you say, tiger?'

'I wouldn't know about that,' said McCullough, not really listening.

'You like soya?'

'That's a strange question.'

'Well,' said Natty. 'I guess I mean: doesn't it bother you that all these animals, all these kangaroos, have got displaced by soya plants? Particularly soya, it being such a dull plant. That on account of *soya* the only place they can roam around now is up here?'

'Well, there are some unmodified roos in the larger suburban belts, where the folk are rich enough to have large gardens and animal-crazy enough to want unusual pets. And there's always Park Antarctica.'

'You got any kangaroos down there?'

'Actually,' said McCullough, compressing all those painful years into two words, 'no.' Park Antarctica had been the logical place to try and cultivate snow-kangaroos. Close to their continent of origin, and with plenty of Antarctic sheep and snow-pigs to provide the droppings. But it had been the altitude in the end that had destroyed them. They had just refused to adjust to the altitude. The memory of all she had put into that project, and how profoundly she had failed, was still there, a miasma of ache. She tried to disperse it with concentration on the now; that was her philosophy. With action.

'Those are all OK,' she said, turning to Natty, slapping the last of her containers with her mittened hand. 'Probably tomorrow I can start bringing them round. Then we're going to need a corral. Anywhere immediately outside would be fine. And we're going to need some dung.'

'You'd better talk to the Three Stooges about that,' said Natty.

The day finished with all five of them in the kitchen together taking evening soup from the soup-nipple. The three soldiers seemed more comfortable eating by themselves. McCullough had lectured them about not fiddling with the kangaroo containers, and then left them to make themselves at home in the hangar. It seemed a cold sort of place, open to the ice as it was, but they didn't complain.

As McCullough got up to help herself to her second bowl of soup, the conversation had got back to the algae. With remarkable stubbornness, Hartmann was still insisting that algae spread was not a problem. Kodwo was shaking her head in a languid sort of way.

'Your problem,' she was saying, 'is that you have no sense of biodynamics.'

'Your sense of biodynamics,' agreed Bronovski, nodding, 'is all to fuck.'

'It's a pattern,' said Kodwo. 'We need to keep it in harmony.'

'And whose biodynamics are inept, I wonder?' Hartmann asked of nobody in particular. 'Not mine, I think. You want to *keep* it in harmony? It's not something you can control. It will find its own level of harmony. That's how nature works.'

'It's a wonder you're here at all,' said Kodwo. 'What are we doing here, if everything is so perfect a self-regulating system?'

'He's here,' said Natty, 'because he's too ugly to make it in the real world.'

'I'm here,' said Hartmann, with a blank expression, 'to give the *sweet-faced* Dr McCullough a helping little hand with her kanga project.'

'If we give the wildebeest chlorophyll hides,' said Kodwo, going back to the core of the argument, 'then the photosynthesis will give them a certain amount of energy. Heat them up a little, maybe.'

'Do you see how elegant that is?' said Hartmann.

'But if they're getting x percent of their energy that way, then they'll eat even less algae. Then the algae will spread even faster.'

'You only think that's a problem because you don't see how beautiful a green arctic would be,' said Hartmann.

'The natural way,' said Bronovski, 'would be to introduce more wildebeest. They'll graze the algae back into ratio. Then the excess beest will starve and die out, and everything will be back to rightness.'

'That's an expensive sort of solution, don't you think?' said Hartmann. 'Don't you think so, Dr McCullough?'

But the last thing McCullough wanted was to get involved in this sort of circular bickering. 'Actually,' she said, 'I'm tired. I think I'll turn in.'

She made her way back to her room, and climbed into her sleeping bag fully clothed. An hour later there was a rattle on the door.

'Who's that?'

'It's me,' said Bronovski.

'What do you want?'

But Bronovski had already opened the door and come in. There didn't seem to be locks anywhere in the complex.

'How can I help you, Dr Bronovski?' McCullough asked.

'If you're feeling chilly,' said Bronovski, with a foolish-looking grin on his face, 'I can help you warm up. There's not much central heating out here, only what we make for ourselves.' He scuttled over and sat on the edge of her bunk. 'Come along, eh, baby,' he said, and stopped, looking ever-so-slightly pained. 'You see, I don't even know your first name.'

'Nor do you need to, *Doctor* Bronovski,' said McCullough. 'You'd really better leave, you know.'

'Come along,' said Bronovski. 'You think you're going to get a better offer? From who, out here? From Hartmann? He has warts. All over his back, take it from me.'

'I don't want an offer from anybody,' said McCullough, feeling weary. 'I'm asking you to go. Now, please.'

'Well,' said Bronovski, blithely, 'since you're asking me, and so politely too.' He stood up, still grinning, and left.

three

The next day McCullough persuaded the three surly interDefence soldiers to set to work fencing in an area outside the mouth of the hangar. They were not happy doing it, but there was certainly nothing else for them to do except sit around playing screen games and perking themselves up with standard-issue jabs of Alertocaine. They slung their weapons over their backs and went out with lasers to cut ice blocks. McCullough had asked them for a wall four metres high, but it was clear by lunch-break that she was going to be lucky to get one half that height.

She, meanwhile, had also found it hard to talk round the Three Stooges, as Natty called them. McCullough didn't get the reference, but the label somehow suited them. They were stooges, in a way; standing in for their Science in a world where what mattered was not Science as such but Technology, and food technology above all. They didn't like the solitude, McCullough decided. That was puzzling too. There were any number of people in the crowded horrors of the northern habitation belts who would have given all they had for a few weeks away from the crush, but these three were always together, as if frightened of being alone. Maybe they had originally come out here thinking the wilderness would be a blessed relief from so many crowds, only to discover that there was something deeply unsettling about all that open space. Maybe they had bound themselves together as a group in the face of the emptiness of it all.

McCullough didn't feel that way, standing in the mouth of the hangar, looking over the plane of ice that went all the way to the horizon. Maybe, she told herself, she was only dazzled by the newness of it all. But now that she was on the ground, rather than hurtling through the sky over it, she found herself strangely moved by the purity of it all.

That wasn't how the others saw it at all. As they took their soya-pottage from the breakfast nipple they complained and whined in their genial way. 'I hate it up here,' said Kodwo. 'It's so desolate.'

'But that's why we're here,' said Hartmann. 'You whiner. We're here to make the desert bloom.'

'*You're* here to make the desert bloom,' Kodwo said to him, 'with your foul algae. I'm here to make the deserts of ice come alive with majestic herds of snow-wildebeest. That's a real activity.'

'And I,' said Bronovski, 'am here to provide the predators. They are at the top of the chain, the snow-lions and snow-hyenas. They are the ones for whom the whole of creation is made. That makes me *more* important than you two, I think.'

'You hardly ever see a lion,' said Kodwo. 'My wildebeest are all over the place. So that makes *me* the more significant party.'

'Not eating enough algae, though, according to you,' said Hartmann. 'Maybe you set their clocks wrong when you genengineered them. Maybe they've all gone into hibernation too early, whilst the sun is still out to nutrify my beautiful algae.'

'And talking of which, *my* circadian rhythms,' said Bronovski, rubbing his eyes 'are all to fuck. I hardly didn't sleep last night.'

'We saw them from the air-truck,' said Kodwo, getting herself another bowlbeaker of soya. 'My wildebeest. *They're* not asleep.'

'Yeah,' said Bronovski. 'And lay off her anyway. It's not an easy thing, this whole genengineering of hibernation in an animal like the wildebeest. Now, my lions, it was easy as pie. Lions sleep pretty much all the time anyway. But wildebeest, they don't like sleeping. They reckon they'll be eaten if they stop hoofing. You had problems with the hibernation gene, *Doctor* McCullough? In your kangaroos, I mean?'

But McCullough refused to be drawn. 'I'm going to bring the roos out of the containers today. I've ordered the soldiers to build an enclosure outside. But I'm going to need some dung for them to eat, and I'd like you to get me some.'

'Picking up shit,' said Bronovski. 'It would be a pleasure, Doctor McCullough, picking shit for you.'

'Perhaps,' said Hartmann, smiling slyly, 'we could provide our own as well? Or even instead? That might save us the bother.'

After they had gone, each taking an ice-car out and buzzing off towards the western horizon, McCullough and Natty handled the unpacking of the containers. The stiff, cold bodies of the snow-roos flopped to the ice floor amongst a rush of bad-smelling steam. 'That's the stasis fluid,' McCullough explained. 'It's pretty volatile, and it doesn't smell good.'

'I didn't figure it was your shampoo, O my captain.' Natty hawked in her throat as if to spit, but didn't actually do it.

One by one, McCullough brought the roos out of stasis, and Natty dragged their white-furred bodies onto a plastic tarpaulin. By half eleven the first part of the job was finished, and the two of them shared a coffee in the kitchen.

'I'll bring them round, and leave them in the corral for a while.'

'Poor bastards won't know what smacked them in their kangaroo chops,' said Natty. 'You can almost feel sorry for them. One minute they're bounding through the wide open outback, in the warm sunshine. The next they have to make a living eating wildebeest shit in the coldest place on the planet. Not much of a trade.'

'These creatures never bounded through the outback,' said McCullough. 'They never bounded anywhere. They don't know anything at all yet. Unless they've managed magically to imbue memories of being tissue samples and computer rendered DNA in the Mount Gambier Animal Adaptation Lab.'

'I'm only kidding with you, honey pie,' said Natty. 'More coffee?' Then, as she filled their globes at the nipple: 'I guess it's been a long time since anybody did anything in what you might call *outback*.'

'You sound like a student radical, or something,' said McCullough, pulling off her mitten and taking the coffee. 'I haven't had that sort of conversation since I was at school.'

'What kind of conversation?'

'You know. All this stuff about the monotony of soya fields, and the dubious morality of relocating animals. Don't you reckon it is better that these animals continue to live in the wild, although adapted? Or should they get wiped out, and only carry on living as pets?'

'I'm no radical, sweet pea,' said Natty, settling down at the table again. 'If I was, I'd be out bombing this place with the terrorists, not caretaking it for the Company. But you got to ask yourself questions, or your mind goes stale. Don't you think? You might want to ask yourself genengineering questions, like you do. You might, on the other hand, want to know why we have to cultivate all these wild areas in the first place. Why turn pretty much the whole of central Africa from tropic to tropic into a huge plantation? Why make over Australia the way they've done? To make sure there's enough food for people like the Three Stooges out there? Would it be such a loss if one of them starved to death, and the kangaroos were left in peace?'

'You really do sound like a student radical now,' said McCullough, the coffee warming her blood and making her smile.

'Bingo, bingo,' said Natty. 'That's exactly what I studied at School. Radicalism and Politics Major, all three years.'

'Really?' asked McCullough, ingenuous.

'No, not really. I studied genengineering, like you. How you think I made the beard?'

After coffee, working outside with hoods up and mittens on, McCullough felt a certain sense of intimacy growing between them. 'You really don't like those three, do you,' she said, feeling bold.

'Those soldiers?' The three interDefence boys had abandoned any pretence of building the wall, and were out on the ice playing at patrols. They had probably hunkered down just out of sight of the complex to enjoy some more stabs of Alertocaine. 'I never seen them before.'

'No, not the soldiers,' said McCullough. 'I mean Bronovski, Hartmann and Kodwo.'

'Oh them. They're harmless enough. They're like kids, really. Some scientists get that way. Maybe being too close to scientific data dissociates them from the way the real world works.'

'Bronovski made a pass at me last night.'

'Surprised he didn't do it on the plane coming in,' said Natty, deadpan. 'Did you take him up on his offer?'

'No,' said McCullough.

'Good thinking, dear, good thinking. He's got a gum virus, one of the incurable ones. And he's not the sort of guy to wear a mouth-prophylactic. He'd pass it on, and you'd be stuck with it.'

'Really?' said McCullough.

'Oh yeah. There's no end of viruses you can get from sex with men. That's why I recommend sex with women until medical science catches up with the infections.' She grinned, her teeth splitting the hair of her beard. McCullough blushed, put her head down, carried on injecting the kangaroos.

Eventually they were all revived, all lying on the mat breathing shallowly. When McCullough leaned close they didn't even move their eyes to look at her.

'It'll take a while for them to come to,' she said. 'Then they'll have to spend a few days getting used to basic stuff; walking and so on.'

'And the getting used to eating shit, too,' said Natty. 'Poor bastards.'

'It's nutritious,' said McCullough. 'They'll get used to it. Don't worry about them.'

'Right,' said Natty. 'And you'll get used to Bronovski hitting on you. You know he'll try again tonight.'

'It would be nice to have a lock on my door.'

'Locks?' said Natty, perkily. 'But we're all one happy little team out here.'

The two of them went through and cleaned up the hangar. Pretty soon they were laughing together at the absurdity of their chores. 'Female domesticity, tidying the house whilst the men are out at work,' said Natty.

'Apart from Kodwo,' said McCullough.

'I count her as one of the men,' said Natty.

'Oh, really?'

Natty chuckled. 'Not in *that* sense. But in the sense that she's one of the Three Stooges, and that's a man's position. Or, maybe, a boy's position. Let's call them kids and have done with it.'

'It's so *stupid*,' said McCullough as she folded the tarpaulin neatly. She watched the laughter come out of her mouth in puffy blocks of steam. Natty laughed with her, although her laughter was a strangely strangled sound, like a high-pitched keening. 'I surely don't get to laugh much when I'm up here by myself,' she said.

'Well I haven't laughed much in, oh, well, *quite* a few years.'

'You got a sob story,' said Natty, nodding. 'We all got our sob stories. Course, some stories are worth more sobs than others.'

'Well, I was thinking more of just having spent so many years in the lab and at the computer, getting these roos sorted out. Not many laughs in doing that.'

'That,' said Natty, 'is not a sob story. That's work. You should be grateful you got work in today's world. You know what they say, cheapest resource in the world is people. It's the only thing in the world that ain't scarce. People are cheap today and everything else is expensive. You build your roos to eat shit; people eat shit in shitty jobs all round the world every single day.'

'I suppose you're right.'

'No, *that* is not your sob story. But you got one, I know you have.'

'And I suppose you do too. I'm bored with this cleaning up.' McCullough stood up, her joints singing. 'I do get stiff. The desk jockey's complaint.'

Natty was grinning. 'You want me to rub your stiff old bones for you?'

McCullough laughed at this, and then paused. When the other woman's gaze didn't waver, she said: 'You're serious?'

'I wouldn't be flippant about a thing like that,' said Natty.

McCullough thought for a full minute, during which time Natty didn't say anything. What kind of scientist was she, she told herself, if she didn't explore? There was something about Natty, a comfortable something. A port in a stormy sea.

'OK,' she said.

So they went back to McCullough's little cell, and Natty rubbed her stiff old bones, and then rubbed some more of her body, reaching her hands in through the front of McCullough's coverall. Pretty soon they were both caught up in it, although never quite caught up enough for McCullough to disengage her analytical faculties, to stop herself thinking 'here I am touching a breast but it's not my breast', or 'the beard is masculine but the body is feminine'. Actually the beard was softer than a man's beard, more like head hair; and neither party exposed too much feminine body to the chilly air. Nonetheless, after a little while she got lost further, and tipped over the edge to where nothing mattered any more. When she returned, her breath was clouding spectacularly out of her mouth and leaving miniature cumulonimbuses in the air of the room. The sweat on her chest and collar bone was starting to settle into a cold crust. She got up and fetched the towel from the sink compartment.

As she wiped the frozen sweat away, Natty sighed in a long self-satisfied way. 'That's better than you'd get from Bronovski, I can *promise* you. Take it from me.'

'Oh,' said McCullough. Then, with a little spurt of panic at the thought of his mouth virus, 'Did you kiss him?'

'Oh he doesn't go much on kissing, specially when the woman has a beard. Don't you worry, my flower.'

McCullough zipped up her coverall, and lay on the bony little bed next to Natty again. 'It was nice,' she said. 'It was.'

'Sound like you're trying to convince yourself.'

After a while McCullough asked: 'Is Natty your real name.'

Natty laughed at this. 'No no. It's a sort of nickname. It'll do though.'

'What's your real name?'

'You couldn't pronounce it,' said Natty. McCullough thought she could read brusqueness in the reply, as if she were being rebuked for wanting to get a fraction too intimate.

'Why Natty, then?'

'I'm from Natal. In Africa. My father part-owned a maize monoculture, stretched a hundred twenty kilometres in from the coast. The reason I say you couldn't pronounce my name is it's a traditional Zulu name, never yet met a northerner who could pronounce it. But maybe you could.'

'That's alright,' said McCullough, already feeling a little distanced.

'I didn't mean to cut you there, my peach.'

'Tell me about your father.'

'Oh, he got squeezed out. He was a fool, really. The thing with Africa being the food basket is that lines to the coast for desal water are the key. You know your history, you know how Africa used to be; just dust and scrub. My father didn't part-own much land, but he part-owned a stretch by the coast, and he thought he'd make his fortune charging the Big Companies water rental for crossing his land.'

'And he didn't? Make his fortune?'

'No. Company VII sent in troops. He got himself killed. Got himself shot, and refused to go in to medictown, and so then he got himself blood poisoning. Then they amputated his leg, then he pushed his glide-chair into the Indian Ocean and drowned himself. Stubborn man, didn't want to bear being a cripple.'

'We've all got our sob stories,' said McCullough.

'What genius said that?' said Natty, grinning again.

* * *

The Three Stooges came back four hours later than they had said. McCullough was beginning to get angry with them. Her roos had started to pull themselves onto their wobbly feet, and they were clicking with impotent hunger. One of two of them staggered back and forth, collided with the rough-made ice walls and fell over. It was pathetic to watch.

Finally the three sleds came buzzing back into the hangar. Kodwo was carrying a plastic sack full of something McCullough hoped would be dung. Bronovski and Hartmann hopped out of their saddles and did a little victory dance.

'What are you so pleased about?' asked McCullough.

'We tracked this herd for an hour,' replied Hartmann, breathless. 'Couldn't work out why they kept moving. Then we saw why: a whole pride of snow-lions.'

'My snow-lions!' crowed Bronovski, flapping his arms like a penguin. 'Beauties! Four lionesses, white as paper, using only the slightest undulations in the ice pack for cover as they stalked – but my God, I couldn't spot them until they made their attack run. Could you?' He was asking this question of Kodwo, who was looking sour-faced. She dumped the sack on the ground.

'Certainly not,' she said. 'One of the bastards came after me. I was at full speed on my sled, and I only barely got away with my life.'

Bronovski and Hartmann shrieked with laughter, and did their little dance again. 'Oh, it's very funny,' said Kodwo, scowling. 'Very funny until I get my face clawed off by a fucking snow-lion.' She stomped off to the back of the hangar and into the complex. McCullough realised she had never seen the woman lose her cool before.

'Oh but it was beautiful,' said Hartmann. 'We took video. Nature in the raw. Blood on the snow.'

'Very nice,' said McCullough. She was trying to be sarcastic, but something about her manner meant that she was never able to put sarcasm across.

'Oh, Kodwo's just worried by the thought that she might have been eaten by a creature I genengineered,' said Bronovski, still laughing. 'That's what pisses her; not that she nearly got eaten, but that she nearly got eaten *by something I made.*'

McCullough checked the sack, and then went outside with it to distribute it to the twitching, spastic-looking roos. They sniffed, and one or two took a mouthful, but mostly they weren't interested. 'You'd better get used to it, guys,' she said. 'It's what you have to live on from now on.'

four

That night, McCullough wasn't sure what was going to happen. She lay in her bed waiting for a knock from Natty, uncertain whether, when it came, she was going to say 'Come in' or put her off with some excuse. She even ran through a few excuses in her head, getting herself ready. But no knock came. Even Bronovski left her alone. Eventually she drifted into sleep.

Disturbance came with a series of cracks, that worked themselves into McCullough's complex, rhizomatic dream as the breaking of the legs of a number of kangaroos. She woke anxiously and jerked upright in bed. Three more cracks. In her sleep-fazed brain, she even thought they were knocks at her door.

'Come in, Natty,' she mumbled.

Then there was a whole string of rattles that sounded more like what they were: gunshots. 'What's happening?' she called out, her voice quavery and dry. She hit the light, and wriggled out of her sleeping bag. A quick sip of water from the tap, and her voice was back. 'What's going on? What's *happening*?'

Out into the corridor, stumbling once before getting the use of her legs back, she came through to the kitchen. Kodwo was there already, standing, swaying a little.

'Kodwo,' said McCullough. 'What is happening? Are those gunshots?'

'I don't know,' said Kodwo, woozy, still half-asleep.

Hartmann came through then, followed by Natty. But McCullough was already moving up the corridor towards the hangar. Through the door, and almost at once she tripped. Tried to keep her balance, but her foot slid in a slime of something on the ice-floor and she went down.

She twisted on the floor to look back at what had tripped her up. It was a body, blood stretched under it glistening in the eternal light of polar summer. The stain looked taut, plastic, except where her foot had smeared it, patched it like a painter's brush. She struggled to her feet.

'Watch it,' she called to Bronovski, who was just emerging from the hangar door behind her. 'It's one of the soldiers, for the love of Christ.'

'Oh,' said Bronovski, looking down. Then he seemed to react. 'Oh God. He's dead. I know what that is, it's dead.'

McCullough was on her feet. She stumbled to the mouth of the hangar and looked out. The roos were still lurching uneasily, jumping heavily from spot to spot. She couldn't see anybody else. She wanted to shout out, to call after the other two soldiers, but with a shaming jab she realised she didn't know their names. 'Hey,' she called. 'Out there. Who's there?'

There was nothing. A vague wind picked fluff from the ice and whirled it in little smoky patches of white. It sounded hissingly in her ears, along with the *plock plock* of her roos jumping, but there were no other sounds.

Natty was behind her. 'The other two soldiers,' she said, breathily. 'They're not in the complex.'

'Christ,' said McCullough. 'Oh Jesus Christ.'

'It's terrorists,' shouted Hartmann from the back of the hangar. 'I just know it. Come away from there, both of you, or you'll be next.'

'Oh Christ,' said McCullough again. Some part of her was thinking, *yes, back inside, safer in the complex*; so she surprised herself when she realised that she was actually summoning up her courage. 'Oh Christ,' she said again, and dashed forward.

The lumbering roos were too dazed to notice her, and she weaved easily past them to the wall. Once there she poked her head up cautiously. She could just see over the top of the rough cut blocks. There were no craft visible on the flawless ice; no air-trucks, no land craft, nothing. Only the empty white stage of the arctic. If it were terrorists, then it was difficult to see how they had got to the base. Unless they'd parked up behind the complex, but what would be the point of that?

She went to the door and forced it open. Immediately on the other side of the wall were the bodies of the other two interDefence soldiers. They were sprawled, their weapons beside them. Crouching down, McCullough put her finger on the muzzle of one of the rifles. It was cold.

She sat back on the cold ice, and stared at the body in front of her. It was incredible. They were dead. That was no joke. This one was hardly bleeding at all, although its head had an oddly deflated look to it. The one a little further on had bled so much his white fatigues looked pink. He looked, McCullough thought randomly, like a Queen at a zone party. The pink warrior. She started to laugh, wheezily, when a shadow fell over her. She rolled and came to her feet screaming.

'Only me,' shouted Bronovski. 'Jesus, you scared me to *fuck*. Why did you yell at me?'

'You startled me,' she gasped. 'What do you think you're doing creeping up on me like that? When I'm sitting beside a dead body?'

'Christ,' he said, bending forward. 'They're both pretty dead. We got to get them in the hangar.'

He grabbed one by the feet and dragged it back through the door into the corral. Without thinking much, McCullough bent down and took the second corpse by the ankles. She walked backwards dragging it after her. It moved smoothly enough, although it left a broad red path of blood in its wake. She backed through the corral, nudging the door open with her bum, and pulled the body swiftly across the white into the hanger. Then she stopped and straightened up.

There was a bright red trail straight through the ice. One or two of the snow kangaroos hopped sluggishly over to it and bent forward to examine it. McCullough started wheezily laughing at that too. There was something exquisitely comic about the ducking forward, the twitching nostrils.

'Jesus,' said Hartmann. 'Your coprophages seem pretty vampiric. You create those beasts so they've an appetite for blood?'

'They're genengineered to be food-curious about anything that shows up dark against the white snow,' said McCullough breathing hard. 'That's how they're supposed to find the wildebeest dung to eat.'

Bronovski went out again and came back with a rifle in each hand. He stacked them in the corner of the hangar. 'Hey, bright boy,' said Natty, her voice high and edgy. 'Why you do that? Move those bodies, why did you do that?'

*　*　*

For twenty minutes, they waited anxiously in the hangar, Bronovski occasionally poking his head out. He and Hartmann went into a huddle, talking in low tones. When the expected terrorist attack did not materialise, the mood lightened a little. But the three corpses in their army fatigues lay on the iced floor of the hangar.

'Why did you move them?' Natty said, several times.

The five of them went back to the kitchen. 'If one of the Company air-trucks flies over,' Bronovski was saying, 'we don't want them seeing dead bodies lying on the ice. That's why we had to move them.'

'Oh,' said Kodwo, 'as opposed to the big red streaks of *blood*?'

'Blood can be anything,' Bronovski was saying. 'Might be animal blood, say. This is a station for monitoring animals, maybe we had to make a kill and dissection or something.'

'Am I missing something?' said McCullough. Her voice was still a little trembly. There had been something drunk, or childish, about the expression on the face of the corpse she had just dragged. Somehow it touched her, and not in a nice way. The eyes had been all white, like an egg with the yolk taken away. Watery. She shuddered. 'I may be missing something, but why does it matter whether the Company air-trucks spot the corpses?'

Four faces were turned towards her. Blank.

'We are,' she said, 'going to call the Company now. Aren't we?'

'How long have you worked for Company III, Doctor McCullough?' asked Hartmann.

'What's that got to do with it?'

'Two years,' said Kodwo. 'She used to work for Company VI in Park Antarctica. Company III poached her two years ago, bought her and her expertise.'

'How,' said McCullough, her brow creasing, 'how on *earth* do you know that much about me?'

'I read your file,' said Kodwo. 'There's no great trick to it. A few favours here, an anonymous download there.'

McCullough glared at her.

'Well, Company VI is a very different thing from Company III,' Hartmann went on. 'Believe me. Or don't – maybe they aren't so different. I wouldn't know how Company VI organises things, but I'd be surprised if it was very different from III.'

'What are you talking about?'

'How much you think it cost the Company to train up those three men? How much to replace them? How much in insurance to their families? We're talking a *lot* of money. You want to call up the Company and tell them this station just lost three valuable men?'

McCullough's jaw actually fell open. '*We* lost *them*? They were supposed to be guarding *us*! Anyway, they weren't Company soldiers. They were interDefence.'

Bronovski made eyes at the ceiling, and Kodwo gasped loudly in astonishment at her naivety.

'Look,' said McCullough, standing up abruptly. 'This is crazy. You think I want to be part of this? We call the Company, they come and sort it out.' She walked to the corner of the room. 'Natty, will you tell them to quit messing about like this?'

All eyes turned to Natty. 'This station caretaking,' she said eventually. 'That's a big job. I wouldn't want to bother the Company without having something pretty nice to tell them.'

'Oh for Christ's sake. What's going on here? We have three dead men in the hangar!' McCullough threw up her arms.

'And we don't know who killed them,' said Hartmann. He was sitting with both his elbows on the table, fumbling with his lower lip. He was squashing it into a peak between fore- and index finger, rolling it back and up.

There was a silence.

'Terrorists,' said Kodwo.

'I *don't* think so,' said Bronovski.

'If it's terrorists, where are they now?' said Natty. 'Why whack these three and then run away? They'd have blown the whole base by now.'

'Maybe it was the soldiers themselves, maybe they did it. Maybe they quarrelled, or something,' said Hartmann. 'How much gunfire did we hear? Maybe one of them killed the guy in the hangar, and then the two remaining went out on the ice and shot one another. How many shots did anybody hear?'

Everybody muttered about being asleep, about not hearing things properly.

'It wasn't that,' said McCullough from the corner, her face in her hands. 'It can't have been.'

'Because?' asked Bronovski. 'Because you thought they were such really nice guys, wouldn't do such a thing? They were trained killers, you know, *Doctor* McCullough.'

'No, I don't mean that,' said McCullough. 'I mean, as soon as I found them was only a few minutes since the shots. For Christ's sake, blood was still oozing out of one of them.'

'And?'

'And the muzzle of his gun was quite cold. I felt it.'

'Well,' said Natty, leaning back in her chair and stretching luxuriously, 'my people. If it was not terrorists, and they didn't kill themselves, you think, what? The kangaroos took up weapons and shot them?'

* * *

There was a silence between them for about ten minutes. One after the other they all went to the coffee nipple and filled their breakfast bowlbeakers. McCullough sat down again.

She took a deep breath. 'OK, I appreciate that we're all pretty stressed by this thing happening,' she said. 'But I want to say one thing. I don't care if calling the Company now harms our careers. I don't care about that. But I would put it this way to you. If one of us is a killer, then do we really *really* want to leave the airwaves empty, to just sit around this station with – let me remind you – three fully charged weapons leaning against the wall of the hangar? Is that what we want?'

Everybody was looking at her.

'Because it is not what I want, OK? Because if one of us killed those three men, in cold blood, then I don't want to have to spend too much time sitting around here waiting for that person's bloodlust to return. If one of us did that – no, actually I mean, if one of you did that, because I know sure as ice is cold that I didn't do it—'

'I don't know anything like that,' interrupted Bronovski. 'I only know I'm not the one. Maybe you *did* do it.'

'You think that's likely?' snapped McCullough. 'Act like a scientist, work with the most plausible possibility. I'm a skinny woman, five foot four. You really think I could have killed all three of those soldiers?'

'How do I know?' snapped Bronovski. 'Maybe you gave them all blow-jobs and shot them when they were distracted. You know?'

McCullough made a scoffing noise. 'Why would I do that?'

Bronovski's voice was rising in volume. 'What do you mean? Why would you give the blow-jobs, or why would you do the shooting?'

'Why don't you go and fuck yourself?'

'Why,' said Kodwo, in a voice loud enough to cut through the squabble, 'would *any* of us kill these guys? Why would any of us? What have any of us to gain?'

'Call the Company,' said McCullough. 'Everything else can get sorted later.'

'No,' said Hartmann. 'No. Not because I killed anybody, which I didn't. But we have to give ourselves time to think.'

'He's right,' said Bronovski. 'And I didn't kill anybody either.'

'You're *crazy*,' said McCullough.

'Stay cool, sweet pea,' muttered Natty.

'Very least we need to do is to think of a story,' said Hartmann. 'Something that might convince the Company that we heroically defended the station, rather than just got startled out of our beds by strange gunfire.'

'That is good thinking,' said Bronovski.

'She has a point though,' said Kodwo, looking at McCullough. 'If one of us did kill the guys outside, then we don't want him to start thinking about going for the complete set. And there *are* loaded weapons in the hangar.'

'How about we all just stay in here,' said Natty. 'We brainstorm up a reasonable story, get the facts all sorted in our heads. Then we can call the Company. Maybe, do the damage necessary to correlate the story, and after call the Company.'

There were grunts of agreement.

'So, that way,' Natty said, 'we all keep an eye on all.'

'Fine by me.'

'Me too.'

'You're all crazy,' said McCullough.

* * *

Soon enough, the Three Stooges were back in their pointless meandering talking. 'Did you see the way two of them bled, and one of them didn't?' Bronovski was saying. 'Man that is odd. That is odd as fuck.'

'I guess he got it in the head, the non-bleeder' said Hartmann, making a wicked-sounding chuckling noise deep in his throat. 'Bullet went in but not out.'

'I wonder how hard it would be,' Kodwo said, 'to work out an algorithm to determine exsanguination after a shooting. I mean, clearly some shots will make you bleed, and others maybe not.'

'Too many variables,' said Hartmann, assertively. 'It's a chaotic system, there's no algorithm.'

'You're just saying that on a hunch,' said Kodwo. 'How can you know it's a chaotic system without any empirical data?'

'Interesting thing about hunches,' said Bronovski. 'There was a study done a couple of years ago . . .'

McCullough felt the urge to scream at them, but squashed it down inside her. 'Shouldn't we be working out our story?' she said loudly.

Hartmann smiled at her. It struck her, if it hadn't done so before, how unpleasant he was. His flat face with its broken blood vessels, his beard with patches of skin showing through. And there was a cruel core to his mind. 'My dear,' he said, his teeth showing. 'You only want to get on the ether to the Company. You only want to hurry us on towards that goal.'

'Well?' she said. 'What's wrong with that?'

'I suppose we ought to work out some sort of story,' said Kodwo, yawning. 'I am tired though. I don't like my sleep being interrupted. It makes me grouchy.'

'You ever tried the Dormalog pills they market nowadays?' said Bronovski. 'They stretch out your sleep patterns, so the literature says. Give you extra hours in the day without wearing you out, or causing you to go on sleep-benders later on where you sleep all weekend, that kind of thing.'

'You got any?' asked Kodwo, sweetly.

Bronovski shook his head.

'Then why bring it up, fool?' still said sweetly.

'You're the weak-willed one,' retorted Bronovski. 'Complaining about being tired.'

'I'm only saying it is three in the morning, according to my body clock,' said Kodwo. 'However bright the sky is outside.'

'I read a paper on those Dormalog trials,' said Hartmann. 'The thing that I couldn't see is the way it enabled them to make claims about quality of wake time. I mean, you can tell that a laboratory pig is awake, but you surely can't tell if it is enjoying quality wake time.'

'Oh, I don't know' said Kodwo. 'There must be lots of ways of registering their synaptic vigour.'

'You're assuming synaptic vigour is equivalent to being bright and alert,' said Hartmann. 'But the whole *point* of the Halász trials was to demonstrate that those are *totally* different subroutines in the mental net.'

'The Halász trials?' said Kodwo, in mock-horror. 'Are you really going to throw those in my face? Do you know *how many* protocols those trials violated?'

'*Science Mondial* had a discussion paper on the appropriateness of the standard protocols for today's science,' said Bronovski.

'Of course,' said Hartmann. '*Science Mondial* is a Company II publication.'

'But it's an interesting point, nonetheless. Don't you think?'

Natty had shuffled her way round to be beside McCullough. She settled beside her with a little laugh. 'Acting to character, aren't they?' she said, in a low voice. The Three Stooges carried on with their passionless bickering.

'What's going on?' said McCullough, feeling some sort of pressure building up inside her. It was intolerable. Why didn't they just call the Company? How could she *make* them? 'I mean,' she said, her voice fizzing, 'what do they think they are doing?'

'Them?' Natty looked at them for a while. 'I'd guess this is just behaviour designed to calm them down. Reassurance activity. Dead bodies, all that shit, that's strange. Unsettling. They're just letting their minds settle back into their usual grooves before they decide what to do next.' She was silent for a little while, looking at them again. 'It's kind of sweet, really.'

'Sweet? It's weird.'

'Well, they do know the Company. And I know the Company too, pretty girl.' She squeezed McCullough's arm through her coverall. 'And it would be better for all of us if we can get the Company people to believe that we were defending the station against terrorists. Or have some fucking story, more than that we were just woken up and ran through and there we were.'

'Natty,' said McCullough. 'There are three men, dead. What about that?'

'Them. I didn't know them,' said Natty, casually. 'They weren't nothing to me.'

'God, Jesus, that sounds cold-blooded.' McCullough felt a startling lurch of panic. What if Natty were cold-blooded enough to kill? What if she were the killer?

'Well, think of it in this light: they are dead, nothing to be done. We are alive. I care about me. I even care about you.'

Suddenly Natty yawned enormously. McCullough, even buoyed up on her outrage and anxiety, caught the infectiousness of it. She yawned herself. Suddenly the weight of tiredness settled on her.

'Me, I'd just like to go back to me bed,' said Natty. 'Or even to your bed, though I guess I'm not going to sleep too well on those narrow little bunks with some other body there.'

'Is that why you didn't come to mine tonight?' asked McCullough, a little startled by her own boldness.

'You know what I want to know?' said Natty, ignoring her question. 'I want to know which one of them killed the boys outside.'

McCullough looked at her, dropped her voice even softer. 'Which one?'

'Well I know it wasn't me, my lovely. And I reckon it wasn't you, I reckon you're not the type for that. So that leaves the three of them.'

McCullough looked over to the three scientists. They were sat around the central table, chatting like students at a late-night dorm party. 'Which one do you think?' she whispered to Natty.

'Me? I don't know. Far as I know, those three do everything together. Maybe they joined a terrorist group together. Maybe they killed the soldiers together.'

'Killed them together,' McCullough hissed. 'Why?'

'Who knows why. Maybe they're being paid to blow the base, and they wanted the soldiers out of the way.'

'Then why don't they just blow it?'

Natty shrugged. 'No notion. Maybe they want to get their stuff out of danger, and then blow it up. Maybe they're just eccentrics.'

'But,' said McCullough, 'if that's so, why haven't they killed us?'

Natty said nothing, and McCullough felt a chilly cramp paw at her abdomen. Suddenly, she felt horribly close to death. It chased the sleepiness out of her brain.

'This is crazy,' she hissed to Natty, her whisper loud enough to attract the attention of the Three Stooges. They all stopped what they were saying and looked directly at her.

The combined power of their stare was too much for McCullough. Her sleep-itchy brain fired up. 'This is crazy,' she said aloud, to all of them. The words came out a little louder than she expected. Their eyes opened wide, startled. 'You're all *killers*,' she told them, her voice breaking a little as she shouted. A part of her was surprised to be shouting like this. 'You're going to kill all of us. You're all killers. You're going to kill me.'

She was on her feet before she realised what she was doing.

five

Bronovski made a lunge for her as she darted to the door, but she got to the handle in time. With all her strength she heaved the door back, catching Bronovski's reaching arm with the metal edge. He howled like an animal, but the sound was fading already because she was dashing up the corridor towards the hangar.

She burst through the door at the end of the corridor into the chill of the hangar. Her breath was swirling round her head in great clouds, and with a sense of terror very distant she realised she was weeping, the tears freezing with little gripping sensations on her cheeks. There was a noise, too; a constant noise, like an alarm going off, a fire-alarm perhaps, sounding a single high-pitched note in a squeaky drone. It was her, she thought. She was the one making the noise. But she couldn't stop, she couldn't help herself. She was going to die. They were all going to die. There was already blood all over the ice.

The guns were still stacked in the corner where Bronovski had left them. McCullough lurched towards them, her feet slipping. She went down on one knee, struggled upwards, and lay the bare palms of her hands on the metal. It was so cold it made her squeal. The metal of the barrel burnt her palm. But there was no time. She hoisted the butt into the crook of her elbow, pulled her hand from the metal with a sickening sucking noise and more pain, and forced her fingers into the trigger guard. The trigger was black plastic, not metal; it was cold, but not painfully so.

Then she spun about, just in time to see Hartmann and Kodwo lumber out through the door. They skidded to a halt when they saw McCullough pointing the rifle at them. Hartmann skidding more fully, was toppling backwards and putting both flailing feet in the air. He landed painfully on the small of his back with a cry. Natty and Bronovski came out through the door afterwards.

'Stop, stop there,' yelled McCullough. The rifle quivered in her arms.

'Hey,' called Bronovski.

'Now, baby, now,' said Natty, putting her hands out in front of her.

'Just stop where you are!'

There was silence. Then there was only the groaning of Hartmann as he slowly lifted himself into a standing position.

There was a momentary tableaux. The four of them at the other end of McCullough's gun-barrel.

'OK,' said Kodwo, slowly. 'Let's be cool. What is it you want?'

'What I *want*,' said McCullough, struggling to remember what it was she had done this for, why it was she had felt she had to get hold of the rifle. 'What I want is for you to call the Company,' she said. Her voice was a bit wobbly.

'Sure, we'll call the Company,' said Bronovski. 'Then what? You going to put the gun down if we do that?'

'You're all killers,' said McCullough. Then: 'I'm putting you all under arrest.'

The gun barrel wobbled worryingly.

'Me? A killer?' screeched Bronovski. 'What are you saying? How dare you throw that at me?' He was still rubbing his arm where she had bashed it with the door.

'You're pretty highly strung, Doctor McCullough,' said Kodwo.

'Watch yourself, baby,' said Natty. 'You be careful with that gun.'

For a moment, McCullough's vision wobbled. A tidal sense of exhaustion shifted within her, swept up and dizzied her head. Maybe she was being ridiculous. Maybe she was acting like a fool. Perhaps – give the rifle to Natty?

Maybe she could lie down, go to sleep. But then she shuddered, pulled herself together.

'You call the Company,' she said.

'*I'm* no murderer,' said Bronovski. 'But I'm starting to think that maybe you are.'

'What do you mean?' said McCullough.

'You seem to be pretty handy with that weapon,' said Hartmann. 'You clearly do know how to use it.'

'That's my theory, definitely,' said Kodwo. 'Maybe she killed the soldiers. She *was* the first person out here.'

'I guess we'd need a motive,' said Hartmann, squeezing the small of his back with both his hands. 'Unless you reckon she's just a psycho?'

'There could be a load of motives. Maybe she's in the pay of the terrorists,' said Bronovski. 'Maybe she's working for another Company, wanting to sabotage the business up here.'

'Shut up,' yelled McCullough. 'You just shut yourselves up.'

'You're the one with the gun,' said Bronovski, casually. Then, suddenly, he was running.

McCullough's heart pounded; she wasn't initially certain what was happening, except that Bronovski's wiry body was in sudden movement. Thinking he was rushing towards her, McCullough's finger twitched on the trigger. The gun screamed; it just screamed. It was the loudest noise McCullough had ever heard.

She had not been aiming the weapon properly, or she would have most likely shattered Bronovski's head with the bullets. As it was, fat gouts of ice came scattering from the wall of the hangar. Bronovski, his mouth open, was diving forwards; not at her, after all, but in the direction of the remaining two rifles, balanced against the side of the ice-wall. Everybody else was ducking in unison, their heads apparently retracting between their shoulders, their knees buckling. Their mouths were open too. They might have been screaming, yelling, but nothing could be heard over the sound of the rifle.

But McCullough only saw these for a moment. The kick of the gun pushed her back on her feet along the ice, and then she was up and flying. The gun was still screaming, sparks and white flames bashing out of its end like lightning strikes, chucks of ice smashing out of the roof as she went backwards. Then there was only silence, and the topsy feeling in her stomach of being in flight. She landed on her back, with all the air in her pushed straight out by the impact. But she was still moving, still sliding backwards.

Her head collided painfully with the base of one of the ice-buggies stored in the hangar, and her body slewed round. She cried out. With a panicky scrabble she pulled herself round and up, found her feet on bent legs, and tried to yank the gun up. But her vision was out, her breath was tight, and her sense of up and down seemed unwired. Trying to raise the rifle to a horizontal position, she thought she was standing straight and was as surprised as hurt by the smack of the ice floor against her chin. It was hard sorting out the up and down; the floor she was lying against felt like a wall she was pushing against. Then there were hands on her, arms under her armpits lifting her away.

* * *

She didn't exactly pass out, but there was a period when nothing precisely came together in her perceptions. The blow to her head, from ramming back into the ice-buggy, had split open the skin. There was quite a lot of blood, much of it on her coverall.

Then she was in her cell, on her back, looking up at the ice ceiling, with her head in Natty's lap. Like a lover. Natty was pricking and stabbing at her head. 'What's that?' she tried to say, but again her mouth was dry. 'Ouch, what are you doing?' The words were raspy. 'Ouch, there again. What is that, acupuncture?'

'My husband was an acupuncturist,' came Natty's voice, conversational.

McCullough tried swallowing, tried moistening her lips with her tongue. Natty, talking as if nothing had happened. Where was her gun? Or had there even been a gun? Was that some past version of McCullough, one without relation to her as she was now?

'You were married?' she managed at last.

Natty sniffed. 'More than once,' she said. 'My last one was an acupuncturist on the personal staff of the King of Hong Kong.'

McCullough tried to digest this information, but her whole head was throbbing so powerfully it was hard to concentrate on anything. 'I used to be married,' she said. 'Promise you won't tell the others?'

'Word of honour.'

'You still married?' McCullough asked, wrinkling up her eyes at the pain.

'No,' said Natty. 'Hold still for a second.'

McCullough sighed. 'Me neither. Breaks my heart to think of it. Why did you and your husband break up?'

'No reason. It just didn't work out. That King of Hong Kong wasn't no proper king, neither. The whole thing was this expensive playboy scam, really.'

'Why,' McCullough tried, speaking slowly. 'Why are you acupuncturing my head?'

'I'm not,' said Natty. 'I'm putting stitches in. You cut it bad enough.'

* * *

Afterwards McCullough slept, or slept again. For a while she thought she wouldn't be able to, with the pulsing pain marking time in her skull. But she did, because the next thing she knew she was alone, and the pain was a little less. Her mouth was so dry she fancied she could sense every single wrinkle inside it. She somehow struggled up and had a long drink at the sink. Then she collapsed back on the bed. The next thing, Natty was sitting on her desk, looking at her.

'Oh God, Natty,' she said. 'What did I do?'

'Now that is a good question. You tell me.'

'I think I got a little freaked, actually.' She tried to sit up, but it made the pain in her head swell alarmingly, like the volume on a hi-fi turned up suddenly. She collapsed back down.

'You should take it easy,' said Natty. 'There are seven stitches in that scalp. You went back at some rate. Caught it against the tread on a buggy.'

'It hurts,' she said, putting her hand up to it.

'No shit.'

There was a lengthy silence.

'I think,' said McCullough, 'I got a little freaked. I shouldn't have gone for that gun.'

'You could have killed all of us,' said Natty, without emphasis.

'I'm sorry, sorry.'

'Yeah,' said Natty. 'Well. It was pretty suspicious, you got to accept that, going for the gun like that.'

'Suspicious? Oh Natty, you got to believe me. I was just scared and wound-up, was all.'

'Well, I believe you. But you need to think about the others, maybe.'

The others. McCullough had a flash of Bronovski diving forward, stretching his arms out and diving through the air like a football player. His mouth an O. 'Why did he go leaping for a gun like that, anyway?'

'What would you have done,' said Natty. 'If it had been him with the gun, and you standing helpless against the wall?'

That silenced her for a while. Then she asked: 'Where are they now?'

'They each took a rifle, made them feel more secure maybe. Then they all went through to their cells to get some sleep. One hell of an interrupted night we've all had.'

'So they're all armed?' insisted McCullough.

'Baby, they're all jittery. They're all sudden believers in the gospel of self defence, you know.'

'But one of them is a killer,' said McCullough, putting her palm over her eyes where the light was hurting her. 'At least one of them. Natty, we have got to call for Company people to come out here. Don't you see that?'

Natty reached over, and planted a kiss on McCullough's forehead. 'I know, slick, I know. They all agreed now, whilst you were laid out in here. They are going to call the Company after they've had a bit of a sleep. Tell some tale about a terrorist attack. Maybe even offer you up as proof, say that you got cracked on the head by one of them.'

McCullough said nothing.

'Well, I suppose you have to work out whether you want to get with that particular programme, get into the pattern of the lie that they are building. It would surely simplify matters, and maybe we would keep our jobs.'

In a small voice, McCullough asked, 'Natty, are you going to do that? Are you going to lie?'

'Surely,' said Natty, in a calm voice. 'Me, I want to keep my job.'

* * *

McCullough slept again, and woke feeling a little better. She got up and tried to examine herself in the tiny sink mirror. The cold had buckled the mirror-surface diagonally, so her face bulged strangely like a reflection in the back of a spoon. There were streaks of blood over her face, and she washed clumsily. Numb fingers traced the tender shapes of stitches in amongst the matted hair on the back of her head. Then she looked at her hand. There was a red line across the middle of it, where she had freeze-burned the palm on the rifle. The sight of it brought back the whole incident. The memory made her head throb more forcefully.

She sighed. Couldn't lurk in her cell the whole time.

Giddily she made her way through to the kitchen. The Three Stooges were sitting around the central table, their usual position. But this time each of them was carrying a weapon. As she emerged, Hartmann said: 'Well, good morning, my dear,' in a sarcastic tone of voice.

'Well well, it's the psycho,' said Bronovski.

'You're the psycho,' McCullough mumbled, like a sulky child.

She started towards them, to take a chair around the table and get something to fill her belly, but the three of them were clearly more jittery than their bland exteriors gave away. With the first step, all three of them reached simultaneously for the rifles balanced on the table; there was a flurry of white where Bronovski's right hand moved, like a loose flapping glove.

She stopped. 'I'm just going to get some breakfast,' she said. She shuffled over to the soya nipple and filled a bowlbeaker, wishing she had some painkillers, not wanting to put herself in the position of having to ask the others for the location of the first aid box.

'That does look like a nasty cut,' said Bronovski, with what sounded like a glib sadistic glee, carefully placing his gun back on the surface in front of him. 'All your pretty short hair is stuck up by the blood.'

'I suppose it hurts,' said Kodwo.

McCullough came back over to the table, and once again the motion produced a reflex in all three, a reaching for the guns. As she settled down McCullough was struck by something. Hartmann and Kodwo reached straightforwardly for the rifle, but Bronovski's hand ducked inside what looked like a silk handkerchief and briefly flourished it upwards to catch it on the palm, before reaching.

That was the moment McCullough understood.

It all came together in her head. For a brief moment everything shrunk to silence in the very heart of her mind; Bronowski keeping his fingerprints from the weapon. His motives, his intentions. Then the world came back to her, and she gasped minutely. The three of them were still chattering on.

'When I was medical,' said Kodwo, 'I did some work with a surgeon who specialised in headwounds. He developed some interesting techniques, ahead of their time really.'

'My theory,' said Hartmann, 'is that we're on the verge of something big with surgery. Mankind I mean. Face it, really, we're still using medieval surgical techniques – cutting and so forth.'

'You three,' said McCullough, croaky, leaning forward with her torso so as not to have to tilt her aching head, and bringing the bowlbeaker to her lips. 'You just go round and round. You're like robots.' She sipped. Her lips were cracked with dryness; they stung as she drank. She was acutely conscious of trying to maintain an unruffled exterior. Wasn't it obvious?

'Interesting thing about the word *robot*,' said Hartmann. 'It comes from the Czech, and it means *slave*.'

'Oh, no,' said Bronovski. 'It means *forced labour*.'

'That's the same thing.'

'It's not at all,' said Bronovski, as if affronted. 'You going to argue with me on Czech vocabulary?'

'Why not,' returned Hartmann, in the same tone of voice. 'You're not Czech.'

'I think you're missing the point.'

'Round and round,' croaked McCullough. 'Did you people call the Company.'

'Oh yeah,' said Hartmann. 'That was your big thing, wasn't it. Well, you'll be pleased to hear we have decided to call the Company later today. We'll do some damage, and tell them terrorists attacked. We're going to tell them that the terrorists gave you that lump on your head too, so you'd better be prepared to back up our story.'

'Or?'

Hartmann shrugged. 'Or we'll tell them your marbles have been knocked completely *loose*. I think your behavioural index thus far into our mission suggests that you have a pretty tenuous grip on your sanity anyway.'

'Ouch,' said McCullough, deadpan. 'Please stop, you're hurting my feelings.' But mockery couldn't touch these three. All of them were grinning.

Her soya finished, McCullough slid off her stool and stood up. 'What time is it?'

'Gone nine,' said Natty, from the corner of the room.

'Well, I'm going to check on my animals. They may need feeding.' She started slowly towards the hangar corridor. 'That is why the Company flew me out here in the first place.'

'Such touching Company loyalty,' said Bronovski. 'You'll be Company pin-up of the month.'

Kodwo was by her side as she pulled the kitchen door open. 'I think I'll come with you,' she said. 'You're in a pretty wobbly state, I think. Somebody should keep an eye on you.' She slung her rifle over her shoulder.

'Whatever,' said McCullough.

She made her way up the corridor with difficulty. Kodwo offered an arm, and after shrugging it off once, McCullough decided not to be an idiot, and allowed herself to be helped.

The hangar, when they came into it, looked a mess. The three bodies over by the right wall, the wide streaks of blood, the great bricks and jagged lumps of ice scattered over floor and equipment alike. McCullough shuffled through the wreckage, and outside.

Most of the dung was gone, which was a good sign. The roos were acting with a little more life; except for one, who was lying on his side, breathing shallowly. McCullough went over to him and bent down. She couldn't see an immediate problem, but sometimes that was the way they went. They just refused to eat, just lay down and died. She stood up, and the motion sent zings of pain through her cranium.

'Uh, Doctor Kodwo,' she said, pinching the bridge of her nose between her fingers, 'I wonder if you could do me a favour?'

Kodwo said: 'What?'

'In the blue-striped pack, on top of the empty stasis box nearest to us, could you fetch me an esuriant injection? I want to try and encourage this one to eat, give him an appetite.'

Kodwo grunted, but went over and brought the hypo. Bending down again painfully, McCullough puffed the stuff through the white fur on its flank. It didn't move at all.

She stood up again. 'Thanks,' she said.

'Oh you're welcome,' replied Kodwo, taking the hypo back into the hangar. 'Isn't it funny,' she called from inside. 'A few hours ago you were trying to shoot me. Now the two of us, we're all politeness.'

McCullough was moving slowly towards the sack containing the last of the dung. 'I wasn't trying to shoot you,' she said. 'Bronovski startled me. I was a little, well, freaked.'

As she scattered the last of the dung she was pleased to see the roos take an interest, and come over to start pecking at it. It was solid as a rock in her hands, frozen hard, but the beasts were genengineered to deal with that.

There was the snick of the door opening, and Natty came through, putting on her mittens. 'How are you two doing out here?'

'I'm not summarily executing her,' said Kodwo, 'if that's what you mean.'

She hefted her weapon uneasily. 'Though there are people who would consider that a small sort of retaliation, after what she did.'

Feeling worn out, McCullough shuffled over to a small pack of stasis algae, and sat on it. 'Retaliation,' she said.

'Look at it logically,' insisted Kodwo. 'Somebody shot those three soldiers. Who is the most likely candidate, would you say? Not me, I know; and I can't see why Natty. And there's no benefit for Bronovski, or Hartmann, in killing them. They're doing well, their work is going well. That leaves you, Doctor McCullough. I don't know you; you're new to this team. You come from a rival Company, so there's always going to be a question mark over your loyalty. You have, shall we say, an attitude. And then you do this thing – you basically go crazy with a gun. You made yourself into the most likely suspect for the killings. Wouldn't you say? I mean, wouldn't you agree? You're a scientist; don't you think the facts support that differential conclusion?'

McCullough looked from Kodwo to Natty. 'Your friend, Bronovski,' she said, and broke off to cough three times, four. Each cough sent spears of pain thrusting up through her head. Even when the coughing stopped the throbbing carried mechanically on.

'Yes,' said Kodwo, firmly. 'My friend Bronovski. I've known him seven years, and you hardly at all. You want me to trust *you*?'

'He's going to set us up. He's going to set you up.' McCullough's voice was barely strong enough to carry. 'Are there any analgesics here?' she said at last.

Natty said, 'Oh, sure. I should have offered already.' She went to one of the packs and fished out a little sachet. McCullough fumbled with the sealing, and pushed two tablets into her mouth. She dry-swallowed them, and leaned back against the wall behind her.

Kodwo was looking at her. 'You think Bronovski is behind all this.' She did not sound as sarcastic as McCullough had been expecting.

'Whose fingerprints are on that rifle you are holding?' she said. Kodwo, as if cued, looked down at her weapon. McCullough went on, wheezily: 'Yours. Maybe the soldier who owned it before, and then yours. Bronovski carried it through from outside, but he only touched it at the end of the butt, and he did that with all the guns.'

Kodwo looked directly at her.

'And,' McCullough went on, 'the gun Hartmann is carrying will have Hartmann's fingerprints. And the one Bronovski is carrying has my fingerprints. But not his own, you notice that?' She stopped, got her breath back. 'He has this handkerchief with which he handles it. You notice that?' There was a pause; the two women were looking at her. 'Now why would he be so keen to make sure his fingerprints don't go on the gun, I wonder?'

'So?' said Kodwo.

'If he had some licit reason for not wanting his prints on the gun, wouldn't he tell you? So, let's say he's planning something. Say he's going to set me up. But if me, what about you? Which gun or guns were used to do the killing, do you think? The one with my fingerprints? Yours? How can Bronovski tell?'

Kodwo was shaking her head, slowly.

'If he's setting me up,' McCullough continued, 'then why not you as well? Then he will be the lone hero.'

Kodwo stood, silent. A minute passed.

Eventually, she said: 'He's my friend.'

'Then you know him,' said McCullough. 'You tell me: how important is the concept of friendship to him? What about loyalty?' She paused, trying for dramatic effect. So easy for that to misfire. 'What about other concepts for him – what about, money, say? What about the sanctity of life? What about, I don't know, getting paid a fortune to mess up this Company by some other Company?'

Kodwo looked at Natty for a long time. Then she looked back at McCullough. Then whatever structure was in her mind, whatever elaborate constellation of ideas, toppled. McCullough could almost see it happen. See the tumble, and the pieces spontaneously reassemble themselves. Bronovski was shifted around in Kodwo's evaluation of the universe. The woman almost sagged. Then she breathed out. And for McCullough, perhaps it was the painkillers, or perhaps the sense that she was starting to get a handle on things; but she felt a quick euphoria.

Kodwo was sitting beside her now. Natty came over too.

'Why?' said Kodwo, in a chastened voice.

'Who knows why,' McCullough said. 'Who *cares* why? The key question here is what do we do?'

'Oh God,' said Kodwo.

'My sense is,' said Natty, coming over, 'that if we try anything, Bronovski will kill us. He's got that inside him, you know he has. He's got the instinct for it, the taste. And he'd kill us as easy as killing those three boys. Why shouldn't he? If he's going to spin a story about terrorists to the Company, then why couldn't the terrorists have killed the three of us as well as the soldiers?'

'This is not good,' said Kodwo, with sudden decision, putting her arm on Natty's shoulder. 'If we go back down, can you call the Company?'

'The equipment's there in the kitchen,' said Natty. 'I'd have to do it right in front of him.'

'We could wait until he goes to sleep, maybe.' She looked at the other two. 'We need to disarm him.'

'He's sitting in there peaceful enough.'

'She's right, she's right,' said Kodwo, gesturing at McCullough. 'I noticed the handkerchief, but didn't really register it.'

'He's your friend,' said Natty, tartly.

'We have to disarm him,' said Kodwo. 'Or we have to get away. Put some distance between us and him. Oh God, Oh *God*.' She stood up, and sat straight down again. 'It all makes a horrible sort of sense,' she said, in a low voice. 'I say we wait till he goes to sleep, and then try to disarm him.'

'No,' said McCullough. 'This is already crazy; this whole situation is already crazy. I say we go. There are buggies here, and we can be away over the ice. Where's the nearest Company III base?'

'There's one south-west, maybe 120 kilometres,' said Kodwo. 'I know the way. I've been there, following my herds.'

'You think the three of us can make it there?' asked Natty.

'In good weather, why not? Ten hours' driving.' She paused. 'I'd like to take some food, but that would also mean going back down to the kitchen.' She shook her head. 'Man it's sudden,' she said. 'I mean, it's a sudden decision. But you're right, we've got to get away.'

'Got to get away,' echoed McCullough. She looked at Kodwo.

'But you,' said Natty to McCullough. 'You think that you can make it there? What about your head.'

'My head feels fine.' And that was the truth, although she had the lurking sense that maybe that was a temporary state of affairs. 'I say we go. How many buggies are there?'

'Four,' said Natty, automatically.

'OK, I say we disable one of them and get away on the other three. We go south-west to the other camp, and we report to the Company.'

six

Natty stabbed the electrics out of one buggy, and then emptied the fuel tank for good measure. With the other three, they pushed them laboriously out by hand through the corral and outside through the door. McCullough needed help moving her one. It was a big, sluggish-feeling lump of plastic and metal, and it felt uncomfortably unwieldy to her.

'Leave the door open,' she said. 'Maybe the roos will be alright. I should have spent a week or so with them, but maybe they'll just have to look after themselves.' She paused. 'When they get hungry they'll go looking for dung. I only hope the nearest herd isn't too far from here.'

Kodwo and Natty were tightening their hoods about their faces and straddling the buggies. McCullough tried to copy, although her head was beginning to hurt again.

'You know how to ride one of these?' asked Kodwo, coming over to her.

McCullough had never ridden one before, but she didn't say so. What would be the point? 'How hard can it be?' she asked.

Kodwo was strapping the rifle to her back. 'It's like a bike. Wring the handle to accelerate, squeeze the lever to brake. It's not so hard.' She stopped, looked hard at McCullough. 'You'll pick it up. Watch out for ditches, cracks, for any larger striation; that can bump you around a bit. If that happens, just hang on to the handles. You'll go up and down in the saddle a bit, maybe, rodeo fashion, but keep hanging on and you'll be fine.'

She hurried back over to her machine, climbed aboard. 'OK,' she said to them both. 'Once we start the engines, it may be that Bronovski will hear the noise and come running. He's armed, so when we start we have to *go*, straight away. Keep your head down, go as fast as you can, till we've gotten out of range.' She pressed the sidebar button and the engine coughed up and started. McCullough followed suit, and Natty.

The thing between her legs throbbed with more vibration than McCullough found comfortable. The fillings in her teeth were rattling, and she grimaced. But twisting the handle and lurching forward, the quality of the vibration changed, became more comfortable, even pleasant. Suddenly she was in motion, sweeping forward. The feeling was immediately exhilarating. She felt as though she were flying. The white ground simply slid by. It was effortless.

The rush of air filled her ears with crinkly white noise, and pretty soon the cold of the environment started to make itself felt. The cold air felt even colder in motion. It froze her face right up inside her nostrils, a bitter ache that spread through her sinuses. She kept blinking her eyes, but they watered copiously, and the tears froze in little spikes around her eyes, little crystals that broke away and scattered with every crease of her blinking. With her left hand she tried pulling the edges of her hood closer around her face, but having only one hand on the handlebar wobbled the buggy, and McCullough's heart jerked in panic. She rammed her hand back down on the handle, and tried to block out her discomfort.

Ahead of her she could see the other two buggies, throwing up little bow waves of ice as they slid forward. She tried turning her head back and found her neck so stiff it barely moved. It was as if the cold were literally freezing her spine, a scary thought. She tried again, with a creaking sound, or rather a dull sensation, in her discs. She was able to see a jolting blurry image of the station behind her. It was already far away, a little black blot against the greater white. She couldn't see whether any of her roos had ventured out of the corral.

Perhaps they were all going to stay inside, too timid or stupid to move. Perhaps they were all going to starve to death.

She brought her face forward again, and hit rough ice. The sudden turbulence was terrifying; the buggy bucked and squirmed like a living thing. She was thrown upwards, clutched desperately at the handles and came slamming back down on the saddle. But then things were smooth again, rattling forward. McCullough's heart was pounding. She was, she realised, wailing; but the sound was lost in the air around her. She stopped making the noise.

After a little while, she became slightly more comfortable with the ride. Another patch of rough ice, and she started to feel she was on top of the experience. Then she tried experimenting, accelerating and pulling herself up alongside Natty's buggy. She thought about waving, but lifting her left hand from the handle even for a moment was too scary. So she contented herself with nodding her head, uncertain whether the motion could even be seen in the voluminousness of her padded hood and coverall.

They biked on for a length of time. McCullough couldn't be sure how long. There was something mantric about the experience after a while, something almost hypnotic. The pain in her face balanced the ache from her stitches, and she slid into a sort of endurance state. It was uncomfortable, rattling, even terrifying, but McCullough went on with it.

She watched the two buggies ahead of her move gently from side to side in motion similar to her own. When she saw Kodwo peel away to the right, and Natty follow her, she readied herself to do likewise. But then she saw Kodwo pull back left and resume her former course, with Natty following her back. She decided it must have been a momentary aberration, and that she would go straight through.

Then there was a loud rushing noise, and her speed fell away. The buggy was juddering violently, and with a lurch the back came up. McCullough was almost too startled to be scared, but she was right up in the air, she was actually flying forward. Some below-thought instinct told her that now was not a time to try and grab on to the handles, and she let go. The world tipped up, white sky changing places with white ground. She splashed into freezing slush.

She lay for a moment, not hurt but stunned. But stabbingly cold water was starting to seep into her clothing, and she struggled upwards as if stung. She was standing ankle deep in slushy water, her buggy buried nose first in the stuff a few metres from her. Still not properly registering what had happened she staggered forward and reached her machine. Its engine was still running, the back treads whirring. She had to crouch to find the switch and turn it off.

By now Kodwo and Natty had circled round and were twenty metres away. They killed their engines, climbed off and made their way over to her. When she arrived, Kodwo was angry. 'What the fuck were you playing at? Didn't you see me change course to avoid this?'

McCullough was just too poleaxed to say anything in reply. She mumbled something, and pushed her shoulder against the body of the buggy, trying to push it back horizontal.

'You have to watch *out* for polynya like this,' Kodwo was saying. 'These are the trickiest things.'

Somewhere deep in McCullough's head there was the germ of an anger starting to glow, *well it's not my fault, you didn't warn me*. But all she could do was blink stupidly and mumble. Her face was pulsing with pain where the cold seemed to have infiltrated deep into her skull, the throbbing of her stitches giving her the impression that the cold had penetrated straight through and out the back. Cold water was dribbling down inside her coverall, snaking death-chill fingers down her belly, her sides, her legs. She felt miserable.

'There's no point in *pushing* like that,' snapped Kodwo, still angry. 'I'll get a line from my buggy.'

She went back to her buggy and payed out a thin steel cable, fixing it to the hook at the back of McCullough's machine. Then she trudged grumpily back to hers, started it up again and rode it slowly away. There was a very human sucking sound and the buggy lurched and came free.

Kodwo dragged it clear of the ice-pond, and McCullough trudged after it. She was, she realised with shame, crying. She never cried. She hated crying.

But now she felt cold all over her body, and her frozen trembling felt very like the fear that probably also fed into the experience. She tried to still herself as she climbed back onto the machine, but her elation at travelling was long gone.

The buggy started again, which was a blessing, and she gently coaxed it round before gunning the acceleration again.

They were off once more. This time McCullough's discomfort was much more acute, much more like actual pain. She was shivering so hard she found herself wondering if she were having a fit. She struggled to keep Kodwo and Natty in view, and to follow every slight deviation in their course exactly. Time bled into nothing, into pain and misery. White sky, white ground, the whiteness of suffering. A desert experience, the human body reduced to a desert, a monocrop of agony. On and on.

On and on. The emptiness of the landscape, which had once seemed to her a tonic away from the crush of the over-populated world, now gnawed unpleasantly at her consciousness. The nothingness of it.

She went over several portions of rough ice, and it was much worse than before, the experience jarring her joints. Now she clung on with desperation rather than with command. Now all she wanted was the ride to stop, for her to be able to go somewhere warm and curl up and sleep. Her head beat time with pulse-throbs of pain.

Kodwo turned through nearly ninety degrees, and McCullough carefully followed suit. After the fact she saw why: a two-metre crevasse. They skirted it for what must have been a kilometre before it started to shrink. Seen side on in motion, the twin sides of the gap coming together had the weird look of two great white lips closing in a smile.

Past the edge of the crevasse, Kodwo turned back and Natty and McCullough followed; they started back, cutting a diagonal across the ice to rejoin their original path.

Then, from white ice to green. It came over as a sort of sideshow to the pain, McCullough started noticing the colour-change of the ice. Patchy at first, but then in consistent blocks, the ice beneath her treads was showing up bright green. It was the algae, the bottom of this invented polar ecosystem: a specially designed strain of wax-stem plants that lived in the very top of the pack ice – if the ice were old enough to have lost enough of its salination. Polar pack at about the age of one year had frozen out enough brine to be drinkable even by humans. The genengineered wildebeest had no problem with it, breaking the ice with their lips and tongues and sucking up the algae like soup.

And, sure enough, where there was green ice there were animals. McCullough started to notice the great white shaggy wildebeest, initially in ones and twos, and then as a great herd of them, stretching out directly in the path of the buggies. Kodwo slewed to a halt, and Natty and McCullough followed suit.

Despite her pain, McCullough found herself impressed by the sight of so many animals. They were the size of cars, at least two and a half metres tall at the shoulder. Their white coats were dreadlocked with shaggy strands that went almost to the ground; their pale grey faces were uniformly pressed downwards, grazing, with albino horns poking out to the sides looking almost pink.

'God,' McCullough gasped.

'Oh it's quite a sight,' Kodwo shouted across. She said something else that McCullough didn't catch, maybe *my babies*, pride at her genengineered creations.

'Will it be OK?' McCullough asked. 'Going through?'

A bit of a wind had got up, so her words didn't carry. She revved, moved a bit closer, and tried again, this time shouting. 'Will we have any problem getting through this lot?'

Kodwo shook her head. 'No,' she called back. 'They'll scatter as we come. They're very wary of anything that could be a predator.' Then she added: 'It's not them I'm worried about.'

McCullough felt the various aches inside her reassert themselves. 'Could we, you know, rest for a bit?' she called.

Kodwo looked at her. 'We've only come about thirty kay,' she said.

'I feel awful,' said McCullough. 'I mean, I'm not usually one to complain, but I do feel bad.'

'Didn't catch that,' Kodwo hollered.

'I feel bad,' shouted McCullough.

Kodwo paused, and then nodded. 'Pull the bikes round, we'll have a bit of a breather.'

'Pulling the bikes round' involved parking them in a line to make a basic windbreak. The three of them did this, and then hunkered down on the far side, huddling together. For a while they said nothing, but eventually they thawed enough to start talking.

'This really isn't the best place to stop,' said Kodwo. 'I mean, this isn't where I'd planned on taking a break.'

'You *were* planning a break then,' said McCullough.

'Sure. Of course I was. But not here. Where there are herds of wildebeest, there are predators. And we don't want to be sitting around in the middle of snow-lions.'

McCullough stared at the grazing animals. They seemed placid enough, milling about, a few of them even moving slowly in the direction of the bikes. 'Surely they'd register it if a lion put in an appearance?'

Kodwo nodded. 'I guess so. Still, I'm not comfortable. We'd better not stay long.'

'I'm thirsty,' said Natty, in a cracked voice.

'God, yes, me too,' said McCullough. 'It's pretty dehydrating, on that buggy.'

Kodwo stamped the green floor with one foot. 'It's pack ice, the salt's gone out of it, you can drink it,' she said. 'Provided you don't mind the piss.'

'The piss,' said McCullough.

'Snow-wildebeest piss *everywhere*. They are ingesting a lot of water, all the time, and they piss it all out again. It's OK, though, it's only urine. It's sterile, you can drink it without ill effects.'

Natty nodded, but somehow McCullough didn't have the savour for it after hearing that.

'I wish we'd brought some food,' said Natty, scratching some surface snow free with her mitten.

'We all had breakfast,' said Kodwo. Then she turned to McCullough. 'How's your head, anyway? You bearing up?'

McCullough leant back against the bike. The back of her head was sobbing with the pain. She reasoned it was just the flow of blood through the injured tissue, but it felt more basic than that. It felt as if her head were gorged on pain, and the gash at the back as a mouth; as if her head were struggling to hold down a vomit of pain that pressed from within, trying to surge up and burst out.

'I'm fine,' she said.

They sat in silence for a while. Natty munched on some ice, then rubbed her beard with her mitten. 'Hard to believe that's doing anything for my thirst,' she said.

'Good to stay hydrated,' said Kodwo.

McCullough's throat did feel dry, so she scrabbled around in the ice between her legs for a while. She wished Kodwo hadn't said that thing about the wildebeest piss.

'You had your suspicions, about Bronovski?' asked Natty. 'I mean, you volte-faced pretty swift.'

Kodwo looked at her, and then looked at McCullough. 'He was my friend,' she said, and then said nothing.

After a while she added something: 'It's logical, though, isn't it? It makes sense that it was him. Of all of us, he's the one with the most motive.'

McCullough said: 'Why do you say that?'

Kodwo stared. 'Well,' she said. 'It is obvious.'

'Not to me it isn't.'

Kodwo turned to Natty. 'It is obvious.'

'Not,' repeated McCullough, her voice rising sharply, 'to me.'

Kodwo glared at her. McCullough saw, with an intuitive sense of the truth of it, that Kodwo hated her. That for her, McCullough was an unpleasant outsider who had somehow managed to mess up a life that had been, until her arrival, ordered and pleasant. It was a chilling moment.

'Well,' said Kodwo, nastily. 'Tell me, *Miss* McCullough, why do you think the Company pays us to do what we do?'

'Putting animals on the ice,' said McCullough, a powerful emotion, possibly fear, possibly hate, warming inside her. Taking her mind off her discomfort and pain.

'That's right, putting animals on the ice.'

'It's an interCompany preservation thing,' McCullough said slowly. 'The grazing territory for these animals is now all cultivated. Has to be, to grow food for the world's enormous population. So it's either lose them entirely, or genengineer them to adapt to the last wildernesses. This is their last refuge.'

'And that's why?'

'What else?' McCullough said sharply. 'You going to try out some half-cocked conspiracy theory?'

'You flare up pretty easy, don't you?' said Kodwo. 'Don't think I'm easily going to forget the way you tried to *kill* me last night.'

McCullough's head trembled, as she searched for the most stinging reply. 'You call yourself a scientist,' she began, but Natty intervened.

'Come on, guys,' she said. 'Now's not the time, eh? When we're safe and warm, you can fight all the time in the world.'

'The reason,' said Kodwo, not taking her eyes from McCullough. 'The reason why Company III pays us all this money, has invested all this resource in Park Polar?'

'Why can't it be for the *right* reasons? Why can't the Company be doing something for the good of the planet? For the good of the animals?'

'Because the Company exists to make profit, the same way people exist to make babies,' said Kodwo, sharply.

'Oh, who's being naive now?' countered McCullough. 'There are other ways of maximising profit, apart from simply shifting product. This sort of project, this wildlife thing, raises the profile of the Company, and that's the kind of advertising you just can't buy any other way.'

'Sure,' said Kodwo. 'And that's true for Company I on the other side of the Angara Basin. And its true for Company VI and Company III in Park

Antarctica. But if you think *any* Company is going to blithely pass up the chance for additional benefits, then you must be crazy.'

'What additional benefits?' asked McCullough shortly.

'Oh,' said Kodwo. 'Meat. What else but food? What else really counts in this increasingly crowded world?'

McCullough scuffed her feet back and forth. Then, almost as if the action might cool her anger, she stuffed a mittenful of scraped ice into her mouth. It was wildly cold, numbing her tongue, but the chill-pain of it suited her mood. She crunched, sucked, and the fluid started going down her throat. It didn't taste of anything except cold.

'When was the last time you had meat?' asked Kodwo. 'I mean real meat?' Her voice sounded a little calmer.

'I don't remember,' said McCullough. But she did. She remembered exactly. It had been at her divorce party. Friedrich had organised the whole thing, invited friends. There had been drink, speeches, and finally Friedrich had brought through a platter from the kitchen and displayed a piece of sea-steak. It had been about the size and shape of two flat hands placed side by side, and had been a strange dark brown colour. There had been applause, McCullough remembered. Everybody there had thought it a splendid gesture at a divorce party, a piece of incredible generosity. Everybody got a strip a centimetre wide and ten centimetres long. And McCullough had managed to smile and laugh through the rest of the evening, before going back to her solitary room and slapping and kicking the dumb walls in a rage. It was *so* Friedrich. The splendid gesture at the wrong time, the thoughtfulness years too late. Idiotic expense. It had all been about impressing his friends, not about her at all.

'Not for a long time, anyway,' McCullough said.

'No, sure,' said Kodwo. 'Me neither. You neither, Natty, I guarantee it. And when we do eat meat, it's that sea-steak. Those big genengineered sea-cows, long as whales, just floating in mid-ocean, attached to their feed tubes. I don't know about you, but sea-steak is just too salty for my palate. Just too salty, and way too expensive.'

'So?' said McCullough, still unable to keep the snarl out of her voice.

'Don't you see? Do you have any idea how much the meat of a herd like this would be worth? On a speciality market, for the super-rich, meat off the hoof rather than the flipper. It would be a serious profit opportunity.'

'It's an interCompany *park*,' said McCullough. 'They can't just poach animals. Anyway, the whole thing is in ecostability. Algae, grazers, coprophages, predators. If you take out too many from the chain it'll collapse.'

'That's why Bronovski is in the vulnerable position. That's what made him the man most likely to sell out to the other side.'

'Because?'

'Because he is the predator scientist, yes? Hartmann is OK with his algae, they'll always need algae, no matter which animals they grow here for food, or for whatever reason. They'll always need some photosynthesising base to the food pyramid. And I'm OK for the moment. At least my wildebeest are proven, at least the Company know they can thrive. Christ, I guess even your kangaroos are OK, I'm sure they can cut steaks off them. But it's the predators at the top of the tree that are the weak link as far as the Company is concerned. OK, they need them as they set the Park up, to give it the interCompany seal of conservation approval, to make it look like they're doing this for the right reasons. But when the herds start to achieve a commercial viability, what then?'

'What then?' echoed McCullough.

'Then you introduce more and more fecund strains of algae, so there's more grazing. So you grow more and more cattle. Then you take out the predators; or to be precise, you replace natural predation with human culling. The whole thing's there, making money for the company; except nobody wants Bronovski any more, don't want his snow-lions and ice-hyenas.'

'Could be,' said Natty.

'It's a possibility, I suppose,' agreed McCullough.

'Look at it from Bronovski's point of view,' insisted Kodwo. 'If you were him, how certain would your future seem to you? How amenable would you be to rival Company offers? Earn money by sabotaging Company III bases? Why not?'

McCullough was sitting forward, trying to keep her head directly over her spine. She found the pain was at its least in that position. A shadow fell over her. She looked up instinctively, and gasped. A monster. She scrabbled backwards, but bumped into the buggy.

'Don't worry about them,' Kodwo said, reaching over to scratch the grey snout of the wildebeest. 'They're harmless.'

McCullough tried to get her breathing under control. The wildebeest head, up close, looked too large for plausibility. Its breath pooled out of wide flat nostrils, smoking around the mouth. Brown eyes the size of hens' eggs were set on the side of a head twice, or three times, as large as a horse.

'I guess I knew the stats,' she said, her voice a little wobbly. 'But I suppose I didn't quite, uh, take on board how *big* these ones are.'

'More heat efficient,' said Kodwo, manoeuvring herself onto her knees without spooking the animal, and scratching it behind its shaggy ear. 'Aren't you, my beauty? My beauty.'

'Lovely,' said McCullough. The breath of the monster was sweeping over her in waves, a vegetative, faintly salty odour. It angled its head a little to focus one of its eyes on McCullough, then moved it back. A stream of clear piss appeared with a profound gushing noise from its hind quarters; it splashed copiously against the ice, spraying urine in a wide arc. Both Natty and McCullough made noises of disgust and wriggled to their feet to get away from the spray, but Kodwo didn't seem to mind.

'You're awfully squeamish for scientists,' she said.

'I'm a genengineer,' said Natty, haughtily. 'That's a kind of technician, you know. I'm no mud-in-the-fields scientist.'

'You,' said Kodwo, leaning forward to breath warmly into the beast's open nostrils, 'are a glorified caretaker.'

'Sure,' said Natty. 'Job market's a bit tight at the moment, that's all.'

The wildebeest, a little skittish as the two women had got to their feet, seemed greatly soothed by the air being blown into its nostrils. For a while, even McCullough was calmed by the scene. Then, abruptly, the beast jerked its enormous head upwards. Kodwo, who had been balancing herself by partly leaning against the thing's snout, unbalanced and fell a little backwards. The wildebeest twitched, shuddered, and started away.

Looking around, McCullough could see that they were now in the middle of the entire herd of the animals. Mostly the beasts had their heads down, grazing on the green ice. Moving only a few steps forward to move onto a new patch of green ice; and with only the occasional raised head, the occasional more coltish run or leap. But then, simultaneously with the startling of the beast by the bikes, the entire herd suddenly poked their heads into the air.

'Uh-oh,' said Kodwo. 'This doesn't look good.'

She got up quickly, and started pushing the bikes apart. 'Time to go,' she said. 'Saddle up, people.'

McCullough climbed onto the saddle, wincing with the pain in her thigh muscles and tendons. It was too painful. She hauled herself off again; stretched the legs, took a few steps to try and loosen up a bit.

The wildebeest jittered again, the anxious movement passing through the herd in a wave. Kodwo, sitting astride her bike, was struggling to unpack the rifle from her backpack, her hands struggling behind her like somebody trying to scratch an itch in an inaccessible place.

'Give me a hand with this.'

Natty hurried over and started trying to untie the weapon. The herd scattered with a tremendous thrumming of hooves against pack ice. With a sense of excitement McCullough heard a second noise in amongst the drumbeating, a grating, rasping sort of sound. It sounded, she realised with a thrill in her heart, like a gigantic cat. This was real nature. This was no simulation.

'Get the fucking thing free,' said Kodwo in an urgent voice.

There was a commotion in the seething mass of wildebeest away to the right, a flailing of hooves, and the startling apparition of a huge white lion on the back of one of the animals. *There* it was! Just as the wildebeest were enhanced size, so the cat was bigger than its African forebears. The wildebeest started to go down as its fellows scattered in all directions from the kill. It lifted its huge shaggy head, and McCullough caught a brief glimpse of a second white lioness, her jaws clamped about the neck of the animal. Then the whole group dropped beneath sight as the animal collapsed, surrounded by stampeding white animals. McCullough stood mouth open, the cold air chilling the back of her throat. As the wildebeest thundered away the arena of the kill cleared, and McCullough saw something she had only ever seen on sims derived from historical documentation of the old Serengeti. The two predators were sitting on their prey; the one at the throat still gripping the flesh as the dying animal twitched, the other on its back biting at it seemingly at random. Where had they come from? Without the camouflage of grass it was difficult to see how they had got so close – more than close, into the heart of the herd!

'Jesus!' cried Kodwo, behind her, in exasperation.

'It's stuck, stuck, it's stuck,' complained Natty.

McCullough started to turn around, wanting to tell them both that there was no need to worry, that the lions had made their kill and wouldn't be bothering them. The words were coming out of her mouth: 'Don't worry.' But as she turned and her field of vision swung round she saw it.

She saw it in the process of jumping, of launching itself from the pack ice. She saw it head on, with its jaws open. Kodwo, who was half twisted round, trying to see what was snagging the rifle on her backpack, wasn't looking in the right direction. Natty, similarly engrossed, and stepping towards Kodwo to give her a hand. But there it was, in flight, its massive white paws stretched out, the claws glinting against the snow, silver. Its eyes level and focused on its target.

McCullough didn't even have time to scream.

With no more sound than a sort of *whumph*, Kodwo was folded over flat, taken from the saddle of the buggy and pushed against the ground. Natty took a glancing blow and sprawled backwards. McCullough, without even thinking about what she was doing, started running towards the bike, towards Kodwo and the lioness.

The momentum of the big cat was so great that it wasn't able to hold on to its prey. Used to the inertia of the giant wildebeest, it was wrong-footed by the way Kodwo's body simply crumpled. It went forward onto its face and started an ungainly feline somersault. As McCullough dashed forward she was suddenly confronted with the lioness's white hindquarters rearing up, its tail floating, right in front of her. She shimmied to the side automatically, and the enormous bulk of the animal half-rolled half-skidded past her.

Against a backdrop of wildebeest dashing in all directions, McCullough was at Kodwo's body in moments. Trying to break her run, she was once again fooled by the lack of friction of her feet on the ice. She slid, and her shin cracked painfully against the buggy.

'Oh *Jesus,*' she swore.

She pulled herself round and to Kodwo. '*Jesus,*' she said again, one hand going to her agonised leg. 'Jesus, Kodwo, you alright?' There was no reply. Kodwo's body was limp, her face pressed against the ice. The back of her coverall was ripped by the claws of the lion, great tears down from the shoulder blades, on either side of the strapped rifle.

McCullough glanced up. The lion was righting itself, flipping round with heart-stopping grace. McCullough could see it flexing its powerfully formed forward muscles. Its mouth came open. A penetrating hiss, a rumbling sort of noise. It looked angry. And as McCullough stared down its maw, past its yellowing teeth, she was suddenly visited with a vivid memory. It was the sort of vividness, perhaps, that attends death. She remembered Bronovski's face, laughing, the day before. She remembered Kodwo, ashen after her experiences collecting dung for the kangaroos. And then came Bronovski afterwards, laughing fit to burst himself. He had said: *She was scared by the thought that she might have been eaten by a creature I genengineered: that's what pisses her; not that she nearly got eaten, but that she nearly got eaten by something I made.* To be eaten by something made by Bronovski. The fear crystallised that element in Bronovski himself, that carnivore aspect of him.

The lioness, its killing-rage dampened a little by caution, puzzled perhaps by the unexpected lightness of its prey, took a step forward. It hissed again, scowling. Then it readied to jump. McCullough wasn't even sure what she was doing. It happened without her conscious mind intervening; or, at least, that was how she remembered it afterwards. Her hands were out of their mittens, and groping about on Kodwo's back. She realised – again, afterwards, when she had time to sift through her sense data – as the hands encountered cold wetness that she was touching the blood that Kodwo's blood-red coverall fabric had camouflaged. But the animal was coming towards her, and her fingers found the knot of the strap-webbing that held the rifle tight against Kodwo's back. The webbing was tangled, knotted. There was no way to get the rifle untied in time. McCullough's naked hand slid up from the webbing, along the cold butt, to the centre of the machine.

She squeezed the trigger. Still tied firmly to Kodwo's back the gun hammered into life. Sparks bolted from the end of the barrel, where it poked over Kodwo's shoulder just to the right of her head. The recoil made the limp body twitch and jerk as if possessed.

The first bullets rammed through the lion's front paws as it readied itself to jump. Shrieking, the beast collapsed forward, bringing its chest and head into the line of fire. Its forward moment carried it forward a little, such that it looked as though it were going to fall on top of Kodwo's head, and probably crush it like a melon. McCullough's eyes were wide, but there was nothing she could do. Then the force of the bullets seemed to take hold, halting the tumble forward. McCullough kept her finger firmly down on the juddering trigger, and watched in half-comprehension as the great animal's body was held in that position, its back impossibly reared up in the air, spastically lurching with each impact, tearing holes in the white fur and bringing up red everywhere. Then the corpse of the lioness shifted, and toppled to the right.

McCullough pulled her finger off the trigger. It took an actual effort of will to disengage herself from the hypnotic state of firing the gun. The whole incident seemed to have tranced her. She sat back, gasping. Sucking in deep breaths.

It was the most terrifying thing she had ever experienced. This was a terror that went very deep.

A massive, shuddering intake of breath. A long exhale. And again. Her fingers were trembling, shaking like a nervous ailment. Another breath. She looked down. The front of her coverall was trembling, because her heart was pounding so hard.

Slowly her breath started to calm itself. Her heart was still thundering though. But as the adrenaline slowly drained away, McCullough noticed with a scientist's detachment that the pain in her shin started to re-emerge. Then her head began to complain, filaments of painful sensation all along the line of the stitching. The thing that struck her was the way those sharp pain sensations had simply gone away during the attack.

Then she remembered Natty. 'Natty,' she called, looking right for her. Natty was sitting up. She raised a mittened hand to indicate that she was alright.

McCullough looked again at the torn-up carcass of the lioness. A wild laugh bubbled up inside her. Overkill certainly; but that had shown the monster who was in charge. Who was at the top of the evolutionary ladder. She raised her arms over her head in triumph, but the shift in blood pressure made the back of her head throb harder so she dropped them down again.

Kodwo was out cold. A thin upward-dribble of smoke, like a plant tendril, was coming from up beside her head. Puzzled, McCullough tried to focus her eyes. What was that? A black twist of something, almost like a trail of fabric. But where was it from?

With a little *pouf*, the hair on the side of Kodwo's head came alight. Yellow-white flames, watery against the green snow, took hold. 'Oh Jesus,' said McCullough, lurching forward. She called out: 'She's on fire.'

Her launch forward brought her hands down upon Kodwo's back, pressing her deeper into the snow. The nerveless body gave no signal that this was uncomfortable, but it must have been – or it would have been for a conscious person. McCullough was intensely aware of the lacerations underneath her hands. Yelping, McCullough tried to shuffle off, take her weight from Kodwo's back and place her hands on the ice. The right side of her head was crackling now with a crown of fire.

'Oh God, Oh God,' said McCullough. She started rubbing at the pack ice, trying to bring up enough snow to put the flames out. But her numb fingers made little impact on the hard ice. She needed the rough stripe down the back of the mittens, specially designed to break pieces from the pack. Did she have time to put her mittens on? The flames seemed to be spreading. She picked up the few little pieces she had managed to dig up and tried dropping them onto the fire. It spat, writhed, but didn't die.

'Oh *God*,' she said.

'What are you doing?' yelled Natty. 'Fuck the snow, just smother it. Lie over her head.'

And McCullough collapsed herself over Kodwo's head, pulling her coverall down at the side to cover the flames. They were extinguished at once.

With that, she rolled off the body and onto the ice, gasping in a relief so intense it was almost painful. The sky. She was staring right up at the sky. The sky, as white and blank as the ground. A desert sky, a barren white.

seven

Kodwo was completely unconscious. McCullough worried at first that she was dead, but there were still shallow movements of her chest. It was hard to detect them through the padding of her coverall, but they were there.

'It doesn't look good,' said Natty, examining Kodwo's wounds. The claws had gone deep in her back, and a lot of blood had come out. 'There's probably bones broken too,' she said. 'Maybe ribs, collar bones. And I just don't want to look at her head.'

It wasn't pretty. The hair had burnt away in patches, and the skin of her ear and neck, and those parts of her scalp showing, was black and puckered. 'Maybe we should pack it in ice, do you think?' McCullough asked. 'Isn't that good for burns?'

'Pack the whole side of her head in ice?' echoed Natty. 'That good for burns?'

'I think so.'

'It would make sense,' said Natty. 'At a molecular level. Take away the heat. But if we pack her head in ice, we would kill her, most like. Particularly with her in this condition. Freeze her brain – not a good idea.'

'Maybe you're right.' She tried to lay a finger against the burnt skin, to feel if it was still hot, but her own flesh was too numb with cold to feel very much.

The herd had gone from around them. It was still visible far away to the right, now placidly grazing as if the lion attack had never happened. But it had. Quite apart from the bloodied corpse of the lion McCullough had killed, the two other lions were contentedly devouring the wildebeest they had killed. Another lioness appeared, trotting happily over the ice to join the feast.

'I don't like being so close to them.'

'Me neither,' said McCullough. 'What if more of them come, and there aren't enough places round the table? They could turn on us.'

'It's less them I worry about,' said Natty. 'Lions are either in hunting mood or not. Now they're not, they're in eating mood. But I worry about the hyenas.'

'Oh,' said McCullough.

'The hyenas are as big as a man, and they are in a mean fighting mood all the time. And they'll eat anything. They'll eat us just as easy as looking at us; they'd eat that lion carcass there. They'd probably try and eat the bikes.'

'We'd better be going,' said McCullough.

'No fucking shit. And where?'

'Where's this camp exactly? The Company III place?'

'I *don't* know. I sit at base, I don't go jaunting about on the ice like the real scientists.'

'Jesus, Natty, but you must know where the camp is? At least, roughly?'

'Oh I know roughly,' said Natty. 'Are you prepared to gamble on roughly? If we miss it, there's nothing between us and the East Siberian Sea.'

'Kodwo knew where we were going,' insisted McCullough, a little desperately.

'Surely. You just wake her up and get her to give us the compass bearing, we'll just go straight there.'

McCullough said nothing.

'Besides,' said Natty. 'We only came about thirty kay. We've got ninety more to that destination. You think we can carry her ninety kay? It'd be a miracle if we could manage her the thirty kay back home, and at least then we can follow our tracks.'

'We can't leave her out here.'

'No,' said Natty, with a nasty tone. 'No we can't. If she'd have done the decent thing and got herself killed we could have, but not with her still *breathing*. Some stupid fucking girlfriend she turned out.'

'What?' said McCullough.

'Nothing. Just she's stupid, that's all.'

McCullough looked down at the motionless body. Then over to where the lions were gorging themselves on wildebeest meat. Occasional noises of tearing, and growling, carried over the snow.

'But if we go back,' she said, leaving the sentence unfinished.

'Me, I don't like it, OK?' Natty came right over to where McCullough was standing. The edges of their hoods touched, their faces were inches apart. McCullough would feel Natty's breath, and it was not fresh. She tried to concentrate, but the pain was building again at the back of her head. More than that, her shin was bulging with pain. She could put weight on the leg, although not comfortably; but at least she supposed the bone wasn't broken. But the pain corroded her ability to think rationally.

'I don't like it,' Natty said again, her voice much softer. The air from her mouth pressed against McCullough's cheeks. 'But we have to take the best option we have, yeah? We'll take turns carrying her, and go back. Maybe Bronovski won't kill us; he didn't before, after all. Maybe he's called the Company in our absence, and we'll get back to find lots of Company people there.' Then, without warning, she leaned forward and kissed McCullough. Her lips were rugged with chaps and sores, her beard tickled. McCullough responded automatically. Her hand came up to grasp Natty's shoulder.

Natty broke away, grinning. 'Come along baby,' she said. 'Baby *baby*. We need to get out of here. How is your head?'

'Throbs,' said McCullough.

'Then I'll take her to begin with. But I don't think I'll make it all the way. We may have to change position after a while.'

They pulled Kodwo's hood over her burnt head, and tied it in place as best as possible. Then they shifted her, pulled her over and sat her up against the bikes.

'That's got to hurt,' said McCullough. 'Leaning back against those bikes with a back all smashed up like hers.'

'She's beyond the caring part,' said Natty. She was pulling at the strap-webbing at the back of her own bike, making a sort of backpack she could tie to Kodwo's own straps. 'I think she might be lucky. If the scapulae took most of the damage, they may have protected her lungs and stuff beneath.'

'God bless shoulder blades.'

'Right,' said Natty. 'I think I'm ready. We lift her, and I'll get onto the bike. You'll have to tie her to my webbing for me.'

They went over to Kodwo. 'Should she be that blue in the face?' asked McCullough.

'Oh shit,' said Natty. She yanked off her mittens, and tweaked open Kodwo's mouth before inserting a finger. A little fishing around, and she pulled it out again. 'Tongue had gone back. Think she's alright now.' She leant forward to listen at her mouth, but didn't stay bent over for long. 'Shit, I can't hear anything. But that doesn't mean much. It's not as if I have a stethoscope. Oh *no*.'

McCullough followed her gaze. A half dozen white dog-shapes were padding over the ice towards the wildebeest kill. Even at a distance, they looked big; their black shadows sliding over white beneath their barrel bodies. McCullough blinked. She could make out their faces, their satanic smiles. They looked wicked.

'They're coming for the wildebeest kill,' said Natty, as she grabbed Kodwo under the shoulders. 'They'll chase away the lions, like as not. But it only takes one of them to get interested in us, and we're all dead meat.' She sniggered, as if she had made a joke. 'Give me a fucking hand here,' she said, her tone steely again.

McCullough helped lug Kodwo's dead weight over to Natty's bike, and then to somehow manoeuvre Kodwo's legs over different sides of the buggy. Together they struggled to attach various sections of webbing and straps together. 'OK?' asked McCullough. 'Shall I let go?'

'Try it,' suggested Natty, her voice sounding strained. McCullough stopped supporting the body and it sagged, and then slowly slewed round to the right.

'Christ Christ Christ,' said Natty, urgently. 'It's going to pull me off the bike.' McCullough grabbed at it, shifted it back. There was a spooky, snickering sound behind her. It sounded like demonic laughing.

Hyenas laugh. They used to be famous for it.

Her fingers started stubbing themselves uselessly. This was no good. She couldn't get the latches on the webbing to catch where they were supposed to. Her heart was spurting, thumping hard. There was a flurry of noise, a combination of boiling-sounding animal fury: hisses, growls, screeches. McCullough looked round; the hyenas were dashing in at the wildebeest corpse, snapping at the lions, dancing away again.

'Try now,' said Natty. McCullough let go. The body sagged, its head fell back horizontal so that its hood slipped off again and Kodwo's horribly burnt scalp was visible. 'We should,' McCullough started to say, and then stopped herself. What was she doing? She had been going to say: *We should tie her head up so it doesn't bang about.* But there was no time for niceties.

'Go,' she shouted. 'Go.' She scrambled to her own bike, climbed on and pressed the ignition.

Nothing happened.

Natty's bike chuckled into life, and started uncertainly away. Kodwo's unconscious head bobbled over the ruckles in the ice, but at least the buggy was in motion. McCullough experienced a freezing in the very heart of her being. She looked over to the hyenas. They had stopped their raiding on the lions, and were looking in the direction of Natty's noisy exit.

One thought came into McCullough's head with absolute clarity. It was that Kodwo was so badly hurt as to probably die. And that, accordingly, she shouldn't be the one to win a ride on the back of Natty's bike. That they should dump Kodwo on the ice, and that McCullough herself should ride piggy-back with Natty all the way to safety.

She pressed the ignition again. Again, nothing happened.

'Jesus,' she said. 'Oh Jesus, come *on.*'

Again the ignition. Again nothing.

She stole another glance at the hyenas. Their heads were on one side now, like intelligent dogs trying to work something out. Maybe there was easier food than the carcass guarded by the lions.

McCullough felt the urge to grin at them, try and placate them. Nice doggy. But she had never known anybody rich enough to own a dog, and wasn't sure what to say. Besides, these were wild. The concept kept snaring itself in her brain, because it was difficult to get around. These were *wild* animals. They followed their own rules.

And now they were going to eat her.

With her muscles groaning stiffly she lifted her leg and dismounted from the bike. Treading gently, never taking her eyes off the animals, she made her way over to the other bike, Kodwo's machine. It was almost as if any noise would have been enough to break the tension, and to have triggered the hyenas into their attack. She settled into the saddle, reached down and pressed the ignition.

It caught, and roared into life. Her hand was twisting the throttle before her conscious command left her brain. With a lurch she was moving.

She pushed the throttle as far forward as it would go, and leant into the direction of travel. There was a bubble of elation. She craned her head round, just in time to see the snap of hyena jaws closing centimetres from her face. It was so close she heard the *click* of the teeth coming together, even over the rush of air. The jaws fell away, grinning; became only a part of a hyena running with rapid lopes a little way behind the buggy. McCullough was frozen, stopped absolutely. Her hand was still forward on the throttle pushing herself forward as fast as the machine would go, but she could not bring her head back round to the direction of travel. Her eyes were hooked on the sight behind. There was the hyena, still dogging the bike. She watched as it prepared once more to leap forward.

Then something inside McCullough fell into place. The ice within shattered. She pulled herself forward and turned the bike hard to the right, away from the side of the leaping hyena. Then she banked and pulled forward again. By the time she dared a look back, the hyena had given up. Speed, she knew, not persistence was the hallmark of these predators. She last saw it trotting happily back to its fellows.

The pain in McCullough's leg smarted, and she could feel a stickiness down there. For a moment she thought that it was blood dribbling down her leg, that she must have cut herself when she banged her shin. But then she realised what it was, that she had peed into her coverall pants without even knowing it.

eight

Their tracks were clear enough, and for about an hour they buzzed along. Natty's double-burdened sled was going relatively slowly, and McCullough easily pulled up alongside her. When they were back on the track parallel to the crevasse, Natty slowed and stopped. McCullough came over to her.

'I can't keep it up,' she gasped. Her face, in the shadow of the hood, looked grey and drained. 'I can't breathe, this fucker is *choking* the air from my lungs.'

McCullough dismounted and helped Natty unloose the body of Kodwo. They lowered her onto the pack ice, face down to spare her lacerated back, with her face looking sideways and the burnt portion of her head uppermost.

'She'll get a frostbit cheek if we leave it against the ice like that,' said McCullough.

Natty was stretching her arms and arching her shoulder blades like an athlete warming up. 'Assuming she's still alive,' she said, grimly.

McCullough hunkered down, and stretched her arm out. Lifting Kodwo's head gently with her free hand she was able to rest it on the arm as a pillow. This meant that she had, more or less, to lie down on the ice next to her. The chill of the ground started soaking through the front of her coverall.

She looked closely at Kodwo's face. Was she still alive? It was so difficult to tell. She couldn't see any movement, and bringing her face closer there was no sensation of breath. It was not a practicable position to take a pulse.

'I think she is,' she said, uncertainly. The blackened skin on the side of the head looked particularly horrible, frayed and flaky.

'Well you'll have to carry her for a while,' said Natty.

They went through the whole ungainly procedure of reseating Kodwo, this time with McCullough sitting against the handlebars of the bike, and Natty ill-temperedly fixing the buckles and straps. 'Try to make sure her head is supported this time,' said McCullough, but as she was saying it, the webbing was taking the strain and squashing the air from her lungs. Kodwo was not a particularly large woman, but her weight was unpleasantly real. McCullough tried to pull herself forward, but the force backwards made her body ache. Her head was starting to pound, the pain pulsing from the stitches.

Suddenly she felt enormously tired. How far was it back to the complex?

'Come on then,' said Natty. Relieved of her burden she fairly skipped back to her buggy.

McCullough tried to take a deep breath in, but the pressure against her ribs prevented her. She gasped. This was not going to be easy. Starting up the bike, and easing the throttle forward, she started moving, but the great sack on her back wobbled slowly back and forward and made it almost impossible to keep balanced. McCullough started cursing. She slowed, reached round with her left arm and tried to steady the lump as if it really were a backpack. But it was too intractable a size, shape and weight.

She throttled up again and once more tried going forward. Past a certain speed and the body seemed to settle; it was still a choking presence, squeezing or rather pulling the life from her, but at least they were going forward, getting closer to the place where she could unload it. She could feel her arms going tingly, where the blood supply was being diminished at the shoulders. And the bike was sluggish beneath her, painfully slow even at top speed, and extremely difficult to manoeuvre – any deviation from the straight line met with a crushing inertial resistance from the weight of Kodwo.

McCullough's head hurt; her leg was stinging; she felt hugely tired and low. The blast of cold air against her skin as she buzzed along seemed to scrape her closely with a stabbing agony. And the presence of the thing on her back was the final straw. She drove on, her vision greying and tunnelling before her, able to concentrate on little more than the little spume of snow kicked up by Natty's bike like a rabbit's tail. Minute moved slowly into minute. It was torment. She tried ignoring the pain, but it refused to go away. So she tried concentrating on it, trying to get inside it: the moaning of her bones, the choked growl of breath in her throat. But that was no good either. It was impossible.

And yet she went on. To her right, now, the crevasse widened slowly. Natty buzzed away in front of her, sometimes pulling ahead into the far distance but realising how far behind McCullough was and then throttling back until she could be caught up. Just as McCullough began to think that she had got into a rhythm, into an accommodation with the constant pressure of pain in her system, everything was thrown up.

She had rattled over some rough ice; but where negotiating this stuff when she was the only person on the bike was one thing, trying to go over it at speed with somebody's body on her back was quite another. She was thrown a little off centre, the body heaved over to that side, and suddenly she was off, crashing against the pack ice to the side of the bike.

The weight on McCullough's back pulled her straight to the ground, and she hit the ice with enough force to knock the wind from her chest. She lay on the ice for minutes, feeling the cold creep into her body, feeling her bones chill painfully, but literally unable to move. Without a hand on the throttle the bike decelerated and finally stopped ten metres from her, its engine throbbing.

Natty was beside her. 'Come on,' she said. 'You have to get up and get on.' She was trying to pull her up, tugging at her arms. 'You got to give me a hand here, she-tiger.'

With a tremendous effort of will, McCullough struggled up. She went over on all fours, and pushed with her legs like a weight-lifter. Natty had brought the bike back over, and helped her get back into the saddle. Kodwo's body flopped about.

'She doesn't . . .' McCullough gasped, and stopped. It was almost too much effort gathering breath, and forming words was harder still. 'She doesn't feel very lively.'

Natty slipped her hand from her mitten and pushed it in at the neck of Kodwo's coverall. 'She still feels warm,' she said. 'Surely she'd be cold now if she were dead.'

'Maybe it's me,' McCullough gasped. She wanted to say: *Maybe she only feels warm because she's strapped to me, maybe that's my body heat you're feeling*, but she didn't have the puff.

But Natty was climbing onto her own bike, and revving up. With a groan McCullough revved her own machine, and pulled away.

She tried watching for rough patches of ice, but it was impossible to spot them until she was almost directly upon them. At the least grinding noise, she took to dropping her speed right down, and that slowed the two of them up further. Her head was brightly pulsating with an inner pain, her leg ached, she felt the cold in every one of her joints. Her nose was producing a thin trail of mucus now, that froze as soon as it emerged from her nostrils; but every time she took her left hand from the handlebar to try and wipe the scratchy accumulation away, Kodwo's body on her back wobbled and she was forced to snatch the handle back.

They came to the place where their tracks turned and stretched away from the crevasse, and Natty slewed her buggy to a stop. 'My turn with the dead weight, I guess,' she said.

McCullough was too exhausted to express her relief.

They changed the body over with more ungainliness, and set off again. Released from her burden McCullough felt a delicious sense of freedom. She had been able to clean up her face, and stretch her aching shoulders. Her bike now felt magically lightened, speedy and manoeuvrable. She rushed on.

Then the air changed around her. The first thing was a series of patches of tiny cloud, like gunpowder smoke, on a level with her shoulders and waist. Shreds of opacity whisked past her. Then, suddenly, she was in the middle of the fog. Everything was grey. It was as if the world around her had disappeared; or as if everything had melted and run in together.

She slowed down, and stopped. Natty was nowhere to be seen. McCullough had been allowing herself to get a little ahead of her fellow-traveller. Now she felt the first twinges of unease.

She fumbled with the switches under a flange on the top of the bike until she found the one that lit the headlight. Then she pulled the bike around, hoping that the light would be visible through the fog. She tried listening for the sound of Natty's engine, but could make nothing out. She tried again, pulling down her hood and turning off the engine of her own machine. Nothing. The fog tasted of sea-air, a chilly seaweedy brine flavour. It got into her mouth, and she started coughing.

When the coughing stopped she cocked her head. There was a faraway chuttering noise, but there was no sense of direction attached to it. She paused, tried to concentrate, when a light swelled up out of the mist.

Natty pulled up right beside her.

'Where did all this come from?' asked McCullough. 'It just came out of nowhere.'

Natty was looking drained. 'Happens like that,' she panted, and then stopped. It looked as though she was trying to say something else, but her eyes shut and she gave up.

'We'll need to go slower in the fog, I guess,' offered McCullough.

Natty nodded shallowly.

So she pulled the bike round and started off again, trying to keep her speed right down. But occasional looks over her shoulder showed Natty falling further behind, and on several occasions her light dwindling into the fog like a lamp dropped into the depths of a grey sea. Several times McCullough actually had to stop until Natty made her way up. On the third of these stops, Natty stopped her engine.

'Can't,' she said, straining at the word, sucking breath desperately. 'Can't. Manage.' She started unbuckling her straps, and Kodwo's body suddenly hinged backwards, bent right over backwards so that her loose head cracked against the back treads of the buggy.

'Jesus,' said McCullough, sharply.

'I couldn't *breathe*,' said Natty, cross, sucking lungfuls of air in. 'This whole thing is crazy.'

McCullough was getting off her bike. 'We can't leave her.'

'I didn't say that.'

'We can't do it.'

'She's not going to make it back *anyway*.'

'She's certainly not if you handle her like that.'

Standing behind Natty's bike, McCullough strained and heaved Kodwo's body into a more upward posture. 'Could we, I don't know, strap her to the front?'

'Do what you like,' said Natty.

'You'll need to give me a hand.'

McCullough hefted Kodwo's body fully upright, and put her hand at the back of her head to support the weight of it. She felt a stickiness in amongst the hair. Natty was unhooking herself from the body with an exaggerated sigh of relief.

'Jesus, Natty,' said McCullough. 'She's bleeding at the back of her head now.'

Natty reached round. 'So she is,' she said, blankly.

'At least – at least if she's bleeding we know she's not dead,' said McCullough.

'I don't know about that, though. She's not bleeding with much force.'

'Well,' said McCullough, unsure why she was pushing the point, 'if she were dead she'd be stiff by now. With rigor; or with the cold.'

'Rigor can take many hours to set in,' said Natty, in the same colourless voice. 'And if she's strapped to one of us, like you say, she's heated a little against the cold.'

'We are *not* leaving her,' said McCullough, the force of her innate stubbornness asserting itself.

Natty peered at her out of the cave of her coverall hood. 'You take her, then,' she said.

'OK,' she replied at once. 'I will. I'll need your help, though.' So, without saying anything more, Natty helped McCullough settle Kodwo's body astride the buggy, this time propping her back against the handlebars, so that she faced away from the direction of travel. McCullough climbed in behind her, clutching her like a mother with a baby. Kodwo's face flopped against McCullough's shoulder.

'That's OK,' she said. 'I can see over her, and I can just about reach the handlebars. This should be OK. And this way she's not pulling all the breath out of my body.'

But Natty was already on her bike and starting up.

Slowly, McCullough followed through the fog. With no rear light, it was easy to lose sight of Natty's bike ahead, and when that happened there was nothing McCullough could do apart from keep her gaze on the ground and try to follow the pattern of tread marks on the ice as they flitted into the circle of the headlight's shine. This was not altogether easy, as the tracks wobbled surprisingly; several times McCullough had to slow almost to a stop and weave cautiously to the left or right to reacquire them. And having Kodwo before her rather than behind her made this doubly difficult. In many ways it was a better arrangement, and it was certainly more comfortable for McCullough. But it was also less stable, which meant that she had to go more slowly.

For an indeterminate period she struggled on over the ice. With time, though, the dead weight of Kodwo started to tell. McCullough's shoulders and the base of her spine began to whine, the pain growing and increasing with each yard they travelled. She tried shrugging, shifting the weight of the body a little, but it made little difference. After a while, it began an intolerable pain. She started thinking about stopping, about giving herself a rest. But, she thought, if I do that will I go back to the journey? A wash of tiredness soaked down through her. Her own throbbing head, the ache still sizzling in her shin. Her sufferings. Her experience had shrunken to this grey world, to these pains and aches, to a going-onwards towards a destination she had no desire to reach, in a land she had no desire to be in. Flitting images, vivid as hallucinations, placed her in a warm shower, in a bed with crisp covers, in the sunshine. Kodwo was dead, of course she was. Why not leave her?

At this idea, as if in cosmic confirmation, the fog started lifting. She passed through a clear place, like a room hemmed in all around by roiling walls of fog. Then, into the grey again, but with breaks, patches of light. Finally, with a suddenness equal to the onset of the fog, it was gone. She was buzzing along a bright white landscape, under a sky of pale blue. Up ahead, she could see Natty's bike.

McCullough stopped, cut her engine, and heaved Kodwo's body off her, trying to lower it gently to the ground but inevitably botching it, so that the body fell with a clump to the ice. Then she walked, stretched her legs and arms, rubbed at her shin. Natty was nothing but a black shape moving towards the horizon.

Kodwo was probably dead. What was the point in taking a dead person back to the base? If it was simply a matter of recovering her body, why not call the Company? They could get out here easily enough in an air-truck and collect it. Why not just get back to the base – it couldn't be much further now – leave the body here. She was so tired. She was not well. Surely nobody could ask her to carry the dead body of this woman, whom she hardly knew, over the ice all by herself? Natty was almost at the horizon now. It was as if McCullough's conscience were slipping away over the rim.

With a sudden sense of decision, she climbed onto her buggy and kicked it up, leaving Kodwo's body lying on the ice. This felt right. She felt an inner release. She was flying, gliding over the ice.

And yet, despite this, she slewed to a halt, angling the buggy round. There was the dark smudge against the ice, Kodwo in her deep red coverall. It looked (and McCullough was conscious of the absurdity of this thought as it occurred to her) *untidy*. She revved the engine of the bike. Leave it, she thought. Leave the body. It's only meat. Dead meat.

She gunned the engine and started off again, circling round in a wide arc to bring her back to the crumpled form. Lifting it from the ice, McCullough struggled to get it upright. Kodwo's face pressed into McCullough's hood as she tried this manoeuvre, skin touching skin. There was no doubt about it; Kodwo had a nonvivid chill about her. Her face was cool. Nonetheless, with a blind stupidity in her heart, McCullough manhandled her body up, and pushed her insensate leg over the torso of the bike. This time Kodwo's body was facing forward, and she sagged over the handlebars. Climbing on behind her, McCullough tried the steering. Deadened by Kodwo's weight it was hard to move, but she could ease it one way or another. It would do, she thought. She was only going one direction anyway: forward.

She started off, lugging the bike over to the tracks on the ice. Then she was moving again, passing shudderingly over the ice. The cold of the air in motion bit at her face again, her headwound throbbing with pain again. But she ground her teeth together and pressed on.

Soon the dot of Natty's bike started to grow, like a black seed in the completeness of white wilderness, white ground, white sky. Pretty soon, McCullough caught up with her.

'I was sort of getting ahead of you there,' Natty shouted across. 'You OK? You want me to take her?'

'She's fine there,' said McCullough.

After another hour's travelling the low roof of the hangar came into view. They halted their bikes together.

'What are we going to do?' McCullough asked.

Natty was silent for a little space. 'I guess we go straight in.'

'What do we say?'

'Say, fuck, whatever. Say we've got to get medical help for Kodwo.'

McCullough looked down at the body slumped over her handlebars. She hadn't moved at all throughout the journey. It seemed clear enough she was dead. 'I guess,' she said.

'Say we're cold and hungry, say we need to use the shower. What does it matter?'

But inside herself McCullough felt it did matter. What if Bronovski were there, pointing a rifle at them as they glided into the hangar? What if he had killed Hartmann? Had it been the proper thing to do, to leave Hartmann alone with a killer?

She pushed the engine into life.

nine

The kangaroos were still milling around the corral, despite the open door. McCullough made a mental note to examine the genes for curiosity and adventurousness when she got back to her lab. If she got back.

Bronovski was standing in the shadows at the back of the hangar. He was angling his rifle from the hip, cool as a sim villain. The glare of the white sky had so bleached McCullough's vision that the shadows were at first completely impenetrable. Only as she glided into the shadow herself did the standing form swim into vision.

McCullough's heart leapt up. She stopped, and Natty beside her. For a long, hanging moment they said nothing, and the hangar was full only with the throb of the bikes. Then Natty shut hers off, and McCullough reached under Kodwo's body to do the same.

Bronovski sniffed noisily. He did not lower the rifle. 'You're back,' he said.

Natty said nothing.

Bronovski took a step forward. 'Is that Kodwo?' he asked.

Still the gun was up, like a magic wand depriving McCullough of the power of speech. Bronovski came a little closer. Then, finally, the tip of the gun went down, pointing now at the floor. McCullough felt something like a catch give way in her chest; her lungs fill with air. She hadn't even realised that she had been holding her breath.

'She's hurt pretty fucking bad, man,' said Natty. 'We have to get her downstairs.'

'She's dead,' said McCullough, finding her voice.

Natty looked over. Bronovski sniffed again. 'You killed her?' he said, questioning, looking directly at McCullough.

'No,' she replied, looking straight back at him.

'Fuck this shit,' said Natty, clambering off her bike. 'We need to get her downstairs.'

'But if she's dead—' began Bronovski.

'Maybe dead,' said Natty. 'We don't know for hundred percent certain.'

'She's maybe dead,' said McCullough. 'She's certainly badly hurt.'

'Then let's get her downstairs,' said Bronovski. 'And where have you guys *been*, anyway?'

McCullough was trying to lift Kodwo from the crossbar. Bronovski was there, trying to help. He was, McCullough could see, wearing tight plastic gloves, the sort genengineers sometimes used when handling toxic samples. As if Kodwo's body were some sort of dangerous quantity.

With McCullough holding Kodwo's shoulders and Natty her legs they carried the body through the door (held open by Bronovski, who didn't relinquish his gun), down the sloping corridor and into the kitchen. Hartmann looked up in surprise. 'Through here,' grunted Natty, nodding her head towards her own cell.

'Where have you people been?' Hartmann was saying. 'And who is that you're carrying?'

Through in Natty's room they lowered Kodwo's body onto the bed. McCullough realised abruptly that she was very hot, sweat starting to tickle its way down her back. She pulled off her mittens, and undid the fastenings on her coverall. It refused to come apart.

Natty was doing the same. 'You've got those straps round you still,' she said. Stripped now to her clothes, she came round and picked the webbing apart. McCullough was finally able to shuffle off the coverall. 'God, I'm *hot*,' she said, wiping her forehead with a sodden sleeve. But Natty had gone. She was back in an instant with a weighty-looking box.

'Get her out of her coverall,' said Natty. 'That's first.' Together they unpinned the front and sloughed it off, sliding it underneath the limp body and throwing it to the floor. The clothes underneath were stiff with blood. Blood had reached everywhere, except for a small patch of white cloth over her belly.

Natty and McCullough crouched down beside the bed as Natty opened the first-aid box. Bronovski, still carrying the rifle, was standing in the door, with Hartmann behind him. McCullough heard Hartmann's voice ('That's *Kodwo*? Jesus . . .') as if from very far away. She was so tired it took a strong effort of will keeping her eyelids from gumming together. She tried to focus on what Natty was doing, mopping at the burnt patch on the side of Kodwo's head with some little cloth. Leaning over her, feeling for her pulse. But McCullough's leg was sending showers of sparking pain up her side now. She sat back, dozily, onto her rump and rolled up the leg of her pants. The skin was broken half way up her shin; edges of skin peeled back and frayed like cloth. There was surprisingly little blood, a tendril of rusty coloured fluid dried down to her foot. But the flesh was open like a puckered mouth, and what looked like bone was just visible. The whole of her shin was a night sky shot through with northern lights, an enormous bruise threaded through with purples, snot-yellow and blues.

The sight of it made McCullough wobble, seeing wounds being so much worse than feeling them. She felt her stomach clutch as if about to throw up, then her head went light. She felt a twisting, swirling sensation, as if consciousness were pouring away down a plughole in her mind.

Natty was with her. 'Don't look at it,' she said, rolling back the trouser leg. 'I'll put some antiseptic on it in a bit, just don't think about it for the moment.'

'Oh God, Natty,' she whispered.

'I'm fine here. You go out into the kitchen, get yourself some coffee. Something to eat.'

McCullough had to summon her voice from a long way away. 'I'm not hungry,' she said.

'Then go and lie down,' said Natty, her attention on Kodwo. 'Get some sleep.'

Hartmann came further into the little room and helped her to her feet. She wobbled, unable to place weight on her left leg. It was still broadcasting the pain. She hobbled through, pushing past Bronovski, getting as far as the table in the middle of the kitchen before sitting down.

Her mind faded out, buzzed, and then slowly focused again. She was tired, physically exhausted; but there was a part of her that did not want to go through and lie down. Her thoughts fizzled clumsily. Her fingers were trembling. She felt like a can of carbonated fluid, shaken to the point of near explosion.

'What happened to Kodwo?' asked Hartmann. The proximity of his voice startled her. He was standing right behind her.

'She is injured,' said Bronovski, also behind her. 'Injured to fuck.'

Hartmann came round and settled himself into a chair at McCullough's left. 'And what happened to you guys? We were worried.'

McCullough looked into his eyes, trying to determine if he were mocking her in some obscure way. But it was hard keeping her head steady. Her leg was trembling, shaking with pain and fatigue. How could he be so calm ? Almost chatty?

'But what *happened*?' insisted Bronovski. 'How did her face get so burned.'

'We were in amongst wildebeest,' said McCullough in a tremulous voice. 'We got attacked by a snow-lion.'

Hartmann let out a low whistle. Bronovski, balancing his rifle across his lap and leaning his elbows on it as if it were a tray or support of some kind, grinned. But he said, 'that's too bad, that's savage. That how she got all cut up, there? She's lacerated badly, lacerated to fuck.'

'On her back,' said Hartmann. 'When Natty turned her on her side to bandage it you could see all the way to the bone.'

The thought of this, the memory of her own wound, brought a violent nausea to McCullough's throat. She clenched her teeth, pressed down with both hands on the ball of her stomach. The feeling swelled, hovered, and then receded.

'. . . quite, though why you went,' Hartmann was saying. 'That's what had us puzzled. And worried. So you went off after the herd again, was that it ? Were you collecting dung? More dung for your roos?'

'I figured you were collecting dung for your roos,' said Bronovski. McCullough turned her head and looked carefully at him. Was he really going to play this as if everything was normal? The long, narrow face had effortlessly taken on exactly the right look of disinterested concern. He even ventured a little smile. 'We were a little thrown, though, that you didn't say you were going or anything.'

Natty appeared at the door of her cell, with the weighty first-aid box in her arms. She came over, and clattered it onto the table, before settling herself into a chair with a sigh. Her face was collapsed with tiredness and something else, perhaps despair.

'She's dead,' said McCullough in a deeper, boomier voice than she intended.

Everybody looked at Natty.

'What? Oh, no, she's not,' said Natty, pulling at her beard. 'She's alive. Just about. Only just a-fucking-bout. I don't see as how she'll survive.'

There was a silence about the table. Then Natty took a deep breath in. 'You moved the bodies,' she said to Hartmann.

Bronovski nodded. 'We thought about it, after you went off to get your dung. We just couldn't see how the company was going to buy the terrorist story.'

'We were wondering about satellites,' said Hartmann.

'Yeah,' said Bronovski. 'Satellites.'

'They'll just monitor their readings and see that there were no submarines, no air-trucks. So they'll ask us how the terrorists got to the base, and we'll have to say that they came on foot. Now, that sounds pretty weird, you have to agree.'

'Weird,' said Bronovski emphatically, 'as fuck.'

'So we reckoned there was a better way.'

'What did you do with the bodies?' asked Natty in a flat voice.

'We . . .' Hartmann spoke with a hitch of hesitation in the sentence, as if embarrassed, 'buried them. About four hundred metres out back.'

'We buried them,' repeated Bronovski.

'Then we scraped all the bloodied ice up and we buried that too. Not an easy job, I can tell you.'

'So,' said McCullough, looking directly at Bronovski. 'So nobody will know what you've done.'

Bronovski looked at her, quizzically. 'That's the idea,' he said. 'That way, as far as the Company is concerned, the soldiers just went off.'

'That's what we'll tell them,' said Hartmann. 'They just went off. Wandered off over the ice. Maybe they got curious, decided to take a look at some wildebeest. Maybe they fell in a crevasse. We don't know.'

'You kept a gun, though,' said McCullough, looking intently at Bronovski.

He looked down at his lap. 'Yes, we did,' he said.

'We reckoned we ought to keep one,' said Hartmann. 'We buried the rest with the bodies. Clearly we don't want the Company thinking their boys had wandered off without their weapons, that would look odd. But we thought we'd keep one for the time being, in case terrorists do, you know, decide to look in. We'll bury it when the Company tell us they are coming over.' He looked over to Natty. 'We'll have to dispose of the one Kodwo was carrying, too.'

'And have you called the Company?' asked Natty.

'Called them a couple of hours ago,' said Bronovski. 'Left it until it started looking like a reasonable time had passed. Time for us to get worried. Then we called them and told them the soldiers were missing.'

'And they said?'

'They said not to worry.' Bronovski cracked a smile. 'Told us they were on manoeuvres, that they'd be back.'

'You'd better call them again,' said Natty. 'Tell them that Kodwo has been seriously injured and will require hospital attention or she will die. She will probably die anyway, but we can't keep her here.'

'Right,' said Bronovski.

'How did she get burnt?' asked Hartmann, shaking his head.

'Just call them,' said Natty, pressing the heel of her palms into her eye sockets. 'It's going to take hours for an air-truck to get out to us, so make sure they send medics and some equipment.'

'I'll call,' said Bronovski. He picked his rifle from his lap and leant it against the table edge as he got up, turning away from McCullough.

She saw the back of his head. His hair was thinning in a swirling pattern, like fluid going down a drain, like iron filings lining up on a magnet. She willed strength into her arms. The first-aid box looked heavy, and her moment would pass rapidly. Then she reached out and grasped the box.

It was heavier than she had anticipated but she was committed to the move now. She grasped either side and dragged it up into the air. Her stretch had brought her off the chair, and she swivelled on her good foot, sweeping the box through. It caught Bronovski at that point on the back of the skull where the cranium overhangs slightly the neck. The rounded corner of the box impacted heavily as McCullough brought the arc of her blow through. The force of the contact jarred the box from her hands, and the first-aid kit fell, clanged off the edge of the table and fell noisily to the floor.

Bronovski made a quiet little noise of exhalation, a *ouaff* noise, and fell straight down. He crumpled in a heap over his own feet as if his spine had been whipped out, knees and torso folding over one another. Only when he was down did he sprawl, falling onto his side.

Hartmann was on his feet. 'What are you *doing*?' he shouted. His voice came through surprisingly loud. 'What are you *playing at*? You are a *psycho*.'

'He was a *murderer*,' she screamed.

'What are you on? You're insane. You have lost touch with your sanity.'

McCullough was breathing heavily. She took steps backwards, almost staggering. Then Hartmann's and her eyes fell on the rifle simultaneously. They both lurched forward, coming together in a scrum, trying to wrestle the gun. Hartmann was stronger, and less exhausted, and McCullough fell away empty handed. By now she was laughing, a thin dribble of laughter that refused to be dammed. She was sitting on the cold floor, looking up at Hartmann, and the laughter was coming out of her mouth like drool. She could not stop herself.

Hartmann's eyes were wide. He pointed the gun down at her as if about to fire, but Natty was on her feet too, calling out to him to stop, to wait. The ridiculous thing, perhaps the reason McCullough couldn't stop laughing, was that she no longer cared whether Hartmann shot her or not. She was so tired that her body had simply ceased functioning. Her eyelids were coming together. The world greyed from above and below, and then it went black. She slumped to the side, went down.

ten

She did not sleep properly. She kept waking, intensely aware of the discomfort of lying on the cold floor, or of the searing pains coming up from her leg. But before she could gather herself, move through to her room, she would fall asleep again. Images of speeding over the snow had infected her imagination. Shutting her eyes brought on the sensation of travelling rapidly, flying over an endless white expanse. Suddenly the snow-lioness was there, flying towards her with claws outstretched and mouth wide.

She jerked awake.

Natty was huddling over her. 'Come on,' she was saying. 'Let's get you through to your room. I want to take a look at that leg.'

McCullough was shivering now, her fingers and feet wobbling. She fought the battle to get upright. Hartmann was still standing by the table holding the rifle. Something about the way he looked made her tremble more.

'Bronovski was a killer,' she told him in a wavering voice.

'He was no killer,' said Hartmann, firmly.

'Come on, through here,' said Natty.

'He was a killer,' McCullough repeated, over her shoulder. Natty took her through and lay her down on the bed. She unzipped the sleeping bag and laid it over her torso. Then she rolled up the leg of her trouser and started prodding at the wound.

Hartmann had followed them through. 'What I want to know,' he was saying, his voice louder than normal, 'is whatever made you think that Bronovski was a killer?'

'The handkerchief,' she said, thinly. Natty's proddings were adding sparkles of over-pain to the constant ache.

'What?'

'She means,' said Natty, 'the way he was so keen to make sure his fingerprints weren't on the rifle he was carrying. That handkerchief. He's wearing gloves now. That's what she means.'

'Is he OK?' McCullough asked.

'Bronovski?' replied Natty. 'He's still breathing.'

'He's probably in a *coma*,' yelled Hartmann. 'All because of this one. She's a menace, a criminal. She is a psychopath.'

'The handkerchief,' said McCullough again.

'I don't believe you,' said Hartmann. 'So he didn't want his fingerprints on the rifle. How does that convict him of anything? So he didn't want to be incriminated – which one of us does? You know how the Company can be. He was just being careful.'

McCullough blinked, tried to make sense of what she was being told. There was something he was missing, something that proved absolutely the guilt of Bronovski. His predator nature. The face of the snow-lioness, grinning with deadly intent as it leapt. It was him. It was just him.

A sharp splinter of agony shot up from the leg. 'Jesus, Natty,' she called out.

'I'm disinfecting it,' she said. 'Just hold still. I'll give you a painkiller in a moment.'

'No – now,' said McCullough.

Natty rummaged in the box, and brought out a fat tablet. 'Get her some water to swallow that with,' she told Hartmann. He let out a gasp, as if in outrage. But he went back out into the kitchen and returned with a cup of water. Propping herself on an elbow, McCullough managed to gulp down the tablet.

'You've got a bit of an infection in here,' Natty was saying. 'I'm going to have to clean it out a bit, bind it up.' But McCullough's senses wobbled, the sounds blurred into one another. She drifted off, tugged back sharply at intervals by the jabs of sensation coming up from her legs. Eventually there was nothing at all.

* * *

There was a patchy period, when she thought she was talking on and on about Friedrich. Natty was at the end of the bed, she thought (it was all a bit ghostly). She seemed to be there, all hunched up; but then she seemed to metamorphose and take on the shape of the snow-lion, hunched and ready to pounce. But the words didn't stop, the drizzle of words from her mouth. All about Friedrich. She had loved him, loved him so much. Even to the point of being ready to give up the research. He had never asked, of course, because he never asked anything. But every evening he seemed a little further away from her. And the further he withdrew, the more she desired him. Big, beautiful him, with his haughty manner, all old-imperial. There was little substance, and little money, in his secondary accounting software, but none of that ever seemed to touch him. Money didn't bother him, but why would it when he had access to her primary Company salary? Still, he grew away from her. Only a very distant chill in the exact middle of his eye, a very slight stiffening in his manner. What could she do? She was crying now, imploring the shadow at the foot of her bed that might or might not have been Natty sitting listening. What could she have done to keep him, to save the marriage? Her whole narrative revolved on this point, the fulcrum between the worsening period of the marriage and the period that came after the divorce party – throwing herself into her work; living, eating and sleeping in the lab. But at that point of pressure, the moment when her whole life hinged and swung about, the whole fog of pain and repression came into focus. As she spoke it, all the emotion came back, and the tears just flowed and flowed. Friedrich standing outlined against the holowall, with his head down slightly. He had said, 'I've spoken to our judge,' and she knew that he had been talking about a divorce, and not about any of the thousand things he could have gone to a judge for. The irony was that, only the week before, one of her co-workers had gone to *their* judge for a child-licence. But McCullough had realised straight away, of course, that was not what Friedrich meant, that was not why he would go to a judge. And the fact that she knew that was not what he meant, carried the real significance. And the realisation sinking in, that she had lost him, that she was alone. She cried, the tears broke from her, and the shadow hunched itself more.

* * *

It was a sort of dream; but also a memory – although more than a memory. Friedrich was leading her by the hand, through the streets. They were going to a party, and McCullough was wearing dainty party shoes; she was worried about them getting trampled by the crush of people around her, so she kept her eyes on the floor. Keeping eyes down, allowing Friedrich to lead her as if she were a child, she watched the clacking, dancing feet and legs of the other people walking with them. Some were hurried, squeezing through the dancing forest, skipping round, feet aimed at spaces as they opened up. Those were dangerous. Several times, the heel of a hard-plastic boot squashed the littlest of McCullough's cloth-covered toes. But there was a bewildering number of other shoe styles, other sorts of leg and feet. Dermasocks, with little metal blisters over each toe to provide the protection that McCullough lacked; old-style shoes, with silver laces; several feet-shoes, pink and brown plastic mimicking precisely the shapes and contours of the feet they encased; hoof-shoes; tuba-shoes; shoes-della-Pedretta, basinet-shoes. The play of light from the street glowglobes laced everything with fluid shadows, so that feet and legs swam in and out of vision.

* * *

So many people. And, here, only the whiteness of the snow desert.

* * *

Take a look, walking down any street. Look up, now. On through the wash and buffet of people, a flow as rapid and shifting as a tumbling stream, and simultaneously as slow and remorseless as a glacier. Faces hurtling up and passing, snapshotted as your eyes blinked. A woman, with a velvet sheen to her skin that is almost a pelt, genengineered presumably; a man with bright blue pupils that look to be dissolving in the washy rheum of his eyes; an old man, wrinkles so deep they looked like scars; another old man, shiftily looking down at the ground. A woman with a bruise on the side of her face, old, purples and yellows, fading like colours bleached by the sun; a brutal-looking man with very white skin, pink eyelashes; a man whose black skin is freckled with pale-brown patches from forehead to chin; a shift in the flow, an interruption in the flood of faces as Friedrich pulls you over to the side of the walkway, out of the glare of the glowglobes. Then more faces pressing in on you: a handsome-faced man in his fifties, his sharply defined features throwing equally sharply defined shadow over to the side of his head; a bald-faced man with a raging pimple right on the end of his bulbous nose, like a nipple; a woman with white make-up framing her black-pupilled eyes, drawing them out of her dark face; a man whose thick eyebrows draw a firm V over the bridge of his nose, over the shallow U of his mouth; another man, very tall, whose face from your point of view is mostly neck, and the dangling skin in the eaves of his chin; a man with a genengineered third eye in his forehead – a grey, shallow eye sitting blankly in a specially built pocket of flesh, blind and sick-looking; a man smiling to himself at some private joke; a woman in a cloth mask; another man who evidently had had the money to pay for genengineering – his skin tone was divided equally between black on the left and white on the right. In a crowd in the smarter parts of town, of course, you would expect to see many more genengineered features, but it so happens you are walking through a poorer district. A large-faced man with saggy flesh the consistency of a piece of bread, all pockmarks and wide pores; a well-tanned bald woman; a young woman, with a ring pierced through the bridge of her nose, and what might have been other rings piercing the ball of her left eye, only it is difficult to tell, she goes by so fast; a man wearing shades that are the exact same tone as his skin, even though it is quite dark now, after sunset as you walk – presumably they are night-vision shades; a woman, her face hidden in the shadow inside her red hood; a short man with hair dyed blue after some contemporary fashion, and gelled to poke up on either side of his head like rabbit ears; another man who catches your eyes and grins; a man sunburnt so badly his bald dome is flaking like puff pastry; a man sweating hard, stars of sweat on his forehead, his cheeks slick, looking like he is on some especially hard-effecting drugs; a man with eyebrows so bushy, and with such prolific nasal and ear hair, it looks as if hair is actually bursting out of his head, as if his head is stuffed with hair like an old sofa; a woman of striking beauty; a man with a worn-out look.

* * *

McCullough shifts in her sleep; in the midst of emptiness her dreams drag her back into the maelstrom of people.

* * *

She woke up thirsty. Her leg was bandaged and aching still, although the pain was a little diminished. She pulled herself up and over to the sink to drink, and then back to bed. Her head felt a little clearer. She pushed shards of brittle sleep from the corners of her eyes, blinked.

Hartmann was sitting in the corner, by the door.

She didn't cry out, although she was startled. He was sitting on a chair, presumably brought through from the kitchen; the gun was in his lap, and he was looking directly at her.

'Feeling better?' he said.

She nodded.

There was a period of silence.

'I don't like you,' he said. 'I didn't when we first met. Now you've all but brained my best friend, I like you even less.'

She nodded again.

He seemed to be pondering something, sagely considering it. 'What I want,' he said, 'is to hear why you thought my best friend was the person who killed those three soldiers.'

McCullough considered.

'Why,' Hartmann persisted, 'was it such a crime, not wanting his finger-prints on the rifle? Tell me that. It was not as if the rifles were the murder weapons. You said yourself that the rifles weren't the murder weapons.'

'One of them,' McCullough interrupted with a croaky voice. 'I only felt one of them. One barrel was cold, but maybe the others were hot. I didn't feel them.'

'So what are you saying? You think that Bronovski went through to the hangar, took one of the soldiers' guns away – why didn't they stop him? Then you think he shot them all, and put the gun back. Is that right?'

McCullough pondered. Was that what she thought? Why had the case against Bronovski seemed so watertight?

'It could have been,' she said, hesitantly. 'You have to admit, he's got it in him.'

'Have to admit?' barked Hartmann. 'Have to admit what? I've known him over a decade. You think you can make a better assessment of his character in a few days, than I can over so many years? What do you know about him – nothing.'

'Somebody killed those men,' she blurted, stung to response by his anger.

'Somebody,' agreed Hartmann, looking hard at her.

'And it wasn't me.'

'You're the one who's demonstrated the violent temper,' he said. 'And you're a woman; you're attractive enough. You could have gone through and somehow talked the boys into putting their weapons aside. Then you could have shot them.'

'Why?' McCullough said. 'Why would I do that?'

'I don't know. Who knows? Maybe you're still in the pay of your old Company. We wondered if that was where Kodwo went; maybe you gave her the slip, and she and Natty went after you. We thought maybe you'd started trying to disable all the buggies, but Kodwo had caught you after one and you'd run off.'

'It wasn't like that,' said McCullough.

'Then when Natty brought you back, wounded, with Kodwo in a worse state, you can imagine how it looked.' He picked up the rifle and pointed it at her, using it like a lecturer's baton. 'It looked like they had caught up with you, and there had been a fight. It looked like you'd tried to kill Kodwo too, but you'd been injured in the process.'

'I *carried* her back,' said McCullough, feeling self-righteousness spark inside her. 'That wasn't how it happened. Ask Natty.'

'Natty's asleep,' said Hartmann. 'Your lover. Your *lover*, did you think we didn't know? We know how Natty is. You think she's going to contradict you, her lover? And I can't ask Kodwo, can I. She's close to death. She's been lacerated, *and* burnt, *and* bashed on the head. All, you say, by a snow-lion.'

'Look,' McCullough began. 'It wasn't that.'

'*You're* the outsider,' Hartmann asserted. 'The three of us had been working as a team for years. Then you come in, from the outside, and everything goes bloody. How do you think the Company are going to see it?'

McCullough felt the first seeds of panic in her breast. 'No,' she said, controlling herself. 'When Natty wakes up she'll tell you what really happened. You go wake her now. She'll tell you. We went off because we were afraid of Bronovski. It was Kodwo's idea. We were heading out to another station – she'll tell you. Then after Kodwo was attacked we realised we had to come back, we had to. That was when I carried Kodwo's body all the way. Well, not all the way, I shared the journey with Natty. But we brought her back. We could have left her out there.'

But Hartmann was only smiling now, his head a little to one side. 'Maybe Natty'll confirm that when she wakes,' he said. 'Maybe she won't.'

'Of course she will,' said McCullough. 'Why wouldn't she?' And stopped. The white face of the snow-lioness flashed through her mind. Jaws open, bristles framing the teeth.

Why wouldn't she?

'Wait a minute,' she said, trying to lift herself. 'Wait. The rifles weren't the weapons used to kill those boys. You said so yourself.'

Hartmann was grinning too intently now. He was lifting the barrel of his gun.

'No, Hartmann, wait,' she said. 'If they weren't killed with their own weapons, then it must have been another gun. No, Hartmann, think – who else even has a gun? Not any of us, because we wouldn't have been able to carry one on the air-truck here. We'd have set off the detectors, wouldn't we. So who else?'

Hartmann didn't seem to be listening. He was getting to his feet. The tiny O at the end of the rifle barrel was mouthing silently directly at her.

'Hartmann,' she said, her words speeding. 'Why won't you listen to me? Listen, it must have been Natty. She'll have a gun, for when she's in the station by herself. That'll be self-defence, don't you see? Even when there's no equipment here, or animals, or scientists, *she's* still here. She has a gun, Hartmann, of course she does. Think about it.'

He was standing up, fully. His smile had broken open into a grin.

'Hartmann,' said McCullough, with increasing desperation. 'Don't you see it? What are you playing at? It'll be her. She was talking to me about her sympathies with the terrorists. It's her.' But McCullough couldn't put into words the real constellation of feeling that sounded the chord within her, the juxtaposition in her mind of the snarling face of the snow-lion and the particular expression in Natty's face. The sudden rightness of it. The falling together of elements, as in a perfect composition; the balance, the harmony.

'You,' said Hartmann, slowly, 'killed my friend. You're a terrorist. The Company will be pleased I put an end—'

And the *crack*.

And the pain. McCullough squeezed her eyes shut, with the pain in her body scattered like glitter blown apart, all her body twitching.

It was moments before the pain resolved itself, located itself in her mind. Her leg, still. The old pain in her shin, nothing new, nothing more.

She opened her eyes. Hartmann was gone. Natty was there. She looked down, and Hartmann was on the floor.

eleven

By the time they were notified that the air-truck was on its way, McCullough was feeling much more full of life. She was even up and moving around, although that took the help of another painkiller, and although she couldn't put any weight on her leg. She went through to Bronovski's room and saw him there, breathing shallowly on his back. His eyes were shut, and his pinched, narrow features gave him a mummified, Pharaoh-like look. Then into Kodwo's room, where little could be seen, only a wrap-bandaged head poking out of a fat sleeping-bag.

Natty was out, burying the last two rifles somewhere in the ice. Cutting a block with the construction laser, hauling it out with the grips, pushing the evidence in and then replacing the block; finally burning off the hump that remained until the pack was as smooth as before. Just like they'd done with the soldiers, and everything else.

McCullough sat in the kitchen, drinking soya potage. By the time Natty came back through, she was onto her second bowlbeaker.

'That's that,' said Natty, climbing out of her coverall. 'Any coffee, my lover?'

McCullough nodded towards the nipple.

'They'll be here in a little space,' she said, as she fetched herself the drink.

McCullough nodded again. 'And we tell them what?'

'It was a fucking mess, that's what we tell them.'

'It was certainly that.'

There was silence between them, as Natty sipped at her coffee. Then she got up, came round, and kissed McCullough. 'I don't even know your first name,' she said.

'Annalee,' said McCullough, automatically.

Natty settled herself again. 'We tell them,' she said. 'We tell them there was a fight. We tell them you and I went out onto the ice, on buggies, to pick up food for your kangaroos. You and me alone.'

'Right.'

'When we got back, we tell them, we found things as they are. The soldiers gone, we don't know where. Only that Hartmann was carrying one of their guns, so that's suggestive, I think. We think.' Another sip of coffee. 'So, we found Kodwo badly cut up and burnt, almost as if she'd been tortured or something. And we found Bronovski and Hartmann together.'

Another sip.

'They tried it with us, so we fought back. We bashed Bronovski, or you did. Then Hartmann pulled his gun on you, so I had no choice but to shoot him. With my Company-issue pistol.'

Another sip.

'What about when the others wake up,' offered McCullough.

'Bronovski, whatever he says, who's going to believe it? And Kodwo, well, I wouldn't hold out any hopes that she's going to be waking up at all, bright girl.'

McCullough looked hard. 'Did you?'

'Did I what?'

But McCullough couldn't think of a way of finishing the sentence. 'What about,' she said, 'what about my head? My shin?'

Natty shrugged. 'You did the head yesterday, slipped on the ice. I stitched it. And the shin, well, you did that out amongst the wildebeest. Didn't you.'

McCullough nodded. Her whole head felt oddly shrunken, packed in soft wadding. The world drifted past her, distant, fey, incomprehensible. People came and went, some people died, some people lived. The pain in her leg was removed far away, pushed to the horizon of her being. The painkillers didn't make it entirely go away, but it was a small thing to her now.

Something else bothered her. 'But what if Kodwo does wake up?' she asked.

'If that miracle happens,' said Natty, with a smile. 'That will be good for her, won't it.'

'Her story won't fit ours,' said McCullough.

'Annalee, my sweet,' said Natty, with a knowing look in her eye, a particular arrangement of wrinkles pointing in towards the brown pupil that expressed world-weariness as well as humour. 'Annalee my sweet, don't you *see*? She won't give them any story until she's spoken to me.'

* * *

And afterwards, after the air-truck had come, with an air ambulance in attendance, and people had gone all over the base, and a skeleton military detachment had been left in position, and Kodwo and Bronovski, and Hartmann's body, had been shipped away in the ambulance – after all the hubbub, when McCullough and Natty made their way into the transparent bubble of the air truck, McCullough was still in a sort of daze. There was a portion of her scientist make-up that pressed her to make sense of everything, but the pieces circled one another. Fragments and splinters in free fall, in a series of mini-orbits about one another.

On the flight back, with nobody else in the observation bubble, Natty came over and put her arm around McCullough's shoulders. McCullough let her. She had nobody else to hug her.

Neither was there anybody else to explain how the pieces fitted together. To explain how Natty and Kodwo had been lovers. To say things like 'I could tell as soon as they came off the fucking air-truck that those boys weren't Company soldiers. They were no fucking use as soldiers, although they seemed surprisingly interested in the equipment unloaded, and they watched every time somebody used one or other piece of technology.' To shake her head laughing at some joke so obscure it left only echoes of unease. Of pointing out the steps by which it had been possible to see that the soldiers were undercover, that the Company had not known which of the trio of Stooges to mistrust and so had mistrusted all of them, setting guards to spy on their comings and goings. 'As if we needed defence against terrorists. What fucking terrorists? That's your absolute fucking grade-first Company misinformation.' To point out, with scholarly over-preciseness by way of a joke, that who needed *fucking* terrorists when any one of the seven Companies would fuck over any other for no more reason than to have something to *laugh* about at board meetings? To laugh herself, in her peeping little way. To launch into a lengthy, difficult-to-follow scientific spiel about a sabotage agent sponsored by Company III, a detergent-analogue that displayed algaeic-bacterial properties, such that once properly introduced it would turn pack ice into foam, into nothing but foam, frothing up coldly over the Arctic Ocean. And had she thought of that? Had she thought how, with so much capital invested in Park Polar, how the Arctic Companies would be hurt, how badly they would be wounded? And conversely, how much the Antarctic Companies would prosper? They were only growing the meat to make money, hiding it under a hypocritical cloak of conservation. Destroy their park from underneath them, and the clever part was that they couldn't retaliate, because the rival park was not floating vulnerably on the sea like a pontoon but founded on solid rock. If they retaliated, all that would happen would be that useful grazing territory would be cleared of ice. And of course she had had her worries, her anxieties that simply destroying the polar ice pack – and that was what was being proposed – might result in raised ocean levels, causing flooding and loss of life throughout the northern hemisphere. But that wasn't it, you see; that was hardly it at all. Because this foam, it would lie on *top* of the ocean, it would if anything *reduce* world ocean levels, since icebergs hide their bulk under the waves. And of course the money, she needed money, they all did. Was her Annalee immune to that need? No, no, no. It was hard enough, though, and there had never been any thought of killing the soldiers, that had never been the plan. Kodwo had gone out to set up the initial detergent-bacterial pods on the bikes, to take them out. Natty had shadowed her, keeping out of the way, just watching to make sure the thing was set up properly. They were being paid enough to set the whole thing in motion, after all. But those fucking mock-soldiers, who could never have fooled anybody. Those fucking boys had come out and caught Kodwo at it. Raised their guns, told her the game was up. And so it was, the game was up, outside on the ice. What were we going to do? Hand ourselves over? What was *I* going to do, let them take my love, my beauty, my Kodwo? I shot the first in the back of the head and he just went down, and then I caught the second on the turn. The third ran – that was how much of a proper soldier he was, he just sprinted away. I had to run with him, back into the hangar, and that's where I shot him. We didn't have a plan, we didn't know what to do. We really didn't. But the others were in it as much as we, they didn't want the wrath of the Company on their necks either. And that bought us time. And then, when you, my little sweet Annalee, had taken against Bronovski, had been convinced that his paranoid skin-saving caution was actually a sign of guilt, we didn't need prompting. We would go with you, go to the other camp, and from there we could denounce Bronovski. Didn't it seem odd to you, how quickly Kodwo changed her mind, how suddenly she agreed to go on that dangerous cross-ice quest with Natty and McCullough? She came because she was my lover and I was hers. We took you with us, although we weren't sure if we could trust you, because we wanted you to be one of us. Only we never arrived, wasn't that the fucking truth. Only, we got interrupted, didn't we. We got interrupted. Oh, I was cross with my lover then. All she had to do was stay out of harm's way, that was all, and we would have been home clear, but of course she didn't. She got herself crushed by a lion, and then my love for her and my anger with her, anger because she was hurt, and then anger because she wasn't hurt enough, and it seemed to threaten everything: then everything got muddled up. And Hartmann was going to shoot you. But I couldn't stand by and watch my Annalee get shot because Hartmann had got the wrong end of the stick, now could I? My sweet Annalee? How could I do that? Because we have to look out for ourselves, and for the people we love, not for the Companies that rule the world and suck away all the money. Because if this first Company will pay us barely a living wage, and this second Company here will pay us a mass of money, we take the second sum, don't we, my love? Don't we, my love?

And McCullough's numbed head hung down against her breast under the stream of words. They seemed to pour upon her like rain. At some point, deeply buried, she may even have realised that Natty was telling her all this to bind her closer, to replace her valuable Company scientist contact (who might so easily die) with another. To fill the space that Kodwo had taken, lover, insider, with another who could be almost as useful. But under the pour of words, pressed down by the weight of them, and the answering yearning within her, McCullough could do very little.

Very little, apart from turning her face up to Natty's, and say, 'Hold me.' And feeling the press of arms about her, burying her face into the coverall fabric, as a comfort. She sat, her forehead pressing into the crook of Natty's arm, and looked down through the transparent floor of the observation bubble in which they sat together. There was a blizzard blowing through the air, obscuring the white ground. Flurries of snow, myriad tiny hailstones, came drumrolling against the sides of the bubble, like sand shaken against a sheet. And then the air-truck banked and flew on, clearing the storm, and the scratched plastic of the observation bubble was bleached all about with the whiteness of sunshine.